BOUND BY FIRELIGHT

Also by Dana Swift

Cast in Firelight

BOUND BY FIRELIGHT

DANA SWIFT

DELACORTE PRESS

Text copyright © 2022 by Dana Swift
Jacket art copyright © 2022 by Charlie Bowater
Map art copyright © 2022 by Virginia Norey

Visit us on the Web! GetUnderlined.com

Educators and librarians, for a variety of teaching tools, visit us at RHTeachersLibrarians.com

Library of Congress Cataloging-in-Publication Data is available upon request.
ISBN 978-0-593-12425-3 (hc) — ISBN 978-0-593-12427-7 (ebook)

The text of this book is set in 10-point Compatil Exquisit LT Pro.
Interior design by Cathy Bobak

Printed in the United States of America
10 9 8 7 6 5 4 3 2 1
First Edition

To anyone who has ever felt voiceless

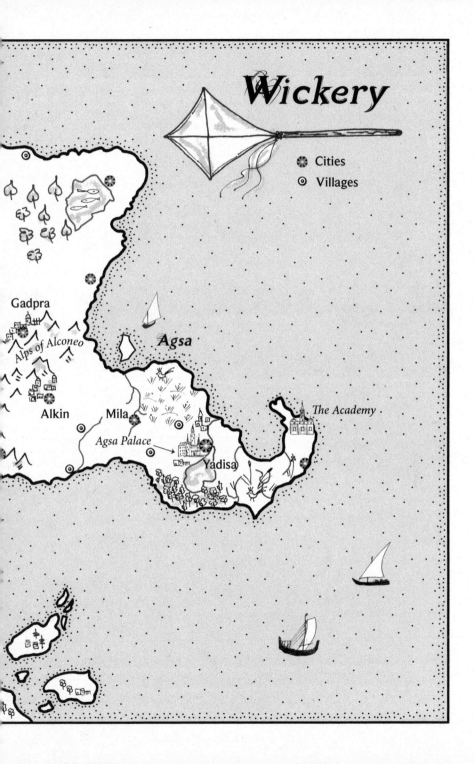

Deities and Their Powers

The Nine Touches

Erif, Goddess of Fire: Rules over volcanoes
◇ **Red Fortes:** Ability to create and manipulate fire

Renni, Goddess of Inner Capability: Oversees personal growth
◇ **Orange Fortes:** Ability to manipulate and heighten senses and the body's physical capabilities

Ria, God of Air: Governs tornados and wind
◇ **Yellow Fortes:** Ability to create and manipulate air, especially for flying

Htrae, Goddess of Earth: Reigns over fields and crops
◇ **Green Fortes:** Ability to create and manipulate wood and plant life

Retaw, God of Water: Controls flooding and tsunamis
◇ **Blue Fortes:** Ability to create and manipulate water

Raw, God of War: Stands on the battlefields of soldiers
◇ **Purple Fortes:** Ability to manifest weapons, shields, and boundaries

Laeh, Goddess of Healing: Watches over the sick and injured
◇ **Pink Fortes:** Ability to heal and enchant potions to fight illness

Dloc, God of the Cold: Dwells in blizzards and avalanches
◇ **White Fortes:** Ability to create and manipulate ice, snow, and other winter precipitation

Wodahs, God of Shadow: Lives in darkness
◇ **Black Fortes:** Ability to camouflage and cast illusions

◇

I Meet Up with the Love of My Life and Almost Throw Him off a Roof

Adraa

The sky crackles with color. Magic jets into the air and explodes in mist and sizzling lights. The festival is in full swing. It's loud. It's blinding. And it's the best thing I've seen in the past two months.

Booths and stalls have popped up overnight. Ornate silk banners in the nine colors of magic are draped and fastened to every frame, making the brocade ones dedicated to the recent fallen scarce for once. The streets flow like a river as currents of wizards and witches hunt for the best food stall or for a good spot to shoot some of their magic in the air and add to the glazed smoke screen of color. Children and the Untouched who can't cast throw powders instead and splash their friends in the face. Although the real Festival of Color isn't for months, this impromptu celebration radiates joy.

It feels like forever since I've seen the populace let loose like this. But if I were to drop from my shadowed rooftop, their happiness would melt. And by all nine gods, that's the last thing I want. For weeks Belwar has been repairing and rebuilding the city, and tonight we celebrate the new western flying station, the reconstructed homes, the life still thriving in this small coastal country. If there is anything my people deserve right now, it's one night of peace, of safety. So I stay nestled in my hiding spot, my eyes on the streams of color bursting in the sky, but my attention drifts to the bloodred magic in my hands condensing into my mask and then disintegrating into smoke over and over again. I know I'm saying the words, pulling the magic from the intricate design of my Touch to create the spell that blurs my face and makes me the Red Woman, and yet I don't quit my muttering.

It settles the heartache.

As do the squeals of kids' laughter below me, sounding bright and full of life. I didn't realize how much I was depending on the festival to showcase how my people might be able to keep going. After my magic was used to cause Mount Gandhak to erupt, killing one hundred twenty-nine people, my country has trudged through grief, repaired the city, and, most achingly, accepted the suspicion that I, Adraa Belwar, did this to them.

I've been living behind my vigilante persona for weeks, and I have to stop myself from plastering the thing to my face once again, right now, and become . . . become anything but the villain the city thinks I am. But I'm trying. I'm trying to feel okay with being just Adraa Belwar for a solid minute and a half as my country celebrates its color and diversity and strength to live on after destruction.

Luckily, no matter what they think of me, I'm still here. Every night I slip past my added security and watch for any sign the Red Woman is needed. That I am needed.

A thud echoes behind me. Footsteps. I whip around, mask adhering to my face instinctively and the bloodred of my magic smoking in my palms as I ready a ramming spell to throw the intruder off the roof.

"Hey. Don't kill me. I brought you food," a familiar voice says.

The lights from the street below illuminate Jatin Naupure, my boyfriend. *Boyfriend.* It's strange thinking of him that way, considering he was my fiancé first, then a weird mix of rival, partner, and crush, though we were hiding our identities from each other for months. And now, he's just . . . my person.

My defense vanishes and my magic evaporates. "Okay. I guess I'll let you sit next to me."

"Don't act like you didn't save this spot for me, Smoke."

I smile at the truth of it. I even kept the shingles warm with some red magic. When Jatin sits a second later, I can tell he notices the heat, but he only smiles and hands over my bowl. Roasted silken fish sitting on a bed of rice and smothered in a spicy red curry wafts into my nose. I take the bowl greedily.

"How's our favorite sociopath?" Jatin asks, scooting closer to me.

I glance down at Nightcaster, who's buying a witch a lamb chop on a stick. It would be somewhat endearing, watching him try to impress her, if I didn't know the true Nightcaster. A cage-casting wizard from the Underground who couldn't open his mouth without saying something revolting. We've been following him for weeks hoping he will lead us back to some scrap of evidence that we can use to prove a group of criminals called the Vencrin and the ruler of the country north of us, Maharaja Moolek, are working together. Or at least that they worked together to try to utterly destroy our cities when Mount Gandhak erupted.

"He hasn't been punched in the face today."

"The night is still young." Jatin pauses. "And he hasn't seen us yet."

"True."

Down below, Nightcaster pulls his bicep into a curl. Even from here I can make out the tattoos that run up his upper arm, mimicking the swirled designs of the gods' Touch.

"Gods," I sigh. "It's sad just watching it." A breeze draws the scent of roasted silken fish back to me and I dig in. "Have I told you this is my favorite?"

Jatin takes a bite from his own bowl and smiles. "I think it was in one of your letters once."

I frown. "I don't remember writing that to you." Maybe it was when I was really young and the letters I sent to Jatin still felt like something my parents were forcing me to do. At the time I couldn't fathom accepting an arranged marriage with the most arrogant boy I'd ever met. When love felt like an absurd question and marriage a horrifying inevitability.

"No, I mean the parchment was stained with it."

I knock against his shoulder as he laughs. "Stop lying."

"I could show you. I kept them all."

4

I side-eye him, my gaze tracing his strong jaw and thick black hair. "You kept them all?"

"What? You didn't?"

"Well, yeah, I did. But you know that post in the Belwar courtyard where we train? I pinned them there as motivation to beat you. Can't say they were well taken care of."

"Even the love letters? I'm hurt, Smoke."

"No"—I soak the rice in the curry and take a big bite—"those I burned."

"I don't believe you," Jatin says, so casually my lie loses its footing.

I open my mouth to joke he's not the only one, but it rings too close to reality. For the past few weeks we've been patrolling the streets, responding to the signal that Jatin created and saving people. We've even made a competition out of it. But that's what I've been doing underneath starlight. In blazing daylight it's councils upon councils with my father and the five rajas of Belwar as they accuse me and call for a truth-spelling trial to determine my crimes.

"Adraa?" Jatin whispers, sensing like always when I've started to spiral and tangle in my own thoughts.

I shake my head as if to clear it. "Hey, thanks for responding to the signal yesterday. I couldn't manage to get out of the meeting."

Jatin pauses. "They still want the hearing?"

I can hear my heart hammer. "My parents are still trying to convince the rajas it's not necessary."

"They'll get through to them. And soon it will be behind us."

His words hit home. That's all I want—for this nightmare to be behind us. But even the roof we're sitting on now has ash embedded between the shingles. The air is saturated with the smell of soot instead of sea salt.

Jatin goes back to his food, scooping up the rice with his fingers. "I saved seven people, by the way."

I drop a piece of roasted silken fish. "What?"

He ignores me, but a smile plays at the corner of his mouth. "And you know what that means."

I shake my head, reconfiguring the tally. It's been hard to keep track after two hundred. "I still think I'm up by two."

"Nope, down two." He smiles full-on.

It melts me even though my inner competitor huffs in irritation. "Don't say it."

He leans in, close enough for me to feel his breath. "Winnin—"

I turn my head quickly to kiss him, interrupting his taunt. I taste the spice of festival food, and, as always, kissing Jatin fills me with happiness and a sense of wholeness. The food is forgotten. His hand roams over my jawline where the Goddess Erif extended and stained my Touch burgundy, like tendrils of lashing fire.

"You know, I've figured out that you kiss me to stop my teasing. It's not a good way to train me."

"Are you admitting that you are trainable?" I joke, kissing him again.

He smiles, but something across the alley catches his attention. I follow his gaze. A woman is lighting a candle in her attic.

The flame seems to totter against the night, as if one hard blow might light up the curtains.

I sigh, the ache returning. "That's a house fire waiting to happen."

"Adraa, you should know, that signal yesterday?" Jatin waits a beat. "It led me to a house fire."

A lump forms in my throat. Two months ago, house fires were a thing of the past because my invention, firelight, brought sustainable light to every household in Belwar.

I know I was the one to do it, to take my people's firelight back to stop Mount Gandhak when Maharaja Moolek infused the volcano with my magic, but the candles still punch me in the gut. I could make more firelight. Easily. But the spell I invented has been labeled evil, an abomination everyone believes I created not to help but to control my people.

I think I could live with that—the vicious misconceptions, my ruined reputation. But house fires? People in danger? I will myself to not cast my mask onto my face, blur out my features, and let Adraa Belwar disappear. Because my other self, the Red Woman? Belwar accepts her, has cheered her on ever since Jatin and I started patrolling in disguise. Belwar loves me when I wear my mask.

Jatin reaches over and clasps my right hand—the one not covered with my Touch—a gesture that I have come to define as not only comfort but also acceptance. Love. "Thank you, Jatin. For being there for my people."

He squeezes again. "I'm here for you too." His expression grows earnest. "I wanted to talk to you about something. . . ."

"As long as it doesn't involve the hearing, my reputation, or the fact that people still think I bewitched you into trusting me."

"It's none of those things. Though that last one is still open to debate if you ask me."

"Jatin," I chastise. "What is it?"

He turns serious again, glancing down at our entwined hands. "I . . ." He's practically stammering.

"Why do you look so nervous?"

He rubs the back of his neck. "Well—"

A light vaults into the sky, red and white twisted together that can only mean one thing: a call to Night and the Red Woman. The glowing blaze is Jatin's invention, a device infused with both of our magic for people to signal us when they are in trouble. It's close. So close that it distorts the colors of the festival, washing away the residue of fun and piercing me with surprise.

Jatin and I only have to glance at each other, and then we're clambering to our feet and running. I reach for my belt and yank out my skyglider, Hubris the Fourth. *"Vitahtrae,"* I cast, and red streams of magic seep into the sturdy wood. As its handle extends and its kited tail unfolds, I throw myself onto it, letting the yellow magic buffer my weight. Someone picked the wrong night to mess with my city.

◇

CHAPTER TWO

Postponed Proposal

Jatin

Being engaged since the age of nine has some advantages, the main one being never having to propose. In the last ten years I don't think I ever processed how lucky or spoiled I was in the art of romance. But, by the Gods, it's bad. Three days ago, I got down on one knee after Adraa beat me in our weekly rainbow tournament, and she thought I had stumbled. She doesn't seem to mind my awkwardness, but she also has no idea that I've been trying to get us officially reattached for weeks.

I wouldn't say it's entirely my fault. We've been busy, the Red Woman and I. Every time my invention sings into the air, we fly into action. And it sings often. I've lost count of how many times it has conspired against me. My best friend, Kalyan, keeps a tally, though.

But then again, Adraa and I are doing what we do best. So here I am, slipping on shingles and unhitching my skyglider so we can dive into danger. Adraa is two steps ahead of me, already bringing Hubris to life. I cast my own extension and levitation spells, ghost-white clouds pulsing into the wood. A roof isn't the best spot for taking off, but that doesn't stop Adraa. Heck, months ago she jumped from a second-story window to chase a criminal. So I follow suit, hitching a leg over my skyglider and shooting into the chilly air.

The source of the signal comes from the East Village. Which could mean a lot of things, but given the Vencrin's ties to the docks near Belwar Bay, it's highly suspicious. Adraa must feel the same because she looks over at me. "Night, do you think—"

An ambush? Yes. I've been awaiting the day the Vencrin use our signal against us. "Signaling for the others now." I cup my hands to my mouth and a blur of white magic gathers there until three beams of light explode upward. But as I watch my signal impale the sky along with all the other bursts of magic from the celebration, my mistake becomes apparent.

"They won't see."

"Then it's just you and me. Like the good old days." I raise my forearm, waiting.

Adraa drops closer and bumps her forearm against mine. "Good old days? You mean three weeks ago?"

I mean every single day I get to spend with her. "What? They weren't good for you?"

She laughs. "I could have done without the one wizard who signaled us to get that monkey out of his yard."

There are some aspects of the signal I hadn't quite accounted for. "Monkeys are no laughing matter, Red."

She doesn't answer, and as we draw nearer to the site of the signal, I understand why. A mob of people inhabits the East Village square, bodies scrunched together, vivid festival clothing brightening the dying day. And they're chanting a phrase that stabs my ears and gnaws at my core.

End Belwar rule.

◇ ◇ ◇

We land silently a block away. People mill forward, pushing toward the square. A platform raised on wooden stilts sits in the middle of the crowd, with a banner depicting the Belwar emblem. Even in the dark, the image of the orange rising sun—Adraa's family's seal—gleams. Adraa doesn't waste a moment. Skyglider hitched to her belt, she's off, maneuvering between people like a dancer.

It takes a moment for me to catch up. "Red, stop. Let's go. No one needs us here."

One glance at her face and I know it's a lost cause. Her eyes scream determination. For weeks she's been desperate to help in any way she can. No signal gets ignored. And tonight won't be any different. "Someone might. I have to be sure."

I yearn to tear off my mask in order to blend in, but neither of us has that luxury anymore, especially Adraa. And at this point I wouldn't dare. This crowd already has their mantra; they don't need much else to push them over the edge. Adraa ducks her head and enters the fray.

The group keeps up their insistent chant—*End Belwar rule!*—and it makes me want to punch something. I feel caged in by their hatred and I can't even imagine how Adraa is feeling. I keep my eyes on the braid swinging down her back, but she doesn't look at me, instead peering around for the source of the signal and the reason we were called into this madness. But I think I know why. And though I hope I am wrong, my gut wrenches.

After sliding through layer upon layer of the mob, Adraa finally stops. "I don't see it anymore," she says, nodding toward where the signal has disappeared from the sky. Her hands shake, and something in me breaks then and there.

"I'm ending this."

She catches my arm. "No, someone here signaled for us. Someone here needs—" Adraa stops as her eyes fasten on the wide platform. I turn to see a wizard gliding down the makeshift stage until he reaches a podium. He wears his lankiness like it was a gift from the gods. His smile sours with each step as if he can't force a genuine countenance for a solid minute. But then again, I'm biased. I already want to knock his teeth in.

With a swift orange spell, his voice booms over the gathered crowd. "Welcome all. Welcome to all the true Belwarians. No matter whether you were born here or not, you came here today to bring light to the real problems of Belwar. We are here to make things right. And to do that, things must change." The crowd applauds. You'd think he had said something profound.

"So I say, no more heirs. No more abusers of power because they were born into power. We should choose. We should raise our voices and get our chance to decide. The gods have forsaken Adraa Belwar and she has forsaken us. She will only rule in ash and misery." The wizard grabs a handful of dust and throws it. It's almost laughable how staged this display is. But no one else is laughing. Worry slices through me and I lean forward and take Adraa's hand. "Come on, Red."

She shakes her head.

"Let us rise!" the wizard yells. "Tonight, as we celebrate our survival, individuality, and power, let us begin making that change. Let us put who we want on the rising sun and let it be a new dawn." He rears back and tears the banner in half. The onslaught of cheers is overwhelming.

"It's quite convincing," Adraa whispers, her voice dead. "My father would like the 'new dawn' part."

I grab her shoulders and swing her toward me. "Hey. Hey! Don't you dare listen to him."

"Why not? There are a few nonroyal wizards and witches out there who can utilize all nine types of magic. Besides, one can become powerful through self-discipline and self-study. The fact that I should rule—or I should have ruled—because of my blood is nonsense. They *should* choose."

"Maybe things do need to change, but that isn't what I'm talking about. They can only raise their voices today because you saved them. Don't forget that."

She pierces me with her gaze. A part of me wants to yell. Why does everyone in this country seem to be losing their minds? Adraa Belwar saved us all. We've been working for weeks to prove it. And I have to prove it, not just because I want to be with Adraa without reservation or even because she's a bloody good leader. If we don't, the whole world will fall prey to Moolek's manipulation. Then there will be no choice.

"You saved *them*. You saved *me*. Please, tell me you won't forget that."

A cheer swells around us as I await Adraa's answer. The crowd has spotted us at last. "The Red Woman! Night and the Red Woman!" they call out. Hands reach out and touch my shoulders, poking and prodding. The news of our arrival ripples through the crowd in energized whispers, and a moment later the orator raises his voice. "Red Woman! You have heeded our call. Come, join me."

So not the ambush we were anticipating, but just as bad. Sometimes, I hate being right.

"Go," a fellow wizard insists, pushing my arm. A mob has power. And not only in its ability to express the need for change or cause such change but also in its ability to shuffle. Without meaning or wanting to, Adraa and I are pushed toward the platform.

Hands reach to tug us upward. There's no escaping now.

"Welcome, honored guests. Welcome." The wizard places two fingers to his pulse point, signifying respect. But he doesn't attach a bow to it, which generates my contempt. My gut wrenches tighter. I have to hold back my desire to flee. Adraa stands firm, and thus so do I.

The wizard turns back to his audience.

"We, the people of Belwar, do not know your name, but we do know your service. And from that we gather you are genuine Belwarians, faithful, honorable, and true. But we wish to know:

14

Do you follow the Belwars, or"—he uses the word *or* not as an alternative but as a decree—"are you here for the *people* of Belwar?"

The crowd cries out in approval. "End Belwar rule!" they chant. "End Belwar rule."

Adraa steps forward, shoulders set. "I stand with Belwar."

The wizard smiles, but he can't even do that properly. It turns down at the edges. "And you, Night?"

"I stand with Belwar," I echo. In truth I should say I stand with the Red Woman, with Adraa Belwar, that she is a fundamental part of this place. Now if only the people here declaring the opposite would come to their bloody senses.

"They stand with Belwar!" the wizard roars, grabbing our hands in his and hoisting them up. I've never felt so paraded about in my life. And my father has orchestrated parades for that very purpose, so that's saying something. I'm following Adraa's lead on this one.

Adraa untangles herself and jerks back. Pride swells in my chest as I watch her, and I unlink my own hand. "I stand with Belwar, and that means standing by the Belwars," she shouts. "The family that came here to escape the discrimination of the North and built this city. I defend the family who will keep defending this country. *Prahtrae,*" she casts, and her bloodred magic straightens the torn banner and sews it back together, piece by piece.

All is silent. For a second I think maybe they'll listen, maybe they'll hear her.

Then come the frowns, the boos, the cries.

"You are no hero."

"Adraa Belwar tried to kill us all."

"She's the monster of Belwar."

"My house was destroyed. Moolek's people are the ones who fixed it."

"The Belwars are traitors. All of them."

The orator scowls. "If you don't stand with us, then you shouldn't stand at all. *Nizlaeh*," he shouts.

I move to pull up a shield as orange smoke springs forward, but someone beats me to it. A purple wall stands between Adraa and the wizard. I glance up, where Adraa's head guard and best friend, Riya Burman, hovers above us, her skyglider's tail a burst of violet and her face concealed by Adraa's invented mask. Alongside her flies Kalyan, my head guard, who lands in a gush of white wind.

Riya swings a leg over her glider and drops from the sky into a kneeling position. The makeshift platform shudders down to its wooden bones.

Riya rises slowly with a glare like death. "Don't touch her."

I can't help but smile. My signal worked after all. Our reinforcements have arrived.

◇ ◇ ◇

Although we have Riya and Kalyan on our side, a square filled with people lies before us, and based on their repetitive rhetoric and the knockout curse just thrown by Sour Smile over there, I think they want our heads.

16

It isn't the first time we've been outnumbered. But it's the first time civilians are the ones gearing up for a fight. Riya isn't helping matters. When the orator makes a move toward Adraa, Riya lunges. A second later, a satisfying crack splinters out into the crowd as the wizard falls to the platform.

"Nasty man," Riya spits, brushing pink magic against her bruised knuckles, "you don't misuse the signal."

"Yes, but it looks like he has some fans," I say.

The crowd heaves forward with screams of rage. *"Sphuraw!"* I yell, creating a wall of curved shields with purple magic.

Adraa and Riya follow suit, crafting our barrier into a dome of bloodred, violet, and white. But it's not enough. A few over-zealous members of the rally have already jumped over it. And they aren't happy. One hurls pink daggers at my face. I dodge. Another fastens wood planks to his arms with green magic and rushes forward.

"Don't hurt them!" Adraa cries from the other side of the platform, blocking a water stream someone has crafted.

Another pink dagger zooms past my nose. "Tell them that!" I holler, freezing the wizard's hands in ice and kicking up a plank to hit the other man in the face. I wince as he falls with a bang. Fighting amicably is difficult.

Kalyan steps up beside me, five shields swirling around him like a turtle shell and catching a dagger and two spears.

"I'm guessing she said no," he says, deadpan. At this moment, he is the most annoying I've ever found him. And as my decoy and head guard, I've seen the guy every day since he was eleven.

"No, she didn't say no," I huff, tossing a wizard over our heads and back into the gathering crowd. "I haven't gotten the chance to ask. Wait—" I block three yellow arrows with a shield. "You thought she would say no?"

Kalyan shrugs. "Fifty-fifty."

"Fifty-fifty? She and I have been engaged for ten years and all you give me is fifty-fifty?" I lengthen my barrier, pushing wizards and witches from the platform. *"Bhitti Himadloc!"* I yell. Sheets of ice spring from my hands, surging upward and barring more people from entering behind us.

Kalyan crafts a whip and catches two more men who are trying to climb the platform behind the Belwar banner. "Ten years, and yet you still aren't engaged. Now she gets to choose."

"Of course, she gets to choose. But—" A wizard takes this moment to barrel over my ice barrier with a funnel of wind. I swing some ice at him, catching him midfall and hitching his flaming yellow hands to the floor. "She still chose me."

At that moment, across the makeshift stage, Adraa sweeps the legs of a witch, then skids, using the heat of her red magic to melt the lane of ice I've carelessly constructed. As she slides, she topples one wizard back into the fray. A flash of red mist, and two other wizards go down.

Kalyan nods in appreciation. "And you are lucky for it."

I can't keep the smile off my face, even when Adraa stands, whirls around, and slips again. "Must everything be ice?" she yells.

I shrug. It's my forte. What does she expect? But I sweep

my hands forward and call back the chunks of ice that divide us. "Happy?" I ask, even as Kalyan's sentiment warms its way through me. I will always be happy if Adraa Belwar chooses me. Now if only we could get a moment to ourselves so I can ask her properly.

Before Adraa can answer, her eyes widen and her hand rises. I turn, but it's too late. Another extremist has crept up behind us, a streak of a blue sword falling down on Kalyan and me. I don't even have time to raise a shield before a barrier of purple covers us. Riya bounds off the boundary above, spinning in the air and kicking a witch in the side of the face. The witch goes down, and Riya turns. "I'd be happy if you would all pay more attention to your surroundings. Gods, how did you survive without us for this long?"

"Obviously with much luck," Kalyan says. "Unbelievable amounts, even."

Adraa runs up. "That's the last of them that slipped in before we got the barrier up. Let's get out of here before anyone gets hurt."

"I think it might be too late for that," Kalyan says. The four of us turn to the barrier, surveying the carnage of splintered wood. Most of the crowd has scattered, but those inside our bubble shield are lying on the ground, knocked out or moaning. Dozens of wizards still pound against the shield, though. Many have glowing red eyes, which can mean only one thing. They're under the influence of the drug Bloodlurst and all that comes with it: more power, less control, and no concern for logic. I've never seen so many drugged.

Three wizards punch the wall with orange magic and the barrier's outer shell cracks. It won't hold much longer.

"What's wrong with them?" Riya shouts.

"They're angry. Their city has burned and they want someone to blame," Adraa says, glancing toward Mount Gandhak.

"Today is not the day to make them see reason." I nod to Riya and Adraa. "You two go first. Kalyan and I will back you up."

Adraa gives me a look. "What about you?"

"I've made it out of avalanches. I can make it out of this."

"After all this time, you're still rubbing that in?" Adraa shakes her head but readies her skyglider. "Be careful."

I smile. "I'm always careful."

Kalyan huffs beside me as he blasts more ice at the base of the shield.

I break the ice at the top and the girls zoom through the opening. The question for Adraa is still on the tip of my tongue, unasked and unanswered.

Kalyan watches me out of the corner of his eye. "Remember that pep talk I gave you earlier?"

"Yeah, you said it would be hard to mess up a proposal with the festival's romantic atmosphere," I answer, unleashing my skyglider once again and preparing to punch into the air so fast it'll blow back the multicolored dome.

"Forget what I said. I hadn't accounted for how bad you are at this," Kalyan notes as we settle onto our skygliders. "And for the record, that's quite bad."

"Well, there's one saving grace. I don't think she even

knows I was trying to ask." With that, Kalyan and I chant into the wood of the stage, coating it in white smoke until we appear immersed in a cloud. When we finally do blast off, the stage ruptures. Two holes puncture its middle.

I might not know how to propose, but at least I know how to make an exit.

◇

CHAPTER THREE

I Get Chased by Light

Adraa

———•———

I don't hear the explosion as much as feel it, quivering through Hubris's wooden handle. I know Jatin, and I know Kalyan. They're safe. I simply hope all those people hyped up on Bloodlurst and blame are going to be all right.

Riya maneuvers her skyglider and levels out close to me, the wind whooshing as a new current catches the glider's kited tail. "So . . . ," she says, stretching out the vowel. "I know tonight didn't exactly go well, but did something else make up for it?"

I didn't expect the flight back to Belwar Palace to be one of silence, but I wasn't anticipating the giddy tone she reserves for teasing me. "What?"

"Is there anything new you want to tell me? Anything life-changing, but also super expected?"

"What are you talking about? You heard what those people said just as well as I."

She sighs. "Never mind."

I know I'm missing something, some hint she's dropping, but what's new? Riya is three years older than me, and though that gap loses some of its relevance each year, there are still times she possesses an all-knowing air.

"Where was Prisha tonight?" I ask. "We called to her too."

Riya shifts her weight on her skyglider. "Hiren keeps asking me if I've noticed anything different. But all I know is she's been acting weird."

"Weird how?" I lean forward. I *have* noticed that my younger sister has been avoiding me. Showing up and being part of this team when a signal rises through the air, but treating me like an outcast when I wear my real face, like the rest of Wickery.

"Moody."

"You realize we are talking about Prisha, right? She's a fifteen-year-old girl. Moody should be her middle name."

"No, it's something else. She keeps missing her clinic shifts."

I swerve Hubris so that I face Riya. "All of them?"

"All of them."

It takes me a second to ask my next question. I need to know how far the hatred for the Belwar name has spread because those people weren't just chanting for my end, but for my entire family's. "Is it because our people don't want to be healed by a Belwar?"

Riya's features soften, which is a hard feat with her thick eyebrows and strong cheekbones. But I know how vulnerable I must look and how devastating the answer must be to elicit such a response. "Adraa—"

An orange light blazes between us. We both pitch sideways. Hubris creaks in protest in my grip. The wind, so peaceful and nonexistent, whirls to life as I spin. A second later, I right myself, find Riya's confused and searching eyes, then hunt for the next flicker of light. The sky is empty of color. The streets may still be painted with it, but darkness has swallowed up everything in our sight and only dim useless candles burn below.

"On your left!" Riya screams.

I turn and duck. Another orange blip of magic veers past my head. I twist and see the spell loop back around and shoot straight for me. We aren't being fired at; we're being targeted.

"It's only after you. Dive!" Riya shouts. I plummet. The blaze of orange follows me even as I zigzag. My quick manuevering isn't working. I pull up hard on my skyglider, but the spell flings itself after me. *Gods!* I don't like things as stubborn as I am.

I plunge again, hitting rooftop level and descending into the no-fly zone. There is only one way to lose this thing and the open sky isn't it. I streak through the alleys of my city. The sheets hung over doorways, designed to notify occupants of black concealment magic, flutter. Archways become obstacles. My glider snags on a clothesline draped with rugs as Hubris's kited tail drops too close.

After the eighth turn, the orange light is nowhere in sight. I career to a stop and cast an orange magic enhancement over my eyes, willing them to see through the murky darkness and catch any new details.

The night is still.

Until, that is, the wind whistles and I look left to see Riya shooting toward me. I freeze and jerk to the right, but it's too late. Riya is there, pushing me. Everything happens so fast, I'm a bundle of unsteady limbs. *"Simaraw,"* I cry out, grabbling for a shield. The light blazes down.

Then it halts. Just like that, it stops. We both watch it through our glowing barriers as the orange light unravels into words— *Come home now*—followed by a voice echoing the message. My father's voice.

Riya and I look at each other and share a sigh of relief even as we gulp down a few last panicked breaths. I've gotten myself into too many ambushes of late. Or almost killed one too many times.

"I didn't know he could do that," Riya mutters as the message fades and then dies. "Send one that sought a single person like that."

I can't seem to find anger or even frustration. Since Mount Gandhak, my father has been trying to develop a spell that will allow him to speak to the entire county at once, an emergency notification system. Like the rest of us, he doesn't want Belwar to be caught off guard again. This must be his newest addition. "He learns new spells like the rest of us," I say.

Riya raises an eyebrow as we make our way to the palace. "I'm just saying it would have been nice if he had debriefed me and the fellow guards during one of the daily security meetings. You know, the ones where we talk about making sure the royal family doesn't fall out of the sky and die?"

"It wouldn't be your fault either way." I meet her eyes. "My death, or my undoing, it could never be your fault."

Riya stares and then drops her gaze to our surroundings—the dark alleyways, the ash littering the corners, the dyes still smeared on the street from the festival. "It's my job, so yes, it would be my fault. Blame is easy to pass around, but it's also hard to get rid of."

In that moment I don't know whether she's talking about me, herself, or the people at the rally looking for anyone to blame for Mount Gandhak's eruption. Or maybe she's talking about everyone at once. When it comes to blame, maybe we are all culprits for letting it fester.

Though my father's new method of sending messages scared me, I'm more frightened that he asked to see me at once.

Since the eruption I haven't spent much time with my father. I assumed when Mom told me she knew I was the Red Woman that Dad did too. But I've learned she can keep a secret. Sometimes too well and too many to count. The opportunity has arisen a few times—me telling him. But I've held my tongue on every occasion. Not that there have been many. He's been busy fighting against the trial that would determine my fate and my so-called crimes. Something tells me I should confess tonight, like it might be too late if I don't spit it out all at once.

After checking his study and the meeting room, I find him pacing in front of the throne. Some of the last orbs of firelight light up the Belwar emblem, which adorns the back wall, the orange sun whose rays thrust toward the ceiling like spears. I used to see hope in it. Now it's a painful, unattainable dream, the sign of a crumbling ancestry that began to fall apart with me. Tonight, I stitched our flag back together. But will I be able to do that in reality, mend what has been falling apart?

I watch my father. I don't think I've ever seen him pace. My mom's the pacer. I'm the pacer. Father is as sturdy as his arms.

"Dad, I need to tell you something—"

He turns, worry clouding his green eyes. "Adraa, finally." He rushes over and sweeps me into a hug. Since I was a little girl my father has been loving, but never physically affectionate. I've learned long ago it's through humor, reassurances, his readiness to teach me the political game of our country that he shows how much he cares. I could count the number of hugs we've shared on a single hand. The only other one in recent history came after I awoke from taking my firelight back from Mount Gandhak—after I almost died. The fact that I'm nestled in his arms right now scares me more than his message, more than anything else that has happened tonight.

"I'm sorry. I'm so sorry," he keeps whispering. "I've failed you."

My heart stops. "Sorry? Sorry for what?" But something deep down tells me I already know. "You could never fail me."

"I *have* failed you. The rajas have collectively overruled me. And now, tomorrow . . ."

I tremble. "What happens tomorrow?" I need him to say it.

My father pulls away and looks at me. "Tomorrow you will go on trial for the murder of one hundred twenty-nine people."

I slowly weave my way to my room. Along the way—along the tapestries depicting my country's history, along the orange-and-pink brocade glowing with the names of my parents, and along the emblems of rising suns I'll never have stitched into my own clothing—a thought snags in my mind like a thorny branch.

It's real. I'm not truly a part of the fabric of this palace. My story will never be woven into its seams. I have failed. It's not simply reputation and rumors anymore. The whole country of Belwar believes it.

They believe I will destroy them.

When I get to my room, I don't know what to do with myself. After coaxing away my tears by telling me to think of this as a new dawn, Dad had said to rest for the day ahead. *Rest.* What an impossible request. Especially when the number one hundred twenty-nine reverberates in my skull and drives me to silence. Silent tears. Silent shaking. Silent hatred.

There's a thump on my window and I'm so startled I feel magic laced and ready on my skin. But a second later, after gathering the courage to brush open the curtains, I find Jatin on the other side of the glass. With a click, a whoosh, and the small jingle of warning bells, the pane flies open.

One look. One look and I'm certain he can see right through me. And he is not here to report in about the rally. Somehow he knows what I face tomorrow without my speaking. I can see it in the crease of his brow, in the warmth and sadness in his eyes. Gods, he has such kind and knowing eyes.

Neither of us says anything at first, soaking each other in, bathing in silence before one of us voices it.

"How did you know?" I'm finally able to whisper.

Jatin glances at his hand, which clutches a tattered, scrunched-up letter. Slowly, he raises his arm and the wrinkled parchment unravels. "I'm the first witness."

My face falls, and I collapse against him as he wraps me in a hug. "Don't worry. The most they will get out of me is how much I love you. It's going to be awkward for the crowd, but I'll muddle through it."

I let out a huffing laugh but choke on it.

"Tell me," Jatin says.

There was a time when I would have bottled all this up, when I wouldn't have let an ounce of self-doubt or vulnerability leak out. But with Jatin? I don't have to fear his judgment. He thinks I'm strong, and he lets me know it. So now I'm blunt as blood.

"I'm scared. Before my ceremony, I voiced my concerns, and everyone reassured me. Then the world exploded. What about this time? What if I can't prove it was Moolek? What if they don't believe me and they really think . . . they don't believe . . ."

"It's a truth spell, Adraa." He lightly tugs my hands away from my body and holds them. "They have to believe you."

I take a deep breath. "And if I tell them *too* much truth? If I let slip the fact that I got all my intel as a cage caster and as the Red Woman? All my evidence comes from under a mask. Every night we scout, and every night we find more evidence of a cover-up. They are trying to bury us, or at least bury me."

"We won't let them."

I pull back to look at him. "Oh, that sounds pretty easy."

He smiles. "I know. We are very impressive. Coming up with solutions like that? I think I just proved why I graduated top of my class."

"It must have only taken you the whole flight here, right?"

"Just about." Then he grows serious, squeezes my shoulders. "But really. They don't know who they are messing with. We—"

The unmistakable sound of splintering glass reverberates into my room.

We both start. "What in Wickery?" I blurt out, but I'm already imagining the worst. Members of the crowd at the rally or the Vencrin following us. The palace under attack. My identity exposed and vulnerable.

White fog flares in my peripheral vision. "You lead," Jatin whispers.

I call upon my magic, red smoke flourishing all the way up to my neck before we slip out of my room. I navigate through the halls, and soon I know exactly where the noise is coming from. I drop all pretenses of camouflage and run for the medical wing.

I think I expected a rogue patient or a distressed Zara, my maid who works as a healer in the clinic, fumbling over a broken jar, but that's not what Jatin and I stumble across. Instead, we find Hiren, one of the elite guards—my sister's, in fact—and son of one of the five high rajas ducking as an orb of mud flies at him.

"Hiren, what's going on?" I shout.

He whips around, his too-large cloak sweeping the floor. He joined Prisha's guard two years ago, a gift from his father, and he's been eager to ascend the Belwar ranks. Now I think he might be regretting his placement. "I've tried to stop her, but nothing will calm her down."

I hear his words but don't put them together until I round the corner. Before me is the clinic, my mother's second home and the place I dubbed "the smell factory" when I was ten years old. Where rosemary is stacked on buckets of ginger and tulsi; chilies, peppers, and cumin are labeled and placed on wood shelves; the organs and blood of goats, pigs, lizards are arranged by date and consistency. Or that's what the clinic usually looks like. Now my sister sits in the middle of it all, covered in dirt and debris. For a second I just stand there, shocked, until Prisha screams and a pink lash of purple magic slices through the air, smashing a bottle of newts' eyes.

"Prisha!"

She swings around and I see her fully, face wet and devastated.

"Prisha, these are good herbs, remedies that are helping people. You know how many are still injured, who are still—"

"Well, whose fault is it?" she snaps.

I stumble back. I let my next words out in a single breath, so quiet I can barely hear myself. "What did you say?" I don't say more than that, because I know the next words would be harsh and brash—too much like the old Adraa Belwar, who rushed into situations. And where did that get me? Where has that gotten us?

Prisha slumps and lets out a sob. "Adraa, I don't know what's going on in my head."

I crouch next to her. Is this what the crowd meant when they said the Belwars were over? Not just because of Moolek's intricate web of plans to kill us all, as I believed, but from the inside out, from uncertainty and failure.

"I'm . . . I'm a pink forte," she gets out between sobs.

I go still. That's what she's upset about? *Fortes?*

"Prisha, you're not sixteen yet."

Prisha jerks upright, glaring at me and then glancing around the room until her eyes land on a cauldron simmering in the corner.

"*Hilloretaw,*" she commands. A blush of pink smoke glides off her fingertips and plunges into the cauldron, pulling out the water. A spiral of liquid levitates in the air before Prisha releases the spell. "Every spell I try is that color."

It's true, then. She's not overreacting. My sister is a pink forte. Goddess Laeh has picked her to represent those who can heal the injured and cure the sick. This is unexpected but happy news to me. But pain distorts Prisha's features. Two years ago, when I came into my forte, it was cause for celebration. In the early years my family had thought I might be Untouched, that I might end up powerless because my right arm is unnaturally bare—dark brown like the rest of me, not Touched by the gods in swirls of magical designs. My stomach cramps. That was only two years ago. The scene before me now—it's not one of celebration.

"Prisha—"

"Don't say I'm not. Don't lie."

"Okay, fine. You are. But pink magic brings miracles, life . . ." I bite back the words. Not like the fire of a red forte. "Not destruction. Not this." I gesture to the clinic. I haven't seen it so ravaged since the earthquakes of Mount Gandhak splattered potions like blood. It took weeks to get it back in order.

"It's been getting worse since I brought you back. That's what did it."

So she blames me. I can see it in her face, in the detached tone she wraps her words in. "Are you saying you wish you hadn't saved me?"

Her tears fall onto the floor and her hair hangs like a curtain around her face. "I prayed every day, Adraa. Every day. I don't want this to be my destiny."

"It isn't. I'm tired of trying to convince you. As much as everyone likes to classify and categorize, you are more than the color of your magic. Pink fortes are not meek or nurturing or feminine just because they can heal. You'll be much more than a potion master or a glorified medic. *You're* going to be a rani." I hate how bitter my voice gets at the end. She will be a rani, probably even the maharani of Belwar, and I . . . I will never hold such a title. And what's more, no one wants me to.

But Prisha doesn't seem to have heard me. She continues on with her rambling. "When you died, I prayed to Laeh. After all these years of avoiding her, practically dishonoring her, I turned to her. I think this is her revenge on me."

Maybe it is. The gods are flawed, I know that now. They are like us, with personalities, and tempers. They make mistakes.

They can screw up entire lives and kill us. I thought I had a destiny, but no, they took that away. Yes, Goddess Erif helped me on Mount Gandhak, but she also allowed Maharaja Moolek to ruin me, to the point that my own sister has doubts.

"Even if it is your destiny, you need to stop being so self-centered. Maybe the gods thought you needed to take care of others for a change."

"Oh, so I'm the selfish one? I haven't seen you in the clinic in days." She looks me square in the eye. "They blame you for a reason, you know."

I flinch, tugging away from her and standing to gather distance from her insinuation. "You believe the rumors then? You believe I would plant my firelight in Mount Gandhak to kill our people?"

Prisha keeps crying, but I hear no contradiction. I hear nothing but guilt and fear and . . .

Not just doubts, then. It's real. This is truly happening. Even Prisha.

"Tomorrow I go to court. I guess we will find out then if I am to blame."

Prisha's head snaps up, and her eyes sharpen. It's clear she wasn't privy to this information. "Adraa, I . . ."

I can't stand being near her another second. I twist away. Jatin searches my face with his eyes, and I shake my head. I don't know if I'll ever be okay again.

I walk past Hiren. "Please get Zara. I don't want my mother to see this mess," I whisper.

I can tell he wants to reply; I feel his dark eyes on me, hear his intake of breath. Right when I think he'll choke it down, his words slam into my back.

"She worships you. More than any god. You." His voice is heavy. I can't force myself to look back at this scene of pain, not when my sister has destroyed me.

"It's hard to watch your heroes fall," Hiren whispers.

I inhale, desperate to keep my composure. "Who says I'm a hero?"

CHAPTER FOUR

◇

Trauma on Trial

Jatin

The trial starts at three past dawn. I arrive as the sun winks over the mountains and cloaks half the courtroom in light. It's not quiet, yet I hear my every footfall as I approach my designated chair.

I've never attended a truth trial of this magnitude. Then again, an heir to the throne has never been on trial quite like this, accused and showcased so blatantly. Being a royal either hides you in the back corner when wrongdoing occurs or places you directly in the spotlight. But this is more than a spotlight. Even though half the spectators are doused in shadow, Adraa will be under the full blaze of the sun, and we all feel it.

This is the first truth-spelling trial in which witnesses like myself are being brought forward. And if that doesn't tell you something, this room—brimming with the most powerful wizards and witches of the nation—does. The five lower rajas of Belwar sit on thrones like mantels that rise above us.

In Naupure there are nine rajas, spread out across our mountainous country, residing in the major cities. In Belwar there are five, one for each village and the outer northern region. I met them all weeks ago, after the eruption, and I've categorized each of them depending on where their allegiance falls. Hiren's father, Raja Dara, is my favorite, as he is the only one I've heard speak bluntly against Moolek's men "cleaning" the city. He voted against this trial. Raja Lal of the South Village did as well. Raja Gupta of the North Village, Raja Reddy of the West Village, and Raja Amin of the East Village are the ones who brought us here today.

In the middle of the rajas, where Maharaja Belwar *should* sit, a bearded man with a thick body and long face reigns over the hall, casting his eyes over the people crushing their way in through the door. The air tightens and my lungs pinch. It doesn't help that more people arrive to fill the rows behind me and their whispers seep down my back. The audience is limited to officials, a dozen Dome guardsmen awaiting orders, and the few people who lost a loved one and demanded a spot for retribution. As if that is what they will find here.

The room does a good job convincing people it's a place of justice. It's shaped like a bubble, as if lies would only get stuck in corners. Nine pillars arranged in a ring impale the space, each with a banner bearing the color of a god. The effect is eerily like that of a temple. I'm nearest the pillar that honors Htrae, Goddess of Earth, who blessed Moolek with his forte. I don't know if it's just a coincidence, but my skin crawls thinking of Moolek beside me.

His men are still stationed in both of our countries, but since the eruption Moolek himself has been governing his "helpful" troops from afar. Blood would be spilled one way or another if he appeared today.

My hope is this will all turn around. Adraa and I will speak our truth, and through our words Moolek will be hunted down. I've had hope for weeks now. My stomach has been sinking ever since.

My father finds his seat beside me, his features expressionless. But his hands shake in his lap and I find his eyes, to try to figure out what he's thinking. Last night, before I flew to Adraa, he'd been disheartened, handing over the order for my court appearance with sad resignation. Now he appears to have rallied his emotions into a mask of stoicism.

"We won't let anything happen to her," I say. I don't exactly know when I became the adult here. I have never wanted the throne or its responsibilities. But since Mount Gandhak, or maybe since meeting Adraa, I've slowly been sieving the weight of ruling from him. Today, for the first time, he looks like he needs it.

He nods, but his face is ashen. "This isn't right."

"You're telling me."

"No, something in the air. Something—"

"All rise!" an amplified voice announces across the courtroom.

The doors burst open and Adraa walks in. She wears a pink and orange sari, traditional, respectable, sleeves down to her wrists. It's there, right where I would have placed a wedding bangle, that purple cuffs glow. The cuffs don't bind her hands, but they do prohibit the flow of magic. Adraa could probably break through them if she really tried. But that's not what today is for. Right now the cuffs are a precaution, as well as a marker to distinguish the suspect.

It's all unnecessary.

Adraa's rich brown eyes fall on me. She looks resilient, collected. To the rest of the room I'm sure she appears confident, but I know that, on the inside, she's trying not to panic.

I nod. Smile. I hate how much it reminds me of two months ago when I reassured her before her royal ceremony, and then she stopped breathing in my arms. My spine straightens, each vertebra knotting itself into stiffness.

The two guards accompanying Adraa stop in the front row opposite mine, next to her parents. Everything stills as her footfalls stop and I feel the eyes probing her. She doesn't deserve this. We should be honoring her. Gods, I will tear this place down if anything happens. I'm primed for it. My head's buzzing—

My father nudges me in the ribs. "Jatin."

"What?"

I look around. Everyone is waiting on me. The judge is staring down at me like he doesn't expect much now that I have missed my cue. "Jatin Naupure," he repeats sharply. "Please take the stand."

So they aren't going with formalities and opening statements and a reminder of why we are here and who is to be cast into telling the truth. Maybe I should be glad they are dropping

39

the facade. But as the crack of my steps echoes off the dome and the sudden silence, I look up at the hard lines of the five rajas, steadfast and waiting, and I know I'm wrong. This is wrong.

Even truth can be twisted.

◇ ◇ ◇

The witness stand is perched alongside the thrones of the judge and the rajas, down a level and facing the audience. Everything about the spot shouts discomfort. The bench is hard. Three walls cage me in. To look up at my accusers I must wrench my neck; the height difference is even more staggering close up. Two candles, which feel out of place here, melt into puddles on the side banister. I want to push them off, to let them spill to the floor so that Adraa won't have to stare at the small pools of wax and be reminded this started because of hate, money, and economics.

I don't move.

A wizard steps forward, a truth-casting Dome Guard with orange bands around his wrists that signify loyalty to Belwar and, above all else, truth. He will be my interrogator. This shaggy-haired, muscle-loaded man who I might very well have caught stealing firelight and working for Moolek will question my motives.

"Are you ready, Raja Jatin?" His voice is low, calm. I'm anything but.

Yet it goes on. The best way is through.

"First, introduce yourself, please."

"Raja Jatin Naupure."

"And, Raja Jatin, as someone of your status I imagine you understand the conditions of the truth spell and accept the terms?" He smiles like we are friends. But a true friend would know I don't like the idea of my status, my birth, or my power as indicators of superiority.

"Yes, I understand the terms." I hold up my forearms, cross them, and touch my fingers to my throat in the ultimate promise. For Adraa, for the truth, I allow and accept the truth spell to be cast.

"Thank you," he says before gesturing to the judge.

The judge stands. "Everyone will now be momentarily deafened, as in agreement with the truth accords."

Though we have all been warned, most of the audience startles as a blanket of magic wraps the room. My ears hollow out and silence rings. This part is expected. Weird and off-putting, but expected. No one is allowed to hear truth spells. Especially me, a royal. What I'm not prepared for is the actual truth spell. Even as I watch this wizard's lips move, his hand flourish, and orange smoke charge toward me, the spell hits with a punch. A flurry of magic rams into my face and dives into my pores. It nestles into my throat like the onslaught of a cold and my body is fighting back. When I open my mouth, it's sticky with saliva. My gums are gooey. It takes everything I have to appear normal, to not grip my throat.

My ears pop, my hearing restored along with the crowd's. The Dome Guard waits, peering at the audience to make sure everyone is focused. Then he leans forward like he's about to whisper a secret. "I'm going to get straight to the point. Tell us, Jatin. You were the only one up there with her." *Her. The enemy. The love of my life.* I bite back a retort, or maybe the truth spell does it for me. "Tell us what happened up on Mount Gandhak when it erupted."

The image of fire bursts into my memory. "We tried to stop it," I finally spit out. "We failed. But Adraa was able to do it. She saved us all." For a truth spell, it's very hard to talk. There's more to the story than that and yet for some reason my mouth truncates the details. Maybe that's the trick of the spell—it elicits simplicity.

"You saw this?"

"No," I say, then pause, waiting for the truth spell to rip out the explanation. No words come, and fear worms its way through me. My truths could implicate Adraa. Because what did I really see? What did I do when the lava was bearing down and fire burned the sky?

"Please elaborate for the court. What were you doing while Adraa supposedly saved us all?"

"I was unconscious. I had . . . burned out." From the corner of my eye, I see my father drop his head into his hands, his body seeming to move in one huge sigh. A raja burning out. The weakness stripped bare for the court.

"Then you're saying you were unconscious the entire time Adraa performed this miracle?"

"Yes, but—"

"But what?"

"I was told. She told me," I say, trying to explain.

"So you were told by the defendant that she saved us all. Has she ever, by chance, lied to you before that you know of?"

Silence echoes like a scream. My fear bubbles to the surface, and I reel in torment. I look over at Adraa, who is sinking down into her chair. Our eyes lock. I always knew our lies to each other would hurt. But we had grown past it. We were together. I mean, blood, yesterday I was trying to propose. We were fine. No more lies and we had lived by it.

I choke back my answer, but the truth spell's syrupy strength congeals in my throat, pulling at my vocal cords. Adraa's eyebrows furrow and finally she breaks our stare. Her eyes shutter closed in defeat, and a curse forms on her lips. It doesn't matter if we have our forgiveness. Lies cannot be undone. Truth cannot be forsaken. And I'm about to hurt her in a way that pretending to be Kalyan never could.

"Jatin, has she ever lied to you before about anything of importance?" the truth caster repeats, sharper than before.

"Yes, b-bu—" I try to stutter out a contradiction, but the prosecution shuts me down before I can get the consonant out.

"No more questions." He turns away.

That's it? They really do just want me up here to tarnish her. To blood with the truth.

I break from the bench. And finally the truth spell yields, and my words come. "Have you done your research? Have you looked into this case at all? Adraa Belwar was unconscious; she was dying when Mount Gandhak first blew. How could she have done this?"

The truth caster whips back around. "Easily. She set it up

for months and when she unleashed her power to detonate the volcano she burned out, went too far. Wouldn't you say her unconscious state, her dying, was very much like a witch dealing with a blowback of immense power?"

The truth spell realigns, ready for more. It sticks to my throat, my tongue. I try to resist. He's wording it all wrong, jumbling it up. His timeline is flawed. Anyone with two copper pieces of sense could figure this out.

"She burned out because she failed the royal trial. We witnessed it," I say.

He tilts his head likes he's been waiting for this argument. A tremor slides down my spine.

"Then maybe, isn't there a chance that she failed her royal trial because the gods were trying to save us? Were trying to kill *her* before she killed us all?"

I refuse to answer. I've misjudged him. I've forgotten how things could be spun. This audience has just been offered an alternative world in which the gods don't only bestow our magic, but actually intervene for the good of Wickery. The truth caster has offered them the idea of a utopia. The nine pillars burn brighter in the sun with the audience's hope. So what can I say?

"Couldn't there?" the prosecutor demands.

I fight it. Try coughing like I might be able to spit the spell from my mouth. I flounder in silence, gagging on nothing, choking on the need to speak like I can't breathe unless I say it. Seconds pass and the question isn't repeated. He knows he's got me. "Y-yes." The truth is wrenched out between my teeth.

Because the truth is . . . maybe. Maybe. But the world is full of maybes. It's also full of lies.

He smiles. *Smiles.* I want to smack it off his face. It's people like Adraa and me and our parents who saved the day. How dare he take away our sacrifice, our choice, *my* choice to have climbed that mountain and to potentially have never returned?

"Then I repeat, no more questions." He beckons to the crowd, which has already begun its clamoring. "The boy is being manipulated. He did nothing. He saw nothing. And he defends her anyway like a lovesick teenager. He shouldn't even be allowed to testify on her behalf."

His words cut me in half. Boy. Lovesick. As if my feelings for Adraa make me foolish and weak, when they have done the opposite in every respect. But instead of voicing this and announcing my conviction that Adraa Belwar took back her firelight and saved us all, I am dismissed. And once again I am left in the quiet, knowing not only have I not reassured her, I have made it worse.

CHAPTER FIVE

◇

My Words Get Twisted

Adraa

I'm so tired of guilt. I'm tired of its weight and its all-consuming gluttony. But most of all I'm tired of its unexpected arrivals and prolonged stays. I wish I could be like Jatin and be confident enough to know that Mount Gandhak wasn't my fault. But thoughts get twisted and people get broken.

Jatin didn't say a single lie on that stand. And that's why I see in his eyes that we are both breaking. We lied to each other for weeks about who we were. It has come back to bite us, and now the guy I love looks at me not with confidence, but with guilt.

I haven't shaken the blame. And if someone like Jatin is so easily consumed, what hope do I have?

I carry guilt.

So maybe . . . I am guilty?

I shake my head. *What?* I turn around in my seat, searching for the source of the voice, realizing a second too late how paranoid I'm being. How loud I'm letting my doubts yell. It was a mistake to look, because I'm met with daggerlike stares. My citizens hold brocade banners over their laps in unity. One witch cries in the back of the courtroom, trying to muffle her sobs. I breathe slowly, a gulping motion like I too am about to let out a wail.

"Lady Belwar," the judge calls. "Lady Belwar, am I boring you?"

I whirl around. "No. Of course not."

"Then please come to the stand."

My chair squeals as I rise. My mother's hand flashes forward and grips my fingers. One squeeze. No words.

Ten years ago my parents coached me for my first meeting with Maharaja Naupure and Jatin, and I threw their advice out the window. I am eight no longer. This time I listened. "Don't look to us, Adraa," they said. "Appear as you are. As a woman capable of stopping that volcano, of leading this country, of not needing her parents' safety."

My mother squeezes my hand one more time. *But we will be right next to you*, it tells me.

I approach the bench. The crying hasn't stopped. The cuffs on my wrists glow, knifing their way through me. I hadn't even realized I had pulled at my magic. Even that crutch, my own magic, has turned against me.

"Do you understand that a spell will be cast willing you to speak the truth and nothing but the truth?"

"I understand," I say clearly. A sheen of sweat coats my body and my throat feels drier than possible.

"And no one has coerced you into appearing today?"

"No."

Foolishly, I glance toward the back of the room. Several people are being led out by their friends and family. A sick part of me wants to know who they knew out of the one hundred twenty-nine. I've done the research. Forty-eight guardsmen under my father's command who were building trenches when half the mountain slid into the ocean and took them with it. Thirty-two Untouched without magic to shield themselves or fly. Fifteen crushed when the earthquakes toppled buildings. Twelve children. Nine shop owners. Eight knocked from their skygliders by debris and a crashing flying station. Three drowned. One baker, who made the best pastries in the West Village.

And finally, one small man who taught me everything I know about skygliders and sold me all thirty-seven of them. Mr. Mittal, the best flier and yellow forte in Belwar, stayed on the streets handing out skygliders to every fleeing pedestrian he saw. It's reported he saved over eighty-five people. I look up again and finally recognize the witch standing in the back. It's Muni, Mr. Mittal's partner in more ways than one. Pain laces through me like I'm hearing his name on the death list for the first time.

This is why you are here. I tell myself to hold back my tears. I could fight and spell my way out of these purple cuffs. I could have not come. But Muni and the rest need to know the truth. We cannot fall to Moolek and this lie he's cast upon me. I don't want to be the monster of Belwar.

"No one coerced me. I want the truth out there like everyone here today," I clarify. I don't want Muni to think I did this. I don't want any of my people to think I did this.

"That *is* what we all want, Lady Belwar." The truth caster turns to the audience. The door opens for another mourner to escape. A sudden shaft of daylight illuminates the aisle. Then, just like that, the door slams and the light is cut off. The truth caster waits for quiet to speak again. "Well said."

◇ ◇ ◇

I didn't expect to hear the truth spell, but through the ring of silence I think I make out an incantation. I didn't expect a voice sounding like syrup. Or for the actual spell to hit me like I'm sinking in the stuff. But here I am. Drowning in what's probably my own saliva because I'm having a hard time swallowing. My throat feels like it has been stripped.

"Let's start simple. Walk me through the day of the eruption."

I find Jatin's eyes. He nods, but for a split second I could have sworn his expression shouted, *Run!*

"It began with my royal ceremony," I start, and then the truth spell unravels the events. It's weird what details it skips over, like meeting Goddess Erif, me begging her for answers and her telling me just how Mount Gandhak was erupting. Maybe the spell is being precise, allowing me to explain only what happened during the day, not whatever one may call the red room. The wizard doesn't prevent me from sputtering along. He asks no follow-up questions until my mouth stops and he and the audience are left with a shell of an explanation.

"So . . . you are telling, us, the counsel, and the people of Belwar here today, that you died, or at least went into an unconscious state after your failed ceremony, where you felt Mount Gandhak's eruption, and you then rose from the dead and flew to the volcano, called back your power, and thus stopped the discharge of your firelight? Did I miss anything?"

"No." The answer falls out, but I shake my head. Isn't that a lie? He summarized it fine, I suppose, but what about the details? I didn't rise from the dead so much as my sister pulled me back from the brink. I find her watching me now, tight-lipped. I look away quickly, facing the wizard again. It's not much better. I've met my share of creeps, cage casters, and Vencrin drug dealers. How is it possible this man looks more put out than someone I've punched in the face?

But I breathe. Because so far, he hasn't cross-examined my every word. He's barely asked me anything. He's flirting with the truth spell's loophole—that I can answer only what has been asked.

I need one more question. And it needs to be about Moolek. *Ask me what happened after I was bandaged and broken*, I want to scream. Incriminating evidence sits right here, inside my head.

They just have to ask . . .

Let me prove myself.

The truth caster huffs. "I think we have had enough confusion about your physical state during the eruption. Let's talk about what we all want to know, Lady Belwar. Did you place your firelight into Mount Gandhak?"

The truth spell floods my throat. I gag on the surprise of it. It's worse than the first time. Syrupy only at the edges, muddy at the core.

A weight presses down on me. A cloud must have moved across the sun because suddenly shadows stretch and lengthen. People watch, waiting, and yet they appear fuzzy and out of place. The five rajas lean in, yearning for this moment.

I do want to answer. It's simple, one word. Let's settle this.

I open my mouth to speak.

CHAPTER SIX

◇

Lies Legalized

Jatin

"Yes." Adraa's head tilts, her eyes flash, and the word falls flat.

Everyone stills. The tight air constricts even further. I reconfigure the question, thinking I must have heard wrong, my hearing still diluted by truth-spell silence. Maybe it's not her answer that rings wrong. Maybe it was the question. Maybe I—

"I'll repeat." The truth caster's voice edges into pure glee, dripping with satisfaction. "Did you place firelight into Mount Gandhak?"

I grip the banister in front of me, slowly standing. *No. No, no, no, no.*

"Yes," Adraa repeats flatly. She looks fierce, angry in a way I've never seen before. And I've seen her angry. I've seen her furious.

She rises from the bench. "And I'd do it again. I'd delight in watching this city burn. You think I gave my firelight, my power, willingly to the people because I'm generous? You are useless.

Belwar is useless. Anyone who ever used firelight, who thought they could harness *my* magic, deserves to die. To burn."

I can't move. No one seems to be able to. Then, the truth caster steps back, his fear evident, but triumph overriding it. "How long were you planning this?"

Adraa scoffs. "Since firelight's inception. Since I was old enough to know I am chosen and any drugged-up commoner playing at power should die." The Touch lacing her neck lights up even though she's wearing cuffs. It should be painful; she should be flinching or cringing at the very least. No. Adraa stands tall, eyes hateful and dark in a way I've never seen before. It can't be. This isn't her. Someone must be controlling her, something—

The Adraa impersonator stares out at the crowd, and for the first time I'm scared of her. Screams follow along with the pounding of feet as the crowd in the courtroom race for the doors.

"Someone stop her!" a woman cries.

"Kill her!" voices shout.

"Shoot her. Shoot her!"

A spark whizzes through the air, a perfectly aimed arrow glowing an angry purple. I watch it for a second, paralyzed. The next moment I'm jumping into the air as every spell to stop it vanishes from my brain. But the arrow is too high and too fast for me to catch it. The spell sizzles past me like a shot.

Raja Dara isn't so slow. A sweep of his own purple magic incinerates the arrow a meter from Adraa's head.

Adraa's parents are shouting spells, building a barrier in front of the rest of the audience. I rush to help and find they've already finished. A glowing shield of orange pink cuts the room in two. Kalyan, Riya, Prisha, and the audience are on one side. The guards, the rajas, Adraa's parents, my father, and I are on the other. My eyes lock with Kalyan's—he's frozen with shock. Riya, on the other hand, pounds on the barrier, shouting her disapproval, which I can't hear.

"Don't let her cast. Contain her! *Himadloc!*" Raja Amin of the East Village yells, and I whip back around.

Shackles of ice bind Adraa's arms to the stand. Her expression changes instantly, like a wall falling. Madness turns to confusion. "What are you doing?" she calls out, the words laced with fear. "What is this?"

What? She couldn't have . . .

My father's fingers cling to my arm, clammy and frail. "Jatin."

Everything happens too fast for me to process. In mere moments my life has fallen apart.

The judge rises. "Enough! I've heard enough. Adraa Belwar, Lady of Belwar, for the truth you have spoken today, and the crimes against your own nation, for the deaths of one hundred twenty-nine people . . ." He pauses, sternness overcoming his face, his decision clear in the set of his shoulders. "This court sentences you to death."

◇ ◇ ◇

The whole scene mists over. And that's when I realize it's my magic building and gushing like a storm, like a wave of unending fog. I'm already running toward Adraa, orange spells of

54

strength and power rumbling off me, so when I knock through two guards no one can stop me.

With one swift strike, the ice cracks. Adraa extends her hand and I haul her from her imprisonment. Then I have her by my side, keeping her as safe as I can in this situation. "Adraa?"

"Do you feel it?" she says, her words a rushed jumble. "I don't know how he got in. Is he here? How—"

"Shh," I say, rubbing her arms. "I know. It wasn't the truth. I know you would never destroy us."

She slowly looks up at me, her eyes wider than I have ever seen them. "What?" Her voice is brittle. "What do you think I said?"

The question pierces me. She doesn't know what we all heard. She doesn't understand why people are cowering, flooding the doorway, or charging forward in vengeance and violence.

Adraa's father speaks. He's not only angry but also heartbroken. "As your maharaja, I order you to release my daughter this moment."

A condescending smile crosses the judge's face. "We the court are not under your rule. You said so yourself when creating us. No one man is above the truth. And how right you were. You heard the truth from your own daughter's lips. Your kin tried to murder this nation."

"We don't give death sentences. It is not the Belwar way," Maharaja Belwar spits.

"No Belwarian has ever confessed to mass murder. This is unprecedented."

"You will *not* kill her."

"I am not scared of you. In this room, in matters of truth and justice, I will do what I feel is right, which is the job you elected me for." As the judge rises, the entire council of rajas follow. Then, one by one, they ready their magic. Raja Gupta in yellow, Raja Reddy in green, Raja Amin in purple, Raja Lal in blue, and finally, with reluctance, Raja Dara in purple. "Don't make it messier than it has to be. Adraa Belwar is guilty, as she has confessed," the judge says.

Maharaja Belwar's jaw sets, ticks. I await the next move, the next shout of denial, the next play to resolve this mess. But it's only us, the audience cut off and silenced by the barrier.

The judge turns, his long face growing longer as he frowns. "Boy! Step away from the perpetrator."

Perpetrator.

Boy.

I twist my head so hard that my neck twitches. "It's 'raja' to you." When I step in front of Adraa, a wave of snow wafts from me to the floor. My magic prickles on my skin, wanting release, like I imagine clouds do before a storm. This will the most difficult fight of my life. Five rajas. My eyes shift to four guardsmen circling like wild cats.

Just try to take her. Just try to take her from me.

Out of the corner of my eye I catch the blue of my father's magic. Adraa's parents are at the ready too. I'm not alone here.

Then my attention is drawn back to the bearded judge, who is eyeing me. "I will not have violence in my courtroom," he says, "so I'm only going to tell you once. Stand down, Jatin

Naupure. You are protecting a criminal, and I will not hesitate to arrest you."

I feel Adraa's hand on my shoulder, burning hot. I can't tell what she's trying to communicate in this moment: *I'm with you in the coming fight* or *Obey them*. The snow won't stop falling, though, my arms crying out like they did the last time Adraa was in danger. Last night I should have taken her. We should have run.

"I will count to three," the judge says.

Raja Amin of the East Village flexes. Purple knives tumble down in smoky tendrils, materializing in his hands like claws.

"One."

The raja of the North Village holds two twisters of yellow magic swirling along his Touch. Raja Dara crosses his arms, the only one with no magic rolling off him like the clashing of a natural disaster.

"Two."

"No!"

We all turn toward the voice. The maharani of Belwar steps forward. *"Niyam Samalaeh,"* she casts. I'm unfamiliar with the spell, but pink gushes over everything, everyone. The courtroom slips into sludge as everyone hesitates, slowed by Adraa's mother. The spell seems to diffuse the tension. Tight shoulders relax. The rajas' knives weaken. And my snow has dissolved, the swirling angry white mist receding.

Finally, Adraa's mother releases us and we all take a breath like we had been drowning in honey. All is quiet until she speaks. "You will not touch her. The only truth I see here today is that my daughter is being sabotaged and persecuted for doing the right thing."

"You heard her as we all did!" Raja Amin hollers. He's the first I'll attack, the most vicious and probably the one who's behind this, maybe even part of the Vencrin. And maybe— a dark thought enters my head—maybe even the elusive Vencrin leader whom Adraa and I have been trying to unmask.

"I don't care what I heard. If she were heartless enough to try to kill us all, she would not admit it like this, in front of this crowd. I know my daughter."

"She's *your* daughter. You are willing to believe her innocence when the facts, the truth, speak otherwise. Take her," the judge orders again.

Maharani Belwar steps forward, her entire stance imposing. "Your wife is very sick. I provide her potions every week. If you sentence my daughter to death, your wife will never receive another drop from me."

"You dare bring my family into this?"

"I dare to bring the whole world into this. Without my daughter, your wife and every last one of us would be dead anyway."

"If it weren't for your daughter, Mount Gandhak would never have erupted!" the judge roars.

"She saved us all, you bloody bastard!" I yell.

And, with that, we are right back where we started, tensed, ready, my arms snowing. I see it then. I think we all see it. The moment the maharani of Belwar gets desperate. The moment she lies.

"I commanded her to do it. I ordered it. So take me."

Everything stills, the maharani's sacrifice vibrating through the air.

The truth caster shakes his head. "I don't need to cast a spell to know that is a—"

A heavy thud interrupts him. I turn toward the noise. The space where my father was standing is empty. It takes a moment for my brain to catch up. I have the impulse to glance upward, like he might have popped on a skyglider and whisked himself into the air to stop all this nonsense and help Adraa escape.

But no. My father has collapsed on the floor, motionless, like the dead.

◇

CHAPTER SEVEN

I Make a Decision

Adraa

I don't know what's happening. One moment I'm answering their questions, and then suddenly the truth spell urges me to stand and proclaim my innocence. I told them of my love for this country and its people. It wasn't my most brilliant moment, but it doesn't explain the death sentence. Fear wraps me in a tight coil. I'm about to shatter.

No one moves. No one seems to even breathe. I'm numb. That's because of the ice, I reason. The ice they wrapped around me because . . . because I leaned forward and told them I had planned on taking back my firelight only at the last minute. That I was sorry it took me a while to figure it all out, how to stop the eruption.

And now my mother is asking to take my place and Maharaja Naupure lies on the floor. No one is even checking his pulse to determine whether he is breathing. It's these two things that, somehow, get me out of my own head. Loosen the grip of fear. I may not know what is happening to me, but I know what needs to happen.

I step out from behind Jatin's protection. "Don't stand there. Someone help him."

My mother rushes to Maharaja Naupure's side. "He's breathing," she announces, and I can tell Jatin finally breathes himself. "Not a heart attack," she continues, "but I don't know what has happened. He needs to get out of here."

The judge speaks. "Fine, release him and your wall." He gestures to the barrier my parents crafted. "And we will take Lady Belwar—"

Mother glares. It's a look I've lived with my whole life. It still scares me. "I will tear this place down before I watch you kill my daughter."

There's a moment's pause during which no one moves, though I see my mother sieving magic into Jatin's father—diagnosing or breathing spells, I'm sure. *Shock* doesn't adequately describe the emotion filling me, because it's mixed with a toxic terror. Maharaja Naupure or me. One of us will die based on the judge's next words.

"Then not death. Life."

All attention shifts to the truth caster.

"What?" the judge asks.

The truth caster smiles. He appears smug, having come up with my damnation. "If we are about to kill each other over a sentencing of death, then how about we sentence her to life. Life in the Dome."

Silence soaks us all like a heavy rain. Life in the Dome. I

don't know what to make of it. But I didn't know what to make of my execution either. *What. Did. I. Say?*

"She's innocent," Jatin bites out.

Am I? comes a voice deep inside my head.

"Is she?" asks a chorus of voices.

I jerk, realizing all five rajas have said the same thing.

Wait . . . wait. Wait. Wait.

Well, whose fault is it anyway? Adraa, I don't know what's going on in my head. I search for Prisha behind the barrier. She holds her head in her hands like a headache has eclipsed her senses. Riya looks pissed, and she keeps shaking her head like something is stuck in her ear. Only a few people are left on the other side of the barrier, and they all wear masks of hostile confusion. Much like that crowd last night, out for blood, driven practically senseless. Much like how I felt when Maharaja Moolek proposed at the temple and pointed the finger at Maharaja Naupure as the one who stole my firelight. There had been a voice in the back of my head then too.

Lucky for you, I needed you both alive. Moolek's voice laces through me.

Oh my bloody Gods!

My legs buckle, but I quickly right myself, gripping the defendant's stand. "I'll do it! I'll take your offer. Stand down, let Maharaja Naupure get to a clinic, and you can take me peacefully!" I shout.

The room seems to feed on tension, waves of it wafting through the air. They have to listen. Because right now, none of them can trust their own minds.

"I will go freely. I'll live my life in the Dome. No one has to fight."

"Adraa, no," Jatin says, his voice an octave lower than I have ever heard it. He's torn in half, the grip on my hand pressing harder and slipping at the same time. I'm torn in half too. Maharaja Naupure, the man who is my second father, lies at my mother's side. If the rajas do what I say, I'm gone, dragged to the Dome. But if we keep standing here . . .

"Please," I beg. I stare, first at my mother and then at Maharaja Naupure. It's a simple trade—my life for Maharaja Naupure's. Because I'm not getting out of this. Moolek has somehow poisoned their minds against me. Mere words right now are folly. My mother stares back, the crease in her brow making her nose look even more crooked. Then, slowly, she nods. I stare at my father next. "It'll be fine. Let them," I say.

"What are you waiting for? Take her already," the judge commands. Guards rush forward, released from the tension.

"Adraa," Jatin says, his voice quaking. We both know what I'm asking of him and what I'm doing to myself. He grabs my right hand; he's an anchor in the madness, the only one who doesn't seem to be affected by Moolek's manipulation. Gods, I love him. I have always loved him.

I look up at him. The kindest eyes in all of Wickery shine with worry. "You're going to have to let me go," I say, before making a snap decision. I hug him tight. "Don't come for me. I need you to—" With a yank, the guardsmen break us apart.

"Let me talk to her. Just let me talk to her for one minute!"

Jatin yells as my hands are bound together in another shackle of purple magic.

As he jerks forward, a wall erupts between us. My family and the rest of the courtroom are blurred by purple. "I need you to figure out how Moolek did this. He got in our minds, in everyone's. Figure out how!" I scream. But Jatin only pounds on the wall, the thumping thunderous. I'm not sure he heard a word I said.

Then the guardsmen tug me away, through the back doors, down the hall, and into a windowless carriage. All I see is Jatin's face and the look of betrayal sketched into his kind eyes.

I let myself be the monster of Belwar.

◇ ◇ ◇

The carriage rumbles up to the Dome, its wheels skimming smoothly over the well-worn grooves in the dirt. The ride lasts ten minutes. Then, with a rickety stop and the click of a latch, I'm thrown back into daylight, where I'm greeted by the stark curves of Belwar's prison rising over me. In a city of sandstone, arches, and shingled roofs, the Dome appears foreign, an invader. It shares the same cream-colored coating as the rest of the architecture in the city, but the curved surface rounding into the sky is magical ingenuity exemplified. I've always found it intimidating, accomplishing its job to inspire fear and an incentive to not break the law.

Terror crawls its way in. I'm about to walk into a prison

where every Belwar criminal is kept. Some of them witches and wizards I put here myself.

With a hard shove, I'm removed from the carriage. Doors shift. Walls open. Darkness wraps around me. And just like that, I am in the Dome. With no guarantee I will ever leave.

A torch fastened to the wall illuminates the cavern. The walls are stone, but mud and grime have scabbed over the smoothness, leaving rough, jagged edges. It feels as if I'm descending into an open mouth, into decay and death. Everything curves, even the aisles and the stairwells rounding into darkness. By the time we take another turn I'm already lost. All fear tactics. All ways to perpetuate the belief there is no hope in here.

I trip on nothing. Or maybe I was pushed. The dirt greets me just the same.

"Get up, Lady," the guard sneers. "I'm sure they taught you how to walk in the palace."

I spit. "It doesn't look like you were ever taught to have manners."

A foot pushes me down, and I crash into the dirt again. This might not be the best time to talk back, I realize, but it's too late. My parents can no longer protect me; Jatin can no longer defend me. I'm beyond their grasp. And I'm a snarky fool merely playing at calmness.

Rough hands haul me up. The guard leans toward my ear. "We are going to have to do something about that mouth of yours."

The other guard huffs. "Let's go. We don't have time for this."

I look at him. Stubby in every aspect besides height. Of the two of them, no one would peg him as the nice guy to his clean-shaven friend. But appearances lie and you can never truly tell who is on your side.

We stop a minute later. Keys jostle into a slot, opening a thick oval door.

The stubby guard grabs my upper arm. "A word of advice if you want to survive? Don't piss off the nice guards." Then he pushes me into a room and slams the metal door.

The room is empty except for one ragged wicker chair. It's also square, which wouldn't be extraordinary if this weren't the Dome. To be honest, I didn't think corners existed here. I must still be in shock, my brain rounding into nonsense. I mean, blood, I'm dwelling on corners.

But then my brain returns to the nonstop terror of the court-room, and I wish the filthy confines of these stone walls were the worst of my concerns. I can't get the faces out of my head, especially their eyes. Jatin. My parents. Even Riya. What could I have said for them to look at me with such horrified disbelief? To receive the death sentence, something my country hasn't doled out in nearly a century? A damp coldness grips me, making shivers dance up my back. I don't think I want to know what I said.

"You did the right thing," I whisper to myself. Maharaja Naupure wouldn't have gotten a healer's attention if we were still in the standoff. And Jatin can figure it out without me. He'll discover why and how Moolek managed to poison so many people's minds against me. I did the right thing. Though when I say the words aloud again, they feel like a lie.

The door squeals open and three men step into the cell. Two different guardsmen and another man, who looms in the shadows.

"Hello, dear. How are we this evening?"

I haven't heard that voice in months, but my ears ring at the sound of it. Only one wizard had the audacity to call me *dear*. Basu, the man who distributed my firelight to the Vencrin, the man I had arrested, steps into the dim light. He has the same hairy arms, the same pudgy face. Only four months have passed, but his features are creased with a level of smugness I didn't think even he could achieve. "It's been quite a while, hasn't it, my lady?"

"You?"

"Yes, me. You thought bringing me to the Dome would be good enough. You thought I had disappeared, afraid of the Vencrin?" He leans toward me, his eyes scanning my face. "Moolek was right. You are easy to fool."

I jerk forward even though the cuffs around my hands protest. But the pain is worth it when Basu stumbles back. I stifle a dark laugh. "Try not to fool yourself because you've aligned yourself with more powerful wizards. You are the same Basu I knew in the East Village. But now? When this is over, I know who to come for. You should have stayed in Agsa."

He smiles, his confidence returning. "This won't end, my dear. You aren't getting out of here. You are a convicted criminal."

"Whatever they *think* I said, the truth will come out. It always does."

"Oh, but who will tell them?" He smiles again. "I can assure you, it won't be you." He nods and the two guards push me into the chair. Then Basu jolts forward, one hand grabbing my jaw. I startle, but I can't move from his grip. "Hold her firm. There can be no mistakes with this one." Hands snake up my arms, holding me in place.

Pain explodes through my jaw as he unhinges it. Every part of me thrashes. He's going to try to make me swallow something, a sleeping pill or something, and I won't let him. But I realize a second too late that I'm wrong. Basu's arm brightens, the blaze of yellow magic igniting and then swirling like a mini twister. His voice wraps around me. He's chanting, a stream of spells I don't recognize.

What the blood is this?

I try to scream, to cast, to escape by any means possible. But I can't. My hands are still cuffed, and these bands restraining my magic glow in bright red as they burn my wrists. My plan to wait this out was reckless. Bloody reckless. Moolek wanted me in the Dome. That alone should have told me to fight from the very start. But I was trying to not be rash. I was trying to not be typical Adraa Belwar.

The air around me whips and snaps. The yellow twister swirls closer and I feel it. I try to clamp my mouth shut, but my jaw is locked open. Vulnerable, my body shrieks. The twister skirts my teeth and dives down my throat. I gag. Hands wrench my mouth closed so fast my teeth clack.

A coldness plunges down my throat, then it's fire, tearing, ripping, snarling. And through it all, Basu is chanting. No one cares about my mother's threats or their compromise of life in the Dome instead of death. I'm being killed from the inside out. I imagine the twister descending, tearing through my internal organs. But right now, it stays in my throat, choking me. I can't breathe.

Basu motions to the guardsmen, and their hands leave me. Suddenly, his hand is pressed against my throat. "Scream for me."

I obey, the wind, the fire, the pain all wanting to be released. I scream—it seems to be the only thing that's left—until the edges of my vision go fuzzy. Then all I see is the yellow of Basu's magic bleeding into mine as bloodred spirals rise like heat off my arm. Screaming overtakes me. I am nothing but noise. Finally, the noise ends. The pressure on my throat pulls back. I crash forward, the chair buckling. Wood splinters, a welcome sound after my deafening wails. I lie there. I lie there and breathe.

From my spot on the cold stone I'm able to make out Basu slumping against a wall, his chant over. The small ounce of me that can think of anything besides breathing is glad he's drained of magic, close to burnout. A guard reaches toward him, but Basu holds up a hand. "I'm fine. Go. Tell him it is done. Tell him the Lady of Belwar is no more."

I want to protest. I want to spit out that I've felt pain worse than this. This is nothing. I've been prepared to die. I've even felt death. This . . . this is . . .

I move to stand and fall to my knees.

Basu reaches for my cuffs, and I realize with a start they have dulled back to purple. "Don't need these anymore." He wipes his hands and then his sweat-slicked face. "Rest, my dear. You do look so worn." He starts to turn, then pauses. "Ah, one more thing. A message from a mutual friend of ours. He wanted me to tell you, don't worry about anyone discovering your identity in here. You truly are nothing of consequence anymore."

Before I can retort, the door slams and only stillness follows.

I open my mouth to scream-cast, to unleash my anger in fire, but walls of silence erupt around me. The designs on my arm remain dull, even the ones wrapping my shoulder. My magic is still there, I can feel it. But my words, my ability to cast, are gone.

Dampness wraps around the shadows, caging me in. Silent sobs rack my throat, desperate to express anguish, but it's futile. The only sounds are the small, wet splashes of my tears hitting the stones beneath me.

There are many times in my life I have felt weak. I know some have seen me like that since the beginning. I'm a one-armed Touched, I can barely cast white magic, I failed the gods' test for leadership. And I've failed my people in letting Moolek's plans and manipulation sneak past me. But I've never been powerless. And I certainly have never been voiceless.

Until now.

◇

CHAPTER EIGHT

Dealing with Death

Jatin

"How could they do this? How did this happen?"

The question has been reverberating in my skull for the last five hours, so I don't even register when it comes from someone else. Chara, my nursemaid since I was four, zeroes in on me as she speaks. But I'm sure she doesn't expect an answer. I don't even know if she's talking about Adraa's sentence or my father's dire state. He is splayed on the bed, his breathing finally even.

We're sitting in the mountainside clinic my father created after my mother died. Sunshine pours in as if the buttery light were bragging. Water drips from the ice roof, splashing the plants and herbs. Frostlight branches cast cheerful shadows against the day.

I will my eyes away from the countertop and shelves of ingredients to my right. Adraa and I sat there while I made her a potion to help her cramps. It was the first real quiet moment we shared instead of a death-defying one. Everywhere is a memory, and I loathe the new one unfolding in front of me. Dad's face looks like Mount Gandhak is still erupting and its ash has embedded itself into his skin.

"I don't know," I whisper. "I don't know."

Chara is over ninety years old, yet her hands feel strong when she rubs my back. I've never been more thankful for her—she's one of the few people left I can trust. That courtroom swallowed my faith in powerful strangers.

"He is strong, just like you. That's how I know it will be all right. He will heal and you'll get her back."

Don't come for me.

How am I supposed to get Adraa back when that's the one thing she asked me not to do? Bitter irony clings to the back of my throat. We played our roles. Adraa sacrificed herself, again, and I was . . . useless. So useless Adraa doesn't want me to even try? Why? Why would she say that? She must know I won't listen, that I can't.

I jump up, my emotions boiling over. With a jerk, I overturn a bench of potted plants. The crash overwhelms the brightness. Ceramic splinters. Dirt explodes. The semblance of order is thrown into chaos. I'm satisfied for one breath of a moment before the image of Prisha hurling newt eyes and sitting in wasted materials in her mother's clinic seeps in.

I'm no better.

"Blood," I curse.

Chara starts, not at the crash, but at my language. I never curse. But what does it mean if I want to curse the whole world?

"I'm sorry. I'll clean it up."

"It's okay, dear. If now isn't the time to break things I don't know if there ever will be," she whispers. It's the same tone people in the palace used after I lost my mother, which means . . .

I can't think about losing them both in the same sentence. Not after this morning. "Has there been any word?" Maharani Belwar set up the cyclone of pink magic floating above my father's head to stabilize him. But after getting him breathing comfortably and announcing there was seemingly nothing wrong with my father—he hadn't had a heart attack or a stroke—she vanished, rightly so. We both have a lot of process, to grieve. But if I don't do something soon and figure out what is wrong with the only family I have left, no plant will be safe from me. Nothing will be safe.

Chara frowns, wrinkles lining her face. "We must give her time. The maharani has stabilized him. She's performed the hard part so I can keep him breathing as long as it takes for him to recover."

"Has his temperature risen?" asks a voice from the doorway.

I whip around to find Maharani Belwar standing on the threshold, wearing the same orange sari from the trial, though the pleats are in disarray and the bottom border, adorned with rising suns, is now covered in grass stains. Her eyes are rimmed in red.

"Maharani Belwar, thank you for coming back. I—" My fingers find my throat and I bow without a second thought.

"Please," she says, her voice weary. "Please, drop the formalities. Call me Ira." Ignoring my fumbling, she steps into the room and kneels beside my father. "And I'm sorry for leaving. It's just . . . I run my tests better in my own clinic," she explains before casting.

I try to catch the spells, the diagnosis and tests, but the words slip by me. Even Chara seems to sit back, and she is one of the best Naupure has to offer. I guess you can't beat Pire Island teachings. Then the maharani does the thing you never want to see a professional do—she sighs and hangs her head, rubbing her temples.

"What?" I ask.

She looks me straight in the eye. "It's what I was afraid of: poison."

"Poison?" I replay my memory of Adraa's trial. My father's shaking hands, his unusual quietness. Last night's tiredness. He wasn't disappointed, he was hurting. And I am the idiot for not noticing. *Don't we have precautions? Did no one taste his food?*

The maharani faces me fully. "I don't think this came from food."

I startle, realizing I must have voiced my irritation. I don't have time for embarrassment, though. "How? How was he poisoned?"

"It entered his body like a spell."

Our eyes both scour my father's frail form.

"A torture spell?" But that doesn't make sense. Torture spells are direct pink magic infusing the body with ravaging pain instead of healing. And I witnessed every spell cast in that room. I paid attention as we all teetered on the brink of war. But maybe that is what they wanted. Maybe someone got to my father as we debated Adraa's fate.

"No. More like it seeped in slowly and then, today, someone released the final dose. A spell we didn't notice, or maybe a potion that reacted to something."

Slowly. Which means this was happening for weeks and I've been neglecting him, running out of Azure Palace every chance I had to answer my signal and spend time with Adraa. "Is he going to be okay? How do we heal him?"

"This echoes a case of mine, but unfortunately that man is still lying in my clinic, in a coma."

Riya's father, Mr. Burman. Adraa's tutor and guard. The one act of violence that started Adraa's entire crusade as Jaya Smoke. Blood!

"You're sure?"

"That's why I left, to make sure. It's not exactly the same—Mr. Burman was attacked with one heavy dose, maybe just a torture spell. This"—she gestures to my father—"like I said, this has been going on for a while. And I'll need time to figure out what spell or toxins were used."

"Does that mean we can't do anything?"

The maharani's eyes shift to Chara, and I detect the meaning. So does my nursemaid. She stands and bows. "I'll follow whatever you put in the chart *as always.*" Chara wobbles out of the clinic, turning only at the last moment to grace us with a firm nod.

As always? Adraa told me her mother's secret, her network with the clinic, her flow of information about the city and its inner workings. But that couldn't mean . . . Not my nursemaid.

"She's . . . she's one of yours." I don't even know if I should phrase it as a question.

Maharani Belwar's mouth twitches, accentuating her broken nose. "Or I am one of hers. She was *my* nursemaid in Pire before you were born." Her smile widens, unraveling a thread of a secret I hadn't even known existed. "We pink fortes stick together. Who do you think helped make this?" She gestures around us, to what I thought was my father's obsession, a fortress of clinic materials to prevent anyone else from dying on this mountain again. But of course, he couldn't do it alone.

When I look back, her expression is hard. "I'll make you a promise, Jatin. I'll do everything in my power to cure your father. But that means I'll have to trust that someone *else* is working to break my daughter out of the Dome."

Silence encapsulates us. A moment long enough to make me wonder if I misheard her. "You want me to break the greatest law of Belwar? A law your husband created?"

"No, not you. I need *Night* to do it." She sees my hesitation and continues. "We won't be able to convince anyone that Moolek's to blame if Adraa is in the Dome."

I agree. But she misunderstands my reluctance. *Don't come for me.* The words pound through my skull. Even with Maharani Belwar's royal request and the mask, Adraa's message was clear.

I grasp the railing of my father's bed, shaking the wicker frame. "And if Adraa doesn't want me to?" I mutter.

When I finally look up, tears fill the maharani's eyes. "Is that what she said to you?"

I nod, sharing her grief. They took Adraa. They took her from us and she let them, didn't allow us to fight back.

The maharani breathes deeply. From the corner of my eye, I watch as she wipes away the tears. We sit in silence for several moments until she speaks. "You know, from the beginning your father said Adraa was made to be a Naupure. And I understood what he meant. Naupure has the reputation for knowing when to push back and when to play the political game. Your entire country is founded on escaping Moolek's prejudice and setting forth your own systems. Adraa has always been an original person who knows when to push back and when to . . ." Her voice trembles. "As much as we hate it, she made the right decision."

I drop my head into my hands. Even if she's correct, the pain still consumes me. I didn't do enough.

"But for me, that night, I saw Belwar in you," the maharani says.

I jerk back up. My name is my country, infused to my identity like rust. "Belwar in me? From what?" All I did the first time I met Adraa was be a rude, spoiled child who got slapped in the face. Not wanting to admit embarrassment, I tried to play down the situation and deny it had happened. That doesn't sound Belwarian to me. Especially when I have always associated Belwar's main attributes—strength and compassion—with Adraa.

"For standing back up after getting punched down, especially when it's hard enough to knock you off your feet."

I manage a smile. "Punched? Don't you mean slapped?"

"Please, we both know my daughter. Even a slap must have felt like getting hit by an orange forte." She's exaggerating, of course, like I've exaggerated for years. Adraa didn't hit me that hard. I had been startled by her fierceness, by the reaction itself. It was the first time someone ever contradicted me, ever told me no.

But maybe I need to contradict Adraa for once. Be like a Naupure—know when to obey and when to free myself.

A new voice rises up in the back of my mind, pounding even louder than that of Adraa's. And it tells me one thing. *Go! Find her. Free her.*

"I'll get her back. I swear to you." As Night. As Jatin. As anyone I need to be.

The maharani nods. "Good. Because I don't pretend to think my threats convinced them. There is a reason they allowed her to live. And every way I look at it, that reason cannot be good."

A chill washes over me. Of everything I have come to learn about Ira Belwar, I know that she is brilliant—and she is almost always right.

◇ ◇ ◇

Once my new conviction to save Adraa grips me, I don't waste a moment. I charge into the armory. Swords and weaponry I hardly use line the walls. A large wooden table and wicker-laced stools are laden with equipment and maps. Heat billows from the adjoining room as more weapons are crafted into being. The place smells of a brewing war. Kalyan, tall and forbidding, stands among it all, sheathing daggers into his belt.

"About time you showed up." My best friend tosses me something and I catch it on instinct. The hard handle of my skyglider, the skyglider Adraa herself gifted to me, presses into my palm. "What first?" he asks.

I extend my skyglider, white smoke soaking into the wood. "We're going hunting."

◇

CHAPTER NINE

Into the Dome

Adraa

Five days pass, and I don't encounter another soul or leave my room. Hours after Basu departs, I fall asleep, and I awaken to find a pale orange kurta and a pair of flying pants by the door. My embellished sari becomes a blanket. In the beginning, in the quiet darkness, I try everything I can to pull magic from my arms and light the space. My power stirs under my skin, but eventually I succumb to the reality that, without my voice, I have no way to release the spells.

I mark time by the hand that juts into my cell to give me food and pick up the empty platters twice a day. By day two, this terrifies me. By day three, I have cried enough to fill the bay. Four days in, and the sadness inside me has settled, but a new determination hasn't yet taken hold. And my eyes still remember the tears.

I can hear rumblings, and every once in a while the room seems to quake with some unknown activity in the depths of the

Dome. But now I'm done. Five days—I think—and I'm ready for this quarantine to be over. Maybe they know it too. Maybe there is a system of abuse and control, because on the fifth day, my door screeches open and the tallest guard I've ever seen stands in the doorway.

After five days without seeing another face, this one sure isn't much to look at. Not that that is any type of requirement or I'm in any way picky, but his teeth appear to be having a hard time deciding whether they would like to rest inside or outside his mouth. "Come on, newbie. Let's go," Jagged Teeth says.

Where? I open my mouth to ask. Forget. Choke on air. I break just a little bit more. But at least I can rejoice in feeling something. In knowing I'm still alive enough to feel something. I clamber to my feet, because who really cares where we're going? Anywhere is better than this damp isolation.

We walk through a hallway that curves like a tunnel. Then the space suddenly opens up. I have to raise my hand against the brightness, even though light only filters down in patches. It's piercing and chaotic compared to the darkness I've been living in.

When I look again, I'm teetering on a jagged cliff as I gape at the Dome's interior. Outside it's all smooth sandstone, but inside I'm met with rough black stone, like cutting into a perfect apple to find it's rotten. In the center of the prison looms a twisted black tower at least ten stories high. Platforms have been carved into the hollow cavernous interior and ring the outer walls. Dangling from each platform ledge is a spherical cage, held up by strands of yellow magic that thread into the tower. Narrow pathways connect the cliffsides to the tower as well, making the place a maze of bridges and dark empty space.

I step back, astonished by the sheer amount of magical power pumping through the veins of this complex. How did I not know the Dome was set up like this? People always joked that the Pire Islanders set their dungeons over the cliffs, floating above the sea. I never imagined that inside this sphere, Belwar did a similar thing. How could I have been so clueless?

The guardsman squints down at me and gestures to the closest bridge connecting to the tower. "Hope you don't have a fear of heights."

He gestures again for me to go first, and I think back to five days ago when I refused to move and got pushed into the dirt. With so little ground beneath me I obey, stepping out on the narrow plank and into the chasm of the Dome.

A column of air greets me as I walk out into the void and with it comes a damp, moldy smell. One that I'll get used to or will get used to me. From this vantage point I can see the dangling cells better. Rows and rows of them, every caged bubble the same. They hover on pads of cushioned yellow magic like the flying stations above Belwar. Each one contains two beds, a basin, a curtain near the stone wall, and two prisoners in matching pale orange outfits.

These orange-clad witches stare as we pass. Though huge, the room is smaller than I expected, and then I realize that all the prisoners, around one hundred of them, are women. There must be another side to the prison where they house the men, another rounded room with cells hanging off cliffs.

The prisoners' eyes stay glued to me and I feel like I'm walking into the courtroom to be judged again. Do they know who I am? Why I was sentenced here?

A buzz zings through the air and I startle as the guard grabs my arm. The whole Dome seems to move. The strands of magic tighten and pull. Before I can figure out what I'm seeing, the cells rise and settle onto their platforms and their doors open. Prisoners pour onto the Dome's outer ledges and head down. Guards on skygliders appear, zooming through the air, yelling at anyone moving too slowly. I notice at once how many of the prisoners are wearing cuffs. I rub my own bare wrists.

"Common time," the guard explains. "For those who have been good." I don't like the way he says "good," but then again, I don't like any of this.

We finally reach the tower and the guardsman wipes green magic across the stone. Leaves grow from the frame, creating a handle the guard yanks, opening the door. He nods for me to enter. I have no power and no escape, so I move into the darkness. I'm met with spiral stairs. We climb until we reach a hallway.

It's quiet until steps echo behind us.

"Whoa, Vihaan. What's this?" A woman emerges from the shadows, her confidence and freedom to roam implying she's a guard even without the uniform. I gaze into the older woman's face, her hair pinned into a bun. She owns freckles like she's collecting them. "A new arrival? You know I always get first look." She surveys me. "Especially the pretty ones."

Something deep and cold in my stomach says the compliment should worry me. Sims, the leader of the Underground, said something similar the first time he saw me. *You're pretty enough to warrant consideration, but maybe . . . too pretty. You don't seem like the fighting type.* I'd proven him wrong. I glance away from the woman. Maybe that is all that's left of me. Pretty.

Vihaan grumbles, "Warden asked *me* to get her."

The woman continues her inspection. "Is this Nira's replacement?" The way she says it, with pain and surprise, makes me memorize the name. Nira. How could I replace anyone in the Dome? Unless they mean I'm taking her bed?

"What cell is she going to?" the woman asks, curiosity dripping from her voice. "My section, I assume."

"Number 317."

She raises her thin eyebrows. "That has to be a mistake. Harini's? She's still—" She stops herself. I swirl the other name around my mouth and memorize it as well. The way she says it leaves me with no confidence my luck will change for the better.

The woman continues. "They can't put Nira's replacement in with Harini. She'll kill her."

"I doubt that," Vihaan retorts.

"Harini put three girls in the clinic this week. None of them were trapped in the same cell with her." The woman pushes toward the door. "Let me talk to the warden with you."

"He said just me," Vihaan responds gruffly. "And the warden gives the orders."

"Fine, go, then." She turns. "Don't want to keep him waiting a second too long."

I'm guessing the warden is impatient, because Vihaan doesn't waste any time. He nudges me into a large, windowed room that glows with magic. The strands from all the cells connect to the tower in this very room. One cut, one spell, and the cells would plummet into the depths of the Dome.

A lanky wizard with light brown skin stands by the tethers of magic, taking in my every move as I enter the room. Although he appears to be in charge, his face is common. If I passed him in the street I wouldn't take a second glance.

"My thanks, Vihaan. That will be all," he says.

"Sir?"

"I want a word with our new arrival. Then you will take her to her cell."

Vihaan and his jagged teeth turn.

"And, Vihaan? Tell Ekani it *will* be cell 317."

The room seems to grow dark as the door closes. I wait for the warden to lash out, to transform into something unmistakably evil, but I don't even get a smile or a sneer. Yet there *is* something unsettling about this wizard that I can't pinpoint.

Finally, he speaks, his voice calm but hard, commanding— a voice made to run a prison. "I don't want a single person in this prison to know who you are. Understood?"

What does he expect me to—

"Blood, just nod or something, girl. Basu didn't take your hearing too, did he? I was told you were spirited. Don't tell me we've already broken you."

My hatred spikes, magic rushing to my hands ready for a spell, but I can't do anything, can't say anything. Slowly, my magic recedes.

I nod.

"Good. It's for your protection more than anything. We can't have you dying the first week, can we? Bad for business." He peers out the window, gazing at the bustle of the Dome from his watchtower. It hits me then, the thing that makes this guy so unsettling. He hasn't blinked. Once.

"What's your new name, then? Spell it out for me, huh?" He thrusts a pen into my hand. I don't know what he wants exactly, seeing as he hasn't offered any parchment, until he points to the packed dirt under our feet. So this is what it has come to? I'm writing my name into the ground like a child learning and memorizing their spells.

I hesitate for a second, but if the last days have taught me anything, lying is easier when there is some truth behind it. *Jaya,* I paint into a lie. The old habit and the older persona welcome me back like a long-lost friend. Simple. And just like that, I'm Jaya again, with no real past and, now, no real future.

"All right, Jaya. Welcome to the Dome," the warden says, wiping his foot across the letters and the last chance I may ever have to communicate.

◇ ◇ ◇

My welcome seems to end there. The next introduction is to my cellmate, the ominous Harini.

The cage that Vihaan guides me to hangs off the cliff like the others with two beds and one basin. When it starts lifting onto its platform, the girl inside sits up on her narrow plank of a bed. She has the coloring of a Pire Islander, dark and beautiful like my mother. Short curly hair brushes her shoulders. She also has a black eye and a swollen lip. Since she wasn't released like the others, I'm guessing she hasn't been "good."

"You have a cellmate now," Vihaan announces as we step into the cell.

The girl stands. Without even looking at me, she grabs a bundle of parchment and holds out the top page. In clear scroll letters it reads, *No.*

This short interaction tells me two things. One, my cellmate is cold, colder than this cell. Two, like me, she is voiceless.

The latter condition makes my throat taste like bile. They do this to others. I had hoped I was a unique case—too spirited, too infamous, like the warden said. I hate how wrong I am. I hate that I left the Dome to the outskirts of the West Village and let corruption and illegal magic find a foothold.

"Isn't negotiable," Vihaan says to the girl. "The north wing is still under repairs. We need the space." He sounds worried. The girl seethes and the paper flutters to the ground. I go still, noting the tension in her legs. That's the only warning of her lunge. She throws herself forward. Vihaan is too fast, though, or he had expected it, because he shuts the door of our cage and leaves my cellmate pounding her fists on the creamy glass.

He shakes his head at her, then cuts his eyes to me. "Try not to die." At least he has the decency to look sympathetic. *Try not to die.* That's what I've been trying to do for months. In fact, I'm only here because I tried to make sure my whole city didn't die.

I hold out my hands as the girl turns, already planning to use the bed as barrier if she attacks. She glares at me, then scratches a phrase on another piece of parchment. When she thrusts it at me, I'm wary, but curious.

We are nothing to each other. Not friends. Not enemies. Don't try to change that. You don't want to be my enemy. She fastens me with an icy stare while underlining *don't* three times without even a glance down. I'm guessing she wants a nod, so I give it. She's about to turn away when she notices me looking at the parchment. I mean, this girl has parchment, a means to communicate.

She adds one more line. *Touch this and you'll wish you were dead.*

CHAPTER TEN

◇

Smoked Out

Adraa

Within a day I fall into the routine of the Dome. Small oval sky-lights open at daybreak and close at sunset, wind-generated like most of the Dome. During the daytime, circular patches of light mark the arena of cages. In the interim, prisoners are released from their cells three times. One, early lunch. Two, afternoon freedom. Three, dinner.

Harini is the opposite of helpful, but she hasn't tried to kill me in my sleep, so there's a small bright side. But do I even sleep, knowing Vihaan's and Ekani's warnings? No, of course not. I need to live, to get out of here. I simply have to bide my time and try to learn how to nap with one eye open.

It's that guard, Ekani, who won't leave me alone. The cafe-teria is at the bottom of the Dome and filled with guards lean-ing against the walls, pretending to watch the prisoners. Ekani doesn't pretend. I find her eyes on me at every meal. Maybe she's still trying to figure out how much of a headache I'll be for her. But I don't want to be anything to her. I know that for sure.

By the third day I've surmised enough about her character to understand. Ekani is an entrepreneur who works people, a female Sims. She may not have his advertising finesse, but she runs her division of cells in a way that generates respect and fear. More importantly, there is a clear understanding between her and the other guards: Don't mess with her section. And don't mess with her Voiceless. That's what they call us—those who have had their voices taken, those of us who used to be powerful—sixes or above, I learn.

There is order to the madness; like everything in life, it's been systemized into a hierarchy. Only here there's one crucial difference: the Voiceless are at the bottom and under Ekani's supervision. I pay close attention to how many of us there are. Nine, I count, including my cellmate and me. Which makes sense. Most of my fellow prisoners are Untouched or Threes at the most. The ones on the street who had to do anything, especially break the law, to survive.

On day six in the Dome, Harini pushes ahead of me, having ignored me since our initial meeting. In a tidal wave of movement, the other inmates make room for her as well. The shuffle of dinner plates scrapes against the lunch counter as cuffed witches jump back in desperation to get out of the food line. Long, tightly woven wicker tables and stout chairs occupy the bulk of the space, and even there I can hear and see the other prisoners getting up and moving away. I have yet to see Harini do anything more than glare, but the other prisoners' actions speak louder than words.

I enter the circular meal room alone and with as little fanfare as possible. And I do what I always do when I enter a public space. I pray no one notices my presence, especially Ekani.

No chance. Her eyes slice into me. She corners me as I make my way toward the back of the food line. A younger girl, around Prisha's age, follows in her shadow. She's short, skinny, and fair-skinned. I've seen her before, darting around the lunchroom on Ekani's orders.

"Still alive, 317?"

Before Ekani can say more, the girl cocks her head and bites her lip. "I know you," she declares.

I'm speechless. For the first time I don't know what I would say even if my voice hadn't been taken. I have no idea who this girl is, but that doesn't mean she doesn't know me. As per Belwar tradition, before my royal ceremony, my identity and my title were unknown to the public. After the whispers and rumors started, everyone wanted to see my face. Everyone wanted to peer at the monster. My parents and the palace staff didn't let them, but over the years many Belwarians met me in my mother's clinic and dozens sat in the trial room.

I'm just about to shake my head in confusion when the girl presses on. "Yeah. Yeah, I really do. Hot blood. Do you know who this is, Ekani?"

Ekani eyes me, sizing me up. I try to soften the fear that I'm sure she can read in my expression. "Warden said her name was Jaya."

A pause. I imagine the warden's unblinking eyes taking in this situation, piercing me to the core, letting me know that one slipup could mean an end to the invisibility I've used to survive the past six days.

"Yeah. *Jaya Smoke.*" The girl cuffs my shoulder in some form of bubbly excitement. "I saw the fight between you and Beckman, the Tsunami, before you went and disappeared from cage casting." She throws her hands up. "You were one of the best." Then she seems to realize I haven't answered yet. "Hey, that is you, right?"

I nod. I've never been more grateful for my Jaya Smoke persona. But I can never show them my arms—because while they might not know my face, everyone knows of the notorious one-armed Adraa.

"Why aren't you saying any— Oh blood, are you . . . ?"

Ekani verifies my disability with a nod.

The girl smiles. "Gods, you're more powerful than I thought. What are you? A five?" Her eyes light up. "A six?" She goes for my sleeve. I block her. She tries again and automatically I grab her wrist, using her momentum to turn her and then twist her arm. I notice her Touch as I do. Her marks skirt only up to her mid-forearm. A clear two. She yelps and squirms. "Let me go, bloody Voiceless."

"She doesn't seem to like being touched," Ekani says like she's repeating an old joke.

When I realize how hard I'm twisting the girl's arm, I ease

my grip and push her away. I'm so reckless. I have enough enemies as it is. I hold my hands up like this will save me, like I can be forgiven.

"Blood," the girl whines.

Ekani seems to find our whole interaction funny. "So she was a cage caster, huh?" She turns to the girl. "What forte was she? Red, I assume."

I'm barely paying attention to Ekani, scrutinizing the girl as she cradles her wrist and glares. Retaliation is a natural feeling. I'm watching her process it, weigh it, retreat.

"Yeah, red," she finally relents.

"Ah, Smoke. Got it. That Sims with his creativity." Ekani smiles and finally addresses me. "I think I can help you out, Smoke."

The girl blanches. "You aren't considering . . ."

"Why not? She's experienced."

"But would they want to test her so soon?"

Test? My skin prickles. *What test?* I don't like the sound of this.

"Your wrist okay?" Ekani asks, and the girl huffs in response. Then Ekani gives me a good once-over, even more calculating than our first meeting. "People like fire, sure, or they used to." With a whisper of red magic, a purple flame lights up on her finger like a wick. I watch it flicker. "But it's just as pleasing, almost cathartic, to watch the fire"—she snaps her fingers—*"burn out."*

◇

CHAPTER ELEVEN

Seeing the Impossible

Jatin

"I don't know anything," the big-nosed wizard pleads. He's been spouting the same thing for the past thirty minutes and I'm almost inclined to believe him. Blood.

Kalyan and I stand in one of the forgotten alleyways where ash has been pushed from the center streets. It clumps like snowdrifts, creating the perfect shadowed spot for an interrogation.

The guy in front of us is named Yipton. He used to be a lower-level Dome Guard, and he was the reason months back Adraa caught on to the fact that some Belwar guards had been corrupted. We didn't see then how they could ruin us. Now Adraa is in a cage, and they're the ones controlling her welfare. I feel sick just looking at Yipton's pleading face.

"You sure knew something that night when you were hauling firelight at Pier Sixteen." We need one person, one bloody person, to give us information about the Dome. This Dome

Guard seems like one of my last chances to crack into their corruption and find out exactly where Adraa is being kept within those thick walls.

"I swear to you, I got out of the Vencrin. That night you and the Red Woman saw us on the dock I was fired, ousted. I don't even work in the Dome anymore. I've been running and hiding since then so they don't kill me. I can tell you how we snatched the firelight, how we shipped it. But please believe me, I had *no* idea what they had planned."

I wheel back to punch him.

A hand pulls at my shoulder. "Ease up. I don't think he—"

I jerk from Kalyan's grasp and walk a few paces down the alley. The Vencrin sobs on the ground. I turn to Kalyan once I'm out of earshot. "He's our last lead. It's been ten days and this is all we have."

He looks me squarely in the eye. "I know."

"We don't even know if she's alive."

"I know."

Repetitive monosyllabic answers used to piss me off at the academy. There was once a time I would have punched something with my losses stacked against me like this. But I breathe. Kalyan's tone says everything. He understands. He'll let me vent.

"Do you think there is anything we can get out of this guy?" I ask.

"No. Unfortunately, I believe him."

"Okay, then. So we move on and ask him . . ." I don't want to say it as much as I don't want to hear it. *What the Dome is like*

95

for the prisoners. It'll be old intel, but I have to know. Phase one of the plan is learning everything I can about the Dome, finding its weaknesses. And that means I have to contemplate what Adraa may be going through.

"You going to be okay?"

"I can do it."

Kalyan gives me one of his signature nods. "Do you want to be the reasonable one this time? Switch it up a bit?"

I give him a look.

"All right, then. We'll play to our strengths."

I crack a bitter smile. Gods, it's nice when your only friend gets you.

I walk up to Yipton and squat down in front of him. "I need you to tell me everything you know about the Dome. How it works, who's working for the Vencrin, and what they do to the prisoners." I give him a hard stare. "What they *really* do."

Terror engulfs Yipton's eyes. "I'll be killed."

Kalyan sits down next to him. "You said you didn't know what was happening with the firelight. You didn't know it was going to be used to potentially murder millions. Help us prevent that from happening again."

"It's going to happen again?" Yipton looks to the sky even though it's calm, quiet, and hours past dusk. What would we even do if it happened again? I push the thought from my mind.

"Maybe," I concede. "That's what we are trying to prevent. So talk. I want everything."

◈ ◈ ◈

As Kalyan and I walk out of the alley, even the strong wind blustering through Belwar can't whip away Yipton's words. The creeping winter chill has finally shown itself in the depth of nightfall. The air cuts me with its jagged edges. It doesn't help that every piece of information Yipton told us makes me want to vomit. Cells hoisted and hung by threads of yellow magic. Swarms of guards at every entrance. Brutality delivered without warning or reason. Corruption on every level. It paints a picture, but it doesn't give me the key to getting Adraa out.

Something shifts in the corner of my vision. Kalyan steps in front of me, but moonlight illuminates the shadowed threat, revealing Riya. "So, this is what it's come to? What you've been doing for the last week?" she says.

"What are you doing here?" I ask. "How . . . how did you find us?"

Riya nods to Kalyan. "We've been writing."

"Comparing notes on the trial," Kalyan finishes.

This shouldn't surprise me and yet Kalyan has been by my side this entire week as we scoured for information. He never said a thing.

"And I'm here to help."

"We're good, Riya."

She pushes forward. "You've gotten pretty bad at lying."

"I don't think he was ever good at it," Kalyan supplies.

"Fine, I didn't want to involve you," I say bluntly.

"Involve me? I'm Adraa's guard. This should be *our* mission."

I don't say anything for a long while. It should be our

mission. But I don't think I could handle any of us succumbing to Adraa's fate. "I have it handled." My boots crunch in the dirt and ash as I turn away.

Riya's voice turns somber when she counters. "Maharani Belwar told me about the poison. How our fathers . . . How it might be the same thing, or something similar."

"I'm glad you know. Stay with him, see if you can find something."

"Adraa and Prisha are the talented pink magic users. I'm useless there." The word cuts deeper than I think Riya will ever realize. "Don't make me beg," she continues.

"You really want to help us do *this*?" I gesture to the alley, to what I know Riya can imagine happened there. Though I don't think she can comprehend the anger, the pain I feel.

"Hiren and Prisha have a plan. I think you should hear it."

"Hiren?" Exactly how many people did Maharani Belwar tell about my mission?

"Prisha's guard," Riya explains.

"I know who he is, it's just . . ." I pause. "Do you trust him?" My only real interaction with the guy was last year on a rooftop before Adraa and I were about to invade a Vencrin drug den. He seemed young. A complete rule follower.

"He's a boy trying to impress his father. The father in question being Raja Dara of the outer north region. And Raja Dara's family has been loyal to the Belwars for generations. His eldest son died in service to Belwar. Hiren is like the rest of us, trying to live up to the legacy and responsibilities put upon him."

I contemplate what she said. In every meeting, Raja Dara

advocated for Adraa's freedom. In the courtroom he saved her from that arrow. "Prisha vouches for Hiren?"

Riya and Kalyan both snort at my question.

"What?"

"Prisha would vouch for him with her life. She has a huge crush on him. Has since she was old enough to know what feelings were," Riya says.

"She does?" I ask, as Kalyan says, "Of course."

I turn. "How do you know?"

Kalyan rolls his eyes. "For having the only established relationship among the group, you are really dense."

"And a little unobservant," Riya adds.

Kalyan nods and shrugs.

I open my mouth to defend myself when Riya returns to the subject at hand. "Raja Dara has been entrusted with the Dome Guard. Hiren has intel and a way in. Who else do you have?" She gestures to where drops of Yipton's blood still sit in the dirty alleyway. I wouldn't trust Yipton with my life, much less Adraa's.

"What's their plan?" I finally ask.

Riya takes a breath. It must be bad. "It involves raiding the Underground, bringing in whoever we can, and using them to get inside the Dome."

I'm silent. Kalyan is the first to speak. "They want us to . . ."

"Destroy our entire undercover operation," I supply. And I'm using *our* loosely because it's Adraa's operation, first and foremost. This plan screams of last resort.

"The Belwar Guard will be raiding the cage-casting ring soon no matter what," Riya says. "But we can get in before the Guard. Ask Sims or any Vencrin you want the real questions before a bunch of guardsmen come busting through the door. Hiren says he can escort them into the Dome and get Adraa's exact location."

It takes all of two seconds to realize her reasoning is sound, that Hiren's plan may have merit.

"What other choice do we have at this point?" Kalyan asks.

I breathe in the chilly air, focusing on the hollowness of the night. This far western part of Belwar has been half abandoned by the devastation of Mount Gandhak and the fallen flying station. My hand bumps my skyglider on my belt. The man who made this is dead. The girl who bought me this is in prison.

"It's just . . . that's . . . Adraa's," I finally say. She spent six months building her cage-casting career. She bled in a cage for information and inside intel. Going in and barking for answers feels like a disservice to her, a betrayal.

"I know. But think about it, okay? Let's all meet and talk through other alternatives. No one can do this alone. Not even Adraa, if she were in your shoes."

"I'm sure she'd try."

Riya looks at me for a long moment. "I was hoping you wouldn't make her mistakes. You created the signal. You created this team. Lead us, Jatin."

◇ ◇ ◇

Up in the air, I twist on my skyglider toward Kalyan, who, as always, seems to be waiting patiently for me to speak first.

"Prisha and Hiren, really? I don't see it."

Kalyan looks at me, eyebrows raised.

"What else am I missing?" I ask. "Have *you* fallen for someone?"

"That's not really my thing." He says this like he doesn't want to elaborate. But he doesn't have to. We've never talked about it outright, but not once has Kalyan brought up romantic relationships as something he wants. "You do know Riya isn't interested in men, right?"

I hold up a hand. "I knew that one."

"Trying to get to know the team, then? Has Riya gotten through to you?"

"So, you're all for this mission to destroy the Underground?"

"I agree with Riya. We've become a team these last few weeks. We should work as a team. And Yipton was our last lead."

The wind howls past us as a particularly cold gust catches our skygliders' tails. Kalyan has to bank to not cross streams. When we meet up again, he says something unexpected.

"If it's fear that you'd fail leading us, you won't, Jatin."

I run through my rationale. Is it fear? Have I avoided involving Riya and Prisha because deep down I worry they won't follow me without Adraa by my side?

"I'll do it," I say at last. "We'll tell Prisha and Hiren tomorrow. We just have to—"

A red blur condenses out of the corner of my eye. I swivel so fast that the white stream blustering behind me curves. I blink as the image comes into focus. A girl is running along the roof meters below us. I watch the form sprint, the red glow of her magic lighting up this patch of darkness. Then she drops behind an archway.

"Did you see that?" I yell, loud enough that Kalyan jolts on his skyglider.

"What?" he yells back, scouring the sky and the ground for a threat.

But I'm not looking at a threat. I'm seeing . . . I *saw* Adraa.

I don't stop to think. I tear forward, plummeting toward the blip of darkness where she disappeared. I careen to a stop, hovering over the roof she ran upon, searching the area for movement. "*Vardrenni*," I cast, enhancing my sense of sight. I'm about to add on hearing when three roofs over I see it. A flash of red, and a female figure skirts the shadows and vanishes again.

"*Pavria*," I chant into my skyglider, pushing it harder, collecting the wind and using it to propel me forward as fast as possible. I see her, below me. She whooshes over a chimney.

I half land, half crash in front of her. She swerves to a stop. My lungs ache. Or maybe it's not only my lungs. My heart's pounding.

We stare at each other. It's Adraa in every physical sense. Long black braid. Athletic build. Even the swirls of magic woven into the black threads of her Red Woman uniform. "Red?" I hate how bloody hopeful my voice is, how much I want to say her true name. But I can't chance it.

For a second, we are statues. Her magic simmers down and she smiles tentatively, slowly, through her mask.

With a start I realize I don't have my own mask on. In fact, I've taken off all spells and enhancements that transform me into Night, so I haven't fully outed myself, but it may be pretty obvious. I hadn't even thought to sneak up on her like she obviously snuck up on me. I thought my mind was combusting into images I yearned to see, and I had to make sure. But, that look, the orange speed spells.

It's real. She's real. Unless . . .

I take a few generous steps forward. "Red?" I ask again, an edge to the question this time. No answer. I lunge forward and catch her hand. She twists out my grip, seemingly furious at the contact. Like I've burned her. She's never, and I mean *never*, looked at me like that. I hoist my hands up, readying my magic.

"Whoever you are, take off the mask and show yourself."

She backs away, closing in on the edge of the roof.

"Stop!" I shout. "Please stop!"

She doesn't stop. She whispers a few words, and red smoke engulfs her.

"Don't," I yell as she drops, then grabs the roof at the last second and swings to the ground. I scramble after her, watching as she rushes down an alleyway and slips into the shadows. *What the actual blood!*

Kalyan careens around the corner and tumbles onto the roof. "Ah, what the heck was that?" He's as calm as ever despite me jetting off without him, so I ignore him for a second. *Because truly, what the blood was that?*

When I turn around, the girl is still gone. I swipe the air where she had stood, searching for any ripple of proof she was using a screen of black illusion magic. Nothing. It was too real for that anyway.

"Did you see her?" I ask.

The shake of Kalyan's head is the last thing I want. No, he had to have seen her. She was right here. *Right here.*

I can't be going crazy. Not with everything else. "She was real."

"Jatin . . ."

I don't like that tone. I fall to my knees. "What am I supposed to do? I need someone to tell me what I'm supposed to do." *Go! Find her. Free her,* a voice echoes in my head, pounding against my skull.

Then, suddenly, the memory of Adraa's voice overtakes my own. *Don't come for me.* I knock my fists against my temples. I can't give up on her. I can't just let her go.

Kalyan sits with me as I crumble in the darkness, warring with two voices in my head.

◇

CHAPTER TWELVE

A Touch of Hope

Adraa

When the nightmares come, I almost expect them. As always, they start in the red room, and I'm alone. Erif's chamber is just as I remember it, bleeding walls and an air of indescribable eeriness. As soon as I'm oriented, the nightmare shifts, and I'm gasping for breath on Mount Gandhak. Sweat drips off me and I see the inferno blowing up in front of me again, the volcano spitting and blasting out firelight in bloodred waves of ash. I panic. The world spins, plunges into smoke.

Jatin is suddenly there, lying in the snow, burned out and vulnerable. Terror suffocates me as I rack my brain for a solution. Somewhere in the back of mind, I know I've been here before. When I realize what I must do—that I must pull my firelight back from the volcano—my voice doesn't work. It fails. I clutch my throat, but no words come out. I look down at my left arm, and slowly the designs of my Touch unravel and fall off my body. I try to yell again. I remember the red room and scream for it. Nothing happens until a voice rings out in my mind: *You are nothing of consequence anymore. You failed.*

Failed.

A foot slams into my bedpost. Everything shudders, and I startle back to reality. I realize a tall man is standing over my bed mere seconds before he grabs me and pulls me to my feet. I fight against the intruder's shackling fingers. But one glance at Harini, who has been woken up in the same manner, and I'm startled into stillness.

She's a solid brick of resignation. No fear, no reaction, no anything. She knew this was coming. Wish I had been warned that Ekani's nice little threat was coming to fruition tonight. I jerk away from my captor. I may not have a clue about what is going on, but I refuse to be manhandled.

When I turn and my eyes adjust to the darkness, I see Vihaan and his plethora of jagged teeth standing next to me. A guard I don't know holds Harini. Ekani stands at the threshold of our raised and open cell. Of course. Is this some sort of initiation? Were the five days of isolation and silence not enough?

I brace myself and dip into a cage-casting stance. If they mean to knock me out, I won't make it easy.

"Come on." Ekani waves a freckled arm. "The ring waits for no woman."

Harini gives me an irritated look as she inspects my fighting stance. Then, quickly, as if she hopes I don't notice, she quirks her head to the side, indicating I should follow. It's the second time she's ever communicated with me.

With that gesture—and Vihaan jabbing my back—I follow.

It might be idiotic to give in so easily, but curiosity and no other real choice forces my feet forward, over my cell's threshold and onto the narrow cliffside.

They lead us down, into the depths of the prison, stairway after curved stairway. Each level we descend, the coat of dust grows thicker, the stench of sweat and something fouler intensifies. Fear strangles my heart, which is pumping heavy and loud in my ears. If I know anything, walking into darkness is never a good idea. But what can I do?

At the end of a hall we come to a rock wall with a fake window plastered on it. The unnamed guard steps forward and sprouts green magic into the frame. It elongates, stretching until it carves a person-sized door into the sandstone. I look over and catch Harini watching me, sizing me up. I assume she's looking for a reaction. But since she gives me nothing, I raise my chin and shade my face into a mask of indifference. I may not know what waits for me in the passage hidden behind this door, but I refuse to show my cellmate, Ekani, or these guards any trepidation.

With a heaving jerk, Vihaan helps the green forte crack open the door. It swings outward. As I'm ushered through, I notice the warm, circular glow along its frame. It must be a sound-proofing spell because the first thing that hits me once I pass through the doorway is the noise. A wholly masculine roar rises through the murk. I'm pushed farther forward, and then I see it.

Before me is a cell-sized, spherical cage-casting ring and a mob of men—guards in disheveled uniforms—encircling it. Inside the cage, two Untouched women spar. With a lunge, one thrusts forward, her fist connecting to the other woman's temple. Her opponent drops to the ground. Not sparring. Attacking.

Ekani's words come back to me crystal clear, their meaning solidifying. She wasn't threatening me yesterday. No, she was being more direct than that. Finding out I'm Jaya Smoke. Finding a use for me. Burnout.

They want me to fight.

I glance around. Beyond the spectacle of the cage there's nothing. No bar. No seating. More soundproofing spells are woven into the walls and ceiling, lacing the room in rainbow strings. Apart from a few candles anchored to the walls, these magic threads seem to be the only light in the place, casting the arena and the two women in a dim, multicolored glow.

If I thought the Underground grimy, this tops it. No fighter statistics cover the walls. Even the cheers bite the air differently, more harshly. No articulate taunts are uttered—just grunting and stomping as the guards take in the fight. The bets are open, silvers and even the occasional glint of golds spilling from pouches right in the forefront. I never thought I would ever appreciate or respect Sims in any manner, but I can't deny he ran the business clean, with a level of decorum I don't think these men could pronounce, let alone understand.

I can guess Ekani's incentive in this mess, and I'm almost disappointed it's money. The motivations around here are staggeringly uncreative. Everyone fits into little boxes of greedy, power-hungry criminals worried about reputation and status. Everyone except Harini, that is. She's an anomaly I can't figure out.

"Come on, Jaya. You'll get your chance to stare later. In fact, you'll be getting a close-up look," Ekani spits. She shoves Harini and me into a room half the size of the dressing room I used in the Underground. Cobwebs lace every bend and crooked frame. When the door is shut, the noise is muffled, and for a second I can think.

They want me to fight.

I'm going to fight . . . without magic.

Harini slinks away from the door, a sense of defeat evident in the slope of her shoulders. Her movement captures my attention. Harini. I'm going to be fighting my cellmate. My cellmate, whom everyone avoids for their own safety, who put, what was it—three women in the clinic a mere week ago? Terror snakes up my spine.

I'm desperate to know who this girl is, where she came from, and how she ended up voiceless in the Dome. She shrugs off her prison uniform, and I try to see how far her Touch weaves up her arm. But then I avert my gaze—it doesn't matter, not when we're both unable to access our magic.

The reality of the situation hits me all over again. My Gods. What kind of nightmare is this? I can't fight like this.

Ekani interrupts my panic by throwing a blouse at my head. "Put this on."

I unfold the small sleeveless garment, the black-as-night fabric slipping through my fingers. It's formfitting and ill-suited for combat. I'm not a fan of showing off my stomach for all of Wickery's underbelly, but that's not why an anxious note vibrates through my chest.

I need sleeves.

I shake my head at Ekani, dropping the flimsy excuse for a top at her feet.

"Don't give me that, girl," she says. "This isn't the time for self-consciousness or modesty."

I shake my head again and trace my arm down to my wrist. Up and down, tugging the fabric at the wrist for added emphasis.

"You want long sleeves?"

I nod. I can tell she's about to ask why, so I pull down the collar of my prison uniform, flashing a hint of skin. Erif's advanced Touch is still coated in burgundy. *Burns,* I scribble into the dust-coated wall to my right. That bit might be overdoing it, but I need to make it clear. Tell her what she's looking at before she inspects it herself.

For once, her features soften. "Mount Gandhak?"

I nod slowly. Feels good to accompany the lies with a truth. Makes it more believable.

Out of the corner of my eye, I see Harini freeze, obviously listening in.

"Bloody firelight," Ekani curses, but a look of sympathy lights up her face. For a second she almost appears . . . kind. "I lost a nephew in the eruption. Best Untouched con this world has ever seen."

Perfect, like I needed another reason to be on this woman's bad side.

"I'll find something to cover your burns."

Slowly, I place two fingers on my throat and bow. The

gesture feels stilted. It's also the first time I've given anyone my respects in weeks, not counting the trial's mandated ones. And while it's partly a ploy to get Ekani to trust me, I also do it for her nephew. For the little piece of pain I *am* responsible for. Gradually, I will collect all their stories. I'll know all one hundred twenty-nine by name, not just number.

"This might be better anyway. Blend in with the blood." When she tosses me another blouse it's the color of my forte, dripping red. It has sleeves and a high collar, and little else. I won't even be able to put it on myself—strings lace up the back to hold the thing together. I give Ekani a look.

"What did you expect?"

I don't know, for a prison to *not* have illegal cage-casting rings, which force its voiceless female prisoners to fight one another while scantily clad? But I guess that was too much to ask.

I slip into the farthest recess of cobwebs and gloom. And only then, in the privacy of darkness, do I peel off my loose prison uniform and wrestle my arms into the tight choli. I would like to think I'm not a clothing snob, but the starched fabric rubs at my neck and shoulders, and constricts every joint I'm meant to move. I've gotten used to Naupure's imported silks and my maid Zara's impeccable style.

Ekani obviously thinks she's given me enough time to dress, as she steps forward and pulls at the laces on my bare back. "Look, I know this is hard." She yanks the laces so tightly I fear they will tear. "But trust me when I say this is a favor. Most of these guards are fine. Most are nothing more than overpowered meatheads. But one or two out there like to use you prisoners for other reasons, especially the pretty ones." Nausea whips through my gut. I can feel her fingers tying a knot midback, and there is a franticness about them that sends a cold wave of panic through me. For the first time in months, that night on the upper deck at the Underground flashes through my memory. Nightcaster's hands. The loss of control and the fear I would never be able to get it back.

One last yank and the blouse is fastened in place. "Stick by me and this will be the worst," Ekani says.

I turn around, and she inspects me. I don't know if she wants a thank-you for this "favor," but I give her nothing. If she asks me to smile, the fight just might begin early. My mother's inside man, Beckman, saved me that night, when Rakesh was on top of me. Is Ekani implying that tonight is a comparable rescue? Doesn't feel like it when she's the one lacing me up and putting me on display. I can't process this sudden change in her demeanor, and I search her face for it. The wrinkles around her eyes suggest genuine concern. But what's the act and what's the truth here? Is she baiting me or warning me?

"Gods, you're almost too attractive, you know. Makes my job so much bloody harder. Just . . . just try to be interesting to watch, okay? And once you fall, stay down."

Her concern finally fractures my facade. She goes tight-lipped seeing my fear. "Come on."

Ekani turns away, and slowly, I follow.

We make our way out to the horde. Unlike in the Underground, the roar doesn't rise until we are in the men's sight. This time I really look at the magic infused into the ceiling. It runs in erratic patterns like cracks. I realize a second later that they *are* cracks. Every fractured inch of this space holds an enchanted soundproofing. Which means they are hiding this from someone. Respectable prison guards, my family, the entire country.

Harini enters the ring first. Like me, she also bargained for sleeves, which means neither of us can see the other's Touch. But again, it doesn't matter. What matters is that she's taller than me, and stronger, judging by her biceps.

For a moment I expect a burst of magic to wash over the arena, like it did in my Underground matches. But there's nothing. Harini just stares, facing forward. Then she throws her head back violently and screams. No sound comes out, yet somehow it's even more terrifying.

My stomach knots. I've been trained in hand-to-hand combat, sure, but magic has always been there. My tutors and trainers made me rely on it above all else. I'm doomed.

This is a bloodbath waiting to happen. My blood.

Ekani pats my back hard, half pushing me into the ring. "Good luck, Smoke. I hope you are as good as everyone says."

Yeah, me too.

⬦ ⬦ ⬦

I was cage caster Jaya Smoke for eight months. I've met my fair share of fighters. But nothing prepares me for this because, well, frankly, I'm ill prepared. I'm powerless.

I think Ekani was joking when she said I might die, but as

Harini rushes me and punches through my guard, the bone-crippling pain suggests otherwise. I fall back against the curved wall, its coldness stinging my bare back. But Harini keeps coming. She's all muscle and fists and rage. Five different spells come to mind that could push her off. Another fist catches my temple and dizziness spins the words. *Think! Not spells. Not casting.*

It's beneath me, I know, but I catch her next punch with my forearm, and with my free hand, grab her short curly hair and yank. It jerks her enough to stop her blows. I gather distance like it's salvation. As though I'm in another world, I note the crowd is booing my schoolgirl tactics. If this were happening during my Jaya Smoke days, I might feel conflicted—these kinds of childish moves would have affected my stats and thus my undercover operation. To blood with all that now. This is the Dome. I don't want to die like this. I'd have rather Moolek left me for dead on the volcano if I'm just going to be another body dragged out back and forgotten.

Harini pulls back her arm again, and I block. A distraction. She drives a fist into my stomach. I double over. *Too slow,* Jatin's voice thrums in my head, a memory from when we practiced hand-to-hand combat. Maybe I really was only fast at magic. Maybe I am nothing without it.

I cough. Blood drips from my mouth. No sound comes out. Why do they find this enjoyable? Real cage casting is a marvel of magic. It's violent, but there is also creative flair I can understand and respect.

I look up at Harini, and I can see the hatred in her eyes. Her eyebrows knit. Self-hatred? She waves her hands at me. *Let's get this over with,* the gesture seems to signify.

I feint left, then push off on the balls of my feet and rush her. She's unprepared for my speed, the full commitment to my attack. I duck a flying fist and catch it with my hand. I've been through too much for this to break me. I yank, and Harini's forearm breaks. The snap of bone echoes. Cheers gobble up the sound.

Be done. Let it be over. I wrench away from retaliation. Too slow.

She gestures outward, and her elbow hits my chest. I fly. I fly like I've been hit by a man three times her size. Or three times her strength . . .

I don't crash into the wall, a saving grace, but I still slide the length of the arena, meters of distance. My sternum aches; my ribs cry out. I gasp for breath as I clutch my sides. My shoulder stings too. I reach upward and my hand comes away with blood. It's a gash the length of my hand. What just happened?

I stare up at Harini. She's taller and stronger than me, yes, but that . . . that kind of strength is magic.

In cage casting we whispered spells, so I'm used to heightening my sense of hearing. I've been trained to seize even the smallest of murmurs to evaluate what spell is coming my way. So I'm sure, absolutely sure, Harini didn't say a single word. Couldn't.

It's fast, but I catch a subtle flick of her hand as she cradles her broken and swollen arm to her body. Then I see it. A small flare of orange smoke hidden under her sleeve.

The crowd roars, pounding on our cage, hands smashing against the creamy glasslike substance. They want us to keep going; they hate our stillness. But I am still because I'm pretty sure my cellmate somehow cast an orange strength enhancer and is subtly healing her broken arm as I'm lying on the ground, bleeding.

For the first time in two weeks, hope finds its way back to me. I smile as I wobble up off the ground, wipe the blood off my hand, and wave my fingers forward in a taunt. Her eyes widen and then narrow in what I can only assume is pure wrath. She wants this to be over, for me to lie down and not get up. I can't say a part of me doesn't desire the same thing. But hope has found its foothold and the stronger part rises up, deepens my stance, and steadies my feet.

I'm going to lose and it's going to hurt so badly. But for however long I can last, I'm going to study her every move. I'm going to figure out how she did that. How this girl, this voiceless cellmate of mine, just performed magic.

CHAPTER THIRTEEN

◇

An Old Acquaintance

Jatin

My father hasn't improved. The poison and, more importantly, its antidote remain mysteries. Nothing has changed but the scenery. Now he lies in his own bed instead of in the clinic. Oddly enough, I can't recall the last time or maybe even any time I've seen my father asleep. He wears sickly like he's bored, and I don't think he's ever been bored in his life.

I don't know if this bedroom setting is better or worse. On the one hand, it means Ira doesn't think an herb or a potion has to be at her fingertips to keep my father alive. But seeing him here, looking like he may never get up . . . feels like this is the end.

I can't let it be.

Ira told me to talk to him, to let him hear my voice, and I wonder if the prescription was meant more for me than for him. Nonetheless, I do it. The first time I felt silly. Now it comes naturally, like a report.

"I've stalked every point of contact that Adraa had in Project Smoke, every empty warehouse where the Vencrin could be hiding. I've found so much evidence of Bloodlurst, you and Adraa would be equal parts alarmed at its quantity and thrilled it no longer seems to be circulating the city streets. But right now, I don't care about the drugs. I need information about the Dome. I need . . ." My voice cracks.

It's been over a week since the trial, and since that last encounter with Adraa's phantom image I've scoured the streets for her. Nothing. Doubt has crept in instead. Voices in my mind. Visions of my hopes and dreams. It's almost the definition of a psychological break.

I can't let anyone know, even my unconscious father. So that part remains unsaid.

Yet I can't keep going like this. One week is already one too many for Adraa. So I've decided to hear Hiren out on his plan to take out the Underground.

I look over at my father and before I realize it, I'm telling him the plan, voicing my concern that Adraa wouldn't want this. "I hope she'll understand. But I don't have any other options at the moment." I stare at his still body. It seems to get frailer every day. "You'd probably have a better idea." He definitely would. Project Smoke was half his, after all.

I rest my head on the side of the bed, feeling the stiff blanket imprinting its woven pattern on my forehead. "Gods, Dad, don't leave me." I take in a steadying breath. "Come back. Help me figure out a solution."

A knock echoes on the door. The soft patter tells me it's

Hughes, my father's servant and Azure Palace's main keeper nowadays. I jerk to a sitting position, rubbing my face. "Come in," I call.

Hughes enters with a bow and a quick, silent step. "Maharaja Naupure," he says casually, like those words don't hold the weight of the country behind them.

A flood of emotions slam into my chest at the words—grief at the forefront. I've always liked Hughes, but sometimes the level of respect and honor sting. Like I am nothing more than my title. "Don't call me that. Don't call me that while my father still lives and breathes."

He gives me his standard frown. "Sir, it is custom when the maharaja is . . . is incapacitated that the next in line—"

"He will not die." If I say this with enough conviction it may come to pass. If only I were powerful enough to make that happen.

"Yes, sir, but in the meantime, you are the reigning leader."

I slump in the chair, not caring if it suggests my weakness. I thought I was ready for this. I thought I could take charge, but I was wrong.

Just months ago, I was prepared to save my people, to sacrifice myself, to rule when they needed me, but I wasn't ready to play at politics or take the throne if it meant losing everyone I love. The price is too high. And yet everyone expects me to grow up and run a country in the blink of an eye.

"Sir, you said to inform you after I gathered information about the rallies in Belwar."

I lurch from the chair. "What did you find? How many?"

He hands over a thick report. I open it so quickly the pages billow.

"Five, sir. All after the trial."

Five. That's practically one every other day. I scan the pages, looking for the answer to my next question. "Same rhetoric?"

"It's not simply about dethroning the Belwars. They are calling to cast a vote and elect a new leader."

Total overhaul, then. "What are the Belwars doing in response?"

"Supposedly, Raja Dara, head commander of the Guard, has volunteered to attend these rallies with some of his men and answer questions, defuse any situations that might arise." I'm relieved to hear it's Dara over any of the other lower rajas, but it's still what I thought. They can't contain them. Can't demand people's respect. Adraa's trial changed everything, broke people's faith. I need time to read through the file carefully.

"That will be all, Hughes. Thank you."

"Sir, I also came to announce a visitor."

I look up, startled. Azure Palace has been all but shut down. Until we get to the bottom of exactly who poisoned my father and how, visitors aren't just showing up at the ice door. "Who?"

"She's waiting for you in your office."

"She?" I don't mean to sound surprised, but in all of Naupure there is only one lower rani and she rules a small section, with just five isolated villages. I couldn't even tell you how many times she's been to the capital.

"Maharaja." He bows, fingers to throat and the whole bit.

I stride toward my father's office. I open the door with force, a show of composure. It evaporates as I take in who awaits me.

"Whoever came up with the tradition to climb that mountain by foot on one's first arrival is both brilliant and a bit sadistic," a chipped voice says.

I don't move as one of my old nightmares walks toward me. Fiza Agsa.

The girl who grew up with me at the academy and tormented me with her flirting and attention to such a degree that I wrote fake love letters to Adraa Belwar. The girl who was so calculating and annoying I pondered which trait would win out in adulthood on an almost daily basis. I had hoped it would remain a mystery. My luck has run dry.

It's strange seeing an old acquaintance after you yourself have changed. It's much like a shift in ground, a re-formation of rock. Similar, but oh so different. Fiza of Agsa, with her caramel-colored hair and light-brown skin, stands before me, a glacier of time and a landslide of stone wedged between us. But she smiles as she stalks toward me like she's stepping over a crack, not a canyon.

"Lady Fiza. Pleasure." I bow. She deserves a more familiar greeting, one between equals, like a press of my arm against hers. I'm going to keep my distance for as long as possible, though. She's come here for a reason, and I need to parse out what it is quickly. I don't want to be flirted with. Not now.

"Hello, Jatin."

I'm surprised, but I shouldn't be. There is a bird native to

121

Agsa with a large, hooked bill that only hunts after blood has been spilled. When walking through the Agsa plains, one can often see the predator's bill rise above the grass. But it's the swiping, charging talons—the thing you least expect—that can kill you. Encounters with Fiza Agsa are a bit like that.

"What in Wickery are you doing here?" I blurt. I don't have time for reunions or games or whatever this is.

She laughs. It's not what I would call attractive, though some might. Some would say the high-pitched breathiness matches her shortness and small upturned nose. But like Fiza's entire being, the sound rings false.

"I don't remember you being quite this blunt. Being back home change you this much?" She approaches the map on the wall, a map of Wickery. Instead of tracing the slender, hooked outline of Agsa, her country, east of Belwar, her index finger taps a southwest point, my capital, the place she's spent hours flying to. "I thought Naupurians were traditionally hospitable."

"I'd say that's an old stereotype. My father built a bluestone palace atop a mountain, next to a volcano, after all." Honor, respect, and class slowly overtook our welcoming nature and open-door policy. Belwar is now the sanctuary most people sail toward. "Besides, you'll have to forgive me, it's . . . I've lost—"

"I know what you've lost."

I swing around the desk and even out some papers to busy my hands. "I don't think you do."

"Maybe you're right. But that's why I'm here." She steps toward me and gestures toward my father's desk in a wide sweeping motion. "Let me help you."

"How could you help me?" I look into her eyes. "Is Agsa willing to go to war for the first time in over five centuries?"

I hear her sharp intake of breath. She should know now how much I've changed since our academy days. I'm not the same boy who accommodated her and falsified an entire relationship of friendship and pleasantries instead of being frank.

"My people might be peaceful, but that's the last word you would use to describe me, don't you think?" She tilts her head, golden-brown hair flipping over her shoulders.

I scoff. "That's about right."

"So I come with an opportunity."

"And what's that? Marry you? Make you the next maharani of Naupure?"

A wide smile swings my way. "I'm glad we are on the same page."

The joke makes me sick, and immediately I'm revolted with myself for going there. I stare her down. Gods, I hate this.

"Is it weird to say I still don't get it?" I say. "The academy was full of powerful men with grand titles. I understand Naupure's draw—the power and the money and the prestige—but why me?"

The question comes out wrong. I meant to ask, have you ever seen beyond my position? Have you ever liked me because of *me*? But that seems too vulnerable and open. And even now, years later, Fiza's very presence makes me put up my guard, fumble for the fake mask I've only recently grown accustomed to not wearing.

"You still don't get power and money and prestige?" Her

sarcasm slices through me. "I thought maybe you had learned a thing or two about ruling, about what it means to be an heir."

What she says resonates, vibrating to my bones. What it means to be an heir. Maharaja. But it feels wrong, out of tune like it always did. Growing up at the academy was hard enough without fellow students like Fiza trying to manipulate me into their way of thinking. Not too long ago, right after the eruption, Adraa said it would be best for me to marry someone else because of our positions, our current reputations. But love, at least the way I love, doesn't work like that. If there is a chance that Adraa Belwar wants to be with me, I'm going to do everything in my power to make that happen.

I sigh. "I'm in love with someone else, Fiza. And I think you know that."

She sighs. "I'm joking, Jatin. I'm here on behalf of my father and Agsa. Nothing more."

"So this is *all* political?"

"My brothers were already out of the academy by our year. Father wanted someone to come who you actually know. You really thought I'd chase you across the world?" She holds up a finger. "Actually, don't answer that. Let me get to the point. I'm here to help you save Naupure. And when this war or these ideas about voting reach Agsa's borders, you'll help us."

So she is tuned in to the current political climate, the *true* climate. But something's off. "Your father sent you to do *all* this?" I've met Maharaja Agsa; he doesn't seem the type to let his youngest daughter wear flying pants, let alone travel the world to salvage an entire alliance by herself.

She pauses, and I know in that moment she's weighing whether to tell me the truth. "My father sent me to investigate Adraa and the eruption."

There it is. Finally, a glimpse of authenticity. And I despise every word.

"Investigations and alliances are two entirely different things," I say, trying to maintain the little composure I have left.

"Agsa might be made up of fields and swamps and simple farmers, but some of *us* understand what's happening. Even though my country won't act in what I predict is a coming war, we don't want Moolek and his ideals overtaking us until there is nothing left. Agsa has its problems, but I think we both understand what life might be like under Moolek's regime." Her magic flutters in black smoke up her arm. Like me, she isn't a red, green, blue, or yellow forte—the only respected fortes in northern Moolek, and the only ones with any rights. We'd both be inferior under Moolek's rule.

"You did always have a good amount of foresight, I will give you that."

Fiza smirks. "I also know of another problem you're facing. A missing Red Woman . . ." Her words trail off as she raises her arms, and mists of black smoke engulf the table. With a whisper, her magic changes to deep red, showcasing the ease of her illusion. She's the only witch I know who can do that.

"What makes you think I care about the Red Woman? Or that I've lost one? That's Belwar business. Masked nonsense," I retort.

Fiza reaches into the folds of her wraparound skirt and pulls out a poster I haven't seen in a long while. After the eruption they scattered to the wind, and then I invented the signal. Adraa and I responding to calls of help changed our reputations almost overnight. Clear as day the old poster reads NIGHT AND THE RED WOMAN, with badly drawn pictures of me and Adraa in masks beneath the words. "You want to pretend this isn't you and Adraa Belwar?" Fiza says. "Fine. But I'm not so into secrets. Let's be blunt, especially since you've gotten better at it."

Her words are crisp, almost friendly. A new level of irritation clings to me like sweat. I forgot what talking to Fiza Agsa was like. It's more than hooked beaks or talons. She's smart. Every word draws blood.

We stare each other down, confidence radiating off her. I feel young and, more than anything, exposed. She *knows*. She knows, and there is nothing I can do about her knowing.

"Okay. Blunt." I step closer. "What do you want, Fiza? Why are you here, really? Adraa is in the Dome. Investigation's over."

"I know, but like I said. I heard you had a problem." She perches on the corner of my father's desk. "I am here to fix that problem." She leans forward. "I hope you will let me."

Adraa in the Dome is more than a problem. But I still scoff and turn away. "She's not replaceable."

Fiza hops off the desk and casts. Black smoke engulfs her arms and I twist back to see her transform. Like rippling water, her magic flows over her frame until it solidifies and snaps into place. And suddenly it's not Fiza Agsa in front of me. It's Adraa. The Red Woman. Embedded red magic infused into her clothes, red mask, black braid, beautiful eyes. The girl I love standing before me with a smile.

I can't move. I can't speak. The only part of me not boiling over in anger is the small part that's relieved to know I'm not losing my mind. But even that is laced with betrayal.

"Please," Fiza says, and even her voice—*even her voice*—sounds like Adraa's. "News of Night and Red Woman's antics have reached Agsa and the academy. The Red Woman is more a symbol than flesh and bone now. And a symbol can be easily replaced. It's only when it disappears that it ruins everything."

"It was you. The other night . . ." I can't comprehend my anger, only that it's bubbling to the surface—fast. I have to know. "What was that? Running around the streets of Belwar? Why didn't you reveal yourself?" She's going to need a bloody good excuse for making me think I was going crazy.

"Wait, you didn't actually think . . ." Her face falls. "Blood. I wasn't trying to mess with you. I wasn't trying to be seen at all. So I ran for it. Then you caught up and I couldn't help myself. I wanted to test my black magic. To see exactly how convincing the illusion could be."

I can't stand to talk to her while she's wearing the illusion. "Take it off. Take it off *now*." My voice is ice, colder than I've ever heard it.

Fiza obeys and with a gush the illusion falls. She seems to understand her misstep because she raises her hands. "Believe me, Jatin, I'm only trying to help you."

"Maybe I don't want *you*."

She scrunches her upturned nose. "But you need me. I'm the only one who—"

Something breaks. The idea of planning the Underground interrogation was already fracturing my nerves. Now this. My glare stops Fiza in her tracks. "Stay in Naupure if you must. But there will never be an alliance. Being the Red Woman isn't a job you can apply for, no matter how much you look the part. Now, leave." I force myself to rein in my anger.

It takes a second because she wants to keep talking, to keep trying to convince me, but I don't stop scowling until she's through the door.

"Oh, and, Fiza?" She whirls around, and I savor the curiosity and hope on her face. "It's tradition to climb down the mountain too," I lie. Then I do what I've wanted to do since I was nine years old. With a whisk of yellow magic, I slam the door.

◇

CHAPTER FOURTEEN

The Art of Breathing

Adraa

I think about Harini's magic all night. Mostly because my body hurts so badly, I can't move enough to do anything besides think.

But eventually I do fall asleep, and the next morning I awaken to the biggest surprise of my life. In the night, someone has re-dressed my midsection, right around the broken rib—and I can narrow down the prospects to one. I glance over at Harini. She's staring at me.

Well, that's creepy.

Then I realize she's . . . she's *crying*. Quietly, of course, with no real sign besides the single tear running down her face. I'm shocked. In fact, I'm so shocked I don't even know what to do. When she sees I've noticed, she jerks her head sideways, embarrassed.

But before she turns away completely, I reach out. My entire midsection panics at the movement, screaming in pain. But I find the dusty, curved wall and smudge two words into its glass-like substance with the pad of my finger.

I know, I write, then erase it with a swipe after I'm sure she's taken it in.

She nods and lies back down on her side.

Bloody Godly blood! Subtlety was never my forte, and now I'm the bloody rani of it.

Then a new idea comes to mind. I can't be all Red Woman about this. She's made it clear that communicating is off-limits, so I'm going to have to make her *want* to talk to me.

I'm going to need some paper.

Slowly I attempt to fully sit up. Every part of my body fights me. Harini is all watchful eyes as I move. Gods, I hope she doesn't try to punch me again when I get close. My lungs seize, and I fall back in pain, barely catching a breath.

The morning alarm rings and the door to our cell slides open. It's lunch already.

Harini stands to leave with a glance back at me. We both know I'm not moving today. Which means I don't get to eat either. When she disappears, I reassess my injuries. I have many bruises, especially along my entire right side, where they bloom above the bandages. I can only imagine the black and purple beneath. It's the possible broken rib that worries me, though. I press a hand to my chest; I still can't seem to purchase enough air.

With nothing to do and nothing to eat, I attempt to sleep. Anything to release me from the pain.

I awaken to sweat. Buckets of it drench my uniform, my bedding, and my brow. It takes me a moment to realize the perspiration is coming from me. Blood. Things have gotten worse.

My entire chest seizes. While I choke for air, I have an idea of what's happening to me. My right lung—it's been punctured. For the first time in my life I'm ill. Deadly ill with no resources, no magic, and no help.

It spells death. My vision clouds, like I'm entering a slow, woozy burnout. I can normally keep awake in these sorts of instances. But magic depletion hits differently than being physically broken. I can't fight this.

A whoosh of a door and the smell of spices bring me back for a moment. I blink hard. Our cell lowers, and I make out Harini coming toward me. She's standing over me, and I've never felt more vulnerable, yet I lack the energy to care. Pain, sweat, and heat squash down all apprehension; I'm too lopsided and fuzzy for apprehension. In fact, what a weird word, *apprehension* . . . so many syllables . . .

Slowly, Harini puts down a bowl of something. A soup or stew, my nose tells me. I will myself to look down, and on the rim of the bowl sit two white idlis, already soaking up the moisture. The image reminds me so much of Jatin that I almost start crying. That rooftop at the festival seems like a lifetime ago.

A freezing-cold hand touches my forehead, and I startle back to our cell. That's right—cell. Harini looks stricken. Then she's there, crouched right beside me, examining my ribs. I wheeze soundlessly.

On the wall, beneath the spot where I wrote and wiped away my message, Harini writes another two-word phrase. I'm just lucid enough to read it. *Trust me.* Right under it, she scribbles something else, but my vision goes fuzzy. I stare, trying to make the words out, wondering if my mind has completely spiraled due to lack of oxygen. I squint hard as Harini lifts me off my bed. Finally, I'm able to read the rest of what's written.

I'm sorry.

There's a smidge of blood woven into the words.

Huh. That's terrifying.

I'm oddly aware of our journey out of the cell. There's banging, a face full of freckles, a descent that rolls my stomach, then the thumping of walking. A husky voice yells out, and the arms around me tense. Then I black out from the pain.

When I come to, I'm on a cot. It's cold, not recently occupied. Dampness lies heavy over me.

"She shouldn't be down here," a hard male voice says. The warden.

"Where else is she supposed to go?" Ekani? It sounds like her. I try to roll and the pain, along with a wave of dizziness and heat, snuffs out my willpower. "She's the new red forte," the voice continues. "You know how important she is to them. If you let another die, we will *all* be killed."

"You don't need to tell me how important she is. How did this happen? The fight was supposed to just weaken her. Test her," the warden says.

A scoff slices the air. "Someone got a little too violent."

A pause.

"What is she saying? I don't understand when she flaps her arms around like that," the warden says coolly.

"I don't know, but I can guess she's saying it wasn't her fault. Jaya wouldn't relent. The willpower on this one. We need to heal her, *now*."

"I'm running a prison here, Ekani. Not a clinic. I'll have to get Basu. This is his problem anyway."

I open my eyes after hearing that name. I'm deep in the prison, in a clinic of sorts, I think. I recognize the tang of blood, the smell of herbs. Two bubbling cauldrons spill the scent of spices into the air, adding to the mixture.

The two of them notice that my eyes are open. Ekani. Harini. The warden is already out of sight, gone to get . . .

I shake my head. *Not Basu. Please*, I mouth.

Ekani's head rises over mine. "You won't die, Jaya. I'm trying to save you." Her words shatter my concentration and a wave of heat hits me. Sweat drips down my forehead.

Staring at Ekani, I forget why I should struggle. I imagine my mother in her place, and the image is pleasant, soft at the edges. When I was eight, after Jatin and I had been introduced, my mother brought me to her clinic. *I think it's about time you started helping me, Adraa.* She had to bend down to look me in the eyes back then. *One punch and you can make an enemy for*

133

life. One potion and you can save a life. And when you save some-
one, they have your trust, they share their secrets with you. The
same thing can be said for our potions. You have to learn nature's
secrets. Even with the best intentions, you can do more harm
than good if you don't respect nature. We used to examine every
shelf of the palace clinic, opening jars. I'd observe and identify
the leafy plants by shapes. I'd feel the texture of different bat
wings. I'd smell the point when a flower had fully dissolved in
a solution. *Let's start with a basic antibiotic. You have your three*
main ingredients: garlic, ginger, and—

Honey. It floats around me, perfuming the air with its sweet-
ness. *Mom,* I try to say, but I'm not able to vocalize the word.
Why can't I . . .

The image dissipates. Something cold pierces my ribs. My
eyes fly open.

Basu stands over me. He holds a knife made of yellow magic
to my left side. *No! No, no, no, no.*

"Hold still, my dear."

Someone grabs my legs. Harini pins my other shoulder to
the table. She gestures, movements I can't grasp. Then I realize
she's gesturing to Basu.

"You know I don't understand you. But if you are asking me
to save this girl, then, yes, of course. I'm trying my best. She's
a dear friend of mine, in fact," he spits through gritted teeth.

The yellow knife of Basu's magic stabs the side of my chest.
Pain blooms in aching waves, and black dots fill my vision, but
not enough for me to unsee a haze of yellow magic diving for
my mouth. I panic. This isn't a healing spell. He's going for my

throat again, tearing out something even more vital. Healing shouldn't be painful. He isn't saving me.

He's destroying me.

My eyes latch onto Harini's face as I scream in silence and a rush of air dives down my throat. She mouths two simple words again—*I'm sorry*. Then darkness takes over.

◇

CHAPTER FIFTEEN

The Meeting

Jatin

Fiza's visit has solidified two things. One: I need a plan. And two: I need help. As much as this mission needs to remain quiet and undercover, I can't work alone anymore. And sneaking through the streets hasn't procured any solid clues. In fact, I think it's breaking me. So I tell Hiren and Prisha to meet me here, in my mother's tearoom, to go over this idea of theirs. It's the best place to formulate and visualize a plan.

When I first brought Adraa here, to this wing of Azure Palace, she spoke like everyone does—quietly, like a single word could tamper with the ghosts of the past. My mother's ghost, to be exact. Funny how I used to feel the same, until it became the place where Adraa and I frequently met to discuss our operations. In this room we felt safe, and confident we could stomp out the criminals hoarding firelight and creating Bloodlurst. We were quite idealistic back then, mere months ago.

"Jatin?" Kalyan jerks me from my reverie.

"Yes, sorry, Kalyan. Bring them in."

The door opens and in walk Riya, Prisha, and Hiren. Riya looks exhausted, but Prisha seems resolved in a way I've never seen before. Like she's standing taller. She appears to have come to terms with whatever raged inside of her the night before the trial.

"Thank you for coming," I say.

Riya glances around, and I can guess her line of thinking. This isn't a war room. This isn't even the most secure of locations. Arched windows open onto rounded balconies. My mother's birdhouses swing, empty, in the sunshine.

"Of course. Kalyan filled us in. But, Jatin, why did you call us *here*?" she asks.

"*Simaraw*," I cast on both doorways. I add an extra layer of soundproofing, just to be safe. Only after that do I speak.

"I want to show you all something."

Hiren steps forward, opens his mouth.

I hold up a finger. "And to hear you out. Please, give me a minute."

I crouch down, taking a moment to appreciate my mother's painting of Wickery, every building rendered in pristine detail. I rest a hand on Azure Palace a moment and then swipe over it and pour so much magic onto the floor that an eruption of fog engulfs our feet. Hiren backs up.

Using my mother's painting and black magic, I've zoomed in on our target and created an enlarged, three-dimensional depiction of the Dome and its surroundings. And there it sits, center stage, in all its awful glory. I've never noticed before the direct contrast between the Dome's spherical shape and the natural slope of Mount Gandhak, but I'm left once again feeling that the Dome is the most artificial thing in Wickery.

Everyone leans forward and stares.

"Whoa," Prisha sputters as she crouches beside me. The smell of spring wafts past me and immediately, like whiplash, it reminds me of Adraa. I can't help but look at Prisha.

"What?" She startles.

"Sorry, you . . . ah . . . you smell like her," I say, already regretting it, knowing how creepy it probably sounds.

Prisha bites her lip. "I stole her perfume from her room. I'm sorry. I . . . I wanted to—"

"It's fine. I understand." I turn to the others, who are still gawking at the detailed map and thankfully ignoring one of the most awkward exchanges I've ever had.

"I always wondered how you knew Belwar so well," Riya whispers, leaning in to touch my illusion. It fizzles a moment before returning.

"Actually, that was Adraa. But responding to the signals these last few months has helped."

I draw myself up to my full height, which is not as impressive with Kalyan standing next to me, but I'm used to that. It's strange having this group of vigilantes staring at me, waiting on me. With a start, I realize we're all used to orbiting around Adraa, me most of all.

"I've brought us all together for one purpose," I begin. I glance at each of my friends in turn. "For the last several days Kalyan and I have interrogated every Vencrin we could find.

None of them know Adraa's location in the Dome or have any insights into her well-being. Alone, I've been failing. But together, we might not. The five of us are going to break Adraa Belwar out of the Dome."

Resolution. Nods. No surprise. Exactly what I was hoping for.

"Good." Riya steps forward. "I just hope you have a *how* wrapped up in this speech, though."

"Yes, but before we get to it, I want to make sure everyone in this room is committed to the cause. We are getting her out, by any means necessary."

Kalyan crosses his arms and nods. Prisha is quick to follow, her eyes wide and sincere as she bobs her head.

Riya looks irritated. "You know us, Jatin. If you weren't going to accept this meeting, I was going to keep hounding you or go after her myself."

I turn to Hiren. He takes me in. "I'm Belwarian," he states like that's enough, like that absolves him of any second-guessing. I think of the rally that night, all those people roaring against the Belwar name, how they wouldn't connect themselves to it now. Maybe he does deserve my complete confidence. It's his idea and his willingness to spill Belwar Guard secrets that brought us here, after all.

"He's the most loyal person I know," Prisha says, raising her chin in defiance. I see it then. The way they orbit one another. Hiren's eyes always finding Prisha's face.

Riya and I share a knowing glance and she tips her head. I guess I have been a little unobservant.

"We just have to be sure," I say. "Moolek wasn't in that courtroom. He didn't make Adraa say what she did. Belwar has traitors within it. The Vencrin leader, for one, is still out there. Nothing we say today, nothing we plan leaves this room."

A silence falls, as I knew it would. The wound is still too fresh for all of us. The pain also dwells on the unchangeable past, when we let Adraa sacrifice herself. The sheer havoc of that moment comes back full force and I have to push it down before it overwhelms me.

"We *need* to get her out. And we need to clear her name as well." I pause. "We also need to know who we can trust. Or, more importantly, who we cannot."

I turn to face Hiren. "As much as I respect your father, and we all owe him for trying to get the hearing dismissed in the first place and stopping that arrow, you speak none of this to him. Can you do that?"

"Yes," he answers without hesitation.

I clap my hands. "Okay, then. Let's go over your plan." With a swipe of the map, I zero in on the alleyway entrance to the Underground and the five of us lean forward, staring at the painted replica of the grimy, narrow space.

"Riya filled you in on the basics?" Hiren asks.

"Invade the Underground before the Belwar Guard can get to it. Question who we can and make sure you arrest someone you can escort in."

"Yes," he says, "but there is one hitch. We need someone important enough to warrant my presence in the Dome. It can't just be a cage caster with no priors and a loose affiliation with the Vencrin. In fact, it can't be any old Vencrin member at all."

Kalyan and I share a look. "We have a perfect contender for the prisoner," Kalyan says.

I smile, the plan knitting together in my mind. Yes, a perfect contender indeed. "How does the man who runs the entire Underground operation sound?"

Hiren grins. "That's what I was hoping you'd say. There's something else, though. I've been asking around, and I found out the Dome was hit during the eruption. The north siding was ripped open. They are operating without one-fourth of their cells."

"Tell them what that means for Adraa," Prisha pushes.

"The north corner was used for solitary confinement and special prisoners."

"So . . . ," Riya prompts, hope blooming in her voice.

"So," Hiren continues, "they had to have put Adraa in the general women's section. She'll have a cellmate. Might even be treated like everyone else. On the one hand this might make it easier to get her out. On the other? More eyes, more witnesses, maybe even more guards."

The whole room sighs. I believe we are all cursing in our heads. And I'm filled with dread at the word *cellmate*. Cellmate as in a criminal, a *Belwarian* criminal.

"I guess one bright side is she's not alone," Kalyan whispers.

I pound a fist on the nearest table. "No. That isn't good

news. If they know who she is and if they think she is guilty, they'll be after her." I don't have to remind them of the added security Belwar Palace had to be fortified with so no assassins could attempt to kill what Belwar has dubbed "a monster."

Prisha wipes at her face and pulls back her shoulders, but says nothing.

Hiren frowns, finally speaking into the drawn silence. "There's another point I was trying to make with this information." We all look at him. "The Dome, the most imperturbable place in Wickery, has a hole in its side."

◇

CHAPTER SIXTEEN

Burying the Underground

Jatin

A hole in the side of the Dome changes everything. Now, instead of disguising our way in, we're going to find that hole and bust it open to create an entrance and escape route. Even with this new knowledge, though, the beginning of our plan remains the same. We need a way into the Dome to find out exactly where Adraa is being kept before we can go back and get her out. Therefore, we need a criminal for Hiren to escort into the prison. Tonight, Kalyan, Riya, and I rip out one of the Vencrin's hearts. We're taking out the Underground and we're arresting Sims.

Adraa once led me here by following a series of hidden messages in the street. I still use them today. An upside-down hammer on a sign. The faded arrow on a hanging sheet. All the way to the window at the end of a long-forgotten alleyway.

"This place still gives me the creeps," Riya says as we approach. "And makes me mad that Adraa came here by herself."

"I know. Project Smoke should never have been a solo act. *Upaphtrae,*" I cast into the window. The green-paned frame cracks as it enlarges and drops like an unhinging jaw.

"Password?" a burly wizard asks from inside.

"A bloody place like this needs a bloody shorter password," I answer. Gods, sometimes I feel like I've missed one of the curse words. Is it two or three? Most of the time I just pray I have the most current rendition of vulgarity.

"Been a long time." He nods. "White Knight."

I wonder for half a second if I should read into this, but he doesn't say more, just lets us enter. The memory-inducing stench envelops me like a dust cloud. Riya and Kalyan don't even wrinkle their noses at the smell of hundreds of sweaty bodies pressed together as they duck under the exposed beams. Professional guards through and through.

When we get to the inner pit, the center of the humid, squishy, smoky glaze, I turn to the only person who hasn't met the Underground's brand of stickiness before—Kalyan. "Thoughts?"

A witch bumps into him, spilling Roloc on his pants. The colorful alcoholic drink glows in different hues, so when he brushes at the splotch it turns from red to green. "Charming."

"Adraa always seemed to think so," Riya jokes.

And just like that, all the muscles in my body tighten. I'm ready to get on with it. It'll be fun to turn this place upside down.

◈ ◈ ◈

Finding Sims is not a problem, and not just because he's a large guy. He's the heartbeat of this place. No fight happens without his say-so. I spot him on the upper deck, aka the wraparound catwalk where most fighters watch the competition. I point him out to Kalyan and Riya with a quick nod. Then, without a word, we split up. Riya heads to the bar, which curves around the large room. Kalyan moves to the outskirts of the roaring crowd. I'm going to the locker room.

The narrow hallway unleashes a flood of memories. Sims interrogating me. Adraa saving me and offering to fight Beckman for leverage. It was here that Adraa and I became partners, where Night and the Red Woman started. And in a few minutes, I'm going to blow the whole operation.

No voices echo down the hall. In fact, the place is eerily quiet. When I step into the locker room I see why. No one's here. I'm about to check the smaller, cramped closet the women use when a bulky figure emerges around the corner.

Beckman. Better known here in the Underground as Tsunami.

One look and Beckman drags me around the corner and shoves me out of sight. "What are you doing here?" the powerful blue forte asks, his voice deep and thunderous.

I push him away. "I could you ask you the same thing. What do you think I'm doing here?" The last time I talked with Beckman, I was shouting at him in this very room as I healed Adraa's head injury. The one he had inflicted. If he hadn't been explaining his own undercover operation to protect Adraa, while also bleeding all over the place from his own wound, I would have taken a swing.

He steps back. "I'm making sure none of them have an exit strategy." He nods to the door, then pauses. "I didn't think it would be you."

"Why not?" I'm just as much a part of this. Even more so.

His eyebrows scrunch. "Because you have an entire country to run."

Gods, why does every single person think they need to remind me of that? I've lived with the burden my entire life.

Beckman's expression softens. "Do you know anything? Any news from the Dome?"

"That's why I'm here."

"Sims and these fighters don't know anything about the Dome. If you can believe it, none of them had to actually serve their time."

"They're about to," I correct. "Glad to see your cover hasn't been blown."

He glares. "No, Lady Belwar performed well that night. Your cover, on the other hand? That's a different matter. Most of this crowd doesn't travel to Naupure, but you aren't exactly anonymous anymore."

"You don't have to worry about me," I say. "This will be the last time I come here."

"What do you need from me?"

I raise an eyebrow. "Get all the innocents out."

This makes Beckman chuckle. "I was told this was simply a raid. What are you going to do? Blow the place up?"

I stare.

He whistles. "She's really rubbed off on you, huh?"

Something inside me warms. It's a nice compliment. "I have a mission."

He nods slowly. "And now so do I." He walks away, but at the curtain he stops and turns back. "You think I could punch Nightcaster one last time?"

It really is everyone's favorite pastime, including mine. "Whoever finds him first."

Beckman chuckles and presses his fingers to his throat, a salute without the bow. Maybe he isn't so bad.

"*Chagnyawodahs.*" I cast my Night mask to my face. Then I replace my white cage-casting kurta for the black one, embedding shield spells down my chest and legs. Next, I build up my magic. White smoke and then crystallized frost wash over the room. The anger I feel toward this place grows until it's layered in the spells, in the power I have inside of me. I walk out of the locker room. I might just get too much enjoyment out of this next part.

One universal fact of life—it's always easier to destroy than create. Though I'm kind of doing both. Frost turns to ice as I encase the quiet back hall in white magic. Crystals crack under my boots as I walk, and then they spread outward, creating a tunnel of bright white. My breath catches the air, marking it. It's only going to get colder.

With a blast of razor-sharp icicles, the door leading to the Underground's stage bursts open. The sound is deafening. Torn wood splintering, ice crackling as it climbs over the frame. It almost swallows the commotion from the crowd inside. Almost.

Stepping through the hole I've created, I press a hand to the wall that lists the fighters' statistics and the current bets. The frost freezes the numbers. Perfect evidence if, say, a troop of Belwar guards were on their way.

I look past the mob of people flooding the entrance and glance up at the upper deck. At my flashy signal, a masked Riya slashes one of the ropes holding the upper deck airborne, then she slides down the plank and lands in the fray below. Sims, on the other hand, tumbles down and hits the floor with a thud. He rolls to standing, but I'm already there, spells primed.

Ice wraps around his arms, anchoring him to the ground. But I don't stop there. My magic billows like mist. I search for Kalyan in the crowd. He and Riya have Nightcaster in the same binding of ice and purple rope. Good, because I'm not done with this place yet.

"Himadloc!" I yell, and throw my arms outward. The Underground is swallowed by fog. For a moment I don't even see Riya or Kalyan. Everything is bright white, like I've transported us into a cloud. Then, with a whoosh, my magic disperses, adhered to the walls in glimmering, shining crystallized frost.

And with it, a stillness overtakes the space. The crowd has made it out. Beckman stands in the entryway, and with one nod he's gone. I inspect my handiwork. Opened and split in two, the spherical cage-casting ring has become a shard of ice spears reaching upward and outward like fanged teeth. The floor is a frozen lake and the bar is a tabletop of overturned drinks and icicles.

Sims is the first to demolish the silence. "You're destroying the place!"

Not exactly. I'm freezing it. "It'll melt," I tell him. "Eventually." Not fast enough to avoid discovery. Hiren and his men should be on their way. "I wanted to talk to you about something in the meantime."

I shout out spells. They may be encased in ice, but I know how many people have white magic up their sleeves to crack open ice shackles. So, I overwhelm them. Chains of purple seep through the ice. Currents of yellow press down. Vines of green converge atop the personal prisons and squeeze. And last but not least, shadows of black illusion make it appear there is no way out.

Rakesh, aka Nightcaster, roars against the restraints. Adraa told me everything about that night on the upper deck when he put his hands on her, how he thought he could take what can only be given. Beckman stopped it, but I'm happy enough to hear Nightcaster's cries now. He deserves every ounce of pain. I just wish Adraa could be here to hear him too.

I drop down from my elevated platform, walk over, and punch Nightcaster in the face. His head swivels at the impact. Beckman's right. It feels good. I should have done this a long time ago.

"I don't want to hear either of you unless you are answering my questions," I articulate, each syllable dripping in its own kind of frost.

"Oh, you've made a mistake, kid. A big mistake," Sims says, shaking his head.

I turn toward him. Riya and Kalyan step closer. The three of us against the two of them. Now for the hard part.

"I don't think so," I answer, gesturing to the icy enclosure. "I've been wanting to do this for a long time. You see, I don't know if I've ever unleashed my full power on anything before." The room glistens. With a whoosh of white magic, I create two cones of ice, their tips like spears. They fly toward my captives. Rakesh croaks out a sound of protest as the shard hovers at his forehead. "I've restrained myself my whole life. I've never wanted to kill before. Funny how things change." The daggers of ice swirl closer. "And how fast."

"I'll tell you what you want to know," Sims bellows. "Blood. You don't need the theatrics. But it will be your head, your mistake."

"Thank you for the warning." I crouch down to his level. "Let's start at the beginning."

"The beginning? The beginning of what? Of the money? Of building this place?"

"No, start when Maharaja Moolek got involved. I want to hear why he hired you. I want to hear you say it."

Sims looks confused for a second, his mouth frowning so deeply I think it could get stuck that way. "See, there, that makes me think you aren't ignorant. You know who you are dealing with. Yet you're still here."

"One more chance." The shard zooms forward and presses into Sim's forehead, breaking the skin. "Why. Did. He. Hire. You?"

Sims sighs and I hate how calm he is. "Let's clear one thing up, because your questions need work. Moolek didn't join me. He didn't *hire* the Vencrin." He snorts. "He created them."

I fall back on my heels. It takes me a second to process what Sims just said. Riya glances around, taking in our surroundings. Our thoughts are probably on a similar track. Because if this is true—if Moolek *created* the Vencrin—then his plans extend not just in complexity but also in time. Mount Gandhak wasn't months of planning and work, but years.

"For what?" I ask. "For Mount Gandhak's eruption?"

Sims's eyes finally find mine. He keeps silent.

Kalyan slaps Rakesh. "What about you?"

"I did what I was told. I got paid. I don't know anything," Rakesh whines.

Sims's eyes flash. "Where's the girl, huh? Where's your leader? Smoke wouldn't want to miss this."

Smoke. A chill runs through me and not because of the ice I've cast around us. Sims knows. He knows one of Adraa's secrets. And maybe mine. "You don't get to ask the questions," I snarl.

"What did Moolek create the Vencrin for?" Riya shouts.

"It wasn't much of a question," Sims says, ignoring Riya. "I have my suspicions." He looks down at the icy shackles imprisoning him. "Not many high-level wizards out there and even fewer who could pull this off. Are you even trying to hide anymore? Though I'm sorry she couldn't be here tonight. Send my regards."

"Yeah?" a girl's voice asks from the entryway. "It's nice to hear you've missed me."

We all start, but I'm the first to swivel around. And there, in the middle of the staircase, stands the exact same illusion I saw the other night . . . and in my father's office. I jerk back around to look at Kalyan and the others. Their eyes are trained on the very real Red Woman duplicate making her way toward us.

My chest tightens and it takes me a second to realize why. For a heartbreaking moment, I thought it *was* Adraa again, the Red Woman, come back to me. It was only a second—a second of wonder and hope and such piercing happiness—but I wish to live in that second for the rest of my life, because now that it's past, my chest constricts, squeezing my heart with anguish and then anger. It's Fiza Agsa again. She went ahead with her plan, no matter what I said.

In the bright ice world I've created, the shadows of illusion hold up. But the way she walks . . . I can't pinpoint how it's different from Adraa's other than that there's a sway to it. But then again, the outfit, the mask, the hair wound into a tight braid and shimmering with illusion. I don't think many could pick up the difference, especially not Sims or Rakesh.

"Answer his question," she says.

Kalyan jerks to attention, but it's Riya who steps forward like she's been provoked, shock and betrayal clear in her body language. But we can't do this now. I hold out a hand, desperately trying to communicate what needs to happen. Because even more shocked than Riya is Sims. In fact, he's dumbfounded.

"There you go. I answered your question. You got to give your regards," I say, my voice cold. "Now keep talking."

◇

CHAPTER SEVENTEEN

The Question of Voice

Adraa

I'm not dead yet.

When I awaken, I'm cold, and I can tell immediately my fever has broken. I'm also back in my cell, like nothing happened. But I know the truth.

Reaching for my shoulder, I feel the soft slope of bandages. Basu wasn't trying to kill me—at least not this time. In fact, he inflated my lung. But blood, someone needs to teach that wizard how to do proper pink magic. Recovery is going to take twice as long as it should, even though I've been healed magically.

I wonder what time it is and then reconfigure the question. More importantly, what day is it? I turn and find Harini just as I left her, sitting on her bed, watching me. Well, at least she's consistent.

For the next few hours, as I do little more than shift my weight and try not to think of the pain, Harini keeps her eyes on me. I have no idea what she's playing at. Is she watching me out of concern, or has she been assigned to observe me?

In my ample spare time, I go through what I do know and what I need to figure out.

One: There was a truth trial, and during that trial, everyone heard me admit to putting my firelight in Mount Gandhak and blowing it up. I'm about ninety percent sure Moolek manipulated the trial, though I don't know how.

Two: I'm unsure what Jatin heard, but if it's what I think it is, I told him not to come for me. Which means there's a good chance he thinks I'm going to try to escape by myself and he's continuing our mission to incriminate Moolek. Or maybe he's taking care of his father and running Naupure.

Three: Maharaja Naupure was hurt during the trial, but he must be alive. News as big as his death would have slipped through the cracks of this place. At least, that's what I tell myself.

Four: It's possible to cast magic without a voice and Harini knows how.

And that leads me to five: For the first time, I know the Dome is more than just a holding cell and an arena for brutal entertainment. Something even more insidious crawls under this place. During my infection I was brought to the clinic, shown a world I wasn't supposed to see or remember. If I wanted to blend in, I would leave it; I'd simply try to survive. But that isn't me. Because something deep down tells me that the prisoners are being hurt.

And I don't stand by and let people be hurt.

So, I'm going to figure it out. I'm going to learn how Harini somehow does magic and I'm going to get to the bottom of that sickly cavern of a medical clinic. Then I will escape this prison. If along the way I ambush Basu, all the better.

But Harini first. I think I've been reading her cold, hard stares wrong, as has the rest of the prison. She brought me to that clinic because it was all she could do. The trust she wanted me to place in her saved my life. Basu performed the magic, but Harini delivered me to help. She's no killer.

So I'm going after her parchment, and I'm going to try to communicate with her. It's risky, but deep in my bones I believe I can trust her. I just have to wait for a perfect moment.

Finally, she leaves for midday meal without me. As soon as the hatch closes and her footfalls fade, I'm moving. Well, crawling. Actually, I'm more like an infant learning how to do a caterpillar squirming maneuver. I want to keep out of the guards' sight, so it's a slow process. Careful of my right arm, I heave one corner of Harini's cot up. Several squirming motions later and the mattress has been ruled out as a hiding place. Nothing. Blood, where does she keep it, then? There isn't a plethora of hiding choices.

With a spasm of pain I haul myself to my knees and pull open the wicker drawer to the one table in our cell. Empty. *Too obvious.* I feel under the desk, my fingers skimming along the woven wicker. Blood. Harini is going to be back any second, and her warnings ring in my head. I can't be caught.

I crumble to the floor, my head resting under the desk, and breathe. The dizziness sets in and it doesn't care about time limits and violent, secretive cellmates who refuse to share. But then, when I turn, I see it: the crisp corner of a page sticking out of the back-left leg. I shuffle further underneath the desk, grab hold of the paper, and feel along the leg. The wicker gives way with some pressure and the side of the leg opens, revealing a hidden compartment. A scroll wound tightly with a rainbow ribbon falls into my hands. I have to search for the pen in the compartment, but one good inspection and I have it.

As I shimmy out from under the desk, my cell shifts, lifting back to the platform for someone to enter. No! I grasp for the ribbon, fiddling with the knot as the cage inches closer. It opens. I peel a page from the bunch and scribble out the first thing that comes to mind.

Too late.

There's a thunk and Harini is standing over me. Fury distorts her features. She grabs for the paper. I scramble and my hand acts on its own, holding tightly to the one thing I can use to express myself. The sheet of parchment tears and I fall back, my shoulder aching.

But more than that, failure tightens in my chest. One chance. I had one bloody chance. And now Harini is fuming over me.

Then she looks down at my message. *I know about your magic.*

Her whole demeanor changes. Fear enters her eyes, and then an added bolt of anger. She swivels around, looking at the other suspended cages as we are lowered over the side of the cliff. But she's come back early. The cells on either side of us remain empty. It would take minutes for a guard to make it here and stop her if she flew at me in a rage. A lot can happen in a few minutes.

Her hands jerk and I brace myself for her fist, but she doesn't hit me. Instead, her arms swirl and orange smoke engulfs us. I realize with a start it's a spell. But without the words, I have no idea what I should prepare for. I sit up fully and watch in amazement, like I'm eight years old again and magic in any form is still a wonder.

I see it then, the glimmer. Oh Gods, it's an illusion spell wrapped around the cell's walls. She's blinding us from the rest of the prison. I'd be impressed if I wasn't filled with pure terror.

I push myself over to my cot, putting as much space between us as I can. With an illusion hiding us, she can do whatever she wants. *You'll wish you were dead,* her note had said.

Harini turns to me when she's done. I want to hold my hands up in surrender, mouth my apology, but I don't move. I wait.

She smacks her hands in some sort of pattern, and letters materialize above her in a dull pumpkin orange. It's a semi-complex purple magic spell I've seen hundreds of times, but I'm plastered in place. So this is how she does it—through hand signs. Seeing a glimpse of her magic in the ring was one thing, but the proof of her abilities stares me in the face, along with the words she has cast to form the question that hangs in the air.

Who have you told?

I read it again. Told? She's joking, right? For our first real exchange, this is pretty lousy.

She nods to my hands and I realize with a start I'm still

holding half a page of torn paper and the pen. *No one*, I write, and hold the paper up for her to read.

We stare at one another. Several heartbeats of silence pass.

Finally, she moves again. *You won't let anyone know*, her orange words read. *And you won't touch my paper ever again.*

Hope soars through me despite the threat.

Teach me, I write out slowly, and offer up the parchment. *I'll keep your secret if you teach me.*

That wasn't the right thing to express, apparently.

What is wrong with you? She jerks forward and grabs me by the collar of my kurta. *I beat you up. I . . .* Above her head the orange words falter for a second before finishing the sentence. *Almost killed you . . .*

Her eyebrows twitch, and a new emotion emerges—regret. It's in that twitch that my fear simmers down. I remain still, calm, and wait for her to release me. Wait for the moment when she figures out the *almost* is the most important element of that sentence. I don't want to have to spell it out for her—literally. Also, I kind of can't, what with her holding me like this.

Harini lets go, shoving herself away from me and moving her hands. *The last time a Voiceless casted she was killed for it, murdered.* She whips around. *Are you willing to do that? Is having your powers back important enough that you would risk your life?*

Everyone else in Wickery risks my life, so *I* might as well join in. It's my life, after all.

Slowly, I pen my answer. *My magic is more than powers.* I

159

pause. How exactly do I make this clear? *It's part of me,* I add, underlining *me* with three bold lines.

Teach me, I mouth, and gesture to my request. *Please.*

We spend a good while staring at one another. She breaks first, understanding washing over her features.

She writes her response in floating words. *There will have to be rules. Lots of rules. You'll follow them.*

I nod, allowing her to sign. She grabs a paper and writes furiously. When she hands the paper to me, I let out my held breath. Then I read.

Number one: Never, ever cast magic in front of a guard. Two: Listen to me always. Three: Never communicate to anyone about anything pertaining to magic or what I teach you.

That's it. That's all that's written. *And?* I write before handing back the paper. Harini sits on the floor beside me and begins listing them. As I watch her I'm taken aback by how quickly our distance and hostility has crumbled. Now we are like two fourteen-year-olds passing notes in class. Or that's what I imagine it feels like—I was always privately tutored. It's nice. I finally relax, my body not on high alert because of the possibility that Harini might try to punch me. Or that the guards in their tower are peering down at us.

Finally, she gives me back the paper, our code of conduct I'm willing to hold myself to. But the paper only reiterates what she wrote before. Saying there are a lot of rules is a stretch when they boil down to one—don't let anyone know.

I understand, I finally write in thick letters. *I get it.*

She abandons the paper, and her magic takes to the air. *I . . . this is important. That's how they got her.*

Who? I mouth.

My . . . The orange mist lingers. *My old cellmate.*

Nira. The girl I replaced. *I'll be careful,* I scratch out.

Her eyes roll at my answer. *I've watched you. You aren't the careful type.* Her hands slow. *In fact, what scares me most of all is you remind me of her.*

It doesn't take more than a moment to write out my reply. *I am careful when it matters. I swear, I won't end up like your old cellmate.*

She winces. A splash of pure pain I haven't seen before.

Blood, I'm insensitive. I'm not just asking for a favor here. I'm asking Harini to risk her life when someone she was close to had her own life ended. But that's further proof I can't let this go. *I didn't mean it like that,* I write.

I figured. It's just . . . It has to stay a secret. Can you do that? Can you keep a secret like your life depended upon it?

I look up at her, at her fear and uncertainty.

Yes, I can, I write beneath her rules, and slide the parchment to her like a written contract. For the first time in days I'm sure of myself. Some things, like life-threatening secrets, are old hat by now.

CHAPTER EIGHTEEN

◇

Unmasking Fiza of Agsa

Jatin

Sims doesn't give me much more. He runs out the clock on our questioning, and when the Belwar guards arrive he seems reassured more than anything else. I wonder, with all his bluster, if he was scared I might lose it. I look down at my hands, numb from the cold. I'm close to burnout, I think, after having unleashed all my magic on the fortress below, but it's more than that. For a second there, under all that power, I didn't know if I would follow the plan without some bloodshed either. If Sims hadn't talked, if he'd pushed me, what would I have done? For the first time, I can't honestly say I would have held back. The thought slices me to my core.

Sims is cuffed and put into a carriage by Hiren, but he leaves with one final, repetitive warning. "This is a mistake, Night. You've made a mistake."

Mistake. It rings in my head. I should feel good—the plan

worked. But even watching Hiren and the other guards haul Sims and Rakesh off to the Dome, something feels off.

I turn toward the Red Woman. Fiza in illusion—that has to be it. That's where all the uncertainty is coming from. Bloody Fiza Agsa.

Riya is primed to attack, body stiff. She's held off because we still have an audience of guards inspecting the Underground, but her eyes blaze between Fiza and me. I can fully imagine what she'll say as soon as we're alone.

Hiren sends the prisoner carriage rumbling down the road before he and Riya drag me down a few alleyways. This part of the East Village hasn't renewed its firelight lamps with candles, so we are covered by darkness. Ash still coats the beaten-up steps and cracked walls, mingling with the grime. It's very much like the place I took Yipton. "How much should I hate you right now?" Riya demands, her tone chipped.

Huh, so not the words I was expecting.

Hiren's no better. "Want to tell me who that is? I mean . . . it can't . . ." His eyes swivel to Fiza, still in her Red Woman disguise and a few paces behind us. Kalyan stands beside her, shielding her from the confused wrath meters away like the stand-up guy he is. We've already exchanged glances and knowing looks. We both went to school with Fiza, and I told him about her unexpected visit.

"It's not." I sigh. "She's simply a problem I need to fix."

"So you created this?" Riya says. "You let someone else put on Adraa's mask? When were you going to let the rest of the team know?"

"Whoa, this wasn't *my* idea," I say.

Hiren's eyebrows rise. "It wasn't? Because it's brilliant."

"What?" Riya and I both practically shout. I'm with Riya on this. I wouldn't call a fellow royal heir masquerading as the love of my life *brilliant.*

"Whatever, whoever she is, *that* protects Adraa. None of my guards will think twice, and now they will spread the rumor she was here tonight. The Red Woman is more of a symbol than a real person to begin with. And now . . ."

And now she has absolutely no possible connection to Adraa Belwar. I glance at Fiza again. She all but said as much the other day.

"I get it, but it's more complicated than that," I finally say.

Riya's not having it anymore. "Who the blood is she?"

"Why don't you just ask me yourself?" Fiza says, her tone playful and not matching the tension in the alley whatsoever. I can hardly stand looking at her, especially up close. The illusion is too good, too powerful. And in the darkness it's even more convincing than in my father's office.

Riya faces her. "Okay. Who the blood do you think you are?"

I sigh and step forward, placing myself between them. "What *are* you doing?" I ask Fiza as gently as I can. I see all the little differences—I hear them too—but that doesn't stop a piece of me from yearning for someone to admit this has all been a bad dream.

"So you do know this person," Riya says, her voice hard and accusatory. I realize in that moment I have never witnessed her anger directed *at* me.

Fiza isn't daunted by Riya in the slightest. She meets my gaze and smiles. "You said it wasn't a job to apply for."

My Gods. "You just hear what you want to hear, don't you?"

"What is going on!" Riya yells.

Fiza's mask disappears, the illusion falling in a wave of red that shifts to black. Riya cringes backward.

"My name is Fiza. I'm a lady of Agsa and I went to the academy with Maharaja Jatin and Kalyan."

Riya looks to Kalyan like she needs confirmation. Kalyan nods and then rubs his temples. The action speaks loudly to what I'm feeling. I was trying *not* to murder anyone tonight. Fiza always liked to try to push me to the brink.

For a moment I think Riya is going to defer to the proper etiquette for when a guard is in the presence of a lady and diplomat of a neighboring country and bow. Nope. She doesn't seem bothered in the slightest. In fact she stands taller. "How dare you put on her face, her appearance, as if the Red Woman is a *costume.*"

"But you have to admit I did help," Fiza says.

Hiren nods. "Agreed. And we need a black forte to cut through the illusion that's covering the damage on the side of the Dome."

Fiza tilts her head and looks at me, her thoughts evident. *You need me.*

Riya is all gestures and pointing fingers. "No! No. We don't need help from someone who disrespects the very person we are trying to save."

Hiren interjects. He's bolder than I had first assumed. "But you have to admit Adraa's secret is safer than ever. Which means *all* our secrets are safer than ever. Including this entire mission." He takes a moment to look at each of us in turn. "You must realize this." He stares at me last. "No one has forgotten what happened in that courtroom, how you defended her. The only reason the lower rajas don't suspect we are conducting a prison break is because of your mask."

His words resonate into the night.

I shift toward Fiza. "Meet us at Azure Palace tomorrow. We have a lot to discuss." Then I turn to Riya. "He's right. The plan is already in motion. We have only one chance at this."

Finally, Riya looks at me without murder in her eyes, and I know that Hiren's words have soaked some sense into her, as they did with me. "I'll be there."

◈ ◈ ◈

Kalyan and I fly in silence. As usual he's letting me process. And there's a whole lot to process. These cold nights flying home with more questions than answers have become a common occurrence for Kalyan and me. Too common.

Riya and Hiren went back home, and I left Fiza to go wherever she's been staying. Normally I'd inquire and offer up one of the many free rooms in Azure Palace, but I can't get past her sudden appearance back in my life, even if I believe in everything Hiren said. We'll talk, and we'll see if it can work, but I will never be okay with the idea of her putting on Adraa's likeness.

"So that's who you saw that night flying home," Kalyan says

suddenly. "You told me and I still . . . Even looking at her to-night . . ."

"It's uncanny, right? Too . . ." I can't even articulate it.

"Too real."

Yes. That's it, exactly. Too real.

"Did you ever think about using black magic like that? Professor Parsa sure never taught us *that* at the academy. And as someone whose career comes from looking like you, I would have paid attention if it had been brought up."

I chuckle darkly. "I'd remember. It wasn't." Kalyan is right that even a year ago I would have tried to master such a spell. But seeing it on Fiza, I'll stay as I am, flaws and all.

A clamor from below drags my attention from thoughts of Fiza. A gathering much like that long-ago night appears to be forming. Hughes said there had been five such rallies since the trial. I haven't gotten the latest report, but I assume these protests have continued each night in some fashion. I just didn't expect them to still be this large. Adraa is in prison. What more do they want?

I drop lower and Kalyan follows suit. "You want to go down there?" he asks.

"Yes." I decide in the moment. I inspect the surrounding rooftops until I find one hidden in shadow with a good enough viewpoint. I nod toward it. "But not to the crowd. I don't want to be a part of it. Only listen." This time it won't be a show. This time Night *and* Jatin will stay out of it. I will give them no room to risk Adraa's secret.

"Good," he sighs.

I look over at him.

"I know the whole world trusts me with your life, but I'm only one man. I can't protect you from hundreds."

I'm also running low on energy and magical reserve. My skyglider feels it now, dragging itself to stay airborne.

"Can you protect me from Fiza Agsa?" I joke.

Kalyan huffs without humor. "I came up with the love-letters thing to Adraa as a joke, a bet that it would make Fiza leave you alone, and look where that got us. She's keener than ever."

"Yeah, what is with that?"

"Some people want what they can't have, I guess." He's staring down at the rally, and when I follow his gaze, I see what he means at once. A wooden stage has been erected again. Instead of a slimy spokesman, though, a tall wizard in full orange garb holds his hands out to the crowd.

"Isn't that Raja Dara, Hiren's father?" Kalyan asks.

"Yes. *Aasrenni,*" I cast over my ears, enhancing my hearing.

"For those who don't know me, I am Sai Dara, raja of the outer north region and head commander of the Dome Guard. I know your concerns and I understand them. These are trying times. The Belwar girl's betrayal was heartbreaking and unprecedented. But know I am a raja of the land, a proven nine to the gods and I'm here for you."

"She tried to kill us all and yet Belwars still rule!" one particularly loud wizard hollers.

"We should choose! We should choose who leads us."

"*You* should be maharaja."

The cries of approval roar through the air so loudly I

deactivate the orange magic so my eardrums don't burst. Raja Dara holds up a hand for silence, but the crowd keeps cheering and shouting for the ability to vote. "That's what he calls defusing the situation?" I mutter half to myself, half to Kalyan. "Gods. I didn't think it was this bad." After the trial, after they made Adraa out to be a monster and locked her up, they're still calling for upheaval.

Moolek didn't hire us. He created us, Sims had said. Is it possible he created *this* too? Orchestrated this strife? But he wouldn't want people to choose a new leader. That's against tradition and everything Moolek stands for.

"This isn't about Adraa," I say, the thought coming quickly.

"What?" Kalyan asks.

"The hatred. This discord. Adraa was used as an instigator, but something else is at play here. There's something we aren't seeing."

I look down at the mass of wizards and witches with the knowledge that the team I recruited is already falling apart. We haven't located Adraa in the Dome yet, and she is still far from free. Even if I do get her back, she's returning to a country that's in disarray and political turmoil, the likes of which Wickery has never faced.

Sims's confidence sends a chill down my spine. Maybe I have made a mistake.

◇
Questions and Answers

Adraa

Even with the promise of magic, I'm still stuck pretending I am weak. My rib, which is still healing, helps a little with the faking, though, and hope has a way of tinting the situation in a new light.

Finally, when I'm able to walk without falling over, I rejoin the daily activities of my Dome mates. I peer at the cafeteria I'm sitting in not just through the lens of survival but also with strategy.

"You put on one of the best shows the Underground has ever seen, you know?" Ekani says after she's cornered me by the cafeteria table. A smile pulls at her lips. Why she thinks I should share in this excitement is beyond me. All I hear in these words are, *Hope you're ready to get beaten up every week until you die.*

Or maybe not. Maybe they don't want me to die. Maybe there was a reason my death sentence transformed into imprisonment within the course of a few tense words in that court-room.

Maybe I could use this to my advantage.

With my new awareness I notice the seven other Voiceless are also kept within arm's reach of Ekani. Most of them are shy girls I can't even make eye contact with long enough to try to communicate with. But even without communication, their body language reeks of abuse.

I glance around at the clatter of conversation at other tables. Fifty other women eat and socialize in the large, dim room. At the table across from me a fight looks to be brewing and yet the guards just stare at us. Normally, I'd chalk the other Voice-less' silence up to the fact that Basu ripped their voices away, but witches with powerful Touches aren't so easily controlled and corralled like this. Look at Harini and me. I don't believe in stereotypical forte traits, but I do think a majority of witches skilled at more than five types of magic exhibit confidence in some manner. They were blessed with or earned their Touches. Yet none of these witches act like it. In fact, most seem like they're trying to blend in with the walls, even more than the Un-touched do. Ekani's presence suddenly doesn't irk me as much.

Another observation is the spectrum of skin tones within the Voiceless. Belwar is one of the most diverse places in Wickery, but it's weird that the greatest variation comes from the nine of us—the most powerful, but the speechless.

Harini and two others fall on the darker side, with what I as-sume is Pire Island ancestry. Then comes me, which in itself is strange. I'm used to being the darkest in the room. Two of the other Voiceless I would guess to be Belwarian by birth. Two of them are Moolekian. And one girl has such pale yellow hair that it's like spun sunlight. She has to be Agsaian, but I've never seen anyone quite like her. I watch them all carefully, noticing that a few of them tremble as they eat. My skin crawls at Ekani's warnings. Even without my magic I instinctively scoot closer to them.

The girl who revealed my secret is named Deepa, I learn. She's a year younger than me, but with a criminal charge serious enough to grant her Dome imprisonment. She's either unlucky or one of the most dangerous inmates. "I told you she was good," Deepa says to Ekani, grasping for praise at my recruitment.

"You *were* interesting," Ekani says with satisfaction, but then she purses her lips. "But next time stay down when it's obviously over."

Yes, heal me so you can break me again. Wonderful. But instead of giving away my thoughts I nod into my bowl, putting on an act of submission. I need them to think that fight was a turning point, that I'm cowed like the rest of them.

"Save yourself the pain and the trip to Basu. He likes his experiments," Ekani continues.

Experiments? The word rings false. Medicine and pink magic—they aren't experiments. Or they aren't supposed to be.

"But that's Smoke's thing. She always rises back up. Don't you think that's why they liked her?" Deepa says.

Ekani glares. "Rising up is good and all, but we don't try to get ourselves killed in the process."

I don't acknowledge her. I continue eating, focusing on that word again. *Experiments.* Is she exaggerating and criticizing Basu's skills, or is that what the clinic is really for? And if so, what is Basu doing?

I can see Harini's jaw tighten from down the table. Her focus appears to be solely on her food, but I know she's listening in.

"Not interested in hearing about your fight, huh?" Ekani eyes me. "Well, this may interest you. Sims's Underground got destroyed last night. Obliterated."

I perk up. I don't mean to, but I do. Blood, I do. The Underground, blown up? The best-concealed secret in all of Belwar gone? After everything the Vencrin did to help Moolek, I can't imagine him dishing out destruction.

Who? I mouth before I analyze how I should play this.

"Ah, so you are interested." Ekani leans forward. "Supposedly, Night."

Jatin! Just hearing the name of his alter ego hurts. But why would . . . ?

"And, of course, the Red Woman too," Deepa inserts.

What? I'm not easily shocked, but her response hits me hard in the chest. *The Red Woman.* I can't exactly question why the Red Woman would be there without giving myself away, but that part has to be a fabrication. Jatin and I are a team. My city still thinks we are working as a team. It's a mistake. Or maybe it's Riya in her mask and a red uniform? But why destroy the Underground?

"From what I hear the Underground is closed down for now. Maybe even permanently, since it seems Night froze it. You know what this means?" Ekani says.

Deepa shrugs, an exaggerated, heaving gesture. "I don't know."

"Our little war room might need to be expanded. There are hungry customers out there looking for entertainment." Ekani looks at me. A shiver slices down my back. "Who am I to deny them of that? This might be the best thing that has ever happened to our little part of the world."

She's baiting me, I realize. But if what Ekani says is true, then she's my only lifeline to the outside world. And she's willing to talk in front of me. Because what could I even say? I'm a Voiceless. For the first time, I am what I had sought to be in the Underground—valuable but disregarded, overlooked and unassuming. Someone who looks unthreatening enough to be told important details without second thought. Basically, I have become the perfect Jaya Smoke.

◈ ◈ ◈

I'm ready to start learning, I write down as soon as Harini and I get back to our cell. Thankfully, Ekani's conversation must have spurred something in Harini too, because she nods and, with a measured glance, begins encasing us in a bubble of illusion.

When she's done, Harini paces, throwing up the message, *Let me think of where to start.* So, I wait.

Okay, here are the basics. Magic does not come from the sounds you make. It is power you hold inside of you. You can communicate in other ways, thus you can cast. She raises an eyebrow. *Do you understand what I'm doing with my hands? That I'm communicating through them?*

I nod. While I know of the language used by those who can't hear or speak, I was ignorant of the fact they could cast magic. Yet it makes complete sense. Much of casting is calling to the Gods. There's no finite rule that says it has to be done vocally.

Good. Because you essentially have to learn a sign for every spell you want to master.

Start with what you are doing now. With purple. I don't want to rely on paper any more than I have to.

First things first. What are you? A six? A seven?

I pause, forcing myself to not check the length of my sleeve on my bare right arm, to make sure it conceals the Touch that isn't there.

I go with the truth for once. *Eight,* I write slowly. *You?*

I don't get an answer. Harini's hands fall to her sides, and her face contorts in a grief-ridden struggle.

Finally, she takes my pen. *You are an eight and a red forte?*

I try to figure out her reaction. She can't possibly know my true identity. But my stomach plummets regardless of hope or reason, because her face is laced with panic.

I may have just given away the fact that I'm Adraa Belwar, the most hated witch alive.

Harini snaps out of it and her hands churn out words. *Okay. We have a lot of work to do, then.*

So my secret, it seems, is still safe. But there is something more going on here. Something scares her about my power or my forte. *What aren't you telling me?*

She shakes her head.

I wasn't going to press, but . . . her reaction. That clinic. Basu being here. The feel of secrets swarming the entire Dome. I have to know. *What's happening in this prison? What aren't you saying?*

She begins pacing.

What about the other Voiceless? What's happening to them? I write fast, pressing the pen hard into the paper to underline my question.

This prison isn't only housing criminals.

What? I mouth.

I mean some of them are. That young creepy girl who follows Ekani around, definitely. But the others . . . Harini shakes her head. *Far as I can tell most of us were picked up off the street or were led here under false pretenses. I caught passage to Belwar from Pire to get a better life.*

It takes a moment to process this fully. But then anger creeps in. Harini came here, to my city, only to be forced into the darkness of the Dome. Wrongly imprisoned, like me. Or not quite like me. Her situation is even worse.

There's three types of groups here, Harini continues. *The Voiceless, who are all at least sixes. The Untouched. And witches who are fours at the most. We call it many things—a think tank, a lab—but most of us call it an experiment.*

What are they trying to do? I write, barely able to keep up and wanting to say so much more.

They are trying to figure out how to make the Touched more powerful.

My hand goes to my throat. *How?* I mouth.

Are you familiar with a substance called Bloodlurst?

I straighten and nod slowly. All too familiar, unfortunately.

That's what they have come up with so far by using us Voice-less. But the people running this place are looking for a better, more permanent solution that won't burnout the user.

My Gods. This whole time I've been after the Vencrin, yet I never came close to figuring out how the Bloodlurst was made or where.

They make it here? I scribble, my shaky hand forcing out the letters.

A firm nod confirms it. Gods, that's why I could never find it! Here, below my feet, they make Bloodlurst.

They need nine, Harini's airborne words continue. *One for each forte. Our last red forte . . . she died. You're here, I assume, to replace her.*

What do you mean?

That's why you are still alive. If I had let you die they would most likely have killed me. Though I don't know if what I did in saving you was a kindness, not when I know that what you face is much worse: the procedure, the experiments. It always takes the largest toll on the red fortes, I don't know why. But the substance doesn't turn red until the end.

It takes me several moments to process the words Harini has signed above our heads. So this doesn't have to do with me being Adraa Belwar. Or maybe it does. What did Moolek say once? That he was glad I invented firelight. That it led him to me, illustrated my power.

Lucky for you I needed you alive. His words echo in my mind.
How long do we have? I write.

They make us fight every week to see if we are strong enough. I don't exactly know how it works, but it'll be soon. Maybe as soon as they think you have healed enough . . .

So weeks. Possibly days. My hand quakes as I write out the next question. *How did she die? The other red forte.*

Harini turns away and sits on her cot. *I don't . . .* Her hands waver, and with them, her spell. *I can't talk about it,* she finally gets out.

Because the red forte had been her cellmate. Her friend. I even know her name from my first day. Nira. Didn't even Ekani say I was her . . . replacement?

I understand. A friend, I write, and then pause, the pen warm in my hand. *But please, I have to know.*

She was more than a friend. Harini sits on her cot and rolls over, toward the wall. She is obviously done with my questions and our magic lesson. Her final words come over her shoulder in an orange spiral, glowing and pulsing bright like a heartbeat.

She was my sister.

CHAPTER TWENTY

◇

Trials and Tribulation

Adraa

We don't mention Harini's sister again. We don't mention any of that conversation, actually. I can't help but be curious about her sister; I'm her replacement, after all. And I need to know more. Need to understand what might befall me. Because I was right: that truth caster offering life in the courtroom must have known the plans they had for me.

But I know I won't be getting any more out of Harini about Nira. The next morning, she puts up an illusion spell, and suddenly it's like I haven't learned my life is in danger and the Dome has been stealing people to experiment on them.

A part of me is relieved. If I fixate too much on the terror of this place or the ticking time bombs that are the experiments, I don't know whether I'll be able to focus.

But if there is one thing the life of a lady has taught me, it is how to dig into my studies.

We start with the foundation of casting, much like I did at

eight years old. Like verbal spells each time we cast we call to the gods. So I learn the nine hand signals that correspond to each deity. Renni is a pounding fist–like motion. Raw is pushing outward, as if I'm conjuring the weapon I need. Laeh is a softer twisting action, gesturing from my body and outward. Wodahs encompasses passing my palms by one another with a flourish. I flutter my hands like a bluster of wind for Ria's. And finally, Erif is waving my fingers upward like fire.

We skim over Retaw, Htrae, and Dloc's movements since Harini can't cast blue, green, or white magic. So we move on to learning the combined hand movements for dozens of spells. Since time isn't on our side, Harini and I decide I can't learn her entire language. Thus, my lessons will be in studying the system of spells, in magic, in enough violence to free myself. Harini seems committed to this plan of action, which tells me two things. One, we truly don't have much time. And two, some part of her must figure we won't know each other long enough to be on speaking terms.

I don't voice my aspirations for fresh air and freedom, because teaching the girl enough magic to not get killed isn't the same thing as taking down the whole system. But if we don't have time, then I need to bring it up eventually. I can't risk Harini backing out of training me. I can't let fear, fear I know she possesses, undermine my plan to escape.

I fix my hands again. Actually, the movements aren't the hard part. I was trained for the royal ceremony, where movement is an extension of intention. Fundamentally, Harini's use of magic makes sense. I've felt it before, many times. Much of pink magic revolves around the gestures I've already used to infuse potions with healing magic. Not twisting your fingers in a particular way may not doom a potion, but it will enhance its effects.

Harini confirmed that this morning. *It's another way to communicate, to express yourself and connect yourself to the gods,* she wrote for me. I had arched an eyebrow at the religious tint, knowing most Pire Islanders don't believe in the actual embodiment of the gods.

Don't give me that look. Just because I'm from Pire doesn't mean I don't believe in the gods.

Huh, maybe I have much more to learn after all. And obviously I do, because after an hour of increasingly grueling practice, Harini writes *connection* on top of my paper in huge letters.

I concentrate. I'm only trying to say hello. It's a simple wave and then a push, the push to Raw I've come to learn accompanies every spell that manifests words into the air, like a send-off. I put every ounce of willpower into the spell. My magic wells up to the surface—pure energy, like a swell of surf or flicker of light when a fire blooms to life. I wave, then push so hard it's like my wrist has connected with a wall . . . and still nothing. My arms remain dull, devoid of even a ghost of red smoke. Magic churns beneath the skin, demanding release.

You're still shouting the words in your head, Harini writes. She's been signing that same phrase for the past three hours. Sometimes all she has to do is look at me. How she even seems to *know* what's happening in my head is next-level witchiness, but the novelty has worn off. She hasn't corrected my hand position in half an hour, so I know it has to do with connection. Or my lack thereof. For a second, the memory of my royal ceremony floods me, the cold terror of Dloc's blizzard that overtook me.

Maybe that's why I'm failing. Am I afraid to allow myself to be completely vulnerable to magic like that again? Or maybe it lies in the fact I still can't cast white magic. There are some things one just can't do.

I let out a frustrated and soundless sigh and flop back on the floor, stretching my wrists. They really do feel like I've been ramming a wall all day.

Harini doesn't move, but her words float above my eyeline. *What? You thought this was going to be easy? Jaya, you are learning an entire system and then mastering those motions into magic you didn't know existed. How many lower Touches assume they can't master more types? Or how many Untouched never even try because they have been taught they can't?*

I sit up and frown. Blood, I don't think I've ever thought about it in those terms. Could that be why I'm stuck as an eight? A part of me is filled with too much doubt. Did I fail one too many times and even my resolve wouldn't have let me pass my royal ceremony?

I shake the thought out of my head. I don't need new doubts or speculations distracting me. I nod at the main component of Harini's pep talk. Every day I'm in the Dome is one day closer to the experiments and one more day for Moolek to get a foothold in Belwar. I must push myself harder. For Belwar. For Jatin. For myself. I will learn this.

I try again. And again.

Hours pass, in which I learn dozens of signs, but at last Harini sends a message to me. *You've learned to trust your voice to cast a spell. Now you'll need to trust the actual magic inside you.* She frowns at me. *You need to get stronger. Physically and mentally.* The words she doesn't write hang between us: Or else you'll die.

◇ ◇ ◇

I'm on my fiftieth sit-up, the scrap of paper propped up on my legs, my hands forming spells and memorizing their meaning with each crunch when Harini shifts in her cot and sits up. Even in the dark her expression says more than words could: a fierce yet drowsy *What the blood are you doing?*

I don't pause for a second. I have to get stronger. Physically and mentally. She said so herself.

Her wicker bed frame creaks as she surges out of it. Her hands move and I've learned enough to catch some words. She mouths them for me too and I get the gist. *Are you trying to get us caught? It's the middle of the night. For Gods' sake, rest.*

I can feel the annoyance radiating off her.

I don't break my rhythm. Wind spell. Concealment illusion. Shield. I have to practice. I have to get out of here, and there's not much time. They will not use me to make Bloodlurst.

She covers our cell in magic, recasting the silent murk into an orange haze. It brightens the room enough that I don't have to squint so hard at my paper.

You've already practiced for hours today. Go to bed, she writes.

I stop at a full sit-up, my rib cage moaning in protest. I shake my head at Harini. I have to learn this. I have to get it right.

She stands, glancing out and across at the other cells. Nothing moves in the gloomy darkness. Even the central guard tower is dim.

Blood, were you like this in school? Never before has a teacher been so dissatisfied with me for practicing.

I flip the paper over and write, *I was worse. Had to prove myself to someone.* Jatin's face lights up in my mind's eye, and the sheer pain of it turns my arms into wobbly goo. I extend my legs and stretch, embracing the physical pain. I hadn't pictured him in a long while. Especially when doing so makes me think of the last moment I saw him, my final words to him. Words that now seem bloated with overconfidence and conviction. *Don't come for me.* Because what? I could handle this? I could escape by myself?

And now? Harini's expression is curious, nonjudgmental.

Now I have something to prove to myself.

She seems to like this response and sits back down. *I understand.*

I pause. *Yeah?* I mouth.

Another person pushing you can only get you so far. It's a good start, but nothing more than that. Everything after has to be from here. She pounds her chest with her fist, but I don't think she means just the heart. She means every muscle aching for me to stop and me telling myself no, not yet. We get stronger first.

Okay, one more practice. No more purple word formations. You're a red forte. Let's try for a simple fire spell.

I perk up and nod, though fear pokes a hole in my confidence. It whispers if I can't master this, my forte, the magic that has always called to me, there's no hope. I shake out my arms. Gods, when did I get like this? How have I let doubt infiltrate my thoughts to this degree?

And that's what I am doing. The royal ceremony, Mount Gandhak, the death threats, the rally, the trial. I'm letting all that noise, even the blatant lies, leech the power right out of me.

Just like they want.

No!

I turn to Harini and watch as she demonstrates the motion, her fingers mimicking the upward dance of a flame. I breathe, and for the first time in a long while I allow myself to go back to the red room. To embrace and visualize the stream of bloodred cascading and rippling down the walls. I failed, but, more importantly, I came back. I stopped the destruction.

I close my eyes.

Connection. Tapping into the well of energy in my blood. Feeling the forces inside myself at work.

I breathe.

Fire. Flames roaring. The blast of heat and power. My power. My fire. My firelight.

I cast the spell.

A ghost of red smoke swirls up my wrist and curls around my dancing fingers. I exhale so sharply that the magic floats away on my breath, but I know, *I know*, I have done it.

I look over at Harini and she's wearing a grin I've never seen before. *About time,* she writes, and the words twirl in the air. I focus inward again and the wisps of my magic light up my middle finger, the tiniest of flames flickering there. A rush of pure joy and hope crashes over me.

I stare at the walls of our cell and then beyond, to the other cells, to the walkways crisscrossing the cavern. Light—even a small, flickering one—really can dispel the dark. Then I refocus on the red magic I created without any sound. Voiceless, but no longer powerless.

They've put me in here because they think I'm the most dangerous person in Wickery. And for a time I might have been. I'm not anymore.

But that's what I'm going to become.

CHAPTER TWENTY-ONE

◇

Torment in Training

Jatin

We have one day before Sims is processed and Hiren takes him to the Dome. One day. And now Fiza is here and part of our team. I understand her usefulness, and having an extra person makes our plan better, especially a black forte. But I also foresee how she could rip the team apart.

As expected, Kalyan has taken up the post of mediator. At this very moment he is standing between Riya and Fiza, a silent barrier as I discuss our plan, using my mother's map room once again. Fiza and I will find the hole and break the illusion. Hiren and Riya will accompany Sims into the prison. Kalyan and Prisha will scout overhead as lookouts and investigate the skylights in case Fiza and I fail.

During the discussion about each person's role in the scheme, Fiza doesn't bat an eye. A soft quiet lies thick in the air. It feels like tension, pulled tight. She says only one thing: "So, I am needed after all."

It's only after Riya and Kalyan leave and Fiza and I are walking through the palace toward the training yard that she utters more than a quip at my expense.

"It's nice to be here. To finally see Azure Palace."

She's alluding to the other day when I practically threw her out. Wasn't much of a tour, I suppose, nor I much of a tour guide.

"It's nice to see you in your natural element," she continues.

I jerk to a stop and cut to the chase. "Something has been bothering me. How . . . how do you even know what Adraa looks like?" The posters have done neither of us justice—that was the whole point, which must mean . . . "Were you there, in the courtroom?"

"Yes."

I shuffle forward, needing movement to process her answer, to occupy my brain so it doesn't spiral back to the courtroom. To Adraa. To my father. And now, lurking in the background, Fiza Agsa.

Too late. I can almost picture her there, beyond the walled barrier, peering in. But I can't imagine what she thought of it. Pity? Shock? A dark thought places her there, smiling. I shake my head free of the thoughts, focusing instead on the golden drapes that adorn the staircase, which is still decorated from the festival celebrating Naupure and Belwar's reconstruction after Mount Gandhak. I should get someone to take them down. That was a lifetime ago.

"I already told you I was here to investigate Adraa." She stops. "I'm sorry."

"What?" Fiza has *never* apologized to me. It's not in her nature.

"It was a bad day. And now you are probably reliving it all." When we reach the staircase, she takes a step down and swings around to face me. "Let me just say this. Something was wrong in that courtroom."

"In what way?"

"In every way."

I stare at her.

"Whatever you think of me, please know I'm on *your* side, Jatin. My father might not understand the full picture, but Agsa needs this alliance." She turns around and before I can find relief in her words, I realize she didn't include Adraa in any of her reassurances.

$\diamond$ $\diamond$ $\diamond$

Fiza fails.

Fiza fails over and over again.

I don't wish to be too conceited, but it's because she won't listen to me. We were going to work on illusion magic together, but that backfired quickly. So we've resorted to basic training at this point, simply learning to work with the other person, and she won't even do that. If we have to fall back to rainbowing just to see what she's capable of, I don't think I'll be able to keep my cool.

It's Fiza and me against Kalyan and Riya. If Adraa were my partner, this wouldn't be much of a match. But that's not the case. Fiza is a trained nine, but there is a stiffness to her movements. We don't flow together in combat like Adraa and I. We never had to train like this to be a team.

"You go left. I'll go right and take Kalyan," I tell her, hoping against hope she'll listen to me this time. I can't help the edge in my tone. I'm a sore loser, and these losses mean something to me, weaken the little hope I have that we can pull off this rescue mission, much less work together.

The four of us face off again. Hiren and Prisha watch from the sidelines, critiquing all of our tactics. Although every time I look over, they're cutting glances at one another like . . . well, I guess they are lovestruck teenagers.

Kalyan charges, somehow reading the tactic I was trying to employ. I'm about to yell rings, one of my and Adraa's most common maneuvers, but stall. Fiza doesn't know any of our calls, my gestures, or the basics of how I fight with Adraa. Riya's attack seizes my attention, and I block a blunted shard of purple magic. The crash of water followed by a thud sounds off to my right, and Riya stops short with an eye roll. I look over and see that Fiza is pinned down again.

She went bloody right.

I stare down at her, drenched from Kalyan's wave. "I said left."

She breathes, in and out, either dazed or angry. A conversation I had with Adraa floats back to me, when I first suggested her sister help us. *She hasn't been trained the same way. She's never had to worry about fighting for her life.* And that's when it hits me. Fiza is me if I had never met Adraa. Spoiled. Arrogant. Willing to play the part but unwilling to sacrifice yourself for it.

"Maybe I didn't want to go left," Fiza huffs as she stands.

"Then you won't be able to pull this off. We are a team, or we are nothing," Prisha says, stepping forward and sounding much older than her fifteen years.

"Oh, and I'm sure Adraa would have seen it all coming and done it perfectly?"

"Yes," Riya says, crossing her arms in obvious disdain. I can't deny it. Even if Adraa hadn't wanted to listen to me, she would have found a way to take her opponents down. No offense to our guards, but Adraa could more than handle this.

"Of course. Lady Belwar would never make a mistake," Fiza scoffs. I don't know if she means to, but with a wild hand wave she gestures to Mount Gandhak behind her. I go rigid.

Riya seems to pick up on it too and she jolts forward. The tension from the other night at the Underground relights like a struck match. "I know you've got everyone thinking they need you here, but if I ever catch you disrespecting Adraa, I'll end you."

"Well. How feisty," Fiza says through a smile.

I've seen Riya angry over the past weeks, but pure fury explodes off her now. She raises her arms, and black and purple blasts of magic swirl in a frenzy. Whips of wind and a layered shield hammer into one another.

"Stop!" Prisha cries.

I reach out to end it before it begins in earnest, but Kalyan holds up a hand to both of us. "Training, right?"

Fiza ducks and backsteps, creating distance. "Adraa didn't seem to teach you the proper behavior of a Guard."

"Criticize her one more time and I'll mess up that overly symmetrical face of yours for good. In fact, just say her name again," Riya seethes.

Fiza pauses, measures out a look, and then opens her mouth. "Adr—"

That's it.

"*Simaraw,*" I cast. Kalyan's thinking is the same as mine because a gush of wind, along with my boundary, pushes both Fiza and Riya back. They land with a thud.

"Stop," I demand. "We end the pettiness now! We don't have time for this. This training isn't to become friends or increase our skills. We need to be able to trust one another." My head swivels between the two of them. "To know we have each other's backs."

I give Fiza a pointed look, and she doesn't even flinch from the criticism. The admonishment seems to work on Riya, though. "You're right. I'm sorry," she sputters.

Blood. The last thing I want is Riya feeling chastised and inferior after what Fiza had the gall to say. In the past few months I've felt more like Jatin Naupure around her, not a soon-to-be maharaja. In seconds I've blown the progress. But it's my fault. I yelled like a raja.

I give the rest of the group a look and then usher Fiza a few meters away. I watch as Kalyan corrals Riya toward Prisha and Hiren, and the four of them launch into a conversation that I wish I could be a part of instead.

I quiet my voice and lean in toward Fiza. "Riya shouldn't be the one apologizing. She's right. If you can't give Adraa the respect she deserves, leave."

"Why do you keep pretending?" she asks, embracing her future rani title with every facet of her being. Her voice is questioning, like I'm the one who should answer for my wrongs, like I just tried to provoke a guard to mess up my face.

"Pretending what?" I ask, my tone coated in exasperation.

"That breaking her out is the correct thing to do."

"I—"

"I'll stop. I won't say anything else about our patron saint. But don't pretend there isn't something inside you saying this might not be the best path. It makes more sense to free her through evidence and truth, not this violence and idiocy." Her hands fly up. "Just—just stop pretending."

"You first, Fiza."

"What?"

"Tell me, what's the real reason you're helping us? This is an awful lot of self-sacrifice for an alliance." The ugly thought that was nagging at me this morning reenters my head. Fiza was in that courtroom, and she's the best black forte I know. What if she has a dangerous ulterior motive?

"I've already told you. I'm here on Agsa's behalf."

I shrug, straining to keep my suspicions hidden. "And I still don't buy it."

"Then I don't know what to tell you." An unyielding glare passes between us. "Guess practice is over."

She turns to go, and I catch her wrist. "Fine, we'll keep playing your game, but for your sake, don't criticize Adraa. Because next time, I won't create a barrier."

"I think I can take a guard, thank you very much," she says with a laugh.

"Apparently not, considering the past few hours."

She bristles. Finally, she whispers, "Why? Why is she worth all this?"

"Because I would be dead without her—and I don't mean that metaphorically. This whole world would be in ash." It's true—for all my selfish reasons of loving Adraa and wanting her back, I know the people of Wickery need her and owe her everything.

"So she's more powerful than me? That's all it takes to—"

"Stop, Fiza." It takes everything I have not to walk away. I despise the sentiment, the competition. "Just stop. She's not better than you, but she is better for me. Do you understand that? Can you accept that I love her?"

Fiza doesn't answer.

I continue angrily. "And if that's all you think of me—that power is all I care about—you don't know me at all."

Her face scrunches and crumbles at the same time. "I know you."

I've never seen such vulnerability written on her face. A

part of me almost feels bad. How awful a trick I played at the academy, on myself and others, to not have been brave enough to be my true self. But that's changed. I've dropped my mask. "No, you don't."

"Don't say that. Don't lie."

"That's not a lie."

She makes a noise like a growl and pushes at my chest. I'm so caught off guard I fall back a step.

Out of the corner of my eye, I see the others starting toward us, but I raise a hand.

"What do you have to be mad about?" I finally ask. "Nothing happened between us. Yes, I may have lied when we were in school, pretended I was infatuated with Adraa and wrote the letters to turn you off, but we were never together."

She scowls at me. "Oh, I know about those letters."

"What?" I ask, confused. I don't understand her tone, raw with contempt.

"I knew about your letters. I knew you were a liar."

She's not wrong. I am a liar. But . . . "I don't understand."

"It was because of those letters I realized how alike we were." She gestures to the space between us. "And I thought you were putting duty and honor above all else, like me. You shouldn't have to marry someone you hated because of it."

I shake my head. "Fiza—"

"But then you go and actually fall for her. And suddenly, it's just me. I'm the only unhappy one."

"I didn't fall. I had *been* falling—since I was nine years old."

Tears stream down her cheeks. "Like I said, you're a very

good liar. Maybe, just maybe, that's why no one here trusts one another," she finally whispers. Without another word, she marches away before I can ask what she means.

Kalyan, Riya, and Prisha approach me slowly after Fiza has left. The girls look at each other. "You're going to have to figure that out," they both say at the same time.

"Preferably before I do." Riya's threat is clear. I run a hand through my hair and nod.

As Riya, Hiren, and Prisha trudge away, Kalyan sighs, the sound the most relatable thing I've heard all day. "Can't say I missed Fiza being around," he murmurs.

I look over. "Huh, I always thought you didn't mind her much. Actually, if I remember correctly, you loved pushing me into awkward situations with her." I force my voice to stay calm, light, and sarcastic. I can't blame Kalyan for my inability back in school to be clear with Fiza, to be up front and truthful.

Kalyan sighs again. "First, we were kids, and it was hilarious watching you squirm and flee. Second, the world wasn't crashing down around us back then. People weren't in the crossfire."

He's right, of course, so I ask what I've been thinking about all day. "Do you think she can do it?"

Can we trust her? Can I?

"Oh, she can do it. She's beyond powerful. In the Underground I really thought Adraa had come back to us. But the real question is, do we want her to do it? What *is* she after, really?"

"I'm trying to figure that out." Hopefully without making her cry and yell at me next time.

Kalyan walks away, and my chest aches. I look at the bright blue sky. The fluffy clouds look tinged with grime, like shadows have singed their bellies.

"Please be okay, Smoke. Please. We need you."

I need you.

◇

CHAPTER TWENTY-TWO

No More Pretending

Adraa

I get better at spell casting in mediocre intervals. Red magic comes in a flurry-like release. Pink, yellow, and black take time, but finally I get there. Purple letters wind their way into the air after hours of failure. Though materializing anything other than words is extremely difficult. The other four, though? I'm struggling to connect.

There's also another problem.

Some magic and spells Harini just doesn't know. I mean, she's only a six. She can't cast blue, green, or white, and when it comes to yellow or pink, she knows only the basics.

The day passes as all days pass here now that I know the truth of what may come, painful and anxiety inducing. Under the cover of night, though, I practice.

I'm memorizing spells and doing push-ups when the jostle of our cell stops me. It's the middle of the night and we're ascending, which means only one thing. Harini and I make eye contact. We both know what is coming. Kicks to bedposts. Rough hands. Another rousing brawl at our expense. But what about after that? Is this simply another cage-casting fight or have we already run out of time?

In a rush I throw the roll of paper under my bed and wrap myself in my blanket. Harini seems to want to fix something, but there's no time, so she lies back and pretends sleep overcame her hours ago.

We do the whole bit as expected. Brutal wake-up call, marched to the hallway, led into a cage-casting arena of multicolored patched lines. But this time I'm scouring the Dome, taking in the geography of the place. It's amazing how much you miss when fear and confusion obstruct your analytical skills.

In the ring, two nonprofessional Voiceless beat one another up. It's sickening. One girl's face smashes into the wall, and she crashes to the ground.

Why do this? I don't understand how this tests us and it can't only be for entertainment. If this *is* an experimental facility, then there's some vital piece I'm not seeing, which even Harini might be missing. One more thing to get to the bottom of.

Ekani suddenly appears by my side and guides me into the locker room like before. This time, though, five other Voiceless are there too, waiting or fixing their outfits. Harini pauses at the threshold, and for the hundredth time I try to read her silence. Is this a warning of an experiment to come or something else?

"Come on, Jaya. You're late, and they want you up next."

I'm pulled to the back, where Ekani stuffs me into the same red blouse. She pulls tightly at the threads around my ribs, right at the fracture. I flinch, but there's no residual pain from a week ago. "Seems more than healed," she announces, like she's some sort of expert. I turn to find her frowning. Her voice drops. "Might want to put on a show, favor it. Let them know it isn't quite perfect."

Why, I mouth.

Ekani squints. Even she can tell I'm different tonight. Now that I can cast magic, I know there must be a fierce look in my eye. Inextinguishable. I couldn't quell it even if I wanted to.

"You don't bother yourself with why. Just . . . just do as I say."

I nod. I can't let any guard or prisoner get a whiff of what Harini and I can do. Even though it's demoralizing and difficult, pretending I'm weak is for the best.

On that note, Ekani pushes me forward, toward the ring.

Ahead of me, the yellow-haired, pale-skinned witch is dragged into the cage-casting cell. She looks weak, stumbling as she enters the arena. I glance behind me at Harini and even she has the decency to look unsettled. A pressure on my bare back signifies I'm supposed to follow.

What am I meant to do with this? I'm not fighting a girl with half my muscle mass.

"Okay, Smoke. You're up." Ekani scrunches her face. "Take her out quick and then we can get on with it."

Get on with it?

Roars from the crowd echo off the soundproofing. The number one hundred twenty-nine ricochets in my head. In all my pity and hope to get stronger I'm ashamed that that number, the faces, the stories of how each died—none of them have tortured my sleep in days. But the reminder seizes my chest and guilt floods me as my pulse jumps.

I tumble into the ring. Before I can even try to escape, the sides rise and I skid back down to the floor. My opponent watches me carefully, numb.

The bell rings.

The girl bolsters herself with a deep breath and rushes me. She throws a weak-wristed punch toward my . . . I don't quite know where she was aiming, actually. I block with my forearm leisurely, self-defense kicking in. Instead of trying to hit me with her other fist or a dozen other techniques, the girl freaks out and twists, catching her elbow in my chest, of all places. And here's the thing: when someone is this new, their movements are erratic, nonsensical. The rules of combat and good decision-making are nonexistent. So while she's a stumbling mess, that doesn't mean I can't get hurt.

She whirls around, trying to blindside me with a punch to my back. I dodge, and she falls forward.

They really want me to fight like this? I glance around, and the audience certainly doesn't seem enthralled. What's the purpose? How am I supposed to look weak and simultaneously beat her bloody?

My opponent rushes me again, and this time I grab her arm and twist it behind her back. She jolts, and I can tell if she had her voice she would be screaming. Up close, I notice scars along her back. Long ones that I'm guessing were caused by magic-created bindings. Bile builds up at the back of my throat.

And for the first time I feel like the monster that Belwar thinks I am.

I sneak a glance at Harini. *Fight,* she mouths angrily. *Fight!*

I know she means that I should pretend to be Jaya Smoke and beat up this defenseless inmate so that we can continue to act our parts. Skilled, but not too proficient. Confident, but not too courageous. But her instruction makes something snap in me. Yes, I should fight.

I let go of the girl's arm slowly and gently ease away from her.

Blond hair flies as she turns and swipes at me, but I only raise my hands and maneuver out of her reach.

The crowd senses the change, and they get riled up for the first time since that cursed bell rang. They pound on the ring's walls. They yell, shout, curse, but I keep my hands up and dodge a few more attempted blows until even my opponent recoils in confusion.

And so we stand like that. No circling tension. Just two fed-up witches calling it. Not today. Not for this audience.

The hatch clicks open and lowers. An angry guard steps into the ring. He slaps the girl in the face, and as she falls, he surges toward me. He pulls back his hand to slap me too, telegraphing the move a meter away.

I think the guard believes I'll just take it, stand here, nice and docile, while he metes out punishment. The thought almost makes me laugh—almost.

I duck and jab upward, one hit in the rib cage, one in the

armpit. He huffs out a sound of hurt surprise. I take the moment to sweep his legs. He falls.

As he lies there, I hope my message is clear: you don't get to hurt us.

The audience of guards pauses for a moment, stunned. It's the hesitation I need.

Harini rushes to meet me. *Don't,* she mouths, panicked and furious.

And for a second I stop.

But I'm tired. I'm tired of everyone telling me to stop, and me listening. I won't sit in a cell swallowed by anger and fear any longer. I won't be their entertainment anymore. And I will make bloody sure not to be the murderous monster they've made me out to be.

A stream of guards rush forward, ready to take me out.

Slowly, I step away from Harini. Then, with enough speed an onlooker might suspect it's orange magic hidden under my sleeve, I tug at the first guard's shoulder and punch him in the face. The crash vibrates through the flimsy floor. A flash of purple magic, a net of sorts, flies at me and I duck easily. From there it becomes an all-out brawl. Because the half-lowered cage-casting shell protects me from long-distance spells, and the plank that leads up to the ring is narrow, my opponents are forced to enter the ring only one or two at a time. It's the best advantage I've had in a while.

I twist. I move. I strike. And I fight for something worth fighting for.

But eventually it becomes too much. Three guards flank me. Then someone rushes from behind. Harini flies forward and punches a guard in the jaw, his head snapping back with a crunch.

Harini and I catch each other's eyes and rush forward together. We weave around magic and spells without casting our own. We take out the guards who haven't fled. It's the middle of the night. We just have to get past this wave of guards. Then, with some black magic, we can hide and camouflage ourselves enough to get to an entrance.

Is this it? Are we going to break out here and now?

A blaze of magic hits my kneecap, and I buckle under the torture spell. It's nothing compared to what Moolek's thrown my way before, but I still seize up from the pain. It's enough for someone to land a punch on my cheek. I fly backward. When I lift myself and bring my hands up to cast, I'm greeted with an array of spears and swords pointing at my and Harini's throats.

The warden himself steps forward. "Stand down. Now!"

We ascend a few levels, and for a moment I think they're simply dragging us back to our cell. Then we enter the murkiest hallway I've encountered in the Dome so far. It is sun-extinguished darkness. Firelight would look beautiful glowing in this corridor.

It catches me then, how for the first time in a long time I feel like myself again. A wild part of me wants to break free of this binding and cast firelight here and now.

The warden and Vihaan bring us to a cylindrical well of a cavern. Nine cells hang in a circle from its cliffs, which are smaller than the rest of the Dome's. And this time there is no yellow magic buffering the weight and holding the cells airborne. At the bottom of the cavern is a dark pool of . . . I squint. Water? Gods, I hope that's water.

When Vihaan tosses me into a new, smaller cell, it swings. One thick rope holds the cage aloft. I crouch into a wider stance to try to catch my balance and finally the death trap steadies itself. Harini is thrown into the cell next to mine.

"Enjoy the silence."

I try to stand upright, to steady myself, and the warden smirks. "Take one more step and this whole prison will know who you are." His piercing eyes scan my cell. "I wouldn't try moving much." Then he's gone, and a deafening quiet overwhelms the space.

Harini and I sit in solitary confinement, our two spheres hanging side by side. It seems a little odd—this being their punishment. But I'm not about to tell anyone the Dome's solitary confinement could use some refining. Even though Harini probably hates me, I consider us lucky. I need to talk to her. I don't have a plan, but I need to bring her into the fold. If tonight taught me anything it's that I can't keep pretending I can do this by myself or that I have time to become proficient enough in magic to fight my way out of here alone. I need her.

But Harini is done with me. She wraps herself in the flimsy blanket on her cot and turns away. I don't need a more obvious sign that she doesn't want to talk.

Suddenly words appear over her shoulder. *What were you thinking? You almost got us killed and you were about to cast in front of them.*

It takes a while for the message to disappear. Then, she writes, *I can't do this anymore.* The letters rise in the air like steam before fading.

I stare hard, willing her to turn over. Finally, Harini gets curious enough to face me. *She would have died if I fought her,* I write in the air with purple magic. I sign *died* for emphasis.

I knew you couldn't be trusted. If you won't listen this is the end. No more lessons.

With magic we could break out. We could escape. All of us, I sign, finally relaying my intentions clearly.

Her eyes close in frustration. *Where would we even go?*

I show her my confusion. What does she even mean by that?

If we did what you said, escaped, where would we go? Some of us have nothing. Others don't want to live on the run for the rest of their lives.

I raise my hands, but she continues.

And there are all sorts of other questions. How? Many of us are twos, threes, fours. The guards are sixes, sevens even. So you tell me. How? Where? With what?

Okay. Okay. I nod like she is making sense. *But what if I said you haven't asked the most important question?*

What is that? Her words seem to huff in irritation.

You forgot to ask with who.

Her eyes narrow. *Don't be cocky.*

My hands still and I do the thing I swore to myself I wouldn't do. I tear the sleeves off my tight red cage-casting blouse. First the right sleeve. She frowns. Then I pull off the left, unwrapping my arm like a gift. I step into a patch of light from the skylight, because every now and then I deserve to be dramatic. The spirals up my wrist condense, rippling across the skin. Red smoke flourishes from my forearm to my upper arm. When I reveal my shoulder, Harini gasps.

Today, I hide no longer. Today, I'm the fierceness of Jaya Smoke. I am the heart of the Red Woman. And once again . . . I slowly and deliberately sign until four crystal clear words materialize in the air.

I am Adraa Belwar.

CHAPTER TWENTY-THREE

◇

Misfired Mission

Jatin

It's windy the morning Sims is set to enter the Dome and our mission begins—ravenously so, like Goddess Ria is trying to knock our illusions off and leave the kited tails of our skygliders devoid of their magical streams. The sky is the color of slate, a dreary dimness that makes you wish someone would cast some light into the clouds.

It doesn't bode well, and I think we all feel it. The tension whips and snaps like our kurtas in the wind. At least the most important pieces of this puzzle, Hiren and Riya, who will be escorting Sims in, won't be affected. Kalyan and Prisha are air support; they're going to see whether we can get in or out through one of the skylights, but they might have a hard time with this wind.

Then there is Fiza and me. A team only because we're the best at using and recognizing black magic, which is what we suspect has been used to hide the hole in the Dome. And because I'm not sure that anyone else can get along with Fiza for more than a minute. Although I have some doubts about myself. Our mission is challengingly simple: find the hole caused by Mount Gandhak and open it even wider.

So far, we've been civil and let the argument from yesterday dissipate. Or maybe sweeping it under the rug is the more accurate description. As we pass over Mount Gandhak, I catch Fiza surveying the volcano and the barren, blackened decay of its eruption. I've done my fair share of staring. I pass this thing every time I fly to Belwar, but sometimes looking at it like this I can see why no one believes one witch could have stopped this thing.

We don't have time to loiter, so I angle a few degrees north and stretch my sight to the large, spherical building nestled at the foot of Mount Gandhak and the corner of Belwar's West Village. Mount Gandhak is ominous, but the Dome stirs fear like the dark recesses of an alleyway might. A walled mystery. Uncertainty of what lies beyond its exterior.

"Like cracking open an egg!" Fiza hollers above the wind.

"Right." Even the metaphors she uses are terrifying. Does the Dome not chill her? For someone so against this plan she seems delighted about the prospect of . . . breaking eggs.

We fly in low, sweeping against the mudslide from Mount Gandhak. We find a boulder askew on the mountainside and land there. Hiren "borrowed" some Dome Guard uniforms for us, so we don't exactly need to hide, but I don't want to risk being seen just yet. Also, it shouldn't bother me that much, but each time I glimpse the orange rising sun on the shoulder or cuff of my uniform, a twinge of guilt winds up my spine. Adraa never got to wear her own crest, and maybe she never will.

Blood, I need to stop thinking like that. I'm going to fix this.

It helps when Fiza and I buckle our skygliders and drape ourselves in black magic, disappearing from view. A guard walks the perimeter. But then, as he reaches the spot where the shadow ends, he stops and doubles back. I watch as he walks, and after a few minutes, he stops again, just meters away. This has to be it. He's guarding the vulnerable area. I crane my neck to look up at the expanse of stone. It's a daunting amount of space.

"*Vardrenni,*" Fiza and I cast, enhancing our eyesight and scanning for any ripple or shimmer in the facade. The wind beats against the curved walls and I rethink our luck. Maybe the weather is with us.

"Hiren said it was on the tenth story," I say.

Fiza frowns. "And that's what? Somewhere in the middle?"

"Yeah, somewhere in the middle. Almost exactly." I point for good measure, and she rolls her eyes. Apparently, there will no sweeping our argument under the rug. This just became the most awkward mission I've been on. And that's saying something.

After countless minutes, minutes we can't afford to lose, we still haven't found anything. There's no hole-sized anything, no hint of illusion. In fact, the wall looks entirely too solid and too real.

"See anything?" I finally ask.

"No . . . nothing. Are you sure that guard of yours is right?"

I scoff.

"What?" Fiza asks, irritated.

"It shouldn't surprise me, you not trusting him." I set my eyes on the wall, going over it again, analyzing every fissure. We have miles of wall to cover and she already wants to try out other theories. "You don't trust anyone."

"That's not true." She looks at me, then up, where Kalyan weaves his skyglider, watching our backs. "I trust Kalyan."

Something in me deflates, knowing she's deliberately trying to get under my skin. "Of course you do. Just keep searching."

"Did I hurt your feelings?"

I shift, the thick fabric of the uniform scuffing against the rock. "Of course not. It's hard to trust a liar, right? I don't expect you to."

"I don't remember you being this moody at the academy."

"A lot has changed since the academy."

She catches me readjusting my sleeves for the tenth time. "You've changed less than you think." I force myself to be still. But before I can figure out what that's supposed to mean exactly, Fiza stands. "This isn't going to work. If that hole is here, the illusion covering it is too good. It's time for that plan B you rattled on about. We have to get closer."

With a sigh, I follow her. Unfortunately, she's right. And that means we have to take out that Dome guard.

Fiza leans down, using the boulder as leverage and casts a black arrow.

I lean forward. "That's a knockout spell, right?"

She pulls back her hand, stretching the arrow into a spear.

The smoke swarms and swirls in a wild frenzy as it's pulled taut.

"Fiza!"

She lets go. I follow the magic for a blink as it cuts through the air. The guardsman tumbles to the ground a second later.

"Yes, it was a knockout spell. You're the most excitable white forte I've ever met."

Because I'm not stoic or icy like Kalyan. I cross my arms. "Are we really going to get into forte stereotypes? You're one to talk."

She unleashes her skyglider with a whoosh and a snap of fabric. "As much as I'd love to chat, don't we have a schedule?"

"So, you *were* listening." As I unbuckle my own skyglider, Fiza smiles for the first time in hours.

"I've been known to do it."

With that small alliance, we streak toward the wall, skidding to a stop as we get close. Then we separate. I have no clue how long it might take to break open this patched hole, and anxiety starts to sneak in. The beginning of a headache twinges behind my eyes. I'm straining them too much. Orange magic wasn't meant to be used for over an hour with no breaks.

But I can't stop, because again—nothing.

Yet I can sense something. Could be a trick of the light over the curved, smooth surface, but then I refocus, step back, and look at the whole picture.

That's when, like an optical illusion, I notice it.

No . . . They couldn't . . .

I speed up to Fiza, who's above me, the reality of it sinking in as I skim against the stone. "I think I figured out why we can't find it."

This piques her interest. "Why?"

I take a breath—*don't be wrong*—and touch the wall. My hand disappears and when I pull back the illusion doesn't break open like normal black magic. Only a glimpse of purple highlights the boundary of a wide-cast spell, but then it repairs itself. It's the best illusion I've ever seen. Seamless and consistently flowing around the entire sphere like rushing water.

Fiza veers back. "It doesn't stop," she whispers. "The whole thing? They put an illusion over the whole prison?" We both stare, neither of us able to contradict the truth.

"Smart," I relent. Without a corner or a seam, our job just got a lot harder. Now, instead of opening this illusion without anyone noticing, we have to find a way to open it, period.

Fiza looks back up. "Good Gods, this is . . . it's almost impressive."

"Do you remember learning a spell like this?" I ask.

"No. Have *you* seen something like this before?"

My mind goes back to that night on Pier Sixteen, the wall of illusion that hid a whole pier and section of beach. "Yeah, once. Kind of." I fly backward. "We need to get in there. If they have put this much magic into the illusion, who knows what the shields or barriers are like."

"We can't tear this thing apart. That's pretty darn noticeable. We're going to have to pull at a seam."

"Yeah, but . . ." I don't want to state the obvious, but didn't we just get done establishing this thing doesn't have seams?

"We'll have to create one." Her expression turns confident. I side-eye her. "You know how to do that?"

I get a smirk in response. "Someone wasn't paying attention in Professor Parsa's class year sixteen."

"He played favorites."

She smiles. "And someone wasn't his favorite apparently."

"The man had issues." Fiza's mention of Professor Parsa's laborious classes has brought back, full force, the memory of his Agsaian-accented voice detailing the delicacy of cracking an illusion without breaking the whole thing. And now we have to do it while hovering on skygliders, meters above the ground. We have our work cut out for us.

And that doesn't include how we are going to find this thing.

"We'll have to trust Hiren's intel," Fiza relents. It's like she's reading my mind, but that doesn't mean I'm going to let her off easy.

"Trust, huh?"

"Good Gods, is that your favorite word nowadays?" she huffs.

A chuckle escapes me, but it quickly ends as what we face suddenly becomes very real. We have only one chance at this. We hover in the middle of our search zone. I glance up again at Prisha and Kalyan making their rounds. No trouble yet. I breathe, wipe the sweat from my palms, and grip my skyglider with my thighs.

Fiza flies to my right and we count to three. *"Driswodahs,"* we cast simultaneously. My fingers sink into the illusion, but there's nothing to grab. I cast the spell again, louder, and tug at the sheen of smoke coating the wall, feeling for weakness or any give. There isn't any. My fingers slip off the surface like it's covered in oil.

On the other end Fiza is cursing. "Yield, you bloody—"

Then I feel it, the illusion spinning and wheeling and swirling enough that my own magic snags into it like a hook. It takes three times as long, but with persistence and the power of two nines it happens—a fissure.

And then, like any tear, it grows. But there's resistance, and it buckles. More than buckles, it seems to scream at Fiza and me. Or maybe that's us, shouting the spell over and over again, demanding dominance. My fingers strain, my grip slipping. *"Zaktirenni."* I shoot an extra dose of strength to my fingertips.

Once the fissure is one meter in length, I scan beneath its surface, searching for anything besides smooth sandstone. A crack, anything.

"There. Below you and to the left," Fiza says through clenched teeth. Without breaking concentration or letting my grip loosen, I slowly turn. There, gleaming under polished sunlight, is a gaping hole.

Hiren wasn't joking. The thing is massive.

"You'll have to jump for it," Fiza says. The hole is nearly half a meter below us.

"You first," I say on impulse.

"Jatin, stop being so bloody stubborn and go."

A part of me says this makes sense. Fiza will swing in, using the momentum or the backlash of this magic to propel her. She'll be able to clearly see her destination while I'll be half flying, half jerked backward. But if she misses, or if the magic rebounds hard enough that she can't handle it—

"I'll be right behind you," she interrupts my thoughts. "Trust me."

Maybe I do love that word too much, because I relent. "On three, then."

"Okay, but make it a quick three. This thing is bloody hard to hold."

"One."

"Two."

"Three!" I shout, and release. Without watching how Fiza fares under its weight, I grab the handle of my skyglider and dive backward. It happens fast. The rush of wind flares, magic glimmers at the edges, and in the next moment I tumble onto a shelf of stone.

Even with the bite of pain on impact, I rise to catch Fiza. But I underestimate her momentum. The next moments blur in movement and light as the illusion whips closed, and all I know in the snap of darkness is her falling on me.

Fiza is completely on top of me. I refuse to move, to reach up on this dark ledge and touch . . . touch something I do not want to accidently touch.

Instead I go with a safe and vital question. "Are you okay?"

"I'll get off you. Just give me a minute."

So we stay like that, noodle-armed and aching, in disbelief it actually worked. More than anything, it's uncomfortable. I count to four, four awkward and horrible seconds, before Fiza rolls off me, and finally I take a deep breath.

Flames dancing across her fingers penetrate the darkness and light up her face, which is way too close to mine. "You going to burnout on me?" she asks between breaths.

I laugh. It's the wheezing sound of adrenaline and embarrassment. "Oh, because that wasn't a bit difficult for you?"

The fire dances between her fingers. "Not at all. In fact, I believe Professor Parsa would be reassured in his favoritism."

"Come on. We don't have much time." I get up and wrap fire up my sore arms as well.

The walls are multicolored, which means wizards of all different strengths and types fortified this hole. As Night, the person who put a few of those wizards and witches behind these walls, it's reassuring to think that the Dome won't showcase its vulnerability. In any other regard this would be a comfort.

"How many protective shields do you think there are?" Fiza asks.

"My guess? Enough to be time-consuming. And loud."

"Maybe you are trying to burn me out."

"If I wanted you dead I wouldn't risk the mission."

"Of course. Sound reasoning. Very reassuring."

"It's one of my best qualities," I say, and then immediately regret it, because the words taste like flirting. They taste all too similar to how I would talk to Adraa if she were up on this deadly ledge with me, breaking through walls.

"The reasoning or the reassuring part? Because I would like to make a case against—"

"Forget it," I interrupt, my voice intentionally hard. "We have work to do."

Thirteen levels later, Fiza and I are again slumped on the ledge. My arms hang over my knees. My hands feel like they're been run through a grater. Or, better put, fire, a tornado of air, a hedge of thorns, a block of ice, and several walls of shields.

But we've done it. Broken holes in every shield, but the last. Mission successful.

Fiza sighs. "We are the only ones who could have done that. You realize that, right? I mean, that was amazing." And she's right. There is a reason they layered every type of magic in their fortification.

But I think she's implying something else with her praise. I could be wrong, but it sounds like she wants to say that Adraa couldn't have helped in the same way. That the ice wall wouldn't have been a team effort.

"Are your knuckles bleeding?" she asks, clutching her right hand.

I look down at my hands, the bruising, the blood, the pain I'm barely tuned in to because my body is so exhausted.

Maybe I'm wrong, though. It's in this moment, in the adrenaline-filled high of not dying and of getting past every obstacle, I think that maybe Fiza and I could be friends. Maybe I can trust her. *Should* trust her and grant this alliance, which she says is her only motive.

She leans toward me and for a second I think she's checking on my knuckles, inspecting the damage. But that's an Adraa move. Instead, Fiza faces me and leans in close. I'm a blur of instinct, flinching away. My neck twinges from semi-whiplash. "What are you doing?" I blurt because I can't think of how else to respond. I know exactly what she was doing.

"I thought . . ."

Frustration rises up in me. "This is why it's so bloody hard to even be your friend, Fiza. I'm sorry, but joking about shared history or accomplishing something together doesn't mean I'm obligated to like you like that. Sometimes shared history is just shared history."

The darkness seems to close in around us. My awareness of our proximity intensifies. Did I do this? Did I drop hints, laugh one too many times when discussing Professor Parsa and our days at the academy? Bloody feelings.

Fiza stands abruptly. "Let's go. We're on a schedule, remember?"

◈ ◈ ◈

Two hours later, and the group is back in the map room. Kalyan and Prisha arrived first and are waiting when we arrive. "Anything useful with the skylights?" I ask immediately, wanting a lifeline of some sort. It was bad enough flying back with Fiza and still not knowing how the mission went on Hiren's end.

He shakes his head. "Too small. Only you could maybe fit."

"How are you my best friend?" I mutter, grateful for the distraction, the laugh bubbling in my chest. Prisha's thin lips tick up in a smile, and I realize I haven't seen her smile in a long time around anyone but Hiren. Though their features aren't similar, there's something in her smile that reminds me of Adraa. And I want to think of Adraa. Kissing Adraa. Holding Adraa. Adraa.

I rub the back of my neck impatiently. I feel unclean. And I'm trying to reason that it's only the sweat and swelling knuckles, but that's not the truth.

"Any news from them at all?"

Then, like I called them into being, the door opens. Hiren and Riya, fully decorated in Belwar attire, enter.

As soon as the door shuts, the most important question tumbles out of my mouth. "Did you see her?"

Hiren hangs his head. No one likes the silence that follows. Silence is never good, and I need good. "She wasn't there."

"What do you mean? You just didn't see her or . . ."

"I looked at every layer. We met with the warden and I had full view from the tower. Adraa wasn't in any of the cells," Riya says, stepping forward.

"You checked them all?"

"Yes."

"Then you missed one or . . ." I search for an explanation; trying to hold on to anything besides the notion that we failed. Beyond anything, I needed this, confirmation Adraa was alive and okay.

"I'm sorry, Maharaja," Hiren whispers.

"Don't." I release the anger. "Please, don't call me that."

Hiren nods, and the rest of the group falls into silence.

The rest, that is, except for Riya. "Solitary confinement," she blurts out.

"I thought we agreed—" Hiren blusters, and then spins toward me. "The chances are slim, Jatin. They aren't using those cells anymore."

I try to thread together Riya's confidence and Hiren's practicality and insight.

"What do you mean, Riya?" Prisha asks, her tone filled with the hope I'm trying not to feel. "You think Adraa's in solitary confinement?"

Riya pushes forward. "This is Adraa we are talking about. If she wasn't in any cell, she must have done something. Tell me one reason why this doesn't make the most sense." She turns in a circle, eyes resting on Hiren last.

The six of us contemplate it. After a minute, we all seem to look up at once. It's the only thing that makes sense—in fact, it makes more than sense. Yet if Riya is right, that means I was the closest to Adraa, since Fiza and I were in the northwest-facing section. I was a few bloody *walls* away from her, and I didn't knock through them. *No, instead you let a manipulative witch press against you, almost kiss you.*

"This might be better," Hiren offers. "Whatever they have manufactured to replace the northwestern corner can't be as well fortified." He looks to me. "Did you find it?"

"We did," Fiza answers for me. "Found. Broken. Ready for us."

Riya seems to inflate. "So, what's the plan? Jatin?"

Today's failure still stings. I was hoping with everything I have that someone would at least see Adraa, could prove to me that she's okay, still standing, still Adraa.

Go! Find her! Free her! my anger yells, pounding its way through me.

I straighten. "No more failed attempts. No more small victories. Next time we go into the Dome, we are bringing her out with us."

CHAPTER TWENTY-FOUR

◇

I Sit in Solitary

Adraa

Harini keeps staring at me. I think I broke her, and for once I'm glad we're in separate cages. I don't think she believes I'm evil, but I'm probably a fool for not bringing myself up in conversation to gauge whether she wants to kill me right now.

Please, cast something, I finally write.

Slowly she weaves her hands through the air. *So I'm guessing you are innocent? That you didn't cause Mount Gandhak to erupt?*

Okay, questions. That's close to believing me. Her phrasing could be worse, much worse.

I didn't, I respond simply.

She nods.

That it? I write. She didn't need much convincing.

She frowns and gestures to our isolated state. *We are stuck in here because you didn't want to hurt one witch.*

She was defenseless.

Exactly. I don't share your conviction, Adraa Belwar, but I can't deny my respect. You are not the villain they made you out to be.

Neither is she. I smile, grateful beyond measure for her words. *So, you'll help me?*

She raises both eyebrows. *Felt good to finally hit one of them, didn't it?*

It did.

I'm up for doing it again.

◇ ◇ ◇

We sleep, disturbed only by the circular skylights streaking down and creating round patches of light in our cells. When I finally do wake, I forget we are in isolation for half a moment. But in the next, I'm out of the lumpiest cot created and hungry to start the day. Because isolation means no peering eyes and no illusion spells needed. I should have rebelled a week ago.

The daylight doesn't do much to chase away the terrors of this cavernous well, though. Below us is an inky-black pool. The rocks lining the walls stab outward like a shark's teeth. The cells swing with the slightest movement, making me feel constantly unstable and lacking any sense of control. It's just the place I'd wish on my worst enemies.

Ironically, in the most heavily fortified cage I've ever been in, Harini and I begin finalizing our escape plan.

We narrow down our three main goals, which happen to be our three biggest obstacles. One, getting out of solitary. Two, getting out of the Dome. Three, using magic to our advantage. If anyone figures out that last bit, we'll be giving up the surprise. And we need surprise.

The hardest part will be getting through the doors, Harini explains. *Shields fortify every exit. It'll take too long to get through them.*

I have an idea.

Harini motions for me to continue.

We don't go through a door. We go through something less guarded but already half open. I point upward, to the holes in the ceiling.

Harini looks at me like I've properly lost it. *Even you aren't that little.*

That's why we are going to make them bigger. What I'm suggesting is a little drastic, but we need to get out quickly, in one loud bang of magic before anyone can catch on or catch up.

Once upon a time I was in a clinic and Jatin made a potion to heal my cramps, but before I realized what he was doing I had assumed he wanted an explosion spell for the mission. I think he believed afterward that I was only joking. But I wasn't. My mother taught me all sorts of lessons in her clinic. I just never had need for a real bomb before.

I can make an explosive in that clinic. I need to get in, and I need time.

Both of those things will be difficult.

So let's get started, I write.

◇ ◇ ◇

When Harini and I aren't discussing our plan, we're going through magic lesson after magic lesson. Once, way back when, Jatin and I agreed year fifteen was the hardest in magic studies. But neither of us had to sit in a confined space with a newly motivated teacher while impending death hovered on the horizon. It's one hell of a motivator.

Even as I practice my hand movements and drills, I run the plan in my mind and realize that, if all goes well, our escape will be quiet. We can't release everyone. It'll be only Harini and me. Then, as soon as I reach Belwar Palace, I'll come back.

This is the only way it's going to work, yet guilt still nicks at the back of my mind. This isn't what the Red Woman would do. This isn't even an Adraa move. If I had to categorize it, it'd be a Jaya Smoke maneuver. Did I just play at selflessness when the stakes weren't high?

I wipe my head clear of the thoughts. To save others, sometimes we have to save ourselves first. I'm no hero—maybe I never was.

The midday sun strikes down, and Harini and I finally take a break. Not a soul has come and checked on us. In a world like Wickery, where everyone relies on magic and power is synonymous with the Touch up your arm, they sure do underestimate those without it. I refuse to do the same. I vow to never overlook a potential threat. So, while it may be painful, I need Harini to answer a few final questions.

I need to ask. What is the experiment like? What might we be walking into if—? I don't let myself finish.

Harini's chest rises in a sigh and she rubs her temples. *I pass out most times.*

The explanation hasn't started out promising.

But I see what they do to the others. Her orange words come slowly.

I wait.

It looks like a simple cut on the arm, not deep enough to kill, but whenever it's my turn, the pain is like nothing I've ever felt. It's like my whole body is burning out.

I think it over. I don't know how, but they must have harnessed a way to take our magic. Bloodlurst is absorbed through the skin. It's a heavy powder, not a liquid, so there's something I'm missing about the process here. With Harini passing out, I don't think she'll be able to tell me. I squeeze my left wrist hard. It's normally the right I'm fretting over, or used to fret over.

I should tell you something else, Harini writes.

Oh no. I nod for her to continue.

My sister, Nira, she and I aren't like the other Voiceless. Basu didn't take my voice. I've never had it. When I came to the prison, my sister and I were the breakthroughs they needed. Bloodlurst was perfected because of us. They've been silencing the girls ever since. During the cage fights, they measure our magic or our willpower or something, I don't quite understand it. But it's not just entertainment.

I take it all in. Bloodlurst started here, with my cellmate.

What was Nira like?

She was . . . The words fade. *She was brilliant. She was ill in Pire when she was young. She lost her hearing, and we found the community that taught us our new language to communicate and to cast. Even though she was the younger sister, she taught me how to write.*

But what I remember most is her happiness. She was a happy person. So optimistic and her smile could melt . . . anyone. She loved those rainbow ribbons. The last one I have of hers is in our cell. When Harini turns back to me, tears fill her eyes. *I need to get it back.*

We will.

They discovered she could wield magic and the next time they took us to the clinic they killed her. They took too much and I don't even know why. Afraid she'd fight back or just too greedy for her power. Harini shrugs, her shoulders shaking as she sobs.

I sigh, angry at myself for pushing Harini. But I have to know. *Do you think that's how Nira died? Burnout?*

Fury marks her face, and her body tenses. *I didn't see it. I was still passed out when it happened. It was only when I woke up . . .* The magic unravels in a smudge and I can't read the last bit. But I don't need to.

Gods. I imagine Prisha for a second, waking up to her . . . I shove the image away.

I have vowed to get out of here and kill every wizard or witch responsible. And when that's done, I'll kill everyone who used her blood to make themselves more powerful.

I stay quiet. I understand her pain but also know it's not that simple. She's talking about hundreds, maybe thousands of people. Some of them innocent kids who didn't know better. Some who had Bloodlurst forced on them by Vencrin.

Harini slumps. *But all of this is absurd. A million things could go wrong. They could kill us on the spot.* Suddenly her hands stop casting and she punches the wall. *We aren't getting out of here.*

We will.

She won't look at me, and I think she already knows what my spell reads because she casts again. *I realize you are a royal, and I know you might have grown up being told you were special, but this place does not work like that. The world doesn't work like that.*

Harini, I write. I force the word to grow large like I'm screaming it. I want her to look at me and tell her what a goddess once told me. When she glances over, I cast. *There is no destiny, only a path of choices. I'm choosing to do whatever it takes to get out of here before they drain us of our power. You in?*

She pauses. I think she expected an apology or a plea.

Let's go over the plan again, she casts.

◇

CHAPTER TWENTY-FIVE

I Begin My Escape

Adraa

The beginning of our plan relies on a guard eventually coming to feed us. Hours pass, and the longer we sit and wait, more than feeling hungry or forgotten, we sense our plan may be foolish. Silly me, I thought this was punishment, not a death sentence. But this is the Dome. We took out a dozen wizards, who are probably demanding more than missed meals as retribution.

Then, when more than half the spots of sun in my cell have vanished, a door screeches against uneven stone. It's Vihaan. Even in the dim light I can make out his tall figure and jagged teeth. I'd prefer it be some nameless guard, but one can't be choosy when trying to bust out of a magic-infused prison.

Okay. This is it.

He ambles nearer, each clack of his boots against the stone floor one step closer to the plan. I stand slowly, making sure to not wobble my cell and to look the part of a hungry, obedient prisoner.

Vihaan steps into my cage and holds up a bowl of plain rice before placing it on the floor. "Sorry about all this."

Me too. Too bad he won't get an apology.

As soon as he turns to relock the door I lunge. The cell swings.

I whisk the cuff from his belt, and with a satisfying clasp it slaps onto his wrists, disabling his powers. In shock, he hesitates. I've knocked him unconscious before the next blink. Well, that went better than expected.

When I look over, Harini stares at me from inside her cell. *I didn't teach you that.*

I'm a quick learner, I sign as I rush to release her. The latch loosens and the door clicks open. *But I recall you wishing I didn't practice so frequently.*

She rolls her eyes. *That might not have been my best advice.* She looks at me and smiles. *I'll apologize once we're out.*

We haul Vihaan onto my cot and settle a blanket over him. We turn to leave, but then I bend down and steal his belt. As soon as I sling it around my hips I feel like the Red Woman again.

Harini gives me a questioning look.

To save time I motion to the flaps on the belt and the sky-glider holster now resting on my hip. Pockets have saved my life before. I'm not about to walk past a perfect opportunity. Besides, how else am I supposed to carry bombs around after I make them?

We enter the long hallway, the only way out. It's quiet, and with every step I feel like I'm emerging from a cave.

We stop at the stairs that lead further down into the prison. Harini will stay here and guard this entry point.

Well, this is where I leave you, I sign before turning to scout the hallways ahead.

A tap on my shoulder makes me turn around.

Hey! Don't die on me.

I nod through my smile. It's the nicest thing she's ever said to me. But she need not worry. I always try my best on that front.

Harini gave me detailed instructions on how to get to the clinic. I've memorized every turn, but it mostly involves sinking level after level until I reach a point where I must be below the Dome. So much for the sense of escape. Instead, there's a smell of damp earth and a feeling of confinement, knowing I'm truly underground and there's no fresh air beyond the stone walls keeping us in. I unlock the door with a slip of purple magic and suddenly I'm there.

The clinic, if it can even be called that, is almost a parody of Belwar Palace's tightly run operation. The small rectangular room lies in semi-darkness, with a wall of cabinets along one side and dirty cots pressed against the other. I thought grabbing the ingredients would take little time, and then I could dig for paperwork or a scrap of evidence of what's going on beneath the Dome. But in all this disorder, I'm going to have to do both at once. And I have to do it quickly.

The drawers are filled with dried herbs and poorly stored

ingredients. It's a healer's nightmare. I'd be dead already if I had ever let my mother's clinic get half this bad. Nothing is kept in the proper jars. The cauldron has a thick layer of grime. The concept of labels is laughable.

Next, the cabinets get jerked open. Cobwebs and dust puff into my face. Good Gods, how does anyone survive in these conditions?

Finally, I scrounge up some fireworth, a red leafy plant that's harmless unless mixed and heated with ashen, a black powder from Pire Island. There's nothing about the experiment, no indication of what ingredients are being used. What's more, there's no paper trail of any kind. Patients of the Dome don't need health documentation, I guess. Which makes sense, given Harini's account of how she ended up here. Who would document mass kidnapping and false imprisonment?

I hear shuffling and the scrape of a lock, which allows me just enough time to duck around a corner and cast a camouflage spell. I peer over my shoulder as Basu bursts through the door.

My body tenses as I clutch the stone wall. I'm here to steal ingredients, find information, and maintain the plan. I should remain hidden. But, like Harini, I have an underlying reason to want to escape and it's more than freedom. I want to return to Belwar, clear my name, and out Moolek for what he has done and how he got into the minds of my people. I can't imagine doing it without speaking, though. A part of me, a strong part, can't resist this opportunity to get my voice back, to seek my own revenge here and now.

Basu rushes to the drawers I was just fumbling through. I shift to get a better look, and the floor creaks. The mucky little wizard doesn't even pause. I could flee now and continue with the plan. That's what I should do.

Harini once asked if having my powers back was important enough to risk my life. With a deep breath I uncast my protection and step from the shadows. This is the answer to that question.

Basu flinches and then rubs his eyes. "What . . . what do you think you are doing?"

We both stare. I keep my expression neutral, one might even say bored. Sheer surprise is written across his face, though. Whatever he expected, *I* wasn't it.

In one clean motion Basu throws a knife. After days of practice, my hands move almost instinctively. A small shield of red smoke rises from my wrists and deflects the weapon. It clatters to the stone floor.

Blood. Why does he always have to attack first? Then again, he wouldn't be Basu if he wasn't afraid of me.

His eyes widen into orbs. "How . . . ? You're able to perform magic!"

While Basu is still puzzling it all out, I unleash a torrent of wind. It pushes him back against the wall and I hold him there. No hiding it now. I stalk forward. Fear enters his wide eyes as he struggles against the air.

"You don't know what you're doing!" he yells.

I cock my head to one side, shooting my hand forward and pressing the wind into his chest.

He whines, "You'll deny it, of course, but me being here is *your* fault, Adraa Belwar. I was simply a wizard trying to feed his family, trying to get by, and you ambushed me and took away the firelight. Then you put me in the *Dome,* where *he* found me. I was about to be killed. I had to be useful to save my life. You think I want any of this? It was this or death."

Blame. How did I know he would bring it back to me? But I didn't force Basu to deal with the Vencrin in the first place. And I certainly didn't give him that horrible ultimatum. I even searched to make sure he was all right. I refuse to take the blame. I refuse to suffer under the weight of his words after what he has done to countless witches. What he has done to me.

Something in me snaps then and there. No more holding back. My sympathy only extends so far.

What do you want from me? To feel bad for you? Think what you want, but this didn't start with me. This started with your greed.

"Agree to disagree, my dear." His arms flame bright yellow. He throws the wind off with a force of his own. My hair whips from the breeze of our magic colliding with one another.

Remember the last time you tried fighting me without backup, I remind him, knowing somewhere deep down he's thinking about that moment too.

"I can't let you go. It would be my death sentence."

You shouldn't be so scared to die. It's not the worst thing that can happen to someone.

"I do know, my dear. And that's why I can't let you walk out of here. It's me or you."

I move my hands. *You took something from me. I want it back.* When he doesn't say anything, I continue. *Give me my voice back,* I cast into the air, the broad red strokes drifting like bloodstains.

He sinks back. "I . . . I . . . That's why you're here?"

A wave of red washes forward. I didn't even realize I had cast. Basu flies, though, pinned to the wall by bands of purple magic. With a clunk, a shield clamps around his throat. Harini taught me that one.

"I can't!" he yells as he grasps at his neck.

My hands weave, smacking my body as I spell out words that blaze above me. *I don't want excuses. Give. Me. My. Voice. Back.*

"It's not an excuse," he wheezes. "I've never done it. I don't even know if it can be done."

I freeze. *You're telling me—* I break, my arms shaking. *You're telling me you took my voice—you've taken voices and you don't know if you can undo it?*

Basu slowly shakes his head. "No one . . . no one has ever asked."

I explode. With one flick the wall of magic bears down, smothering him. But he is still able to scream. A scream that tells me no one has tarnished his vocal cords. *I wonder why, you monster. How could they ask?*

"I meant . . ." A new level of fear enters his eyes as he braces against my wall. I know what he meant. No one has ever asked him to put back a voice because the Voiceless are nothing. Terminated threats. Delivered death sentences. Why would the

Vencrin or Moolek want to restore anyone's power? Who would have ever asked to right a horrid wrong when they don't care?

"Pavria," Basu wheezes, and the small gush of air keeps him from being crushed. I let it happen. I drop the shields holding him in place. He crawls across the floor, making his way to the door millimeter by millimeter. It's sad. Pathetic. And yet, I am still unsatisfied.

In fact, I'm a ball of emotions. I should be running and casting the ingredients together and following through on my and Harini's plan for escape. But I can't fully give up and give in.

I call strength into my body and hoist him up by the throat. My thumbs find the groove under his mandible and press, hard. *Today. You. Try.*

He struggles and strains but refuses to answer me. *I'm not letting go until you try.*

Then he smiles, his eyes focusing on something behind me. "You sure about that?"

◇

CHAPTER TWENTY-SIX

Breaking the Dome

Jatin

Everything goes smoothly until it doesn't. Hiren gets our uniforms just fine. We meet up without suspicion or a tail. Everyone seems focused, and even Fiza seems reassured. Ten minutes into flight, though, the sky opens up and releases its first autumn rain. It's the kind of storm that obliterates any leaves clinging to their branches.

"Should we wait until tomorrow?" Prisha asks, swooping in close to me.

"No. They'll notice we destroyed those walls sooner than later. It has to be today."

Hiren lightens the mood with, "The noise may mask our approach," which actually brightens my spirits, especially when a loud bout of thunder rages above. Then Fiza counters with, "Yeah, by it's going to be near impossible to find our hole." She points as the Dome comes into view. We look at it through the pelting rain and gloom.

"Even this rain won't take that illusion down. I didn't ask before, but how many wizards created it, you think?" Fiza asks me.

"One," I answer.

"One?" she scoffs.

I've been thinking about it more and more, especially last night when sleep wouldn't come. The leader of the Vencrin, the purple forte wizard in the black cloak. Everywhere I turn, I find an illusion smothering Belwar. What I thought was a recent team-up of two separate entities is actually a long-standing partnership. So, we have two wizards with bad intentions, one unknown and the other the wealthiest and most powerful wizard of Wickery. I always thought Moolek was the bigger threat. But last night it occurred to me—what's more threatening than the unknown, especially when all we know is how powerful it is?

"Just one," I answer.

We're soaked by the time we reach the Dome and take out the three guards hovering around its outskirts. But that's not the hard part. Like I thought, Fiza wasn't wrong. It takes time and energy to find the hole. The rain continues to stream down my face, forcing me to cast an umbrella of blue magic just to see. Eventually, Fiza and I find it and let the others through. Hiren and Prisha take over on the other side and hold the illusion open for us. I land on the ledge inside in a puddle.

"Was that hard for you?" Hiren teases, sweeping hair from Prisha's face.

She blushes and rolls her eyes, then grabs his hands. "You're the one still shaking. And you call yourself a black forte."

"What do you mean, call myself? I am a black forte."

I'm almost taken back by their blatant flirting. Okay, Kalyan and Riya were right. It's almost sad how I missed it all this time. I turn to see if anyone else noticed, a pang arising at the thought that Adraa and I would have shared a knowing glance and a similar quip. Everyone else seems focused on drying off. Fiza is even warming up Kalyan, laughing at the fact that he used blue magic to slick all the water from his clothes, leaving himself still cold. Did we become a full-fledged team right under my nose?

"Jatin?" Riya whispers.

"Yes." I step toward the one shield yet to be broken. "Wait for the next thunderclap."

◇ ◇ ◇

We step into the Dome, round a few corners, and emerge onto a cliff of black rock. Before us is a chasm with cells on twenty different levels. Hundreds and hundreds of spheres dangle off the cliffs, each with its own landing post. With the storm and the lack of light, walking into this place is like walking into a dungeon.

"You looked through all these cells?" Prisha asks, the disbelief in her voice echoing what I'm feeling.

"Yes, all of them," Riya says.

A Dome Guard emerges from around the next corner and the six of us duck back. "Come on, like I said, we're near solitary confinement. Follow me." Hiren waves a hand.

We dive into the Dome's inner hallways, and even though they are confusing and mazelike, I can still visualize the struc-

240

ture of the Dome. The outer shell is like the innards of an ant-hill, winding and elaborate and leading up or down to the next level, with the middle hollowed out so that the cells can hang over each cliff.

Hiren leads us deep into the catacombs, the air stifling with the smell of mud and grime. The humidity makes me feel sticky.

A wizard guards the door to solitary.

"Okay, it's right beyond that door," Hiren says.

"I can take him out," Riya volunteers.

I hold her back. "No, let's use him."

"*Kuntaraw*," I cast, materializing a spear into my hands. I nod at Riya. "I'll hook his left shoulder. You got the right?"

Her smile gleams. "Do you even have to ask?"

The others stand back as the two of us line up our shots and fire. White and purple streams of smoke cut through the air and stab the guard's clothing. A black spiral follows right behind, latching onto his mouth and cutting off his cry as he's pinned to the wall. Riya and I look back at Fiza. "You forgot about the noise," she answers.

"Thank you," I say.

With a whoosh of magic, I paint my Night mask on. One by one so does the rest of the team. Then I unfold from the shadows and press an ice knife against the guard's throat. "Take me to Adraa Belwar."

His chin juts upward, away from the blade, but he manages to nod.

So far, so good.

After being unhooked from the wall, the guard doesn't waste a moment unlocking the door and leading us down a spiral staircase. It feels like we're spiraling into doom. But it's only a few more minutes before he leads us to a pit with orbs hanging in a circle. Rain leaks into the cavern from the skylights and patters against the lake meters below.

Only one cell is occupied. In it, a witch lies facedown and motionless.

Adraa.

"Wh-wh-what have they done to her?" Prisha stammers, jolting forward.

Hiren stops her. "Wait, these cells can't take much weight. They aren't stable."

The guard seems to deflate in Kalyan's grip, revealing what he had hoped would be the end of us.

I look at my team and hold out a hand. They all know if it can only be one of us, it will be me. "Adraa?" I call, my voice almost swallowed by emotion. She's there. She's *right* there. But she's not moving, and my stomach drops like it's fallen into the pit. Slowly, I walk into the cell, find my balance as the cage wobbles, and then drop to my knees. "Adraa?"

She turns her head. A stranger stares back at me. Same hair color, same dark skin, same build. No, not same. Similar.

Because it's not her.

I pull up her right sleeve, and above the cuff that disables magic are the designs of a three. The shock of it all knocks

242

me back. But I am very much done with look-alikes. "Who are you?" I ask, more harshly than I intend to.

She answers confidently, not even a tremor or a note of confusion in her voice. "Adraa Belwar," she says like it's the truth.

$$\Diamond \ \Diamond \ \Diamond$$

"No. No, you aren't. So cut the act," I whisper.

"It's not an act," she says, her voice warped, slurring at the edges like she's . . . *Oh no.*

"Prisha," I call, holding out my hand. "I need you. Come. Carefully," I warn as the cage sways.

Prisha steps in lightly before falling beside us. "What—" Prisha immediately halts. "Good Gods. She's drugged."

"Can you help? What do they have her on?"

Prisha looks up at me as the witch's head swivels between us. "Something strong."

"What the blood is this?" Riya whispers from behind us. "What kind of messed-up— Where is Adraa?"

"I don't know." I turn my attention back to the guard, whom Kalyan still holds in a wristlock. He squirms as I focus in on him. "But we are going to find out."

Kalyan must have wrenched the guard's wrist backward, because he winces. "Hey, hey, I'll tell you what I know. It's just not much. Please, don't—"

Fiza leans down and half slaps, half pats the wizard's cheek. "Gods, stop sputtering and tell us, then."

"They told us this was Adraa Belwar. But if it isn't, then I . . . I never saw her," the wizard whines. "She's the most important and deadly prisoner we have ever had. They wouldn't have assigned her to the likes of me."

I sigh. So he's useless.

"But I've overheard the rumors and the other guards talking. Theories and ghost stories, I thought, to scare us new guys."

"You talk a lot. Get to the point," Kalyan says, giving him a shake.

"Some think she's in the part of the prison unknown to most of us. The haunted Underground, they call it. Others say she's not here at all. That she never existed."

Prisha looks up. "Doesn't exist?"

"We need more than theories and ghost stories," Fiza demands. "Do you know where the real Adraa Belwar is being kept?"

"We got our orders from high up. We were told to keep quiet to avoid panic and to avoid being killed. They were going to kill us all."

"If she's not here"—I steel my voice, trying to not let it or myself break—"then where is she?"

Each of us looks at the other in turn.

"What the blood did they do to her?" Riya shouts, hitting the black stone wall.

Think, Jatin. They are all looking to you. Think!

Scrambling, I veer back to the decoy witch. "Prisha, any way to sober her up? She might know something." But we all know I'm grasping.

Prisha's pink magic hovers above the girl's forehead. She appears to have passed out. "This is going to take hours."

"Hiren?" I ask, noticing for the first time that he's pressed himself against the wall, the situation shattering his resolve.

"I . . . I don't know," he says at last.

I push myself out of the cell and back on the rocky cliffside. *Find her!* a voice yells. *Think!* No more rash, impulsive actions. I peer at the other cells dangling around us, at the center path below.

What didn't I see? Where did I make my mistake?

Mistake.

I wheel around. "There's someone in this prison who knows." I face the guard. "You're going to lead us to another cell."

◇

CHAPTER TWENTY-SEVEN

Experimentation of the Nine

Adraa

The warden stands in the entrance with Harini sagging against him. Her right eye swells purple. Her hands are bound, not in cuffs but with rope. We have failed. Harini's expression says as much. Her words come back to me, less like defeat and more like an omen. *A million things could go wrong. We aren't getting out of here.*

"Stand down," the warden says, holding a knife to her throat. The light catches its gleaming blade. He wouldn't kill her. She's too important for their experiment. But maybe they really do need *only* our blood.

I pull back from Basu. He coughs and chokes on fresh air.

I can't take the chance. Not Harini. Not anyone.

I wave my hands and red smoke gushes from my arms, wrists to shoulders. We have to make it a proper standoff, don't we? It won't end like this. *How?* I cast. How did he know I was here?

"You think I don't see everything that goes on here? This is *my* prison. Now, what part of 'stand down' do you not understand?"

Before I can move or talk my way out of this, a flash of yellow magic sweeps up my leg. I'm knocked to my knees; a dizziness and fatigue takes over.

No. Not something as simple as . . .

My eyelids flutter in a deep heaviness, sleep beckoning.

"We can't wait any longer. He wants the next batch today and we don't even need the ring results to tell us she's fine. Tie her down and get the other Voiceless. I'll leave you to it."

I wrestle against the sleep spell, but I should know, magic is always too hard to fight. And I'm so very tired.

◈ ◈ ◈

Water splashing my face wakes me up, and I gasp and spit. We're still in the clinic. All eight other Voiceless lie on wicker tables. One for each of the gods. Lambs brought here for slaughter. White, black, pink, purple, blue, green, yellow, orange, and then, finally, me—red.

It's exactly as Harini said.

"Good, she's awake. We can start."

Both my sleeves are ripped off. No one has time to worry about my bare arm and what that means for who I am. I notice the light-haired witch I saved lying on the table next to Harini's. A yellow forte. She's staring at me and my identity laid bare. Our eyes find one another's, and she frowns.

Then something on the other side of the room takes my

attention. A huge pile of pale white powder sits on a platter. Bloodlurst? If I'm right, it's enough to enhance hundreds.

With a knife Basu slices open the arm of the witch on the other side of me. None of us can hear her screams, but I know she's crying out. Her blood drips in long streaks down and into the powder. Harini was right, it's not much blood. In fact, it's the kind of scratch a mediocre rendering of pink magic could fix. Something else is happening—the dull powder glows bright white. Ice crystals rise into the air. Then the witch passes out, going limp against the bindings.

A chill runs through me and real fear tangles in my throat. It goes quickly after that. Quicker than could ever be expected when it comes to complicated magic such as this. I watch as one by one each of these powerful women is drained of her magic and the powder changes color. From ice crystals to sweeping shadows to the brilliant shine of pink to hardened spikes of purple. Blood and soundless screams and unconsciousness.

Even after seeing it with my own eyes I can't piece together how it all works. They have somehow figured out how to steal our magic through bloodletting. I didn't know such a thing existed.

As they work on the dark-skinned Pire Island witch and the powder turns blue, I refocus on the rope binding me to the table. I twist and tug, fighting my restraints. It's just rope, simple rope, and yet I think they use it to prove how powerless we really are. The strand binding my right hand has a frayed edge.

Maybe I can work with that somehow because I have to get out of this. Or I'm going to die on this table.

Before I know it, Harini is crying out silently next to me. She's grasping the rainbow ribbons tied around her wrist and I realize how we both deviated from our plan. Yet, I'm glad she has them. The substance shines pumpkin orange, Harini's pumpkin orange. She falls limp like the rest, her head tilted toward me. My throat tightens, imagining the same expression, the same outcome, when Harini looked at her sister, Nira, for the final time.

Basu smiles as he moves to my side, blocking the sight of Harini. "And now, it's you turn, my dear. We've been expecting you a long while. Finally, we get to see what you are made of. See how powerful you really are. Please, don't disappoint." He raises the knife. "This next part is going to hurt."

I struggle against the rope, trying to move my hands in any formation to cast. Nothing.

Basu frowns. "Feisty until the end. Quite inspiring, my dear." He leans closer. "But it's either you or me."

The knife descends, a flash of silver. Then pain. When the blade digs deep into my skin, a new level of agony engulfs me. My blood patters to the floor, and my vision fuzzes at the edges, a numbing sting like burnout radiating up my arm, telling me to stop, stop casting, stop using up energy I don't have.

But I'm not. I'm not casting. And yet . . .

My blood drips, splashing the floor in an unceremonious and unnerving patter.

So this is how they do it. This is what Bloodlurst is. Not an herb or a potion infused with my magic. My actual magic, flowing out and dripping down my arm.

I watch, my vision blurred. I couldn't do it. I couldn't escape and no one rushed in to save me. Only the darkness comes, in waves and then all at once, blackout and burnout collide, and there's just one last thought as I sink into the inky blackness: Is this how I die?

Adraa? Adraa, is that you?

◇

CHAPTER TWENTY-EIGHT

Sims Talks

Jatin

Sims sits comfortably in his prison cell. Well, as comfortably as a man two heads taller than me can in a sphere that's hanging off a cliff.

"Open it," I tell the guard. The cell takes its time rising up to the walkway. Sims nods to me as I burst into the space. Kalyan, Hiren, and Riya handle any guards passing by. Three men are already tied to the cliffside. And I've already told Prisha and Fiza to stand back and let me do the talking, to not intervene unless I give a signal. But I already don't appreciate Sims's smug expression, like he's been waiting for me to show up.

Seeing my mask, his cellmate leaps to his feet. "You're the bloody freak show that put me in—"

With one word I throw the man against the wall. He crashes to the floor with a thud. Sims doesn't move. In fact, he almost seems uninterested.

"Thanks for that. The guy wouldn't shut up," he finally mutters.

I ignore him. "What was it? What do I have wrong?"

Sims crosses his arms and leans back on his bed. "Poor manners, for one."

The white mist of my magic flares. "Don't make this harder than it has to be."

"And why should I answer to *Night*?" Sims grumbles. I know he's messing with me, baiting me to see what I'll reveal.

"Because underneath, you know I'm more than that." I take the biggest gamble of my life and wipe off my mask in one clean stroke. "At one point you even named me."

Sims smiles again, pleased. Too pleased. He must have doubted himself for a second in the Underground. "And to think when we first met, I pitied you. Thought you were some obsessed Smoke fan sneaking into the back rooms. Did Smoke ever tell you that if she hadn't intervened, you would have been another bloodstain in the alley?"

"That's probably not what would have happened," I whisper. My magic blazes.

"Ah, true. But it isn't every night a royal nine barges into an establishment such as mine."

"Where is she, Sims? What was my mistake?"

He cocks his head. "What am I to you?" The cuffs on his wrists click as he brings his hands together.

"Right now? Someone refusing to answer a single question."

"It's best to establish a relationship first. An understanding. We haven't even talked payment."

"I'm guessing you want out of here."

"Obviously," he says with a nod. "And enough money to start a new business."

I came here because Sims is a lesser evil. But he has the information I need. And I have to find her. *Free her!*

"Okay, done. Now talk."

"I want to talk to the girl first."

I grab him by the collar of his orange prison kurta and jerk him to his feet, then think better of it and throw him against the wall. Blood, Sims is heavy. "We're done negotiating."

He chuckles. "You're messing with your whole persona, kid. No respect for consistency. You don't get to play bad cop, not when the Red Woman is your partner." His eyes flit to Fiza. "Now, I want to talk to her."

"Why?"

"I want to know who I'm doing business with. Always have."

"Red!" I call, and nod for her to join me. Riya and Kalyan go rigid, but they trust me. Fiza steps into the cell lightly. Even close up, her illusion holds, even as Sims analyzes every movement.

"Talk, Sims," I command.

"It's nice to formally meet you, Lady of Agsa."

Before I can say anything, Fiza drops her illusion. It ripples downward, revealing her true form. "Can't say it's mutual," she answers.

"Ah." He smiles, his whole countenance lighting up. "It's always nice when you've guessed right." Then he begins.

"Adraa Belwar was brought here to get everyone to believe in the show."

"I know. So tell me where she's being kept."

"She was brought to the Dome. That doesn't mean she's still here, Raja."

"What?" He can't mean . . . She's not gone *gone*. They wouldn't kill her.

"She didn't even stay here a single night. They had other plans for a red forte of her caliber; probably have for a long while, ever since her first fight in my Underground. Do you know how these things work?" Sims taps the curved wall of his cell. "They aren't just clear curved walls, they analyze how powerful a Touched is. It's how cage casting started. Dueling, even a mere fistfight, is always the best way to really see what a wizard, or in this case a witch, is made of. It just happens to make for bloody good entertainment too."

Although this is news to me, I don't want to indulge his tangents and time wasting. "I don't have time for a history lesson. Tell us, Sims! Where. Is. She?"

He sighs. "I don't know what it's called. To really keep a place a secret, you don't name it. All I know is that they took her where all the powerful but unwanted go." He looks directly at Fiza. "Adraa Belwar is probably the first public figure they have stolen, but certain promises had to be fulfilled. You need *real* power to raise an army."

Powerful but unwanted? Raise an army? What is he talking about? "Who's *they*?" I shout. "Moolek?"

"What did you say?" Fiza whispers to Sims.

Some revelation spins in her eyes. Looking between her and Sims, I finally understand. Sims wanted to talk to Fiza not to gather information or verify our secret identities, but because she can decode the vague clues Sims has just laid out before us. Names. Stolen. Promises. Army. To her all that spells out a location. "Fiza?" I ask, the not knowing killing me.

She looks at me and then at the rest of our team. "I know where she is."

◇

CHAPTER TWENTY-NINE

Return to the Red Room

Adraa

I come to in a land of red. At first, I think it's a nightmare like the hundreds I've accumulated over the past year. Erif diving into my mind, and then my mind diving into memory and the terror of death and my failure at my royal ceremony.

But then the dizziness settles, the solid walls gleam red, and I know I'm back. I'm in the red room and that means . . .

"Adraa? Is that you?" Erif seems to materialize from the walls, a figure of pure red with fire hair and coal eyes. Every article of clothing she wears is drenched in shades of red, just like before. Yet in my understanding, in my ability to process all this, her hair seems to nuzzle her neck instead of lashing out. She seems more real and unreal in the span of a second.

"I thought I sensed a haughty eighteen-year-old. What are you doing here? Are you trying to get yourself killed?" she asks.

This can't be happening. "Blood! Am I dead . . . again?"

My hand rises to my throat. I can talk. I *can* speak! Of

course, the first thing I say is a curse. Mother would be . . . unimpressed.

"Not even close, or at least not yet." Erif tilts her head and peers into the hearth that resides in the middle of the room. "But you are bleeding all over the floor."

Sure enough, woven through the flames, an image of me tied to that table appears, my arm cut and bleeding. And this time the memories leading up to my appearance here are clear and in focus. The Dome clinic. Harini's face. Basu's smile. I check my pulse, and it holds a dull but steady rhythm. That's different.

Cautiously, I ask, "So . . . no volcano is erupting? Wickery isn't coming to an end?"

"No," Erif says. "I was in the middle of tea." She lifts a red teacup up, as if any of this is normal. "I wouldn't be making tea during the end-time, and I would surely never call a guest. However, since you're here . . . do you want some?"

I lean forward and check the hearth again. The fire has changed. Now the flames burn in a million little tufts like thousands and thousands of witches and wizards. I didn't notice that before. Or maybe it wasn't like that last time? Blood, this is weird. A million similarities. A million differences.

"No," I answer. "Thank you," I add quickly because the last thing I want is to piss her off. But right now she is as calm as I've ever seen her—soft and warm, like a fire that crackles and exudes life, taking away the shiver of winter.

Erif is the literal embodiment of fire. Danger. Destruction. And today, today I guess it is warmth, comfort. And tea?

"That's probably for the best. I don't exactly know what it would do to you." She examines the hearth again. "But it would most likely be all right since you're powerful enough to get here on your own now."

I step forward. "How did I get here? How does any of this work?"

"Oh." Erif's eyes widen. "Never mind. So you are still somewhat of an idiot." She nods to herself. "That makes more sense. I was about to say you were a little overzealous with the bloodletting and essence spilling. Next time save some for the journey back."

Bloodletting is bad enough, but essence spilling sounds way worse. "My essence?"

"Your connection to me and to magic and to the beyond." Erif gestures to the dripping walls. "I'll stop there. Some things are better left unknown."

Wonderful. It's not like I won't be mulling over *essence* and *the beyond* my entire life now.

"But you truly weren't trying?" she asks. "I felt you calling and calling and—"

"I wasn't trying to get here. Who would—"

I stop, a realization striking me cold even in the heat of the red room.

The memory of a velvety, manipulative voice comes back like a bad dream. *You had your first death. Once you've had your fifth, I'll be impressed.*

Clearly this is something of a habit for Moolek. Is this one of the fundamental things about magic that Moolek knows and we don't? Is that where some of his hatred comes from? Our ignorance of this realm of our gods?

"That's rude. I'll have you know many of my fortes would love to talk to me," Erif says matter-of-factly, and I notice her hair doesn't flare when she speaks, so I believe that was a Goddess of Wickery making a passive-aggressive joke. What kind of life have I led that I even know that? "Though to tell you the truth," Erif says, looking almost shy as she sets her teacup down and sits, "you were my first."

I decide then to utilize everything my mother has ever taught me about manners and politeness. I sit down across from Erif. "Thank you," I say, because what else does one say? She helped me save my country, after all.

"I understand why Htrae invites her blessed over so often," she continues. "I guess it is kind of nice, when you aren't choking, whining, or being a complete idiot."

I was right, then. Htrae, Goddess of Earth, has visitors like Maharaja Moolek.

"Htrae?"

"We aren't all the same. Some of us are more welcoming than others. The other day Laeh was telling me to be more gracious, but she's one to talk. Half her Touched don't even believe in her anymore. I don't think she could open a portal for her fortes even if she wanted to. Wouldn't want anyone dying on her. Though that is how Wodahs likes to invite his, through death only."

She's speaking quickly, but I'm pretty sure she just spilled secrets of mortality and afterlife and . . . My brain hurts.

"Is there anything you can tell me? What of the coming war?"

"Coming war? It has already begun."

"What happened?"

She glares at me. "The volcano. Your imprisonment. The unrest. No wonder you are losing. You didn't even know it had begun?"

I try to sort all that. I did know. But this isn't how war should be waged. Through deception and falsehoods. I have a million questions. What happened at my trial? How did Moolek manipulate my country? But only one thing truly matters. "What are they going to do next?" I ask.

Erif tilts her head. "The future is too hard to pin down. It depends on you."

"Me?"

She sighs. "I can't believe you are my . . . Never mind." She looks me in the eye. "Haven't you figured out your importance in all this? You and a few others are the blurry pieces of the puzzle, which makes things complicated and undefined. It's what Htrae told her blessed. It's why Moolek has come for you."

"Can you make me more powerful, then?" I touch my throat. "Give me my voice back?"

She points at my neck, the side of it, where the netting of designs is burned into my flesh. "You are already the most powerful red forte there is. Any more special treatment and the other gods might spite you. Dloc and I have—"

Suddenly, the fire crackles, cinders flying like the hearth has coughed. It convulses again and the fire seems to shake. Then a bright red light peers out like a beam. The Bloodlurst. They must be done.

Erif snaps toward the fireplace. "Adraa, you need to stop releasing your magic. Now."

I look down at myself. Blood appears, drenching my forearm. "I'm not doing anything," I say, pressing the wound and trying to stanch the flow.

She shifts back to the fire, dropping to her knees in a flutter of red silk. "You've got to get back. I see what's going on now. Blood! Those greedy bastards are taking too much. If you don't wake up soon, you'll die." She looks at the fire and then at me. "I'm going to have to push some magic back into you. It might burn a bit." She smiles and grabs a poker from the fireplace. I remember this all too well. It is going to hurt. A lot.

"Is there any other way to do this besides getting stabbed?" I frown, my displeasure evident.

Erif sighs. "You're very ungrateful, you know that?"

"I wouldn't say it's my biggest flaw."

"That's for sure. It was . . . somewhat nice to talk to you too. Now, please, next time could you wait for an invitation?"

"I'll try."

"That's all I ask." And with that pleasantry taken care of, Erif, Goddess of Fire, stabs me. Not through my chest like last time but into my forearm. I'm happy to report it doesn't hurt nearly as bad as the first time she impaled me. I think we could even be . . . friends?

"One more thing, Adraa, in case you haven't realized it yet. The day of the eruption"—she touches my neck again, right on the Touch she burned into me—"I gave you a little of *my* essence to survive. Because those wizards are using *your* blood to make their substance, your essence has a little bit of my power as well. You can't let them have it. It's more powerful than you can imagine. It needs to be destroyed."

Terror climbs through my gut. I look down at my arm, at the fireplace. "Why do you always bury the lede?"

"My apologies. But I couldn't have you forgetting. Destroy it, Adraa. Destroy every single grain of it." Then she pushes me back into the flames.

CHAPTER THIRTY

◇

I Figure It Out

Adraa

This time when I come back to life, I'm coughing. I realize right away it's because I'm on fire. Literally. Flames rage over my arms. Just like when I call forth and cast fire, they don't hurt, though. All I feel is heat and rage.

Erif really isn't subtle, is she? Though when have I ever seen the Goddess of Fire be subtle? Bloody cryptic, yes, but not subtle.

"Put it out!" Basu shouts. "And take it." Other male voices yell and footsteps pound the floor.

I think I feel water trying to extinguish me, but it's a laughable attempt. I'm the red room brought to life. This is pure magic from Erif herself. Though maybe not, because it feels like my power too. The ropes have long melted away, so I raise my hand and the bloodred flames blaze in a roar of acknowledgment. Upon closer inspection, I realize the flames are coming from the gash on my arm.

I'm not casting my magic as much as leaking it.

Men scream. "She's alive!" one yells, and I don't think I've heard such terror in a long while. Not since I awoke after Mount Gandhak. Only this time I haven't stopped a volcano—I am my own inferno.

I try to peer past the fire, to sort through the clouds of black smoke choking the air. Smoke. Not magic, real smoke! My fellow Voiceless lie tied to their tables, still unconscious. If I don't dull this power somehow, they will die.

But I also have a job to do. Erif gave me this power for a reason, to destroy the Bloodlurst. My not dying might have been part of her thought process too, but I don't like to fool myself. As I take in the scene, I already know the drug is gone. The floor is wiped clean. The disorganized cupboards have been thrown open. Other guards rush to the doorway and surround me, none with Basu's short stature and hairy arms.

A guard in front of me swings with a blaze of purple anchored around his fist. I duck and use his force against him to push him out of the way. I swipe my arm forward and Erif's power blazes outward. Wizards fly through the air from the sheer force of it. Glass shatters, walls crack, the noise of destruction explodes through the air. I run from the room. Up ahead, Basu is about to round the corner. He turns, and we make eye contact. One piercing moment that seems to slow as his face transforms into terror.

"Stop or she dies!" a scared voice cries.

I whip around to find a guard, ashen and bruised, hovering over the blond witch, knife to her throat. Good Gods, this is getting repetitive. I can't let Basu get away. I can't. But a line of blood trickles down the girl's throat and I know the guard will kill her.

As I raise my hands, preparing the shot, I catch movement in my peripheral vision. Harini sits up. The ropes tying her down have burned away.

My fire dims to look like surrender.

"Good. Now—"

I expect an orange spell to fly through the air, but instead Harini stands and hits the guard over the head with the nearest thing she can find—a jar of beetle wings. He thumps to the floor. Harini wobbles, catching a table for support. Burned out.

When I glance back at the hallway, Basu is gone. I'll have to catch up with him after I get everyone out safely. The flames on my arms extinguish and I run over to Harini. She looks at me wide-eyed. If she didn't believe I was Adraa Belwar before, this has settled any doubt.

Okay? I sign to Harini, and she gives a small nod.

Erif's explosive fire has proved to be the distraction we needed. It's good to know that my plan with the bombs would have worked. Funnily enough, all the materials are still on my belt. I'm surprised they didn't do more than throw it in the corner. That's what happens when they think they have the upper hand. Thank Gods we still have Vihaan's stolen skyglider.

Harini and I check each girl's pulse and untie their ropes.

How long until they wake up? I ask, wishing I could do more, cast a diagnostic spell to make sure.

Harini can't cast words into the air, but she moves her hands into words all the same. *Hours* is all I catch.

I look down at my hands. Even with magic at my fingertips, even with the healing spells in mind that could possibly help, Harini doesn't know them, so I can't use it. I can't help them.

You don't know any spell?

She shakes her head.

We can't carry them out of here. Harini can't even cast. So that only leaves . . .

We go. We escape. In a few hours' time I'll have them in the Belwar clinic and in my mother's care. I'll tell Father of the terror happening under his nose. We'll come back with an army of our own. And then I can get Jatin and the others to help find Basu and the Bloodlurst.

Gods. Jatin. Just the thought.

I'll come back.

It hurts to leave the other Voiceless. Even as I set up shields to keep any Guards from entering the clinic, it feels like I'm imprisoning them in a tomb, like I've become what I hate most. But I don't know what else to do. It could be Erif's power fading, but I feel my physical capabilities waning, the toll of the experiment and Erif's magic hitting me.

Guards are running through the halls. With a shield of concealing black magic, I half run, half drag Harini back to solitary confinement. No one else is heading this way. It's the least likely place we'd go, which is why we choose it. Harini sits down as I unleash Vihaan's skyglider, flying to the skylights above. With

Erif's magic I don't need a bomb. I use what she gave me and blast the hole open.

It explodes with an earth-shattering noise. I swerve out of the way as rubble rains down. Then I fly, quick and swift, the taste of freedom *right* there.

When I do get to the lip of the prison, I edge toward the open sky, the horizon filling my line of sight. But as I turn, the cityscape of Belwar doesn't greet me. No, a screen of purple floats above and covers everything like a dense fog. I reach out gingerly, a part of me afraid it's not an illusion but another barrier I hadn't accounted for. When my fingers touch the smoke, a splotch of the illusion whips away. I swipe my hand across it and push myself upward.

My eyes have to adjust to the sudden daybreak and streaks of pink, the sun having just peeked over the horizon. How long was I under? Hours, or a whole day? I lost count of how many days I've been in here. That changes now.

When I peer out at the outline of steep mountains, I twist, realizing I must be facing Naupure. But even as I turn every sense tells me this is wrong. The air is too dry and cold. The smell lacks sea salt. The stars shine too bright. And the landscape is one continuous array of snow-covered peaks.

I take a shuddering breath and stagger back like I've been punched in the gut. Almost slipping off the wayward skyglider, I steady myself and shoot upward, into the sky. This can't be right. It's simply dark.

I fly two meters, enough for my vision to stretch for miles.

"*Vardrenni,*" I cast, searching for the lights, the sounds, the flying platforms, the bay and further into the ocean. Nothing but trees and mountains and the complete silence of isolation. What the blood? This can't be right.

I dive back down to Harini. She signs, but I haven't had the time to learn her language. Yet I can read her worry, her concern. Her fear. Harini's hands stop, then slowly sign one question. *What is it?*

I look at her, not bothering to collect my features into anything other than horror. *It's not what. It's where.*

CHAPTER THIRTY-ONE

◇

Fly Forward

Jatin

I've never been so confused in my entire life. "What do you mean you *know* where she is?"

"It's a long story. I'll tell you on our way."

"Our way where?" I yell as we push our way back down the halls.

"To Agsa. To a very different kind of prison."

We tear up the steps. Kalyan freezes a guard to the wall and apologizes. I'm right behind Fiza, the others following and peppering her with a volley of questions. "How do you know?" Hiren asks. "What kind of prison?" Riya shouts.

Fiza doesn't answer.

We track our way back to the hole. Fiza throws a sharp jab of magic at the illusion, fighting to pull it open by herself.

"Fiza, what is going on?"

"Adraa's in trouble. Do I need to say more? You want to sit around and talk, or do you want to get flying? Bloody trust me."

"Driswodahs," I cast in answer, and tear the smoke screen open. She's right.

◇ ◇ ◇

We fly for hours. We don't have time to plan or coordinate like we did getting into the Dome. We don't even have time to talk, Fiza's moving so fast.

I fly up to her multiple times and she blows me off again and again. Her responses vary from "talking slows us down" to a simple shake of her head and "I can't."

We fly over the Belwar border, rushing past one of the last big flying stations. No one has slept in hours and I'm worried Kalyan or Riya are going to burnout and drop from the sky.

When the next flying platform winks into sight, I make my decision. Prisha must see it too, because she flies up next to me.

"Jatin, listen, Riya and Kalyan are too proud, but if we keep this up they'll die," she says, sounding a whole lot like Adraa.

"You're right. *Pavria,*" I cast, hunching down to gather speed and catch up with Fiza. Armoring myself with a tone of authority, I point ahead. "We're stopping."

She doesn't say anything, simply nods.

We land thirty minutes later on an unattended flying platform floating above the Alps of Alconea. It's a small one meant for nothing more than catching your breath. There's no little inn or restaurant, just five meters by five meters of floating stone. A domed roof with cups to catch rainwater is the sole amenity.

It's late, so only the bright snow on the peaks rising to meet us in jagged angles hint at the landscape. That's enough for me to know it's the last place one would want to burnout.

My muscles ache in protest. I think they'd abandon me if they could. I believe I'd let them too. For the first time in my life I have windburn, so even my skin is irritated with me. I can officially declare this has been one of the worst days of my life.

Kalyan slumps forward and almost crushes Prisha, who catches him before I can assist.

"Three hours ago, we passed a place with pillows." Hiren scowls at Fiza. "Tell us, is Adraa in that much danger?"

We all turn to Fiza, waiting for answers. Kalyan and Riya prop themselves up from where they've fallen to the ground in exhaustion.

Finally, she turns. "Yes. I believe she is."

◇ ◇ ◇

Riya and Kalyan fall asleep fast. I watch as Riya tries to fight it, glaring daggers at Fiza. But even in hatred, exhaustion wins. I should be getting sleep too, but I can't spoil the one opportunity where wind isn't swallowing my voice.

I approach Hiren and Prisha, who are deep in whispered conversation.

"We should go back. Your parents will murder me knowing you are gone and I'm the one responsible. I don't know if I can even be your guard after this, let alone—"

"Hiren, I know. But she's my sister. And if she's in as much danger as Fiza says, I have to go."

"Exactly—danger, unknown danger. Let Jatin figure this out."

"Hiren, you know the last thing I said to Adraa. I can't let that—"

They spot me and turn away, hushing their voices with magic. Prisha gestures wildly as she begins to cry. She and Hiren hug. I trudge to the north corner of the station, where Fiza peers into the expanse of darkness.

"It's so quiet this time of year," Fiza says. "Or maybe Agsa is always quiet compared to Belwar and Naupure."

"I need to know how you know about this place, whatever it is," I say. "And how did Sims know you'd know?"

"Jatin, why do you always ask the questions you don't want the answer to?" she says, still not bothering to turn toward me.

"Because those are the most important ones. And as someone once said, I need to work on asking questions. I'm trying to get better at it, especially when my enemies seem to be one step ahead of me."

She twists. "Do I really look like your enemy?"

"Why don't you tell me, so I don't have to keep guessing? It's bloody tiring." For a second she doesn't flinch. Then her face betrays her. She's grappling with something. Something that terrifies her. A chill, colder than any wind, cuts me to the bone. What could be worse than the Dome? What is so bad that Fiza is forfeiting our trust and the alliance she came to Naupure for in the first place?

Finally, she meets my eyes again. "So many of the wizards in my life—my older brothers, my father—they yell and shout when I don't do what they say. They try to control me. At the academy you were the only one who didn't treat me like that. I need that Jatin now. Trust me. I promise you, I'll find her."

"I'm sorry, Fiza, but you've driven us hard all day, which tells me two things. Adraa's life is in danger, and you're scared. I need—"

She steps back. "Maybe I'm sick and tired of what *you* need." She sighs. "Right now, I need to sleep. We both do."

"Fiza!" I plead, reaching for her hand. Before I can think it through, I step close to her. "What do you want?"

She gasps at our close proximity and raises her chin to look me right in the eye. She rises up on her toes. I feel her breath on my lips and I'm terrified of what I'm about to offer, what I'm willing to do.

"You'll never accept me if I tell you the truth," she says.

"That's not true," I say, so desperate for an answer I can't tell whether I'm lying.

"And what are you willing to do for it?"

I pause, and we stare at one another. I don't know if I'm able to say it aloud. She knows, though. I can see it in her eyes.

Suddenly, she pulls back. "I'm not that desperate. I won't accept fake."

Before I register what I just did, she turns and strides off.

I let her go. She promised to help find Adraa. That's what I have to focus on. I slump, a mixture of relief and self-hatred tearing through me. It feels like my brain is burning out, the emotions pouring out of me too quickly. *Good Gods. What's wrong with me?*

For the first time, today's events come back in full focus. The rajas of Belwar sentenced Adraa to life in the Dome and then found a look-alike witch to take her place. Adraa was whisked off, out of the bloody country, for who knows what reasons. Ira Belwar's words come back to me. *There is a reason they are keeping her alive. And every way I look at it, that reason cannot be good.*

Find her! Free her! The pounding mantra in my mind accompanies me to sleep.

◇

CHAPTER THIRTY-TWO

I'm Going to Find Some Answers

Adraa

I fall to my knees, staring down at the well of dark water and feeling like it's sucking me in the longer I look into its murky depths. How did this happen? I saw the Dome. I *entered* the Dome. I'm . . . I'm not in the Dome. I piece together my memories until something doesn't fit. That cell they took me to when they stole my voice. Square. No windows. Those two guards I've never seen since. There was some movement, slight and unsettling, but nothing akin to . . .

I was in there for five days. Maybe it wasn't to break me, but to deliver me to . . .

Far as I can tell most of us were picked up off the street or were led here under false pretenses, Harini had written. It was there the whole time. I look at Harini now, who's staring, awaiting answers and for me to fly her out of here. Good Gods!

I stand, jerking toward the entrance.

Harini signs. All I catch is the word *where.*

Change of plans. I'm getting everyone out. And I'm going to find some answers.

She blocks my path, gesturing to the door like I've lost it. And maybe I have, because we almost got killed and I'm going back.

You don't have to come. I can fly you out now. This isn't the Dome. I don't even know if this is a real prison. But we aren't in Belwar. I can't pop to safety and then come back for everyone else left in this terror. I will not leave innocent people to become fuel for the Vencrin. *But I'm not saving myself until they are all free,* I cast into the air.

Harini is a flurry of movement, signing fast. I watch every motion. I see my name and then at the end one descriptor—*selfish.*

I don't know if she's calling me selfish or willing me to be selfish, but either way I've made up my mind. I was selfish the day I decided to take my royal ceremony test to become a rani when I knew Moolek was planning something. I won't make that mistake again. A true rani helps her people.

I shake my head. The action says enough. In fact, it speaks volumes.

Besides, bad people, wizards like the ones capable of kidnapping innocent people and destroying them, will always think the worst of others. Quite frankly, altruism may be the last thing they expect. They'll assume we escaped when we'll actually be right under their noses.

Feet pound down the hallway, finally coming in search of the explosion. I sweep my hands up in black magic as Harini and I crouch near the door. Perfect timing.

I use the wizards' momentum against them. It only takes a push, and they fall with a scream and an eventual splash. Under the cover of my illusion, Harini leans over the edge in interest and then turns to me. *You have a plan?*

I just threw out a rational and easy escape, so I settle down to think. To get our fellow Voiceless out, we'll need help. And to get everyone out, I need to get to the warden's tower.

As I think, Harini works her hands and slowly a wisp of orange magic sings into the air. Her burnout's wearing off.

I've got to get to the tower and release the rest of the cells. I need you to create a distraction big enough that I can get there unnoticed. Then you need to go to the clinic and help the others. I'll meet you there when I can.

I unbuckle the ingredients from Vihaan's stolen belt, and smooth out the herbs and straighten the wicks.

Is this . . . ?

I read her confused face and smile. *The distraction? Yes.*

Harini and I build bombs. By the fifth one I've come to yet another decision. These will be more than a distraction in the end. Once everyone's out, I'd like to see this place burn. I'll need to track down the Bloodlurst made from my blood eventually, but why let the facility keep standing in the meantime?

We wriggle back out of the cavern and I give Harini a share of the explosives. We've gone over how to light them and how long she'll have to get away, but I still feel uneasy about her being involved. I glance at her one more time. *Are you going to be okay?*

She rolls her eyes. *Gods, you're sentimental. Don't die, Adraa.* Before the words fade, she's rounded the corner.

Without a spell to conceal the sound of my footsteps, I bend my knees and tread lightly. I ease a glance around the corner. Three guards stand between me and the nearest narrow pathway to the tower. I clutch a bomb, take a breath, light the wick, and throw it as hard as I can in the other direction. The vibrations knock silt from the cavern-like walls. It reminds me of Mount Gandhak. But it has the desired effect. The wizards run. Then so do I.

I'm vulnerable for the next few minutes, even as I wear a black magic camouflage. Vulnerable to shots of magic. To countless spells that could stop me. And that doesn't even account for any clumsy accidents on my part, like falling off this bloody thing. I sprint toward the tower, one careful step at a time, until I reach the door, pull at the vinelike handle, and throw myself in. The stairs are clear as I blast up them.

It's quiet when I get to the windowed room. And even more ominous when I open the door.

The warden turns slowly, deliberately, and meets my eyes. "This is a fine surprise. Every guard I have is searching for you, and yet you come running straight to me. Thank you for making this easy."

So this is why no one pelted me with magic while I was crossing the chasm to get here. Why the tower wasn't fortified against me. He wanted me to come.

The warden rolls up his sleeves and his Touch tells me of his power. A yellow forte, and a seven or an eight at least. Maybe even a nine. He lifts a pair of glowing cuffs from his kurta and throws them at me. "If you don't cuff yourself immediately, you can be sure that once this is over, your friends will undergo indescribable pain."

All these wizards really think they are so good at threats, especially him.

You can be sure this won't be easy, I cast, kicking the cuffs to the side and rushing forward, arms already blazing.

Erif's magic ignites. Right as my bloodred magic is about to reach the warden, another color—purple—flashes from behind him. I swerve, ducking and rolling. When I lurch upward, the warden is falling forward, slumping to his knees, those un-wavering eyes rolling backward. Then he lands on the ground with a thump. Ekani stands behind him, hand raised. "I shouldn't have done that," she says. "But I guess today is as good as any to finally fight back."

Pure shock hits me. Ekani. She just knocked out the warden. Ekani, the guard.

"What are you staring at? Is this a prison break or what?"

I snap to attention and rush over to the mechanics of magic that line the walls. Hundreds of wheels hold the cells suspended. I pause for a second, trying to figure it all out, then Ekani pushes forward. "I can do it, but as soon as these cells open, guards will be here in seconds. I can get the women out," she reassures me. "There's a back door in the fighting arena that only a few of us know about. You'll find us in the mountains, heading south. But we'll need a dis-traction."

I gesture toward the controls. *Do it,* I write in the air. *And leave the guards to me.*

Ekani casts. Her spell sets off a mechanism that pulls each and every cell up to their platform, then she casts another that unlocks the doors. We both look at the dozens of women stepping out of their cages, unscheduled and unguarded for the first time.

I nod my thanks, still unclear why she's helping me. But I don't have time to spell out my questions. From our vantage point we can see guards rushing toward the tower. Six of them. Others are already airborne and trying to corral the escapees. We run from the room and down the tower.

"Don't underestimate them," Ekani warns.

I nod again, when, from the depths of the prison, one of the bombs goes off. An alarm, which I didn't think this place was equipped with, screeches in answer. Even beyond the alarm's cry, the heavy pounding of footsteps echoes off the walls. They're coming fast.

Go, help the others. I sweep my hands toward another walkway. *I'll handle them.*

◇

CHAPTER THIRTY-THREE

Second Time Is the Charm

Jatin

Nothing of distinction marks our journey or our destination. One moment we're flying over endless mountains and forests, and then suddenly Fiza leads us into a descent. The rest of us seem to hold our breath. I wait for the ground to flatten into farmland, for wooden structures that dot the landscape like most, if not all, Agsa villages. The descent doesn't stop, though, and neither does Fiza. Kalyan and Riya and I exchange frowns; we're all thinking the same thing.

"Is this where she kills us?" Riya asks darkly.

Okay, so we aren't all thinking the *exact* same thing.

I open my mouth to respond, when I see it, rising above the tallest trees like a boulder. But it isn't a rounded mountaintop or even the domed roof of a temple. It's a fortress I've seen only once before.

I'm looking at the Dome's mirror image.

Hiren swerves his skyglider to line up with ours. I realize a second later we've all halted midair. "I thought there was only one of those," he marvels.

"I guess not," Riya answers.

"But what's it doing in the middle of the nowhere?" he asks.

"Being a secret obviously," Prisha says. "Especially if even you didn't know about it." I have to agree with her logic there.

Fiza turns back to us.

"How are we going in?" Riya's arms start to light up as she talks.

"Not arms blazing," Fiza says. "The best way is the easiest."

"Now you feel like sharing. How's that?" Riya practically snarls.

"Being escorted, obviously." Fiza drops through the trees to the ground, latching her skyglider on her belt as she lands.

"What did she just say?"

"She's gotten us this far," Kalyan reasons, following Fiza's descent. My best friend has gone with the flow his entire life; I shouldn't be surprised that he hasn't stopped now. I plummet after him, falling through the autumn canopy and into the dense understory.

Riya eventually follows suit and buckles her skyglider with a snap of her belt. "I don't like this, Jatin. I haven't liked any of this, but especially *not* this. She practically announced she knows this place, and this place knows her."

"But we already knew that, didn't we?"

So we walk forward. Once the tree line breaks, the Dome replica looms, half the size of the real Dome, but from this angle the curved walls seem to continue upward for miles. It sits in a field with nothing marking the location but one long dirt road. A half-abandoned wagon sits off to the side. Nothing moves. No birds fly overhead. Trees rise crisply into the air with no sway. Catching the light above, I can see that a black illusion spell reigns over the structure, but it's clearly not a powerful one since I can see it without magic.

Fiza turns. "Okay, so I'm going in and then—"

"No," I interrupt. "That's not happening."

"Jatin, you think they won't recognize you?"

"It's time for answers, Fiza. Who are they? What is this place?" I feel my friends press in and around me, circling her.

"Start with how you know Adraa is in there," Riya says, as stone cold as I have ever heard her.

Fiza raises her eyebrows, and I know she's about to say something snarky and defensive. Then the ground rumbles and a trail of gray smoke billows from the side of the structure. An alarm blares. Then the gates rip open and a bunch of men dressed in orange Dome uniforms burst out and take to the skies.

Adraa!

"Change of plans!" I shout, charging forward.

I whip out a rivulet of magic, disrupting the nearest sky-glider's tail stream. The wizard falls and tumbles to the dirt. He moans as I grab his collar and lift him up. "What's happened?"

"She was pure fire!" the guard hollers. "I've never seen anything . . . I value my life more than that." He kicks out, breaking my hold, and takes off running, not even bothering with flight.

I turn to the gate. *"Tvarenni,"* I cast, and sprint. The others follow.

We pass a few fleeing guards, but they don't give us a second glance. Whatever Adraa has done, it's scared the sense of duty right out these wizards and witches. Then we enter the walled fortress, which is even more a maze of tunnel-like hallways than the one we just left.

"What now? Where is she?" I ask Fiza.

"I don't know exactly. Based on what Sims said, though, she's here."

"Oh, she's here," Riya and I say simultaneously.

"You heard that wizard," I add. "We split up. Riya, Prisha, Kalyan, try to find the cells. Hiren, to the guards' quarters. I'm going to find solitary confinement."

"I think this place has a basement. I'm going there," Fiza says.

"Wait," I say as they all start to move. I unpocket the orbs of firelight, which glow to life in the darkness. "Here. If any of you find her and she's hurt or burned out, this could help."

"What are we supposed to do with this exactly?" Fiza asks, taking one of the most precious spells I own. It's some of the last firelight Adraa ever created.

Riya steps in. "You let her take back her magic."

Fiza frowns. "Are you telling me Adraa can reabsorb a spell?"

"How else do you think she stopped Mount Gandhak?" I say, before running down a hallway.

I'm coming, Adraa. I'm almost there.

◇

CHAPTER THIRTY-FOUR

Saved by the Red Woman

Adraa

I'm standing right inside the tower, the sounds of an army bearing down on the other side. I have to buy Ekani time to lead the prisoners to safety and I have to get to the Voiceless and help Harini so we can get out of here. I just have to get through this fight. By myself. My first instinct is to throw open the door and charge the wizards. But I stop, examining the wood. I don't have green magic to manipulate it, but as voices shout on the other side to surrender, I come up with a plan.

Zaktirenni, I cast into my legs, and kick open the door with enough force it explodes off its hinges and flies through the air. Guards shoot spells at it, creating a cloud of multicolored smoke. I wait until the firing stops, for the tension to heighten, for the fear to set in.

And then I step out of the tower, my upper body engulfed in flames, the last of Erif's magic pouring through me.

Most of the guards on skygliders flee right then and there. Others turn and run. The ones that do stay hesitate.

Round two. This time without limits.

I run forward, letting the flames encase me as I craft barriers of fire and then punch them outward in fireballs. It works well. The narrow platform doesn't give the guards room to run or duck. I fight my way through those who don't dive off on their skygliders, rolling, twisting, and beating the guardsmen back.

I need to get to the platforms so I'm not out in the open. Arrows of magic rain down on me and a blazing blue one slices the top of my shoulder. I infuse energy into my legs and run for it. When I make it to the cliffside and stop, the fire goes out, the end of Erif's power.

There are only two guards left standing.

"You!" the one on the left shouts like a halt, as if I were trying to hide. *"Astraraw,"* he casts, and another blue dagger hurtles toward me. I sidestep it and charge forward. One of the guards is Untouched, and he pulls a knife at the same time the blue forte manifests a sword. Without conscious thought, I drop and slide forward, crafting a shield above my head as I ram one foot into the Untouched wizard's kneecap. As he crumples, I swing my other leg to knock the other wizard over. He jumps and sweeps his sword down. I raise my shield and it narrows to protect my arm. Blue and red clash in an angry purple, spraying the walls like dye.

We hold like that, a breathless second of sheer strength bearing down and trying to break one another.

"You trying to be a hero, huh? Trying to play at being the Red Woman?"

I start to form a wind spell with my other hand to throw him off me, but the blue forte guard beats me to it. A gust blows me back, right to the edge of the jagged cliff. I twist to sit up and cast when my muscles spasm and my Touch dims like a light. No!

Because it's occurred so many times before in my life, I know at once what is going to happen, what *is* happening. The Bloodlurst experiment and that fire. I'm at my limit. Erif was right. They took too much, and I've used up the power she gave to me. I'm about to burnout.

Tingling numbness seeps from skin to bone and then there is no "about to." I *am* burning out.

The guard doesn't seem to understand. As I slump in the dirt, he pauses, probably thinking I have some trick up my sleeve. I wish I did. I *really* wish I did.

"What's wrong? Not feeling well?" he sneers, but it's also laced with uncertainty. Those flames terrified him. If only I could conjure them again.

He reaches for me, but I have enough energy left to duck and roll. A boot connects to my ribs. I release a soundless cry as I'm sent reeling backward.

"So you finally burned out, that right?"

He grabs my arm and drags me to my feet. I've never had anyone grab me like this during burnout. If they had, I'd be firmly acquainted with the agony and spend the rest of my life avoiding such a fate. It's like he's crushing my bones. Then he squeezes, and I crumple.

He drops me, my shoulder screaming at the impact.

"You aren't getting out of here alive. No one is coming to help. The real Red Woman *isn't* coming to save you."

"She isn't coming because she's already here," a voice says from the darkness. A red whip lashes out and wraps around the guard's waist. He jerks backward, like he's being sucked through a tube. A cracking thud echoes off the curved walls.

A woman steps from the shadows. And not just any woman— the Red Woman.

We stare at one another. Me at her. Her at me. It's eerily like looking in a mirror, like living in another dimension. I know my vision gets murky during burnout, but this is next level. How much blood did I lose?

She runs toward me and pulls something bright from her pocket, offering it like a gift. I look up at . . . at . . . firelight. Firelight! This is definitely a dream, right? My mind red rooming into delusion and introspection? Am I supposed to behold her and see my other self? The one more capable of this pain and torture. The one I created to frighten the Vencrin and empower me when I felt weak.

"Here. Take it. Do whatever you do." The firelight falls into my lap and the heat of it wakes me up. I pick up my firelight, the red ball of magic and light flickering in recognition. Or maybe that's my imagination.

Harini never taught me the signs for my firelight spell, obviously, but I still try, signing fire, calling to Erif, and motioning both hands toward myself like I did on Mount Gandhak. Above all, I concentrate on the intention.

It works—the magic, *my magic,* absorbs into my Touch. The designs on my wrist brighten and then dim. Months ago, at the top of an erupting volcano, that spell was the hardest thing I've ever attempted. I should be surprised I can do it without my voice, that it worked at all. But that spell has become a part of me, like firelight, ingrained in my magic. I clench my fist, then open it. It's not much, but it's enough. With a little bit of time I'll be fine.

"You can thank me now," my impersonator says.

My eyes flicker upward, and I start at the sight of the black uniform, the shield spells embedded in red swirls, the mask adhered to her face. This is real. She is real and . . . and she hasn't cast the mask properly—it's just smoke concealing her face without all the extra infused magic. I throw out a spell to fix it. She startles, her hands flying to her face. But understands what I'm doing pretty quick, because she stills.

"Whoa. That's . . . wow," she whispers, turning her head from side to side. "I can see everything."

I sign and the words float between us. *You can thank me later.*

❖ ❖ ❖

As my impersonator and I run through the hallways, I try not to stare. Gods, this is beyond weird. After a few cutting glances, I notice there is a dusting of shadow around her hair, making the braid swing a little unnaturally. Illusion spells. She's wearing a smoke screen of black magic to cast her in my likeness.

It's bloody impressive, but why?

Finally, I can't take it anymore. I need to know who I'm following. If this place has taught me anything, it's about whom to put your trust in. My list is quite short.

I tug at her elbow and sign the simple question into existence. *Who are you?*

Before she can answer, orange and green spells sizzle overhead, one missing me by a few centimeters. We duck behind a pillar.

"My name is Fiza, Lady of Agsa," she says as she fires a spell over her shoulder.

A Lady of Agsa? That's unexpected.

I weave my hands. *I assume you know who I am.*

She nods like the word *unfortunately* should follow.

But maybe I'm reading into it. And maybe it's my own . . . face. Do I always look *that* serious and angry? I mean, Gods, no wonder I frighten people. With the mask, the uniform, and the whole thing . . . I'm scary.

I hold back a smile because a part of me kind of likes it. I made some fine design choices back in the day if I do say so myself.

An eyebrow rises above her mask. "Why are you smiling?" she asks.

I wave her question away.

A blaze of green smoke twists over the corner of the pillar. I cut it off and stamp a shield into place so we are covered.

More importantly, who sent you? I ask.

"Who do you think?"

I don't know if I should be impressed with this witch or hate her. It's already bloody annoying casting a conversation during a shoot-out. Now I have to try to do it with the likes of Miss Fake Me, who answers questions with questions.

Orange arrows hit my shield hard, the last one piercing it. Okay, I'm done.

With a sigh I pull another explosive out of my belt, light my fingertips on fire, and then throw as hard as I can. I watch as the pouch of herbs soars past the guards. One eyes the bag as it flies overhead. I can see the moment when he decides to shoot it down.

Blood!

"What in Wickery was—"

I haul her down, pulling up the shield like a blanket. A second later the hallway explodes, much closer than I had planned. When the smoke dissipates, the wizards are down and the hallway is cleared. I finally turn to the girl. *I don't know who sent you. That's why I asked. So why don't you bloody tell me?* I sign.

She stands and looks at the two groaning men. "Your guards, your sister, and your . . . and Raja Jatin."

What? All of them! My heartbeat picks up at the thought of Jatin, here.

So he didn't listen to me. I can't say I'm mad. Though . . . I look at her one more time. I swear if Jatin tried to replace me in my absence, he's a dead man.

Another pair of feet echo down the hall, coming for us, but

this time the girl, Fiza, unspools her magic like rope and throws it out, tying it around the wizard's hands and pulling hard. The man collapses amid the black char of the explosion.

Did everyone at the academy learn the rope trick? I really need to learn that spell.

I glance at her, my gaze drawn to the heavy Touch up her arm. One sleeve is pulled up to her forearm. It's enough for me to see it, the red splotch on her elbow. Fiza notices me noticing and quickly flips the cloth back down.

Bloodlurst user. No, an addict.

A commotion that sounds a whole lot like a fight clatters from below us. One look and both of us face the stairs. I push her to the back of my mind and tune in to my senses, the full-out battle we seem to have landed ourselves in.

"Sounds like they need my help," Fiza says.

Her help? What do I look like to her? Powerless? Who took down those hallway guards? Or at least most of the hallway guards . . .

She charges ahead before I can correct her. I'm left to follow.

Blood. Is this how Jatin feels being my partner?

◇ ◇ ◇

As we get closer, I already know where the noise is coming from—the cafeteria.

Fiza rushes to barge in, but I hold her back and signal how

we should throw the doors open at the same time. I make the hand movements and then hold up three fingers.

"I can't understand you."

I try really hard not to roll my eyes. What's a simpler scouting message than "on three"? So instead I ready myself and gesture to the door. Let's just go whenever she feels like it, then. What good is synchronization and teamwork anyway?

Fiza plows her way in and I quickly follow suit, slamming the door open hard in case anyone is on the other side. My hands jet out, ready for an onslaught. But no one notices or cares about our arrival. All the action is meters away, where a swarm of guards converge on the other side of the hall.

Flashes of smoke and color light up the fight. More uniforms stream from the southern corridor and the mass of bodies grows ever bigger. They're all running here, toward the prison's very center. Which means one of two things: either Harini and I succeeded in freeing everyone and they have already escaped, or we have epically failed and now the biggest threat is . . .

A wizard is blown backward, iced to the ground, and when I follow the path of the white mist, I see him.

Across the hall Riya and Kalyan fight on either side of the love of my life. He looks . . . I don't know. Angry. Exhausted. Commanding. But more than anything he looks good. This is the closest we've been in weeks. So *good* is an elaborate understatement. He's here. He somehow found me when I don't even know where I am.

Jatin glances up a second later and our eyes lock. All the

thudding terror washes away as he lights up and smiles. Disregard *good*. He's the most wonderful thing I've ever seen. And Gods, I almost forgot what that smile could do to me.

His eyes flicker to my left and I whirl my arms to craft a shield as a sword slashes down on me. A guardsman roars as he presses down on my boundary, but with a twist of my weight he careens to the side. I untangle the sweep of red magic into wind and shove it at the guard's chest. He blows backward in a jumble of limbs and crashes against the wall.

My name rings across the chamber as Jatin yells for me. I glance over at his group, overwhelmed by a surge of responders. So much for the plan of distraction and sneaking everyone out of here. We're going to have to fight our way through.

I already feel my arms tingling, but I push through. I'm back in a ring, doling out a punch instead of fire. Jatin does the same, shoving forward and through the circling horde of guards. They fan outward, and I see Prisha dueling with two swords in her hands, and Hiren next to her wrapping a shadow of black smoke around a guard's torso.

Then I'm back to Jatin, who barely looks at the guards he's tossing in the air. I start to count the distance. Five meters. Three guards run up on my right side, and I kick a table at them, pinning them against the wall. Four meters. I take a food tray and hurl it at a guard's head. Three meters. I can feel the cold surge of ice as Jatin entraps someone. Two meters. I twist and create a blast of wind.

And then he's there, right there.

We stand in front of each other, a second of unsureness

bridging the space as we gulp in air. "Adraa," he whispers, and, like the first time we kissed, we both move at the same moment. His arms encircle me, embracing and lifting me up at the same time.

"I'll never be late again," he whispers into my hair, over and over again. "Never."

I inhale his crisp mountain smell, taking the moment in full before having to translate what's happened to me, what Basu and the rest have destroyed and why I don't answer him right away. With his arms still wrapped around me, Jatin turns his head and I bend as well, wanting his lips on mine.

But he doesn't press in for a kiss.

He speaks. One little word.

"Adraa?"

CHAPTER THIRTY-FIVE

◇

Break Out

Jatin

"Adraa? Say something. Are you okay?"

Her face crumples. She opens her mouth and then closes it. Tears fill her eyes, and I can't tell whether it's relief that I'm here or anger that I couldn't get here sooner. Because blood, I'm not just late. I should never have let any of this happen.

I slowly cup her cheek. "Please, say something."

She doesn't. Instead she gathers my kurta in her fists and smashes her mouth to mine. I kiss her as though I'll never be able to kiss her again, what I had thought and feared for weeks.

"Gods' sake, you guys really need to find a room," Fiza snaps, shooting off boundaries like she's throwing daggers. I'd happily take a room instead of reconnecting in this madness. But what can I do? Our life is madness now.

Adraa pulls away and looks at Fiza, who is decked out in her Red Woman illusion for some reason.

"I can explain that," I start.

I expect anger or cutting sarcasm. But all I get is a raised eyebrow and a small shake of her head.

"Adraa?" I realize a beat late she *still* hasn't said anything, hasn't answered me. "Adraa?"

Biting her lip and pulling back, she swishes her arms in a circle. Her mouth doesn't move, no spell is cast, and yet one word, my name, appears above her. *Jatin.*

What in Wickery? "How did you . . ." Did she just . . .

A movement later, and her bloodred words smear and new ones replace them. *Jatin, I can't speak. They took my voice.*

◇ ◇ ◇

Anguish and anger rise in me like a flood. "How? Why?" I sputter, questions battling for attention until the biggest one slams into me and refuses to unhook itself from my thoughts—*who.* Because someone took her voice. They bloody took her voice.

"You can still cast?"

She nods and with a smile shoots a stream of red smoke at an approaching guard. I watch him fly backward with a roar and marvel at her all over again. Oh, she's going to rub this in for a long time. I don't think I can adequately and truthfully declare, "I win," ever again. Today, though, I'll happily admit defeat.

"Adraa!" Prisha yells, unweaving the ribbons of twigs from the wicker table and tying a wizard down with them. It's impressive.

"*Simaraw,*" Riya shouts, and a purple shield cuts across the room. That done, Riya and Adraa run into each other's arms.

"Gods, I missed you." Riya glares at me over Adraa's shoulder. "You couldn't have put up a barrier so we could all have a proper reunion?" Riya hugs Adraa even closer. "Please, don't leave me alone with them again."

"Sorry, Riya," I confess.

"Hey! We weren't all that bad," Hiren chastises as he slumps to the ground. Kalyan simply shakes his head.

"Yeah, I guess most of you are okay." Riya pulls back and side-eyes Fiza, who is steps behind me, mask still in place and fitting her well, better, actually, than I've ever seen.

Prisha approaches slowly, her face cautious. "I want to say how sorry I am. I messed up and—" Adraa wraps her in a hug before she can say more.

Riya seems to catch on then. "Adraa? Are you okay?"

"They took her voice," I say, so Adraa doesn't have to spell it out again.

Riya presses at her throat. "They what? That's possible?"

Prisha pulls back from her hug. "Someone took your voice?"

Basu, Adraa writes in the air.

We all stare. Recognition singes my resolve. The distributor who sold firelight to the Vencrin is behind this? "I'll kill him."

Riya takes a step forward. "And if Jatin can't, I will."

We do need to find him, but we can discuss this later, Adraa signs.

"You're right. Let's get out of this place," I say.

Adraa pulls back. *We can't*, her red words read.

"Why not? What am I missing?" I ask.

Adraa shakes her head, then her hands move. I wait. *We*

298

have to free all the prisoners. This isn't a prison. It's a facility making Bloodlurst.

Bloodlurst! I stare at Adraa. All these months. All this time! It wasn't under our noses; it was miles and miles away.

There are seven witches still down in the clinic. We have to get them out. I need your help.

I don't exactly get it, how and why they need this whole place to make Bloodlurst, but there isn't time for questions.

A second later, Riya vocalizes my thought. "Change of plans, then."

"I wish someone had said something a little sooner. I wasn't trying to knock any of them unconscious," Kalyan says dryly, gesturing to the dozen or so men on the other side of Riya's boundary, who have risen up and are preparing their own defensive spells.

Hiren looks offended. "You weren't what?"

I reach into my belt for the firelight and offer it to Adraa. One by one the others follow my lead. Adraa moves her hands and absorbs her magic, bloodred glowing up her bare arms. I noticed her revealing top when I saw her across the room, but I think the rest of the group finally clues in, because Riya pipes up with, "What the blood are you wearing?"

Adraa waves a hand and gives Riya a "don't get me started" look.

Hiren chimes in with "I like—" before I stop him with a glare and Prisha swats his arm.

"We can do this nonsense later. Let's get out of here," Fiza says as a streak of magic hits Riya's shields.

"You ready for this?" I ask Adraa.

Want to make this interesting?

"That depends. What's the winner get?"

She raises an eyebrow and steps forward.

I'm winning regardless.

CHAPTER THIRTY-SIX

◇

I'm Asked a Question

Adraa

Jatin and I dive through the shield as Riya opens it.

I want to ask them all so much. I ache to speak, to shoot out my questions, but Jatin needs his mouth to shout out spells. It'll have to wait. But as I trip a guard, I realize just how battle worn these men are. Jatin must sense it too, because he takes a step closer to me.

"Your parents are fine," he says before he frosts someone to the wall.

I take out a guard and point to Jatin, mouthing, *Dad?* so it's clear. He tries to hide it, but his shoulders slump. "My dad is very sick, but very much alive. Your mom thinks it's poison."

Someone poisoned Maharaja Naupure?

"Prisha is fine, as you can see. Pretty broken up about where things ended with you, though."

I nod, digesting it all. Family okay. Belwar not in peril. Now we just have to get out of here, get everyone to safety, and get

my Bloodlurst back. Though there's still the whole issue re-
garding my trial and Moolek's influences.

Have you figured out how Moolek got into everyone's heads?
I finally ask.

"What do you mean?"

I frown and take down the last guard with a firm punch, and
then twist back around. *I told you that. At the trial. I yelled it to
you.*

"I . . ."

I step forward. No. It can't be. Not when all my hope rested
on the fact that while I was in the Dome, Jatin was figuring it all
out. I can tell the others are paying attention to us, but I don't
care. *I told you to investigate Moolek. That somehow, he got into
all our heads, made the lies seem believable.*

I look to everyone else, the people I love and trust beyond
anyone else. *Tell me you haven't all spent the last month trying
to rescue me?*

All eyes remain on mine, but no one opens their mouth to
answer. Evidently, yes, they had.

The Red Woman impersonator glances at the others. "Am I
allowed to say I told you so now or should I wait?"

A rumble of footsteps comes from the hallway. Everyone
tenses, questions and sarcasm forgotten. My heart jumps to life
and my hands rise, ready for another round of combat.

"Yeah, okay, I'll wait," the Red Woman says, just before a
new horde of guards rushes to attack.

◇ ◇ ◇

We work as a team, using the terrain of the half-destroyed cafeteria to hold off the new guards. I'm hunched behind an overturned table next to Jatin, shooting spells over our shoulders.

He won't end the conversation. "Adraa, I'm sorry, but—"

I shake my head. *I know. There was no stopping you.*

"You're right. There was no stopping me. I had to come. I couldn't let them take you away when you saved our countries. And if I had had any idea what they were going to do to you I would have come sooner."

I'm taken aback by the fieriness of his speech. But I have to remember this is Jatin, the boy who pushed himself to be the best wizard in Wickery, who pushed me to be the best witch. And while I might do anything for my country, Jatin will do anything for the people he loves. And he loves me.

"Adraa, I need to ask you a question."

His seriousness makes me still. But at least it's not "I need to tell you something," which conveys catastrophe. It's a question. I begin to nod, when a spiral of yellow smoke breaks the wicker table in two and rushes between us. It's a wind spell, not an arrow, I realize a second too late, and the shield I build gets blown back with me, across the floor.

I scramble to my feet. Jatin does the same, meters away.

I search the battleground of the cafeteria. Stone and wicker litter the floor. Prisha and Hiren are dueling a wizard to my right. Riya and Kalyan are taking down three to my left. Fiza stands at the exits, pinning guards down as they try to rush at her and escape. None of the guards are that strong even if they are fresh to the fight. Then I see his eyes.

The warden. A very pissed-off warden. Ekani's knockout spell must have finally worn off. His clothes are rumpled, his hair askew, and his eyes, once calm and sharp, have a new frantic edge in them, one that spells desperation.

"This!" he bellows, engulfing his arms in a swarm of magic. "This is *my* prison! You will not destroy it."

"Think we found our new target," Jatin mutters.

The warden steps forward, wobbly and unsteady. "Face me. One-on-one. Finish what we started without letting others fight your battles. Let's see what the real Adraa Belwar can do."

It's sad, truthfully. I feel a mix of pity and disgust. The warden is still weathering the effects of a knockout spell, yet he thinks he can prod my ego enough to make sure no one helps me? A year ago, I might have relented to his goading. Might have tried to save the day and fought alone. But then Jatin came into my life and taught me the value of partnership, of trusting others to support you.

Before I can cast my response, Jatin yells to our friends, "Cover us!" Then he turns to me and grabs my right hand. "Together?"

I smile, understanding exactly what he means. Mirroring one another we push forward and combine our magic. A stream of red and white surges toward the warden and pins him to the wall.

"So about that question," Jatin says brightly.

I look over at him. Really? Our friends are making sure ten guards won't ambush us as we hold an unstable wizard against a wall, and he has a question? I have dozens—like how he found me and where exactly is this prison anyway—but we can talk about that later.

Jatin and I step forward, our magic surging. "I tried asking during the rebuilding celebrations and I should have just done it then," Jatin says. "I should have done a lot of things differently."

The celebration? Right, he did want to tell me something. After everything I had almost forgotten.

The warden roars under the pressure, and Jatin and I press back, gaining another step. Then another. "*Pavria,*" Jatin casts. The enhancement to our combined magic is too much. The sheer concentration of it pushes the warden to the floor, and his yellow smoke vanishes in a flash. He falls to the ground in a heap, much like he did in the guard tower. Complete burnout. It's wonderfully ironic.

I rest my hands on my knees, exhaustion nestling in my muscles.

Jatin tosses a wizard over his shoulder. He's *still* talking. "I know this might not be the best time."

I stand up straight and write, *You're telling me? We're a little busy.*

"I don't want to lose my chance again," he answers as he dodges a fireball and then an arrow-shaped icicle. I blast a guard away with a spiral of wind. "And I don't want to lose you."

A guard bursts in between us and Jatin says, "I'm kind of in the middle of speech here," before hitting him over the head.

There's something different about Jatin right now. More confident, but it's not the confidence peppered with arrogance or performance. He's just . . . more himself. More sure.

We sweep the legs of a few incoming guards, creating obstacles for the remaining reinforcements.

Go on. What do you want to ask?

He smiles and grabs both of my hands. "Adraa Belwar, will you marry me?"

◇

CHAPTER THIRTY-SEVEN

Awaiting an Answer

Jatin

I know. I know I should have waited for a moment in which Adraa and I weren't sweating and battling for our lives. I know I should have made it romantic to try to express every single ounce of love I have for her. It's a lot of weight, proposing. Especially for royal heirs like us. But I couldn't stop myself. I'm not going to overthink it any longer.

When I said I want to make this interesting, I was referring to a bet, you know, Adraa writes with a smile, delight spinning in her eyes.

"I know. But for weeks now I've been in agony, not knowing whether you were being hurt. Whether they had killed you. So there is no pressure now. You can say no. I can handle a no, knowing you're alive."

Instead of answering, she moves her hands to cast a bubble shield around us. I mimic her and add my magic to hers.

Then, amid a full-on brawl, in a bubble all our own, she

grabs the collar of my kurta again and kisses me. It's one of the best kisses of my life, because in every Touch I know she's answering me, saying yes. I'm kissing my fiancée, the person who will be by my side through anything, including the fight that still rages beyond our shields. It feels like it's not words or power protecting us, but our sheer will and love. With Adraa in my arms I feel safe. I'm home. And while it's dim in the Dome, colorful spells light up the darkness around us, and it's better than any festival or celebration could have ever been.

"Just to be clear, that's a yes, right? Yes?"

She nods and her fist moves up and down before she pushes magic into the air. *Yes.*

I lean in to kiss her again, when a body hits our shield and slides down it, unconscious.

Prisha slams a fist against the barrier like she's knocking. "Are you two really making out in the middle of all this? *Again?*"

"Okay, I admit this could have been more romantic. We should probably get going."

Adraa smiles and holds up three fingers. I already know exactly what she's thinking. We turn back-to-back.

"One." I survey the scene.

"Two." I plan my spell.

"Three." I aim.

Our shields explode outward. Guards yell as they are blown back, into the fray. We both used yellow magic, and the result is a twister-level wind blast. The rest of the guards fall. Truthfully, they never had much of chance against the seven of us.

"Okay," Fiza breathes. "Okay, we get it. You guys are powerful."

Riya squints. "Adraa, earlier on . . . did I see you take out one guy with *just* a punch to the face?"

"She must have used orange magic," Prisha reasons.

Adraa turns slowly and smiles. Her hands flutter and then words rise in the air. *I learned some stuff in prison.*

We all stare at her. I've never been so turned on in my life. My fiancée is bloody amazing.

Kalyan leans forward and whispers in my ear. "Never, and I mean never, make that woman angry."

"That's how I know I'm smarter than half the country. I already knew that. This lot, however? They'll realize soon enough."

"You mean the half not already traumatized and running for the hills?" Riya interjects with a laugh.

I survey the room. "I think I won," I say, turning to Adraa for a reaction, my grin unstoppable.

Adraa tilts her head before casting in the air. *Maybe it's a tie this time?*

"Fair. Now let's get out of here."

CHAPTER THIRTY-EIGHT

◇

Destroying What Tried to Destroy Me

Adraa

We descend into the depths of this place, and I lead the way. As we turn the last corner, a shadow moves inside the clinic. I stop and hold up a hand, signaling to the group to ready themselves for yet another fight. Everyone seems to heave a breath of resignation, but they tense and prepare themselves just the same. Tendrils of black smoke coat Hiren's arms.

I hold up three fingers, and Jatin and Riya signal which way they are going to fire when we barge in. On my count we swivel around the corner, seven of the most powerful Touched in Belwar standing on the threshold, arms blazing.

There are no guards, though. Only Harini jolting in surprise as she helps one of the Voiceless to her feet. I scan the room and breathe a sigh of relief to find they are all awake. Most are sitting up and nursing their arms. Scared, of course, but not unconscious.

Where have you been? Harini throws the words at me.

With my friends, I write. Jatin comes up beside me like it's his natural spot. I'm kind of in love with it.

Harini scans the group, her eyes landing on Jatin last. *You didn't mention reinforcements in your plan. I would have gone along with it much faster if you had.*

Unexpected arrivals.

Well, we need the help. She gestures to the other girls.

Come on, let's move, I cast for the others before stepping forward and helping one of the Voiceless.

"What's happened to them?" Riya asks as she helps one of the Pire Island girls stand.

Harini moves her hands, and I'm so thankful. I need the break, and she's better at communicating. *The same thing that's been happening to us. Their Bloodlurst experiments.*

"You're telling me this is how they make Bloodlurst? By stealing people's voices and bloodletting?" Jatin asks.

I nod with a frown and turn my arm, showcasing the wound. This one straight and red and *fresh.* Jatin hisses through his teeth.

I move my hands, bloodred smoke rising above me. *I think that's why in the trial they sent me here. I was needed to make the Vencrin's newest batch.*

"Blood, I'll kill them."

We need to get it back. It's powerful, Jatin. I pull down my blouse's high neckline to expose Erif's red Touch. *And it's not just my power.*

It seems to hit some of them then. Hiren steps in and vocalizes it for the rest. "Wait, wait, wait. Are you saying the Vencrin made a batch of Bloodlurst with not only your power but also the power of Goddess Erif herself?"

I nod.

"New mission, then. We find all that Bloodlurst and destroy every last grain of it. How much was it?" Jatin asks.

Enough for an army, Harini writes.

"An army?" Riya breathes. "Jatin, what Sims said . . ."

Sims? I write out, surprise hitting me hard. What does Sims have to do with anything?

"We interrogated Sims. I thought he was speaking nonsense, but he said something about a witch being promised to create an army."

Shock and fury thrash inside my chest, but Jatin continues. "We'll get it back, Adraa, but we need to go."

Not before we destroy this place, Harini's words rain through the air.

I look back at the cabinets of herbs, a plan forming in my mind. *Start getting the witches out of here. I'll be right behind you.*

"Adraa, I'm not leaving you," Jatin protests, as I knew he would.

I'll be two steps behind.

He doesn't relent.

Please, Jatin. I need you to help get them out. They won't be able to move fast enough. I will.

Finally, with one last look at me, he helps one of the Voiceless out of the clinic.

I gather up piles of red fireworth and black ashen and fuse it together like all the bombs I made. A blast of magic joins mine, and I expect Jatin or Riya, but it's Prisha standing there like a warrior.

"I know what you're planning, what you're making. Let me help." We lock eyes and I nod my thanks. Never underestimate a Belwar girl.

Prisha gets busy pulling jars of herbs from the shelf. "You know, Mom only taught us this so we wouldn't accidently blow up her clinic."

I give her a look and gesture around this rotten place. I stuff any papers I can find in the heart of the jars. So much for evidence. I can't have it replicated in any capacity. When Prisha finishes the fourth bomb, I pause. *You're pretty good at this*, I sign with a smile.

She doesn't appreciate my bad joke. "I don't know exactly where to start, but I'm so sorry," she says, tears sliding down her checks.

We'll talk later, I reassure her. *Will you help me with the last bit?*

She wipes at her face. "Of course. You're my sister. And what are sisters for if not to help destroy an experimental facility in the middle of nowhere?"

I wouldn't have worded it quite like that, but she does have a reputation for destroying clinics. Together we douse the edges of the cabinets with a burst of fire.

Then we run.

◇ ◇ ◇

The bomb goes off as we reach the entrance, where Jatin is waiting for me. He looks past me as the ground rumbles its displeasure. "What did you do?"

"Run, you idiot," Prisha answers for me, and unhitches her skyglider.

Jatin listens and we sprint down a tunnel-like hallway. "Fly with me?" he asks as we bypass the gated front door, torn from its hinges. "We were short on skygliders."

If I had my voice, I'd quip about him asking for a ride. When he meets my eye, I think he knows what I'm thinking, because he smiles. "Come on, Smoke, I don't believe for a second you'd leave me here."

I unbuckle Vihaan's substitute. My friends hover in the air outside of the prison walls, all the Voiceless seated behind my friends on skygliders. Prisha zooms into the air like a pro. I swing a leg over the handle and settle behind Jatin as he yells out the spell. We spring into the air as an explosion booms behind us.

I turn to look one last time at the stone walls of the facility. A trail of smoke billows into the sky from the Dome's bottom left side.

"I'm still unsure what you did in there, but we've started to get a reputation for setting things on fire after we leave," Jatin whispers.

Because they won't let us go without one last fight, an arrow sizzles through the air after us. Riya and Prisha turn to fire back or shield us, but I have a better solution. Time to return the last of the herbs I stole. I throw my last bomb. It rains through the air, exploding in red smoke, an extension of myself.

Everyone's slack-jawed, Jatin most of all. "What was that?" Hiren cries out.

Jatin gets ahold of himself first. "I thought way back when . . . I thought that was a joke. You really can *make* explosives?"

I raise an eyebrow and smile. I wouldn't joke about explosives. He gets me immediately and rubs the back of his neck.

"You're terrifying, Adraa Belwar. And I'm so in love with you."

◇

CHAPTER THIRTY-NINE

The Power of a Good Sisterly Talk

Adraa

After searching for thirty minutes, and before the sun begins to dip behind a number of mountains, we find Ekani and the others. They have made a camp on a bald spot on one of the nearby peaks. We drop more than descend into their camp.

Both parties are windblown and tired. A few of them exhibit the telltale signs of their first real flight. Deepa, for instance, sways on her feet, whimpering about her thighs. Some of them are first-time fliers too.

Ignoring her, I take account of the rest of our mismatched group. There are eighty-six in total. Most seem dazed at the prospect of fresh air, woods, and their first taste of freedom in who knows how long. This won't be the easiest of journeys back to Belwar, but I'm confident Dad will know what to do and Mom will know how to repair any physical ailments and malnutrition.

But there is so much to be done before then. We have to get to Belwar safely and then find my Bloodlurst before Basu gives it to the Vencrin or Moolek or both. He already has hours on us, but I can't leave these women.

Before I can begin to process who should do what, Jatin doles out assignments: food, shelter, and nightly watch. I observe him as he takes command, and a new wave of admiration cascades over me. I wasn't imagining it in the prison. He's changed.

For now I know where I can be most helpful. Some of the Voiceless need medical attention if we hope to fly out in the morning, so Prisha and I go to work. We don't have any herbs, but we clean and sew up lacerations, numb some gruesome bruising, and I fix a few broken bones, all before darkness conquers our camp.

One by one, Jatin, Riya, Kalyan, and Hiren come check on me, bringing me food and water. Riya even gifts me an untorn black blouse, which I quickly change in to. I get more affection, love, and food in the span of an hour than I've had in weeks.

Prisha has been quiet, though. When she approaches, I realize she's only been biding her time until we could be alone.

"Can . . . can we talk?" She winces as soon as she says it. "Sorry, I mean . . . ah—" Immediately, I raise my hands. *It's okay. Let's talk.*

We make our way outside the circle of people. As soon as we reach another, smaller clearing, Prisha charges in. "I didn't get to say everything I wanted in that . . . clinic place."

It's okay, I repeat.

"No, it's not. I need to apologize. I need to do so much more than that, but that's where I should start. And I don't want to admit it, but I don't think the things I said were *all* Moolek. He didn't manufacture all those feelings. They were just pulled to the surface."

I realize with a start I'm cutting off her apology and settle my hands. I gesture for her to go on. Even if we are ready for forgiveness, we still need to let the other speak, to apologize in full.

"I love you, Adraa, but I've always been envious of you."

Okay, I wasn't expecting this. I point at myself dubiously.

"You're so perfect. Prettier than me. More powerful. Funnier. Better at fighting. I mean, blood, Mom and Dad arranged for you to be the maharani of Naupure, and I'm pretty sure they'd prefer you over me when it comes to leading Belwar too. *I'd* prefer you over me."

When I raise my hands to contradict her, Prisha slowly places her hands over mine. "Give me one more minute." She breathes. "Even with all that envy, I was just as drawn in as everyone else. I loved you for being both Adraa and the Red Woman. I wanted to be on your team. So when this voice came into my head and tore it down, I . . . I lost it. No, that's not right. I broke." Tears well in her eyes.

I grab her into a hug, not bothering with words. I hold her tight, conveying everything I can.

Finally, I pull back and sign, *I love you.* Pausing, I add one more thing. *I wish I could say that aloud.*

She nods, tears falling. She wipes them away quickly. "About that, I've been thinking. All fall, I've been helping Dad work on voice and sound spells to create the new alert system. I couldn't be in the clinic. Not when every patient criticized you. Dad and

I discovered some interesting things, new spells. Can . . . can I try?" Her hands light up, a pale pink glow pouring off her palms in waves like her magic is overflowing.

You think you can? I ask. In that prison I'd assumed only Basu could return what he had stolen. I hadn't even thought of any alternative—my gifted pink forte sister.

She gives a weak smile. "Everyone thinks when you died at your ceremony, I pumped you full of pink magic, but mostly it was yellow, to keep you breathing. I want to try. Will you . . . will you forgive me enough to let me try?"

I will always let you try, I sign.

I lie down on the ground, and Prisha presses her hands to my throat. The diagnosis spell washes over me. If this were anyone else, fear would be running through me faster than hope. But I trust her. She's my annoying sister who smirks and teases and, yes, we've been competitive. From the outside looking in, we are siblings who just bicker and push each other's buttons. But I taught Prisha her first potion, not Mom. I was there when she failed her first test. We're sisters, with all the complications that come with it.

"I think I know what they did. Dad and I have been working on amplifying sound, but we had to study the opposite as well. It was like a tornado, right?"

I nod.

A tunnel of pink wind twists above my mouth, and I clench the grass with my fists and shut my eyes tight. It's Prisha. It's my sister. It's not going to hurt.

It hurts.

This twister is smaller and slimmer than Basu's, but it gags me just the same. It's the panic, the memories of the last time Basu messed with my throat that wound me. My entire mouth grows hot. My lungs seize as I stop breathing, and I open my eyes and try to calm down. Prisha's face twists in concentration above me, and I focus on her. This isn't Basu. She'll stop if I signal.

Then, a second later, something tight in my throat loosens. It's like a rope knotted around my vocal cords has been untied.

I gasp. Like in the red room, I hear myself.

Prisha hugs me tight. "Adraa?"

"Yeah," I choke on the sound, the beautiful sound. The first I've made in weeks. I refuse to be humble. My voice is bloody amazing, even choked with emotion.

She laughs at my answer, pulling back. "Yeah!"

"Oh my Gods," I say. I *say*!

"You were right. Laeh blessed me so I could help. So I could help *you*."

I push the hair back from her face. "Not just me. Besides, you still are more than the color of your magic. More than that one spell."

"Well, you could say the same for yourself. You are not bound by firelight."

"Yeah, I've been trying to tell people that for months."

"Is that a . . . joke?"

"Yes, they are pretty hard for me to pull off in written form. Don't go over as well. It's been torturous that for weeks no one has appreciated my sarcasm."

"A true travesty." That mischievous little smile of hers tips up the corners of her lips.

"You are going to be an amazing rani," I tell her.

"I . . . I'm nothing compared—"

I stop her there. "Don't compare us. Don't let others do it and, more importantly, we are going to stop each other from doing it."

"Okay. I can get behind that."

Gods, she's matured.

"What are you going to do first?" Prisha's eyes widen and her eyebrows rise. "Jatin! Go talk to Jatin." She smirks. "Or maybe don't talk."

A blush fuels my cheeks. Jatin and I have a lot to discuss. "You're right. I should go find him. Talk to him." Gods, talk. I'm going to talk to him. "In the meantime, will you heal the other Voiceless? Basu didn't take Harini's voice, but you could help the rest."

Her hands glow. "I'll try."

◇ ◇ ◇

I reenter the clearing and everyone looks up from a cobbled-together dinner. Everyone but the person I want to talk to.

I spot Kalyan, taller than anyone else, building an earthen tent off to the side. If anyone is not going to make a big commotion or ask questions about my being able to speak again, it's him.

"Hi, Adraa," he says in greeting. "What do you need?"

I take a deep breath. "Where's Jatin?" I ask.

Kalyan's eyes widen and his magic stills, mirroring his shock. Like I thought, he simply points. "Taking first watch."

"Okay, I need to talk to him about a question he asked me earlier."

"Finally." The widest smile I've ever seen blooms across Kalyan's face. "He only tried seventeen times."

"Seventeen? When? How did I miss—"

"I'll show you the documentation when we get home. For now, put us all out of our misery."

◇

CHAPTER FORTY

I'll Say It as Many Times as You'd Like

Jatin

I've found the edge of the mountainside, quite a ways outside the camp and past a wall of dense trees. It offers a vantage point of the entire southern valley. And, most importantly, a great expanse of sky. Adraa joins my watch as the sun reaches the peak and floods the valley in rich deep orange. She sits and leans into me, and I reach my arm around her to bring her even closer. Together, we watch the sunset, the peacefulness of the sun saying good night to the vacant mountains. Kalyan will be pleased with the color. However, the orange signifies only of nature's peace. Wickery still teeters on the brink of destruction.

"Remember that letter, the one right before I got home last year? Before we *met*?"

Adraa nods.

I gesture outward. "Didn't I say I would take you to the Alps of Alconea one day?"

She gives me a look and shakes her head. I imagine the huff of a laugh that would come with it.

"Yeah, remind me to never make ignorant promises again," I say.

She seems restless. I nudge her shoulder and hug her close. "What's wrong?"

Slowly, reluctantly, she weaves her hands through the air. *If I could talk again what is the first thing you would want to hear?*

"Like when you get your voice back?"

A nod.

I think I know where this is going. "Come on, Smoke." I tug her even closer to me. "You think I care you can't speak?" I squeeze her hands. "As long as we can communicate in some way. As long as you're safe. That's all that matters."

She smiles. *Thank you for that, but I still want you to answer the question.*

She seems to take this question seriously, so I think for a moment. *My name* and *I love you* jostle for first place. Then I realize what it would really be.

"I would want to hear you say yes." I look over at her quickly, making sure that didn't offend her. "Not that I don't think you meant it, but Gods, I've been trying for weeks. Maybe even fantasizing about it a little too much."

She pulls me into a hug. "Yes," she whispers in my ear. "I'll say it as many times as you'd like. Yes."

For the second time in our relationship, the world stops and spins, and my mind whirls in confusion and elation. "What?" I bolt upright, squeezing her shoulders. "I mean how and . . . and . . . yes?" She just said yes. Out loud.

"Prisha has become an extraordinary pink forte."

"You let me ramble for two minutes when you could *talk* again?"

"I've gotten used to the quiet. And I didn't know . . . I didn't know what to say. I was trying to be romantic."

"Must everything be a competition? Maybe let me have that one thing?"

Her face scrunches. "Never."

I start laughing and she follows suit. "Blood, it's good to hear your voice again, but I meant what I said. What matters is you."

She smiles. "Good. Because if you had made one joke about nagging, I think I would have pushed you off this mountain."

"Pushed, huh? Not punched?"

"Oh Gods."

"I'm sure you would have left me with a skyglider, right?"

Adraa smiles. "Probably."

I reach for her cheek and cradle it in my palm. "In all seriousness, I love your voice. And Gods, I love your laugh. But more than that, I love the way you think and your sarcasm."

"You and your compliments." But she smiles into my hand, kissing my palm, to let me know how much she loves it.

I pull out the gold wedding bangle I've been carrying with me. "It was my mother's."

"Jatin," she breathes before holding out her left hand like she always has because of her Touch. Instead, I slowly slip it over her right wrist. "So you don't forget I'll always be your other arm. Though it's very unlikely you need me."

Her hands move to cast the words in the air, making the gold gleam. *I do need you.* She leans in close, and I don't even let myself savor the moment before her lips touch mine. I kiss her deeply, with everything I have.

Her hands glide under my jacket and suddenly buttons are being undone, clothing slipping away. The wind howls, but her skin is fire under my hands and the coming nightfall is the last thing on my mind.

A mist of red smoke rises off her arms and I sweep my hands over them and then find her waist. With a few shuffling movements, she's straddling me. The new level of closeness does something to us both. A frenzy takes over. Our mouths move against each other like we may never get the chance again, and I know that we've both thought it.

We make up for lost time.

I pull her impossibly close, chest to chest, heartbeat to heartbeat. One hand weaves through her hair, the other on her lower back. And *her* hands. They cup my jaw and reach into my hair, sending a current of familiarity and intimacy straight to my heart.

I realize how desperate I am to just feel her in my arms. For this to not be a dream. I open my eyes to check and find a flush of pink smoke wrapped around us. The mist of white blurring and mingling with bloodred. Even our magic wants to cling to the other. Adraa stares too and everything about this moment evokes a surge of emotion so strong my lungs seem to fail.

"I really thought I might never see you again," I breathe. I don't mean for the words to be coated in such emotion or to feel tears ambush my eyes, but it happens. Adraa gazes at me, and suddenly I'm watching her eyes fill too.

"Me too. And I really thought I might not be able to say I love you again."

We're both crying then. A happy, overwhelming relief. And just like that, our franticness slows and we're hugging one another, not even letting the wind or an inch of chill come between us.

"You can tell me now," I whisper.

She snuggles closer, head buried in my shoulder. "Don't be greedy," she says, but then, not a moment later, "I love you."

My magic wraps around her like a cocoon. "I love you too."

And that's how we stay, enfolded.

When we finally come up for air, she begins speaking. I pull back to watch her face. I could do this the rest of my life.

"I know I didn't really say it properly in there, but thank you for coming for me. I was wrong to tell you not to. And to be anything but grateful when you did."

I squeeze her hands. "Like I've told you before, I would have come no matter what." I brush back some strands of hair I've unleashed from her braid. "The whole time I had this voice inside of my head telling me to find you, to free you."

Adraa stills. Something shifts between us, and I feel it down to my bones. "What?" she asks slowly. "What did you say?"

"Nothing. Just this idea that I had to find you no matter what." I grapple to reclaim our happiness, to reorganize this moment. I hate the sudden, spiking fear that laces through her question. It scares me to my core.

"You said a voice. It was *like* a voice or it *was* a voice?"

I understand her meaning finally. My stomach sinks to the ground with a thud. I search my memory, and that time on the roof comes crashing back. A voice, a feeling foreign and outside myself to the point I thought I was losing my mind. And that night I had put it all on the fact I had seen Fiza as the Red Woman when the biggest illusion was right there the whole time. "Oh my Gods."

"Jatin?"

I stand, fumbling with my belt, searching for my skyglider, then realizing I don't have it with me. "Oh Gods."

"It wasn't your voice, was it?" she whispers.

"No. But how . . . Why . . ." I stare at her. "Why would he want me to save you?"

She looks to the horizon. "I can think of only one reason." She chokes on the words, but she doesn't need to say them. The answer falls into place, just by looking at the wild horizon and the mountains spreading in all directions.

Moolek has been sending me personal messages since the trial for one reason only—to get us out of our countries and out of the way.

◇

CHAPTER FORTY-ONE

Fiza Fight

Jatin

"We're leaving!" I holler. The camp seems to flinch, and everyone jolts awake or at least upright. Many of the former prisoners scan the tree line. I'm scaring them. I know I am, and I hate it. I also hate having to tell them why they can't follow us to Belwar or Naupure, to promised sanctuary. If Adraa and I are right, then nowhere is safe, especially our capitals.

"I'm going to talk to the guard who got them out." Adraa starts to redirect to the large group, then turns back around. "Got any money on you?"

I pull a modest bag of gold off my belt. "How much do you need?"

"How much do you have?" she asks.

"We've been engaged half a day and you already want all my gold." I don't let the joke sit long enough for even an eye roll before tossing her the pouch. "Here."

Adraa snatches it out of the air and runs. That friend of hers from the prison—Harini—notices, and the two of them move their hands in communication as they rush toward the dozens and dozens of women from the prison.

"What's going on?" Riya asks as soon as she reaches me.

"Pack up camp. We have to go. *Now.*" When her face falls and Kalyan runs over with a wary expression, I realize I'm doing exactly what Fiza did to us. Issuing demands and creating tension without explanation. My expression softens. "I promise I'll explain everything as we fly, but Adraa and I think that Moolek is unleashing an attack on our capitals."

Prisha stumbles back, and Hiren catches her. "I should have stayed," she murmurs, turning to him. "You were right."

"Jatin, are you sure?" Kalyan asks.

"I'm going to find out." I march toward Fiza.

"Did you know? Have you doomed us all, Fiza?" I yell, not bothering to conceal my voice or my anger.

She starts. "What are you talking about? Know what?"

"That this"—I spread my arms, gesturing to the mountainside—"is another one of his traps?"

"What are you yelling about this time?"

Suddenly the theory I've been cradling since our training falls out of my mouth. "Are you working for my uncle?"

"What?"

"You are one of the best illusionists in the world. You can impersonate the Red Woman perfectly. You were in the courtroom that day. Did you set up Adraa? Make it *appear* she was admitting guilt?"

Fiza merely scoffs. Her eyes dart to something behind me. I

glance to find the rest of our team listening in, including Adraa. "You work fast," Fiza says to her. "I'll give you that. Feeling a bit threatened?" Then Fiza is focused back on me. "Nice to finally see how little you think of me. You going to truth-spell me, Jatin?" She shakes her head. "There are people in this world much scarier than you." Her eyes connect to Adraa's over my shoulder again. "Your girlfriend, for one."

"Fiancée," I say, just to be mean.

Her eyes go right for the bangle and rest there for a beat too long. I can see the flash of pain before she can hide it. "Well, you work fast too, then, huh?"

"Just answer me."

"No! I led us here. I gave you what you wanted"—Fiza gestures to Adraa like she's some sort of prize—"so don't you dare accuse me of being a traitor."

"Exactly, you led us here!"

She shakes her head like someone caught in a lie and not knowing what to say next. "I don't even know what you are saying."

Adraa pulls at my arm. "Jatin, she may have been influenced like everyone else."

"I have my own mind," Fiza retorts. "And I don't need to justify myself anymore to you people." Black smoke curls around her arms in anger. "In the academy you were always the one who saw the real me. Now you are just like the rest."

"Cut the crap, Fiza. Don't call me a liar when you won't even tell us the most important truth. How did you know Adraa was in that place?"

"Bloodlurst. They make Bloodlurst there," Fiza finally says, her voice strained and powerful at the same time.

We have the whole camp's attention now. "And what does that have to do with you?"

"She's a Bloodlurst user," Adraa says. "And she knows where her supply comes from."

We're all shocked into silence. Then Riya turns murderous. "*That's* how you know this place?"

"How do you know?" I ask Adraa. I know Fiza better than anyone here, yet I failed to see it. But as I piece everything together it's the only answer that makes sense.

"I've seen the marks on her arm," Adraa responds sadly.

Before any of us can move, an orange spiral of smoke coils right toward Fiza. She flinches, and I pull up a hand, but it's Adraa who screams out a spell. A red shield manifests, stopping the pale orange smoke from crashing into the lady of Agsa. The orange forte Harini turns on Adraa then, arms spiraling wildly. When it looks like she's going to start shooting at Adraa, Riya dives forward and tackles Harini to the ground. "Calm down before you hurt someone or get hurt," she tells the former prisoner.

Adraa holds out her hands between us all. "Harini, there's no proof it was Nira's magic."

Harini signs furiously. I have no idea what she's saying or why she's attacking.

"I know. I *know*. But please let's talk this out."

Harini tries to buck Riya off, but she remains firmly pinned.

My eyes lock onto Fiza's. I see the exact moment she gives it all up, gives me up.

"I'm done." She springs onto her skyglider in one rush of fuming black.

I feel for my own skyglider and realize I still haven't gotten it back yet.

Adraa places a hand on my shoulder. "Jatin, I'm sorry, but we don't have time to chase her down. We *have* to get back."

"But she could be alerting Moolek," I reason, though even that rings false. I don't know what to believe. All I know is that, for once in her life, Fiza didn't look like she was hiding talons for a killing blow. It looked like *I* had just cut her open.

"All the more reason to beat her there. We have to go," Adraa says.

She's right. We have to get home.

CHAPTER FORTY-TWO

◇

Piecing Together the Puzzle

Adraa

Riya keeps Harini pinned until she's calmed down and Fiza is long gone.

"You good?" Riya says in apology and warning while getting off her.

Harini frowns, looks Riya up and down, and signs, *You can't protect that girl forever.*

"I don't care to. I protect Adraa. Besides, what were you going to do? Kill her?"

Yes, Harini signs.

"Oh blood." Riya side-eyes me, practically begging me to take over.

So I do. Moving my hands, I cast. *You aren't a killer.*

You don't know what I am.

I sigh. Harini's right, but I do think I know her character by now. She saved me in there. But, then again, so did Fiza. And I have no clue what's going on with her.

Harini continues. *If that witch ever used Bloodlurst, then she used me and she used Nira. She's one of the thousands responsible for my sister's death.*

I take a moment to process that. *I'm sorry. But you are talking about thousands of people. Are you going to kill them all?*

She shakes her head roughly. *I don't care how . . .* Her hands change directions. *I will destroy it. All of it and all of them.*

Then destroy the substance, not the people. I switch to my voice. "I'm going back to Belwar. I believe they will be distributing the new batch there and using it against my people. Come with us. Help me stop it."

Harini hesitates, like she wants to say more, but finally she nods.

"But no killing. If you can't promise me that, then leave with Ekani and the others."

Her fists tighten. *They deserve it.*

"Maybe. But you have to promise me."

I hold out, each second another moment we aren't flying toward Belwar. But Harini knows more about Bloodlurst than I ever will. I need her.

I promise. She brings the words up for Jatin and Riya in a clear orange haze. I watch as they share a wary and confused glance.

In war there are some that don't deserve to be spared, Adraa. Your mercy could be your downfall.

◇ ◇ ◇

We fly high into the air. We eat up sky, the clouds unusually close and the wind understandably bitter and aggressive. I can't get Harini's words out of my head.

Ekani and the rest of the women are staying behind. I gave Ekani Jatin's bag of gold to get her to either lead the witches back to their homes or protect them long enough that I can make sure Belwar is the sanctuary I promised them it would be. That is, if I'm not too late.

Maybe I'm overreacting, but I know I'm right.

I wish I wasn't. I wish the sinking feeling could be explained away. But it all fits. I sort it out in my mind one more time. Moolek. The trial. My imprisonment. The Bloodlurst. I dip closer to everyone and start talking.

"I know this will sound ridiculous, but I think Moolek has gotten into all of your heads. Led you here to rescue me so that Belwar's and Naupure's capitals are left unattended."

The group was waiting for my words. They all lean closer.

"What are you talking about? Moolek didn't make me want to break you out of that despicable place," Riya says.

"Maybe not all of you," Jatin interjects. "But I've been hearing this voice in my head for weeks, maybe even longer. And I led you here. I asked you to come on this mission even when Adraa asked me not to."

"Yeah, but Adraa, no offense"—Riya waves a hand in apology—"would have said something like that no matter what. This doesn't prove—"

"So there was no nagging voice in the back of your head telling you to find her? To free her?"

336

Riya's face falls. "That was just . . ."

"The exact thing I was thinking too. Nonstop," Jatin says.

"It was easy to break into the Dome. Too easy," Kalyan adds.
Another piece of the puzzle. Distract everyone who cares about
me long enough to take my magic and get inside their heads so
when they found the truth, they would rush to save me.

"What does this all mean?" Prisha breaks the silence. "You
think Moolek told us to help you so we would be gone? What
are we flying into?"

"I think if Moolek ever wanted to start a war, a true war, he'd
be strategic, decisive, and use the element of surprise. This is all
three." I hold my breath, liking the next thought even less. "None
of those wizards in there used Bloodlurst to enhance themselves.
Basu was gone. They have enough to supply hundreds, maybe
thousands. I think we are flying toward a full-out attack."

"Mom and Dad," Prisha whispers.

I nod. *Mom and Dad.*

"We'll be facing Moolek's men and Bloodlurst-enhanced
Vencrin."

"They are practically one and the same, Adraa. Moolek *created* the Vencrin," Jatin says.

"What?" That can't . . . He couldn't . . . "That means—"

"He's been planning this for years. Sims told us. He was
right about that place." Jatin waves a hand. "I have to say, I
believe him. In a roundabout way, I think he's on our side—or,
at least, he's not on their side."

Every new detail enhances my fears. Moolek and the Vencrin
leader. They've been out there planning this. It can't get worse.

We fly in silence for a moment. Then I ask the question I dread most. "Who else has heard something in their head? Something that may have sounded like your own ideas, your own doubt, but has . . . it sounds different, persistent and angry?"

Kalyan shakes his head. But Prisha and Riya look stricken. Prisha speaks first. "I . . . something inside me told me you were guilty leading up to the trial and then in the courtroom."

"Anything else?" I cry over the wind. "Think, Prisha. I know you don't really believe these things. But was there anything else?"

"I . . . I think it told me to destroy Mom's potion room."

Jatin and I share a concerned glance. "Was there anything in particular? Any ingredient? Something Mom hasn't been able to replace?"

"I don't—"

Riya sucks in a breath. "Twistgrass."

The plant instantly comes to mind, as does its rarity. Oh Gods. No. It just gets worse and worse every second. "You're sure?"

Riya looks dazed, but finally nods. "Something in my head said it wasn't important."

"What is it?" Jatin asks, almost sounding scared.

"Could be nothing, but . . . but twistgrass is an essential ingredient to create an antidote for certain rare poisons. It's also only found on Agsa prairies."

"My father," Jatin breathes.

I nod. "Your father."

"And my father," Riya adds.

"What?" I ask. Jatin said his dad had been poisoned, but Mr. Burman is a different case. A coma that . . . oh my Gods.

Riya verifies it. "Your mom thinks they are linked."

"With time we'll be able to save them both. But we can't do it without twistgrass."

Which means if Jatin and I are right and an army is invading our countries, Maharaja Naupure won't be able to fight back. I bite my lip, trying to not cry. "How long until we get to Belwar?" I ask Jatin.

"To not burn out doing it? At least two days."

I glance around at all the skygliders in the air. "And what if we don't stop?"

"Adraa, it's impossible." He peers behind him. "One of them will fall asleep or burnout before we get halfway there. Believe me, Fiza and I tried it on our way here, and I almost killed us in doing so."

A wild thought enters my brain and won't let go.

"I don't like that look," Jatin says.

"We double up. Sleep or rest as our partner flies and then switch off."

"But that will still mean stopping at every flying station to switch out. And the next one isn't for miles."

"Or we just do that . . . without landing."

◇ ◇ ◇

The rest of the group doesn't like my idea, but I won't slow down or stop. Every hour could mean lives at risk.

The plan is simple. That doesn't mean it isn't a little bit on the reckless side, but it's the only thing I've come up with, and it's already been an hour.

We're going to attempt to jump on each other's flying sky-gliders midair. Which means I have to create a patch of air to hold my weight for a half second as I condense my skyglider and hop onto Jatin's. Below us, our teammates have created a patch of wind that will slow our fall if we slip. And further below that, Kalyan flies, the last line of defense in my outrageous plan.

"This is just like that one night on the roof." The time I dove into the sky to chase after the Vencrin leader.

Jatin chuckles. "I hated it then too."

"You'll catch me, right?" I playfully ask, willing away the nerves.

"Always," Jatin responds instantly. Blood, my fiancé is hot.

The patch of air only needs to take my weight for a moment. One single moment in time before Jatin catches me and I'm on his skyglider, in his arms. I take a breath, then step onto nothing but a sliver of my magic. At the same time, I have to close the skyglider.

"*Yayhtrae,*" I cast, and the wood contracts into its compact form. In a fluid motion I slide it into my belt. As I do, though, my foot sinks into the magic, and I slip. Jatin grabs my hand, and I half throw myself, half topple onto him. We turn sideways and roll. His arms hug me tight enough to hurt. The wind whistles through my hair, throwing my braid into havoc.

We both come up breathing hard. "I said *always*, and I mean it, but that was a little too close for comfort," he whispers in my ear, still not releasing me from his hold.

I take another deep breath and look around at our friends. "Wasn't so bad. Who's next?" I ask.

Has she always been like this? Harini writes in the air. We all read it quickly, before the wind whips the words away.

"Yes," the group answers in unison.

◇ ◇ ◇

Kalyan jumps to Riya's skyglider next, with a little more grace than my attempt. Harini, stubborn as ever, says she'll take the first shift alone. Prisha doubles up with Hiren, and Jatin fills me in on their flirtation the past few weeks. Prisha has always had a crush on Hiren, but apparently it has developed into something more. I watch them with new eyes; their closeness verging on full-on cuddling is blatant.

"Huh, I wouldn't have guessed you'd be the first to catch that," I say to Jatin.

"Why does no one assume I can be observant?"

I turn to face him, smiling. "When did you realize I liked you again? Was it before or after I had to tell you to your face?" I smile wider. "Also, Kalyan said something about seventeen attempts—"

He smothers me in a hug, his arms engulfing me. "Forget I said anything. Let me hold you." Then, so quietly I almost miss it, Jatin whispers, "Let me hold you forever."

My body warms at his words. I've been through so much. *We've* been through so much. It's nice to know we can weather even the harshest of storms and still come out together.

We fly like that for hours, burning through nightfall and then daylight. Me asleep in his arms. Him asleep in mine. We land on only a couple of platforms for mere minutes to switch positions and go the bathroom.

"We're flying on skyglider number five, by the way," Jatin announces next time we are airborne. "Nowhere close to your thirty-seven, but I'm trying."

"I will forever regret telling you that," I say.

I can tell he's smiling without even looking. "Hey, I've kept my end of the bargain," he says.

True, he never mentions the night he took an arrow for me and we fell asleep on a roof. "That was the first time I really knew I loved you," I say.

I peek behind me. His eyes light up, soaking in the information. "Oh yeah?"

"Yeah, it was awful."

He shakes his head. *"Sankraw,"* he casts. Our names dangle in the air, a zero under his and a one beneath mine.

"Looks about right," I agree before settling into my last nap before we reach home. We've been in the air for hours, just over a day, and we should be close. But I force myself to sleep, retaining as much energy as I can.

"Adraa." Jatin's voice wakes me up. I start, and he hugs me close so I don't tip us over. "It's just over the next ridge."

I straighten and look toward the horizon. We're on the brink of Belwar territory. Right over the ridge we'll be able to see into the coastal valley of my city.

"Nothing out of the ordinary yet," he whispers in my ear.

I nod. Jatin speeds up and the others follow. We all watch the mountains grow closer. Then, like daybreak, we emerge over the barrier. In the distance Belwar sits peacefully, the sunshine of a beautiful day gleaming in a shimmer of ocean breeze and city smoke.

We were wrong. Paranoid. A divine sense of relief overwhelms me.

Gods, I've never loved being *this* wrong before. The group share happy smiles all around. Prisha slumps back on her skyglider so far, she's practically lying on it. We glide forward, moving toward our beautiful, undisturbed city.

Suddenly I feel a twinge in the air, the press of powerful resistance. A purple fray of woven threads, tendrils of smoke whipped and tied together. As we pass through it, I know immediately what it is.

An illusion, meters thick.

It knocks Prisha sideways. She fumbles in the air, and I reach out instinctively, getting close enough to place a hand on her back and stabilize her. She releases a breath of relief, but then she spots something behind me and all that air is sucked up once again in a fearful inhale.

I turn, and that's when I see it for myself, take in the entire picture.

Riya cries out. "Belwar, it's—"

She can't seem to finish the sentence because my country is—

Burning.

Screaming.

Dying.

Flames roar in patches all the way to the bay. Black ash and smoke rise in a dozen little plumes, each competing to block out the sun. We can hear the noise, the screams of panic and pain, from here. All over my city the desperate signals for the Red Woman and Night shoot into the sky, dulled only by the smoke from the fires.

"Gods!" Riya shouts. "There's over a hundred of them."

"How . . ."

My knees weaken. My hands slip on the skyglider from their trembling. Because it really was a trap all along. And we fell into it again.

◇

CHAPTER FORTY-THREE

Signals Singeing the Sky

Jatin

"Blood!"

"What do we do, Jatin?" I don't even know who asked it, but the whole party turns to me. Adraa glances around and a part of me breaks. The city is in danger, blazing in panic. And seven pairs of eyes are staring me down, including Adraa's. I can't panic too.

"We split up and figure out what is happening." I say it with as much strength as I have left in me. Only to Adraa do I turn and tilt my head in question.

She gets it at once. "I was thinking the same thing."

"My father," I say. Although in the distance no fires or signals soar into the sky over Naupure, I can't abandon my country again.

"I know. My parents." A pause. "We both have our countries to look after and then . . ."

"Whoever can get to the other first," I finish.

Riya grabs Adraa's hand. "I don't like the idea of splitting up. We've been separated for too long. I'm not leaving your side, not again."

"Come with me," Adraa tells her.

Prisha whips her skyglider toward both of them and Adraa holds up a hand. "Will you go with Jatin to Naupure? His father needs you. There's a chance their clinic may have twistgrass."

Pain shreds Prisha's voice. "Adraa. I'm more than a healer. I can fight."

"I know. Gods, I know. I saw you at the prison. But you remember that time I told you the world will need pink magic one day? Well, the day has come. You're needed there. Maharaja Naupure needs *you*."

Prisha's brow furrows. I want to reassure her that this isn't some scheme to get her out of the way or away from danger. Adraa is doing what she must. My father needs a healer and Belwar needs Adraa. But we don't have time for reassurances.

"Please, Prisha. You're the only one I trust," Adraa says.

The change in Prisha is immediate, her skyglider already hovering in my direction.

I can see that Hiren is torn. But Prisha pushes forward and kisses him. We all stare as a surprised Hiren totters from the sheer force of the kiss, and then cups Prisha's cheek and kisses her back.

Adraa twists toward me with a raised eyebrow, and then she leans in to kiss me too. It's quick and it feels like the kind of kiss you give someone when it's your last. I pray it's not.

Adraa pulls back. "Be safe."

"You too."

She moves to disembark my skyglider and I stop her with a hand on her elbow. "Wait, Adraa"—this hurts to suggest—"put your mask on before you get there. You're still—"

"I'm still Adraa Belwar." With that, she twists her hands. Red smoke condenses and then paints her face in a glow, and the Red Woman—the real Red Woman—appears before us.

Then she jumps off my skyglider and falls several meters before gaining control of her own skyglider.

I watch to make sure she's okay, and then Kalyan, Prisha, and I jet toward my home as Adraa, Riya, Hiren, and Harini head toward Belwar Palace. Only meters away, my stomach drops. Once again I don't know whether I have made the right decision . . . or yet another mistake.

◇

CHAPTER FORTY-FOUR

The Real Battle Begins

Adraa

The four of us dive toward to the palace, avoiding the bursts of signals that swallow the skyline.

As we near the rooftops, a stream of light explodes right in front of us. I skirt to the right and peer down at its owner, unsure whether that burst was meant to knock me out of the air or call for help. The familiar frame of a witch comes into view. Willona, my family's head maid and the woman who's cared for me my entire life. An armed man clad in green comes up behind her. As we close upon Belwar Palace, the streak of light abruptly burns out and Willona slumps.

"No!" I scream as she falls to the shingles.

I crash-land, and before I can think about it, I sweep the Moolekian guard off the roof. He goes down screaming. I didn't even see his face. I rush to Willona and clutch her shoulders, pulling her away from the edge.

"Willona?"

I don't even have to do diagnostic magic to see she's gone. Light has left her eyes and her pulse is nonexistent.

Riya says something, but all I hear is my blood pounding. A scream knocks me out of it. I jerk toward the sound coming from the east wing. "I'm sorry, Willona. I'll come back for you, I swear it."

We drop into the courtyard, its dirt littered with footprints. I sprint to the side entrance I used to get to the training grounds every day. A girl lies slumped against the door, a hole the size of a fist dead center in her chest. She's one of the delivery fliers from the clinic who distribute potions and messages throughout the city for my mom.

I crouch, hating myself that I don't remember her name. "Hey, hey! It's going be okay."

"Red Woman?"

"Yeah, it's me." A healing spell starts on my lips.

"Don't. I . . . can't move. . . ." She pulls back her hand and amid the blood is a flourish of smoke working away at the hole. Immediately I know it's not going to be enough. The fact she's still alive is impressive in and of itself. "I'm going to die." Her eyes peer behind us and she shoots an arrow of purple magic that knocks a wizard from his skyglider.

"I'm going to do what I can to guard this door," the girl says.

"What happened?" Hiren asks.

"They came in the middle of night. We held them off all morning. A bubble shield went up around the palace. Then, an hour ago, Maharaja Moolek suddenly appeared in the throne room. Took out"—she coughs, wet and bloody—"all our defenses. Then he just . . . just left and this wizard in a cloak . . . he . . ."

One heartbreaking detail hits me like a ton of bricks. An hour. I'm late by one single hour.

There's a crash, and someone screams down the hallway. My attention snaps toward it.

"Go. Help them," the girl slurs. "I'm going to guard this door."

We enter the remnants of mayhem. Shredded tapestries, columns crumbling to such a degree they appear chewed. Holes and lines carved by arrows and spears crisscross the walls. Someone pulled a mango tree through an arched window, whether as a barrier or a weapon, I'm unsure. I cut away its branches with green magic and continue on.

I walked down this very hallway the night my father told me about the trial, wondering how I could live up to the history of this place. Now all that history is in ruins.

We turn the corner into the foyer before the throne room and face the blazing, colorful carnage of battle.

"The Red Woman!" someone yells. "The Red Woman is here!"

Eyes from both sides fasten on me. It takes a moment to take the scene in. Loyal Belwar guardsmen, exhausted and fighting for their lives against Moolek's men. Vencrin sailors. Belwarian citizens, like those at the rally. Some of them have red-soaked irises.

Bloodlurst. Harini's word spear the air as she charges forward, and the word turns into a literal spear she fires with an intensity I hadn't witnessed before.

"No, wait." I push forward to stop her, and something flashes in my peripheral vision. Instinctively, I raise a sword to deflect it, and the smoke of my blade skates across a yellow stream directed at my chest. I slice it in half, the spell weak, or at least weaker than me. With momentum and force, I strike at the wizard who attacked me with the pommel of the purple sword and swipe at the backs of his knees. It's brutal, as brutal as I have ever been without killing a wizard. But Willona lies on our courtyard roof. A few guards lie dead at my feet. This isn't the time for forgiveness.

Riya senses the change in me immediately. For a moment she stares at me, at my blood-spattered pants; the next she answers with a roar and engages the invader who has sprung up to attack us. Hiren falls alongside his guardsmen, but I don't have time to dwell on it. I'm a flurry of movement and action.

We carve our way forward, adding to the bodies littering the ground. Bodies I recognize. Guards who have served my father for more than half their life. Servants who have cooked my family breakfast. Some wounded, moaning and screaming with no one available to heal them or even press a hand to help stanch the flow of blood. I'm watching my people bleeding out in front of me. If possible, it gets even worse as we approach the throne room.

The sudden widening space and light do nothing to dampen the scene. If I thought the hallway we climbed through was bad, it's nothing compared to what lies before us.

War.

Off to the side my father spews magic in every direction,

taking on thirty wizards simultaneously. I search for my mother, but don't see her or the bright pink of her magic. In the middle of it all, a shadowed figure looks on, still, too still, except for the unnatural sway of his cloak. One doesn't have to be a black forte to identify that it's an illusion. It reeks of it. But even then, I would recognize the figure from the night Jatin and I broke into that Vencrin warehouse and I chased him down until we both almost died.

He hasn't seen me yet, though.

"Cover me!" I call to Riya.

I line up my aim. *"Zalyaraw,"* I cast, and let the red arrow charge its way through the crowd, all the way to him. A shield rises up out of the shadow and disintegrates the arrow. But it got his attention. He looks directly at me and I step from behind a pillar.

"Ah, there she is." The Vencrin leader's cloak flutters unnaturally. "The Red Woman." He amplifies his voice so it echoes across the room. A swarm of Vencrin, Moolekian guards, and Bloodlurst-infused Belwarians turn my way. "I was wondering when Belwar's hired hand would show up."

I pause, resisting the urge to spit words in his face. I wait a beat to see whether he'll say more. So many have guessed at or surmised my real identity. If they know I'm Adraa, then silence might play to my advantage.

"Not the homecoming you expected?"

Again, I only stare. If I answer I may confuse him for half a moment. But if I don't . . .

"What's wrong," he says, laughing, "speechless?"

There's the confirmation I needed. I'm glad I stayed quiet. If he knows my identity, then he doesn't need to also know I have my voice. I move my hands and push the words skyward. *Who are you?*

"Hypocritical, isn't it?"

I glare.

"That the one girl who demands an identity hides behind a mask herself. I'll show you my face when you show Belwar yours."

His cloak billows unnaturally.

Hypocritical, isn't it? I write. *That someone who wants me to show my identity won't even come here in person.*

A foot emerges from the darkness. Slowly, the gloom and the purple magic unbind themselves like an unspooling ribbon. Legs, then a torso dressed in embroidered black. The cloak, the shadows, it all falls away until a neck and face appear. But purple mist cascades, around the face, blurring and whirling to conceal any features. If I weren't so startled, I might laugh. It's a pale imitation of my mask.

It is bloody creepy, though.

"I'm very much here, Red Woman. I couldn't miss this."

◇

CHAPTER FORTY-FIVE

Breaking Down the Ice Door

Jatin

Unlike Belwar, it's quiet on the other side of Mount Gandhak. After another hour of hard flying through the smoke of Belwar, we land just outside the inner gates, off to the side of the main pathway up the mountain. My capital appears lifeless. A part of me wants to send Kalyan down to investigate, but I need him here with me. It's only the three of us.

"The birds aren't singing," Kalyan says, and I realize at once why the silence sounds so foreign.

"No goats either," Prisha adds. "Is it another illusion?"

Gods, I hope not. "We have to be ready for anything."

"Should I go to the clinic and look for twistgrass?" Prisha asks, though she sounds reluctant. Adraa may never forgive me, but something tells me we need to face this unknown together.

"No, keep close. Once we get to my father safely, we can search the clinic."

Prisha smiles and the three of us cast spells: enhanced

eyesight, enhanced hearing, shield armor over our clothes. Then we cross the front yard. Prisha, Kalyan, and I look at one another and prepare ourselves. But we don't cross any boundary. Everything about my palace looks the same as ever, daunting and cold. The ice door glints, still fully intact.

"Utsrig Himadloc." I blow the ice door apart. *"Simaraw."* I cast a shield in front of me, and we charge into Azure Palace.

Nothing. It's as if a blanket were suffocating the sounds of the place. Kalyan and Prisha stiffen next to me.

"I don't understand," Prisha says.

A scream sounds above us, on the stairs—a girl's scream. The noise explodes through my ears as I pull back the orange magic, wincing. Prisha cries out and does the same.

Seconds later, a splash of green smoke blasts against the landing, and a witch with light brown hair tumbles down the stairs. As she hits the floor, her body seizes, and she twists toward us.

Fiza.

When she sees the three of us, her eyes bulge. "Run!" she chokes.

A tall wizard steps onto the landing, dripping in emeralds and green silks, a wicked smile smeared across his face. "Ah, Nephew. You've returned home. Aren't you punctual?"

◇

CHAPTER FORTY-SIX

I Learn What It Means to Lose

Adraa

I fight my way forward as the Vencrin leader does the same. It's eerily similar to how Jatin and I crossed the cafeteria toward one another. Only this time I'm barreling toward the Vencrin leader, not my fiancé, and he's killing my guards, my people, to get to me. Blood flicks across my face as my sword cuts too deeply into a Bloodlurst-enhanced wizard's arm. He's Belwarian. My gut thuds and hardens in piercing agony.

I'm a meter away, preparing my arms for the blast of fire. But a bright orange blast throws the Vencrin leader back before either of us can even shout out a spell.

"Thank you for the distraction," my father says, stepping forward, "Red Woman."

I don't have time to respond before another Vencrin charges forward, trying to take us down. The group my father was fighting merge with Vencrin on my side. Wordlessly, my father and I fight back-to-back. He doesn't know who I am, yet there is still a level of trust. Together we build shields, together we dodge and weave, and together we fight. Moolek's men. Vencrin. Dome Guards. They fall one by one. The circle around us lessens. Harini, Hiren, and other Belwarians fight from the corners. Riya attacks the enemy to my right.

"Stop, Vivaan. Stop or I'll kill her," a deep voice announces.

We all turn to the Vencrin leader, who is holding a girl hostage.

It's . . . me.

Or an illusion of me, but it's so impressive that even Riya does a double take. The Vencrin leader presses a knife to the illusion's throat.

My father's voice hollows out and his arms slacken. "Adraa?"

"I know what you'd sacrifice for the ones you loved. And I think you know what I'll do to get what I want. Lay down your arms and call off your men, or I'll kill her." The illusion winces exactly like I do. Then it screams in fear, in pain, in horror. It's a sound I've only emitted once.

Even I stumble back in surprise. Bloody Gods. I know *that* scream. It was the last one I uttered before Basu . . .

Scream for me, he had commanded.

"Stop!" my father bellows, his voice amplified tenfold and filling the entire throne room. The clashing battles behind us grow still.

No! I can't let him fall for this.

"It's fake," I urge my father. "It's not your daughter." I conjure my magic. All I need is one good shot of fire or a sharp purple spell and he'll see.

But he's singularly focused. Completely vulnerable to this manipulation. "I said stop," he orders the Vencrin leader.

Even with all these witnesses, even with everything I risk, I reach for my mask. "It's not—"

"*Red!*" Riya screams from across the room. I turn. It's only a second, a flash of purple. Then orange engulfs my vision and I'm careening to the floor, pushed out of the way. When I look up at my father, he stands in a halo of light, the sun peering through the window behind him. He looks like a god.

I sigh in relief. He saved me. He must have known it was a trap, known that the illusion was a distraction and seen those arrows come out of nowhere. Arrows headed toward me.

Then he slumps, the sun streaking forward in his absence, and I see arrows, wooden arrows, sunk into his chest. He falls to the floor with a thud.

I can't do anything. I can't move. My dad, he's . . .

There's a volley of purple magic, then another familiar color—violet—rises like a wave, catching the spell.

"Adraa!"

I look up. Riya has cast a bubble shield that encases us.

My father, he's bleeding. I've moved without processing it. I'm leaning over his body.

"How long can you hold it?" I shout to Riya.

"As long it takes!" she yells and another layer wraps around us. "Is he . . . ?"

Something snaps in me then, and instead of moving in slow motion, time shifts to lightning speed. Three arrows: one in the shoulder that looks like an easy mend, one digging between his ribs, and one very close to his heart. He's conscious, staring at me as I break off the shaft.

"I'm going to pull this out and then I'll be able to heal you," I tell him. I yank, quick and forceful, and he grunts. I stanch the first wound with as much pressure as I can. *"Laeh!"* I scream. My hands feel wet, and I expect to see his blood coating them. But it's not only blood. A thin purple liquid pools around the wound. I sniff it, and the odor brings me back to the clinic, to the one or two lessons Mom taught me begrudgingly. *You'll have to know what can hurt people, what can poison them, but only to combat it.* And Prisha's caution: *I think it told me to destroy Mom's potion room.*

Thuds explode around the shield. A swirl of yellow smoke smashes against it, the magic smearing and billowing.

"I can hold it!" Riya screams, but her voice chokes. She glances at me. "Why aren't you healing him?"

"I—" My brain knows the truth even if it won't vocalize it. *I don't think I can.*

Dad looks at me then, his green eyes blinking into focus. "I've always wondered why you would help us. I didn't understand you, couldn't trust you." His voice forces me back to him. "But you are good, aren't you?"

For a split second I'm confused, until I realize I'm still wearing my mask.

"I don't think I should be asking you this, but my wife, my two daughters. My oldest, please help free her. She is not the killer they all—" He coughs up blood. "She is the best of us."

I tear off the mask, a shattered screen of red ripping at my face. "I'm here. I'm free, and I'm right here."

His eyebrows furrow as he takes me in. "Adraa?"

"Yes. It's me. It's always been me."

His head thuds back, his eyes crinkling in a laugh for a moment before he grimaces. "I should have figured that out long ago, shouldn't I?"

"No. I'm so sorry, I lied to you. I've been lying, lying to everyone."

"I'm just glad you are here now. I'm sorry," he chokes. "I did fail you."

I clutch the wound near his heart. "I've told you before you never failed me. You could never fail me." I sob. "Dad, it was poisoned. I don't—I don't know if I can stop it. And we don't have an antidote."

"Go to your mother's clinic," he murmurs, and I sob again, wanting to do what he says more than anything in the world and knowing the poison must have taken effect if he thinks I could even make it to Mom's clinic. Then he lifts a hand to his mouth and whispers into it. A glowing ball of his pale orange magic manifests around his fingers, almost the shape and brightness of firelight. But I recognize what it is at once. He hands it to me, and I take it so carefully it's like I'm taking his soul.

"For you and for your mother and your sister."

The tears come. He thinks this is it. *Knows* it. I'm cradling his goodbye. "Dad, no," I sob. "What can I do? We just need to think of something." For the first time since he fell, I scan our surroundings instead of his wounds. Cracks spread in a web on the surface of Riya's shield, and my sobs hitch.

My father sucks in a breath. "Just . . . just be here with me."

I focus back in on him, only him, and cling to his hand. I don't think he can feel it.

"Did . . . did *I* fail you?" I don't even realize I've said it out loud until his eyes clear and he looks at me with an intensity I've seldom seen from him.

"Never," he says. And he says it with such strength that it doesn't make sense to me when he falls still. It doesn't make sense when he doesn't move.

"Dad? Dad!"

No. *No.* I . . . I can do something. I pull up my sleeve. With enough magic, I can fix him, or I can . . . I'll go to the red room and pull him back out.

I search for a sharp object and break a splintered end of the wooden arrow.

"Adraa!" Riya hollers. "What are you—"

The crash and clamor of battle fades as Riya tugs me away from my father's body. I'm screaming at her to let me go, shouting that if I can release enough of my essence, I can get him back, but I realize a second later that more arrows are buzzing through the air. My father is punctured again in the shoulder and it's then, when he doesn't react at all, that I know I've lost him.

My father is gone.

And Belwar Palace is being attacked from the inside out.

They came to kill him. My illusion, my magic, helped them do it.

I want the world to stop. I need it to stop. And suddenly it does. My brain shuts out the noise. The chaos of the fight slows down. I'm behind a pillar somehow. Behind that, I'm under another dome of purple. Riya let the old one break to craft anew. Then a pumpkin-orange color joins the purple shield. Harini. They're both standing over me as rays of color burst around my head and into the walls, lighting up the room. The smoke tears through the tapestries and I'm transfixed, watching as the rags of my ancestors convulse, as curses riddle their way through the fabric and crumble the wall underneath.

"Adraa!"

That's my name, I think.

"Please, Adraa. We can't do this without—"

A spear crashes into Riya's shield. Instead of exploding back into smoke like all the others, it slices forward, piercing the shield. The sound is like steel cutting through glass. Cracks radiate outward.

"Oh," Riya murmurs. She stumbles as she turns, her left hand reaching to her upper right shoulder. Blood seeps through her fingers. "How did they—"

Just like that, everything comes back. The noise roars to my attention.

"Riya!" I scream, jolting forward and catching her before she falls. Her body collides with mine. The purple magic spear is gone, but the wound is gushing red.

Harini stands above us, holding her shield, the only thing keeping us alive. Another spear lodges into it and a web of cracks engulfs my vision. Harini and I cast, swiping our hands to create shield after shield as a rainbow of magic is thrown at us. Each shield is sliced with the strongest purple magic I've ever seen. I snag the eyes of the wizard throwing them at us. His eyes are bloodred. *My* bloodred.

"Kill her!" the Vencrin leader's deep voice bellows.

Riya grows limp in my lap.

No! The world explodes—I explode. Magic rages from my twisting hands. I push upward and smoke engulfs everything, a screen of red separating us from them in a dense mist. Purple magic slices through it with a whoosh, but I build another shield and tear Riya's blouse so I can see the wound. No purple substance. No poison. I can save her. I will save her. Carefully, I gather her in my arms, and with Harini covering me, we run.

◇
Fighting My Uncle

Jatin

I don't waste another second. *"Himadloc. Bhitti Himadloc!"* I shout, crafting a sheet of ice like a runway toward Fiza. Combining it with an orange speed spell, I skate toward her and build a shell of ice long enough to hold Moolek off as I grab her in my arms.

His own white magic shears the ice in half, and shards fly everywhere. Kalyan and Prisha are there to give me cover long enough to maneuver to the side and away from the blast.

The smoke clears and Moolek stands, perfectly still, nothing out of place but the angle of his lips, which are now turned down.

He descends one step. Prisha stumbles back.

I've never met my uncle in person. He's different from what I imagined, and yet exactly as Adraa described. Light brown complexion. Handsome. Tall. Strong-jawed. For a second I wonder if that's where my sharp features come from. It sickens me to my core, and for the first time I'm glad I have my father's smaller build. Anything to connect me with the man who loves me and separate myself from the one who despises everything I cherish.

"The younger sister and the trusted guard. Not the pair I was quite expecting." His arms blaze. "Before we start, tell me one thing: Did you free Adraa?"

White clouds condense on my arms. "She freed herself."

"That's quite less heroic. I set it up so nicely for you too."

Go! Find her. Free her! The words pound into my head like a command.

Standing in front of him, hearing his voice, I don't know how I didn't recognize what was happening from the start.

"Get. Out. Of. My. Head." I've never experienced anger in this way, coating my skin, pumping through my veins. He is the last connection I have to my mother. That made me feel guilty before, the blood we shared, her memory pulling me back, the belief that he saved me on Mount Gandhak because he felt it too. That ends now, because I don't care. My mother lives on through my father, through me. Today, I'm cutting the toxic blood out.

Moolek laughs. "I'm not currently doing anything. But what I *have* done? That's a different matter. Now hand over the Agsa girl. She's taken something from both of us."

"You should have run," Fiza wheezes to me.

"What are you even doing here?" I frantically whisper, feeling helpless as she spasms in my arms. A torture spell ripples through her body.

"Your father is still alive. I—I didn't . . . I didn't l-l-let him . . . ," Fiza stutters, trying to breathe. "I got here in time. He's hidden. He's safe."

"What?"

"They aren't the only ones who can perform a good illusion spell," she says with a wicked smile before passing out.

Moolek sighs, taking another step down. "Now I'm going to have to wake her up and start all over again. Don't give me that look, Nephew. Agsaians should know by now not to involve themselves. They aren't strong enough for the rest of the world. Bloodlurst can only do so much."

Gently, I lay Fiza on the floor and try to process it all. Fiza saving my father. Hiding him somewhere in the palace. Moolek standing in front me.

"Don't tell me you feel something for the Agsaian girl? What would Adraa think?"

Before any of us can move, green smoke shoots toward Prisha. It hits her in the chest and she crumbles in a heap of spasms and screams. Another torture spell.

I jolt forward and a vine of green smoke wraps around my legs. I blast it apart, but the threads multiply. *"Agnierif."* I hit the threads with fire and run toward Prisha, to get her out of the way and shield her before Moolek shoots again. But as I'm running and dodging his spells, I realize I'm reacting, defending. Shields and fire and ice blocking spell after spell of green smoke. Kalyan doing the same thing off to my left. I'm so consumed with saving my friends, I didn't realize he's pushing me backward. As soon as I step on a piece of the ice door,

Moolek casts so fast I don't even glimpse the green smoke flaring through the air. The door rebuilds itself, caging me in it. Ice crunches around me, enfolding me, tightening.

Before I can shout out a releasing spell, a binding shield attaches to my mouth. Water, vines, chains, wind all twist their way around my limbs and torso, and within seconds I'm encased in a prison of all types of magic. Next to me, Kalyan is tied in a similar cage, only his is glued to the floor. Moolek mutters spells faster than I've ever seen a wizard cast. We're both useless as Prisha suddenly stops screaming.

"What do you think? I got word about the little prisons you forged in the Underground. Innovative idea. Thought I'd put my own spin on it. You forgot pink magic. And the possibilities are endless with pink magic."

Kalyan hollers and I turn my head as much as I can to see his prosthetic leg, the one crafted with magic, being ripped apart. Magic shredding magic.

"Stop!" I scream through the binding.

"Sit and watch, or I will kill them all."

Moolek doesn't even wait for confirmation. A glow of forest green erupts around Fiza. She awakens with another cry of pain.

"Ah, there you are. Good of you to join us again."

Fiza spits, but Moolek tilts his head away. "Are you trying to pretend to be Adraa Belwar again? I don't know if spitting is quite her thing. Jatin, any thoughts, preferences?" He rips the binding from my mouth.

"I'm going to kill you."

"We can work on your threats later." He turns back to Fiza. "Tell me where you put him." His voice is cold.

"No." Fiza laughs like she's drunk. Her throat trembles and I know the torture spell is still coursing through her.

"Do I need to torture my nephew? Because I will. It won't be fun, but he is one of the only people you care about, so you aren't leaving me with many choices."

She doesn't answer and I wonder if she even heard him.

"Don't tell him," I say.

Her eyes, very much alert, find mine. Then she speaks. "There's a map in the office. And behind it you'll find a secret room. That's where I put Maharaja Naupure."

"Wonderful. Thank you. Now the torture can be just for me."

He turns toward me, smiling gleefully. He doesn't see when Prisha rises, throwing off his torture spells with her own magic. She casts. A wave of pink smoke liquifies the ice door. In one heartbeat I fall as the water rushes forward and solidifies around Moolek instead. Prisha's eyes lock with Moolek's widened ones. "Figure out who you can torture. I'm a bloody pink forte."

With a roar she sweeps her hands and Moolek is sucked farther inside the wall of water and ice and washed down the hall.

Prisha falls to her knees but still casts from the ground, breaking apart the rest of my prison. I join in, and together we release Fiza and Kalyan, who both tumble to the ground. Fiza looks like she's going to pass out again.

"That won't hold him long," Prisha rasps.

I turn to Kalyan. "You three run. Get as far away as you can. I have to get my father out of here."

"We aren't leaving you alone," Kalyan says.

I stand up on shaky legs. "I leave and my father dies."

"Then I'll stay too," Kalyan says.

"Kalyan, you can barely walk." His prosthesis is almost completely shredded.

"Never stopped me before."

I look at him hard. "Okay." Our forearms press into one another's and then I'm helping Prisha and Fiza through the ice door. "Promise me that whatever you hear, you won't come back." Then I reenter my palace.

◇ ◇ ◇

I'm not halfway up the stairs when a shot of green magic strikes the spot right in front of me. If I didn't have orange magic jolting through my muscles, I don't think I would have dodged it in time. Kalyan retaliates with streaks of white, and I hear Moolek grunt as if hit.

In desperation I tear down the golden celebration banners and throw them in the air, one more visibility barrier. Arrows pelt the fabric as I run down the hall, but they all miss me. The door to my father's office is just meters away. *"Tvarenni,"* I cast, running with everything I have.

I'm almost there.

My calf explodes in pain, and I fall on my face. Turning,

I find an arrow pinning me to the floor. Before I can yank it out, the arrow puffs into smoke, then bursts into yellow magic. The wind knocks me back, and through the door. It rips off its hinges as I crash against the desk.

Moolek strolls into the room, glancing left and right like an inspector on a mission.

Black explodes across my vision. "Why?" I ask as I try to stand. "Why him?"

Maharaja Moolek laughs. "Because he's in my way. *Bandharaw*," he casts, and cufflike purple magic flies from his fingertips and into my chest. I'm nailed to my father's desk. "But it also has to do with how much I hate him." His voice drips abhorrence.

Moolek grins as he rips apart the map in one clean stroke. Then he pauses. Behind it, there's no false door. Instead, there's a portrait of my mother, the one that hung there throughout my childhood, the one that I thought my father had replaced long ago. I've forgotten some of the painting's details. The gold necklace that matches her wedding bangles. The ringlets that sweep across her forehead. The brightness of her yellow sari, edged in mountainous blue peaks.

As Moolek roars, two things are clear.

My father isn't here. And Fiza lied.

CHAPTER FORTY-EIGHT

◇

A New Kind of Potion Room

Adraa

I'm in the east wing, which means any minute I'm going to run into Mom's potion room. In the back of my mind I wonder if I ran here because it was my father's last suggestion to me. It's the least defensible position in the palace, with wide-open rooms and a long line of windows. In fact, it's the worst place to hide. But I can't double back now.

Harini doesn't question me as we sprint, even as the Vencrin leader's deep voice vibrates through the walls with threats I can't focus on. I know part of her is as frantic as I am. Riya is still bleeding in my arms, and the wizards following us are powerful, too powerful.

I point to the door, struggling under Riya's weight, and Harini opens it for me. We barge into Mr. Burman's room. The clean fresh light of afternoon, the frostlight blossoms on the bedside table—everything is perfect and untouched. Probably the last sources of peace left in this mess. Only Mr. Burman is gone.

As I place Riya in the spot where her father should be, Harini throws boundaries across the threshold. If we can't defend this door, then Riya is . . . she'll end up like . . .

Her blood stains the clean white sheets. I scream away a sob.

Help your friend. I'll hold the door, Harini signs.

It's not poison, I tell myself. It's not poison. She'll be okay. I collapse beside the bed, not bothering with a chair, and pour every ounce of pink magic I have left into Riya's shoulder. The wound inches closed, but there's so much blood and the cut is too deep. It went clean through.

I think of the girl outside the gates. This is what my magic in Bloodlurst was able to do.

"Please," I beg to Riya's still form. "I can't lose you too."

Harini casts. *How bad—*

The door explodes open and Harini flies across the room. Fragments and splinters burst outward, showering Riya and me. Green smoke billows and shreds Harini's shield. *"Dvaaih-trae!"* I scream, re-forming the wood back into its frame as a barrier. A swarm of color pounds against mine. Red, yellow, and green build in a swirling bluster, with timber fragments and my magic the only thing separating us from them.

For a moment it holds them back. Then, with another ear-shattering crack, the door flies apart once more.

Three Moolekian guards with glowing red eyes bear down

on us. Slowly, I stand up and raise my hands. "I'll give you *one* chance to walk away."

The one in front chuckles as he takes another step forward.

"She gave you a warning." From behind me a beam of bright pink magic jets through the air and blows the men down the hall.

I turn to find my mother, hair unkempt and dirty, blouse torn. But *alive*.

We stare at one another. Harini gets up from the corner.

My mother glances at her, then at Riya and then back at me. Her arms come to life in a blaze of pink. "Who are you?" she asks slowly.

I start at her question. Then I realize what I look like. Masked as the Red Woman once again. And even though Mom knows my secret, there has been more than one Red Woman running around. Illusions forcing us to doubt our own minds.

I peel off my mask in one clean swipe. "It's me, Mom," I say.

"Adraa?" she cries. "They said you were here and I . . ."

"Dad . . . I tried . . ." I rush into her arms.

"I know. That faceless man made an announcement. They have declared victory, though half the city still fights." She looks at my face, tears streaming down her cheeks. "You were with him?"

I nod, unable to speak, and hug her close, crying into her shoulder.

"Have you seen Prisha?" she asks, her voice choked with worry.

"She's with Jatin at Azure Palace."

"What?" That seems to rattle her, and I pull back. "We have to go," she continues. "It's not safe here. Come with me."

Harini picks up Riya in one strong swoop. I thank her and we follow my mother into the potions room. It's trashed, but nothing like Prisha's fit. Everything has been broken. Plants lie crumbled and torn. Jars litter the ground, their shards like teeth.

"I couldn't let them think this place hadn't already been sacked," my mother says.

"You did this?"

"*Gahahtrae.*" My mother's magic dives into the floor and pushes the great cauldron from its spot in the corner, two meters to the right. Then, with a heave, she pulls open a trapdoor. "Quick."

Harini doesn't waste time. I give Mom a look as I follow Harini and climb down a small staircase. I expected—well, I didn't expect a trapdoor to begin with, but I assumed, at best, that it would be a small space for us to hide. A labyrinth greets us. Tunnels upon tunnels stretch in five directions. Candles hang from the walls, lighting up the caverns. Mom flashes a hand and we enter the center tunnel. We pass cell after empty cell. A dungeon.

Harini tenses. "You don't have anything to fear," I say, though this place gives me the creeps too. It's too much like the prison for my liking.

We reach a wooden door, the Belwar crest carved into its face. Mom knocks out a rhythm and infuses the door with magic, the half sun glowing to life. It swings open, revealing a large room with a cavern-like hole at the center.

I stand frozen at the threshold of a miniature replica of the prison I've lived in for the past few weeks. Cells hang over the platforms, just like the Dome. But inside the cells are plants, potion ingredients, and an entire clinic.

And people. Witches, children, and palace healers. Hiren and some of the guards who were fighting with us in the throne room have made, it down here. Alive. Still hanging on. After the carnage upstairs, I go weak-kneed with relief. They look up at our arrival. One woman sobs, probably hoping for someone else.

A battle-worn Mrs. Burman appears to be in charge of the group. She rushes forward and takes Riya from Harini, then carries her to one of the cells with beds. Beds that are occupied by wounded guardsmen and civilians.

"I thought . . ." I keep looking, turning. "I thought the dungeon was abandoned. That you hated having a prison below us."

"I do hate it, and it is abandoned. Abandoned so I could use it to my liking." Mom waves a hand. "I needed the storage space. And some of my informants can get out this way. It's even been a safe house. Beckman used it for a few weeks after Mount Gandhak when we were unsure if his cover was blown."

More of her spy network, then.

Suddenly, arms wrap around my shoulders. Zara, my maid, cries out in joy. "Adraa! You're back. You're alive."

I hug my ever-optimistic friend. "Zara!" I'm so glad she's safe.

"Come on. We need to talk. And you should get some rest." She glances at Harini. "You both look like you need it."

The crowd grows silent as each person takes me in. I no longer wear my mask. And I know they still think I'm guilty. They must think I broke out of the Dome.

Mom brings us to a cell with a bed. Harini heads toward an area where they are giving out food. I sit down. "Is there a reason everyone looks scared, besides the obvious?" I ask.

Zara fills me in, her voice growing quiet. "They made an announcement that if the Red Woman doesn't show herself to the new maharaja, he'll kill us all."

So that's what the Vencrin leader had said, his plan. Flush me out. Make me sacrifice myself. They probably need me to make more Bloodlurst. Or kill me in front of Belwar to discourage any further uprisings.

"We need to discuss a plan. Sooner or later they'll find this place," Mom says, and I know how right she is. "But rest first. I'll get you food."

Zara begins healing the scrapes, cuts, and bruises on my body. I lost track of the damage. "We won't let them get to you," she whispers.

A light laugh escapes me. "How long have you known, Zara?"

"Since after the trial. When the Red Woman wasn't saving people anymore. When the signals went unanswered."

"My substitute didn't fool you?"

"You wouldn't have let a week pass. I know what you are."

I humor her. "What am I, Zara?"

"A hero."

All the adrenaline that's been pulsing through me washes away and my arms tingle with impending burnout while my mind throbs with grief. I slump sideways. Zara grabs me and helps me lie back.

"I'm okay," I try to say. There's still so much to discuss, to do. But I'm crumpled on the cot, my left arm like jelly.

"You can quit pretending," Zara says. "We know how strong you are. You don't have to keep proving it."

Mother returns with a bowl of rice for me, and I eat quickly before falling asleep.

◇ ◇ ◇

A bustle of movement and a clatter wake me.

I start at the sight of everyone clustered in the doorway. Mrs. Burman, Zara, Hiren, Harini. But instead of murmurs of fear or the rush of an attack I hear exclamations of reunion. Prisha is at the threshold with Fiza, of all people, being taken from her arms.

"Prisha?" I get up and stumble forward. Mom beats me to her and hugs her tight. I'm still across the room when I see Mom lean down and tell her. Dad. Gone. Prisha collapses. When I reach them, I pile on, focusing on their breathing. The three of us safe, alive. After moments of grief, and Hiren coming over and holding Prisha, I finally ask.

"Prisha, where's Jatin? What—"

She cuts me off with a tearful look. "Maharaja Moolek was at Azure Palace. It was an ambush."

"How many men?" I ask.

"Just Moolek."

"And Jatin?"

"He and Kalyan stayed to protect his father." I fall back. Deep in my heart, I don't know whether Jatin is strong enough to fight Moolek one-on-one. I definitely wasn't.

"Moolek saved Jatin last time. Saved us," I find myself saying aloud. "He won't kill him." I have to hold on to that hope because I can't go to him.

"You're right," Prisha says, but tears keep falling down her face.

"They knew what they were doing, separating us," Mom says. "Last night I was told someone was dying in the East Village and I was needed right away. It was an ambush. I didn't think they had gotten so daring. But we are together now, and I'm going to get us out of here." Her voice is reassuring and strong.

"I'm *not* going to run," I say. Mom and I stare at one another. "This is our home. We make one last stand. They want the Red Woman. They want me."

"We have to escape for now. We don't know what we are dealing with. *Who* we are dealing with," Mrs. Burman argues.

"I do," I say, my voice cracking.

Heads turn toward me, everyone in earshot focused. I step forward.

"He's the leader of the Vencrin. He's working for Maharaja Moolek and has been from the very beginning."

I tell them everything I know. About the Bloodlurst and my magic. My theories on the trial and his illusions. By the end, my mom is wiping tears from her eyes.

We need a plan, Harini inserts, her words cutting through the air. Everyone looks up, surprised, and after one long blink, Harini continues. *What have you come up with, Adraa?*

"I have something." I look at Mom, then at Prisha. "But you aren't going to like it."

"As long as it doesn't involve you sacrificing yourself and trying to do this alone," Prisha asserts.

"I'll be turning myself in," I concede. "But this time I won't be alone. Prisha, tell me more about the sound spells you and Dad worked on."

◇

CHAPTER FORTY-NINE

I Fight

Adraa

It's easy getting captured. All I have to do is step out of the dungeon and into daylight, where they are waiting for me. Five Vencrin bring the Red Woman back to the throne room, and I find their leader relaxing in my father's chair, basking under my family's emblem. My whole life I've wondered whether my ancestors meant for the sun to be rising or setting. Now I realize it is dependent upon the person who sits there—what hope Belwar has for a future.

I move my hands. *You don't have the right to sit there.*

"And you had no right to break out of the Dome. You were sentenced to life in prison for what you have done." He holds out a pair of cuffs. "Put these on and come peacefully."

You murdered the maharaja of Belwar in cold blood. Where are your cuffs?

"You've come alone to say this?" His purple mask scrambles into a sneer. "Or write it?"

Like I thought, he thinks he's already won and I am some voiceless witch who can't make a sound. I don't want him to know I have regained my full capabilities.

The cloaked Vencrin leader leans forward. "If you didn't come here to surrender, do you want to fight me?"

In answer, I shift into a fighting stance.

"The thing is Red Woman. You can't bait me. And this conflict doesn't begin or end with you or me." He waves his hand and five red-eyed Vencrin step forward.

As I retreat to gather distance, a roar of footsteps and battle cries thunder from outside. Another window breaks as magic bursts through. All of Prisha's messages must have reached the people of Belwar. Everyone capable of fighting has emerged from the dungeon. Behind me the battle for Belwar has begun.

You're right. It's not just about you and me, I cast. *You involved my entire country. Many of us won't go silently.*

"Go!" the Vencrin leader yells to all his men. He strides off the dais toward me. "You just led more of my people to their death."

They are not your people. They will never be your people.

I have to get him to the courtyard, away from his reinforcements. Away from this room where he can cast illusions around any pillar. I need daylight and wide-open space to have any chance.

I charge forward, lighting my arms with fire and my muscles with speed. He does the same. We close in on one another. I create a fireball and arch back to throw it.

His whole form blurs at the last minute, and the fireball flies across the room. An illusion. All an illusion. Like a shift in time and space, he materializes behind me. Something sharp hits my head. I duck as best I can, veering away from death. When I'm fully upright again I run. Down the hall. I just have to make it down the hall.

He follows as I hoped. I can hear the pounding of feet heavy trailing me. I whip sideways and shoot an arrow behind me. It snags on another illusion that poofs into ash, and I pause. No, he has to follow. Not an illusion. His true self.

I open my mouth to taunt him. It's all I can think to do. But out of nowhere, a hand grips my throat. More black magic. I fumble for the hand, all my training to get out of a hold like this evaporating in an instant. Two hands grip my throat, and I'm lifted up the wall with the strength of orange magic. He emerges, purple mask and all, rippling like mist. "This time I will silence you for good."

The pressure on my throat intensifies.

I beat down on his wrists, but they are solid, purple smoke flaring in agitation. I can't get a sound out to cast. But then I remember—I don't need sound anymore.

Pavria. I sign the spell and my magic releases in a blast of wind. The Vencrin leader skids backward.

I take the chance to gulp in air, my lungs grateful. I grasp at my own throat and stare him down. He's only a few steps away. But I want to make sure he hears this next bit.

"You. Can. Never. Silence. Me."

The satisfaction of seeing him pause is worth it.

"You *really* thought Moolek would give you Belwar after my

father and I had fallen? You are nothing more than a puppet." I rise up. "And I won't let that happen."

"Do you imagine your country won't rip you to shreds if you show your real face?" he says with a chuckle. "Red Woman or Adraa, either way you are doomed because you are nothing but a monster to them."

I stare at him as he articulates my every fear from just weeks ago. But I don't live under my guilt or my doubt—and especially not my fear—anymore. I'm not the same witch. All I can do is hope my people accept me as I am.

No more hiding.

I let the flames burn high up both arms, hot enough to incinerate my sleeves.

The spell of my mask disperses in smoke. I've already gotten my voice back, but this feels like the moment I truly restore myself.

"I'm Adraa Belwar, Lady of Belwar. I'm also the Red Woman. I'm a ruler and protector of my people. I saved us from Mount Gandhak and I have never done this country harm."

I focus on the Vencrin leader. "Just me and you, Vencrin. I'm not afraid to be judged. Are you?"

The purple magic unglues itself then. And I'm staring at Raja Dara.

One of my father's five most trusted men. The man who runs the Dome Guard, who led me off Basu and the Vencrin's trail for weeks. The wizard who saved me in the courtroom from an assassin's arrow. An arrow that would have ruined *his* illusion of me. Of all the rajas, I never thought . . .

Prisha enters my mind. Prisha and Hiren. Hiren, his son. Did he betray us too?

Anger and grief boil together. "Raja Dara, you drugged my people? You helped steal my firelight? You killed my father?"

He shakes his head like he can't fathom my ignorance. But I need him to say it.

"What? Not proud enough of your work to admit it?"

"I'll admit it when you're taking your last breath."

I back up like I'm afraid of him. "The Belwar line won't fall so easily. And I think you already know what happens when you try to silence us."

He cocks his head. "Who needs silence when I can rewrite your words?" Before me, a girl appears. It's me. Or at least an illusion of me. Orange-and-pink sari, the exact one I wore to my trial. "Yes. And I'd do it again," she says with my voice, only it's angry and hateful. She stares outward like there's an audience soaking in her words. . . .

I pound a fist of fire through her, smearing the purple smoke and black magic.

Another doppelgänger appears, jolting forward with a deadly glare. "I'd delight in watching this city burn. You think I gave my firelight, my power, willingly to the people because I'm generous? You are useless. Belwar is useless."

I falter. Is that . . . is that what I said at the trial? Is that what my people heard?

"The voice wasn't perfect, but then I got your real one. It makes it very convincing," Raja Dara says.

A third illusion pops into being. "Anyone who ever used

firelight, who thought they could harness *my* magic, deserves to die." She bends down and looks me right in the face. "To burn."

I'm absorbed in this last phrase when a blast of purple smoke shoots at me. I only have time to raise my arms in a small red shield. It's not enough. I'm blown backward, through the door and into the courtyard. Then I tumble into the dirt over and over again until I lie still.

◇

CHAPTER FIFTY

The Battle Inside My Mind

Jatin

I think I'm about to die, but I'm still relieved. Fiza and Prisha got away. Kalyan has time to flee. Adraa and the rest are facing whatever is at Belwar Palace, but I know she can handle it. She can handle anything. The bigger threat is standing in front of me, staring at my mother's portrait as I'm shackled to my father's desk. Though I know it will take too long, I work in whispers, casting spells to cut myself loose. I'd rather die facing him head-on.

Finally, he turns, not a stitch of emotion showing on his face. "You can wait here." A purple spell latches to my mouth and then he leaves.

As Moolek rampages through the palace, I try to figure out where Fiza might have taken my father. Crashes reverberate throughout my home, each roar of frustration giving me hope that Fiza's illusion is too strong or her hiding spot too clever.

I can't say exactly how much time has passed before he

comes back. Only that, by then, my back aches from the angle and my pant leg is soaked in blood. Moolek stares at the portrait again like he can't look away. "You don't look much like her." He draws closer to me, green knife in hand. Then his arm falls. "And yet I still don't want to kill you." Instead of stabbing me, he removes the magic from my mouth and shifts the bindings so instead of bolting me to the desk, they twist around me like rope. I fall to my knees before him. Even in my terror, I can't help but wonder why. Why do any of this? Why Adraa and Belwar?

A mist of green smoke covers me. "Does it ever anger you how weak your father is? How much he has placed upon your shoulders? Mine was similar, you know. Very demanding." Moolek pauses, watching me.

He glares when I don't respond. "It's always about that girl with you. I honestly don't know which one of you is worse. I got into Adraa's mind months ago, and the secrets, the lies, and the doubt I found there? Blood, it barely took anything. But yours is a bit different. Yours, I can play with."

Go! Find her! The thoughts rage, screaming in my mind.

I shake as if that will rid me of him. "Get out of my head!" I shout.

He ignores me. "You know what the saddest part is?" He laughs. "The emotions I've let all of your people feel? They came from the both of you. They are your thoughts. Your own doubts about whether you can lead them. Because, deep down, neither of you believe you are good enough." He leans forward. "You say you don't want me in your head, to manipulate you? Then don't make it so bloody easy."

He pauses.

It clicks then, why he's telling me all this, why he's talking to me instead of continuing to kick down doors to find my father. He's trying to search my head for his location. He doesn't understand me, so he's poking through everything he can think of. Every insecurity about my father, my leadership ability, about what Moolek has done to Adraa and me. The only reason he's still talking is because he can't get in again.

He doesn't know me. Not truly. I realize then he needs some insecurity, some guilt or doubt to infiltrate our minds. Yet in these past weeks I've grown stronger. I've become confident, too confident for his mind games. Because now, with Adraa free from the Dome and my father as safe as he can be behind Fiza's magic, the last thing I feel is guilt. I know I've done everything I can. I haven't failed.

Moolek's features turn murderous. I've blocked him out and he knows it. "I think it's about time we checked in with our friends. I am quite curious what they are getting up to, aren't you? You'd like to see Adraa one last time, right?"

Is he about to tie me to a skyglider and take me to Belwar? Before I can answer, he lunges forward and grabs my arm. With a whoosh, green smoke billows around me like vines, eclipsing . . . everything. At first, I think it's a cage of purple magic surrounding me. I start to shout some counter, anything, when my body lurches, and suddenly I'm moving. I feel stretched. My skin pulls taut. The air is sucked out of my lungs and a rush of wind swoops past my head. An array of rocky green landscapes shifts before me.

And just as my panic spikes—it all stops.

Suddenly my father's study is gone. We're outside, on a roof overlooking a courtyard. The Belwar courtyard, in fact. Moolek stands next to me, still fastened to my arm, vines of green smoke unraveling around us.

A blast shakes the ground, and the palace doors explode open. A figure tumbles out and rolls over and over in the dirt. "Oh, look. We're right on time. She's trying so very hard too," Moolek says.

My attention snaps to where Adraa lies still, bleeding.

It's an illusion. It has to be. My uncle is trying to destroy me, to get back inside my head.

"This isn't real," I counter, keeping my voice steady.

"That would take far too much energy and magic. I'm not going to burnout just to put on an exciting show for you. I have people for that. Allies."

The wind gusts in my face as evidence. The smell of ash, blood, and Belwar's famous sea salt engulf my senses. I don't know how it's possible, what new spell he's mastered, but Moolek has really transported me here.

"This will be—what? The third time you've failed her? Gods. Not what I would call the best partner."

He leaves me tied up, a spectator to Adraa's demise. "Let's watch."

But something shifted on our way here and I nudge a hand free. I'm going to do more than watch.

CHAPTER FIFTY-ONE

◇

I Free Myself

Adraa

Blood. Everything hurts. It's all going as we planned, or at least close enough. I wanted to get him out to the courtyard, but I didn't think I'd be *thrown* out. And I definitely wasn't expecting to see myself like that. . . .

I reach into my belt. My father's message still glows in orange, and beside it, Prisha's pink orb pulses, capturing every sound. My people won't get the visual of Raja Dara's illusion, but they'll hear him admit to rewriting my words.

I pull myself up and scan the roof for my team planting orbs of magic to replicate what I captured in that hallway. Prisha began to leave her perch at the sight of me being tossed out of the door, but I hold up a hand.

Then Raja Dara emerges from the doorway. The whole courtyard seems to still. I scan for Hiren, whose eyes are fixed on his father. He's obviously in shock. But is it shock that his father revealed himself or shock that he's the force of evil behind this coup? Prisha turns to Hiren, betrayal written on her face. And I watch as she builds a blade and charges.

Raja Dara sees none of it as he lumbers toward me. "You've already lost, Adraa. This is mine." He gestures to the courtyard, to the palace.

"But before that, it was my training field. *Taruhtrae!*" I scream, ripping the mango tree out from the hallway and throwing it, roots and all. *"Agnierif,"* I breathe after it, and its trunk and the very flammable frostlight blossoms littering the ground are engulfed in a torrent of flame.

I twist again, looking for Prisha. She and Hiren are fighting on the southern rooftop. A dance of flashing swordplay. He betrayed us. My plan is falling apart. I turn again and something catches my eye on the western roof. I do a double take. It's Jatin with Moolek. And they are battling, huge gushes of white and green smoke slamming into one another. What is Jatin doing here? How did he—

Out of the branches and foliage, a blast of purple magic engulfs my vision. I don't know what spell is barreling toward me, but instead of dodging I shoot my own power at it. The purple and red smoke collide in an outpouring of magenta, and then billow into a condensed wall. Raja Dara pushes harder and I push back, digging my heels into the dirt as swells of red magic pulse out of me.

I can't take it anymore. If one of us doesn't relent, then we'll both die. With a scream, I push the magic up and over my shoulder. It strikes the pillars of the north quarters but doesn't stop there. The sound of ruin and destruction erupts in a barrage of stone as the palace's foundation crumbles.

When the smoke clears, the north wing is flattened. The hallways, the archways, the tapestries, the rooms adorned with Belwar history—it's all gone.

Raja Dara laughs. "There hasn't been a red forte ruler in over a hundred years, in any country. Do you know why that is?" He circles me. "Because while they are powerful, all they bring is destruction. I think you know it too. I think you understand, deep down, that you are not what is best for Belwar."

"Tell yourself whatever you want," I spit.

"No, I know. How else do you think Moolek was able to manipulate everyone? He used your emotions, your fears. Literally."

What? "That's not possible."

"Isn't it? Every ball of firelight you created has your magic and your intent. There's a sense of you within them. Moolek might have instigated the eruption, but it was your power that destroyed Belwar. The whole city has been living with your sense of inadequacy, your doubts, your fears. What do you expect of your people, having to bear such a toxin? It's no wonder they wanted to see you dead."

No! That can't . . . And yet it all makes sense. The last few months, the courtroom. Everyone thought the same way because it was my thoughts, my doubt. From my own firelight and the very ash of Mount Gandhak spewed over my city. Prisha was wrong in the Alps. I might not be bound by firelight, but my people have been.

Ice wraps around my right arm and fastens it to the ground with a clunk.

"I'm a lefty," I huff in anger, already moving to break the ice. But another spell sizzles through the air like an arrow. It slams into my left hand and pins it to the ground. My body slams down with it.

"Oh, I know," Dara says. "I know quite a lot about you."

"*Agni*—" I start to shout. But before I can complete the casting, another spell hits me in the face, sealing my mouth.

"I know all of you. I know your weaknesses. I know your strengths. Just as I knew your father's. He was too gullible for his own good."

"Adraa!" someone shrieks.

I scream through the ice, or try to. How dare he call my father gullible? My father embodied kindness. He led a country based on equality, truth, and fairness. But all I get out are muffled moans. The frost bites at the slightest movement, crystallizing and climbing below my jaw and over my cheekbones.

"You think you've learned a new skill? It's not so *impressive* when it can be so easily canceled out."

Stuck in this position, I can see the battles raging around me. My people storm through the rubble, meeting the Vencrin and Moolek's men in a fray. I see the rest of the team. Mrs. Burman, my mother, guards, and healers rise to meet them.

Raja Dara takes slow, easy steps toward me, and I know. I know this is the end. Pure hatred lines his eyes. He doesn't care if Moolek wants me alive. He's going to kill me himself.

A shot of black smoke hits him in the arm as he raises it. I glance over and see Hiren. Hiren firing on his own father alongside Prisha. Pink spells blast at Raja Dara. He fires back, whisking a disk of wind at them.

They are buying me time to escape.

But this isn't something I can escape. I can't access my magic. The frost climbs down my throat, the cold biting at my skin. The icicles grow higher up my arms.

"Adraa!" I hear Jatin yell. Then green magic engulfs him.

I have to get out of this. No one can save me but myself. Jatin will be killed if he even turns away from his fight with Moolek.

Most spells have a counter, a way to undo what has been cast. But to break ice, truly break it, I need white magic. I don't have it. I'm an eight.

Still, maybe I can counter it. With strong enough red magic, maybe I can break it. Ice crawls up to my shoulder.

I focus in on the firelight spell, my spell. *Erif Jvalati Dirgharatrika!* I yell over and over in my head. Then I stop.

No. I don't need words, or even my hands. I have to trust my magic, my intention. Myself.

Erif Jvalati Dirgharatrika. My firelight. *My firelight.*

Magic sings through my blood and I concentrate on its power. My power.

Feeling returns to my numb fingers. Heat.

The ice cracks. The sound is loud enough to turn Raja Dara's head. "How—" he sputters, a moment before my left hand bursts from its trap and the roar overwhelms the rest of his question. Bloodred smoke billows from my arm. In my palm,

I hold a ball of firelight, the first one I've made in a very, very long time.

I look at it, the glow stronger than ever. And deep down, somehow I know it will last longer than two months. It's perfect, the image I always had in my imagination. What I wanted when I crafted the spell in the first place. A mini sun shining from my fingertips.

It takes a second for me to understand what just happened. It's Prisha, watching from the roof, who supplies the answer. "Mind casting. It's real."

I turn to my enemy, the man who killed my father. Flames, like the ones Erif gave me when I awoke from the red room, engulf my arms. This time, the fire is mine. "Is this impressive enough for you?"

Crisp, clean steps echo across the courtyard as Raja Dara strides forward over shards of ice. "You one-armed bitch."

I almost laugh. "You should really learn more about who you work for. And you call me ignorant?"

He pulls out a pouch I'm all too familiar with.

"Careful, burning out permanently is the real bitch," I tell him.

He pours the Bloodlurst onto his arm, a surge of bright redness unmatched by anything I've witnessed on the streets or in the Underground. Something, a feeling in my gut, pulls me to the substance. It seems to call to me, pulsing.

Raja Dara rises with a new sense of strength and reassurance, magic wafting off him in a mighty purple mass, his eyes blazing red. Yet all my doubt fades away.

"Oh, you made a mistake there," I huff, almost wanting to laugh.

He marches toward me with a wicked smile. "No more witty comebacks."

"Fine by me."

One spell. That's all it will take.

His hand reaches out.

"*Sara Mayin Tviservif,*" I whisper.

It happens all at once. The magic that infused the most potent batch of Bloodlurst jerks out of his body. I close my fist, and gusts of purple smoke surge out of him. A light show of recent spells he's cast decorates my vision. Swords. Daggers. Ice. They seem to scream to life in a final echo of power. Then Raja Dara falls, limp from burnout. His cries come to a halt. His arms dull to black, then his Touch withers away. Permanent burnout.

He moans, clutching his arms. "What? How . . ."

"I might not be a nine, but I know how to control my magic."

A black rope drops from the roof and wraps around Raja Dara.

"Son!" Raja Dara roars and cries, pleading one last time.

Hiren walks toward him "Don't call me that ever again."

The binding tightens. Another wraps around Raja Dara's mouth to stop his pleading. Hiren's disgusted face says enough.

I turn to the western roof, where Moolek and Jatin stand opposite each other, flinging spells. My mother and Prisha close in, providing backup.

The more alarming threat is the battle raging through the rubble and swarming toward the palace. Vencrin with Bloodlurst beating back my people and guards. They haven't seen their leader fall, and they don't care, enflamed as they are with power. Raja Dara was right. This battle is bigger than the two of us.

"They are too powerful," Hiren says.

I whip around to Hiren. "Watch my back?"

"What are you going to do? What's the plan?"

"I'm not going to let them have my magic."

Help me out, Erif, I pray. *I'm doing your bidding here.* I don't know if she's listening, but I feel stronger.

Destroy it, Adraa, a voice whispers.

"*Sara Mayin Tviservif.*" I say it. I sign it. I will it. "*Sara Mayin Tviservif.*"

A wizard breaks loose from combat and charges me, aiming an ax at my head. "That's not your power," I say, and with a whisper of red smoke I pull the Bloodlurst out of his Touch. The wizard drops, collapsing in the dirt.

"Gods!" Hiren cries.

Not gods. One goddess.

"*Sara Mayin Tviserif!*" I scream. Bloodred washes over the battle like a fine mist. Slowly, my magic, heightened by Erif herself, pulls at each and every enemy who was selfish and desperate enough to drug themselves before battle. Wizards fall. Unconscious. Burned out. Powerless. My people stop fighting, most of them slumping to the ground in exhaustion.

I turn around and Moolek himself is staring at me. I can barely stand, but I refuse to fall under his gaze. It's over.

◇

CHAPTER FIFTY-TWO

Moolek's Undoing

Jatin

I've held my ground on this rooftop fighting my uncle for what feels like hours. My leg has buckled under my weight. My wrist is broken. I've defied death. Prisha, Harini, and Maharani Belwar herself are here for backup. As a team, we've fought off Moolek as Adraa fights her own battle below.

But when Adraa screams out a spell and her red mist fells my uncle's army in a single sweep, I think he truly knows he's out of options.

"No," Moolek murmurs. "No." He and Adraa stare at one another from across the battlefield.

"You have failed," I say. "We are both stronger than you will ever know."

A burst of pink shoots out, aimed at Moolek's head. Then a volley of arrows. He dodges them all easily, growling and tearing his gaze from Adraa.

"You never did have good aim, Ira," Moolek spits.

"Are you sure about that?" Maharani Belwar yells.

Moolek holds a hand up to his neck, his palm coming away bloody and coated in a purple substance that makes him pause.

"Sorry, I don't have the antidote yet, Moolek," Maharani Belwar says.

Our arms glow with power, one last stand from all of us. Ira and Prisha in pink. Harini in orange. Slowly, a crowd gathers in the courtyard. Belwarians. Belwarians who may not know the whole story but who saw Adraa Belwar disarm the enemy. Guards fly or climb through the rumble. Hundreds appear to be readying themselves. Untouched draw their swords. Magic lights up the crowd as one after another fortifies for the last fight.

And then, finally, Adraa's arms blaze with real fire.

I hold up my own hands, crystallized in pure white ice. "What are you going to do, Uncle? Run?"

A bolt of pink from Maharani Belwar hits him in the knee, and he staggers. Vines climb upward and around him, and I watch as he tangles himself within his magic like a cocoon. All at once, we cast. Hundreds of voices and their spells blaze toward him. A rainbow of colors clashes with green.

Moolek lurches, and green smoke billows up around him.

Then, in a whoosh, he's gone.

◇

CHAPTER FIFTY-THREE

The Red Woman Revealed

Adraa

"Adraa!" Jatin shouts my name.

"Here," I call, slumped in the middle of the courtyard. "I'm here."

"Let's get you to a clinic." He bends to pick me up, and for a moment I almost let him, almost let myself fully collapse. He's limping and looks in about the same shape as I feel.

"No, wait. I have to do something first," I tell him.

"Adraa, you're bleeding."

I cling to the rubble, finding my footing and straightening my spine. "I'm always bleeding nowadays."

Prisha and my mom rush to me. I hand over the pink ball of light, which captured Raja Dara's admission. "Now, Prisha, send them free," I tell her.

"Are you sure?" she asks.

"We've won today. You don't have to reveal yourself," Mom says with conviction.

Jatin holds my hand. "You can still be the Red Woman."

It's tempting, the act of hiding, putting on a mask. But I don't want to hide anymore. "They need to know the truth. Moolek's manipulation is still there. This is the first step in breaking his hold on us." I pause, trying not to cry. "My dad died today because of this lie. I don't want to keep living it."

No one says another word. This is my decision.

Prisha raises her hands. With a rush, pink orbs fill the sky, each one repeating the conversation Raja Dara and I had in the hallway. A thousand little messages of truth. Raja Dara's admission of murder, me revealing my identity, him revealing his. His explanation of the trial, and how it was an illusion. All of it. I got it all.

I climb further, up to the ridge of what used to be the north wing of Belwar Palace. The city unfolds before me. A mass of people waking up from their anger and manipulation put down their weapons and pull back their magic. They all seem to be looking at me.

"My name is Adraa Belwar, Lady of Belwar, daughter of Vivaan Belwar and Ira Belwar. I'm also the Red Woman. I meant only to protect you. When Mount Gandhak erupted, it was with my firelight, but I didn't place it there. In fact, I took my magic back. I tried to save us all, and I won—at a cost." I suck in a breath. "A few hours ago, our maharaja, my father, was killed by one of our own, Raja Dara, with the help of Maharaja Moolek. They were able to do this by poisoning our minds, manipulating us. Today I promise you, this will not go unpunished. But I'll need your help. We can't let Maharaja Moolek's hate control us any longer."

No one moves. For a second I wonder whether this is going to work. Moolek's power could be too deeply ingrained. My own doubts have been infused in the minds of my people.

Then, slowly, Jatin brings two fingers to his throat and kneels. As soon as he bows, a cascade of people follow him in a wave of respect and reverence. Emotions rise within me. Shock. Honor. Happiness. They envelop me as I soak in this moment.

A part of me wants to sit down, to rest. But Moolek thinks we, as a nation, can't stand against him. So I remain standing. And as thousands pay their respects, silence falls at last. A nice silence. A silence I don't mind living in for a moment as I take in a city full of people deciding I am worth it.

"No! They can't . . . they can't want you," I hear Raja Dara choke from the courtyard below, where Hiren still guards him. "You are a liar. A one-armed Touch. A royal ceremony failure. You're a bloody *eight*."

I look down at Raja Dara, and for the first time his words don't faze me. They don't mean anything at all.

"I think their choice is clear," I say in response. Then I bow to my people, two fingers to my throat. "And that is all that matters."

CHAPTER FIFTY-FOUR

◇

Fiza's Goodbye

Jatin

After everything, after Adraa is put in a clinic bed, my bones are healed, and Moolek's men have been captured or tracked down—an easy feat since most have burned out—I return to the destruction of Azure Palace.

Maharani Belwar's first orders in the aftermath of the battle were to hunt down as much twistgrass as possible. And once she procured it, she created the antidote only hours later and rushed it to my father's bedside.

My father is not only alive but awake the next time I see him. And while he's not jumping up to greet me by any means, the awareness in his eyes, the life there, makes me break down before I'm even in his arms.

Chara steps aside. Kalyan nods from the next bed over. After Moolek had transported me, Kalyan found my father in his own quarters under Fiza's powerful illusion magic. I guess

I should have known. Fiza always said she trusted Kalyan more than anyone else.

"Is it true? Is he really gone?" Father asks me, and I know at once by the agony in his voice that he's asking about Maharaja Belwar.

I nod into his chest. "I couldn't save him." I refuse to tell him that it could be boiled down to a choice, a father for a father, a friend for a friend. I'm sure one day when I'm strong enough to talk about how I rushed to defend Naupure and protect him instead of helping Adraa, my father will forgive me. I'm even sure everyone will understand. But right now I don't want my explanations to sound like excuses.

"How is Adraa? How is Ira?"

"Strong. Stronger than they should have to be."

He coughs and Chara rises to get some herbs to calm him. After he settles back down, he looks at me with eyes that seemed to have aged a lifetime. "Naupure needs someone strong leading them."

I squeeze his shoulder. "You'll get better soon."

"Better? Yes. Soon? It won't be soon enough."

"You always said strength is more than standing."

He smiles weakly. "You're right. But we're at war. We'll need all the strength we can get. Naupure requires it. Jatin, I need you to be maharaja." The words are firm. It's how I imagined he would say that phrase one day, but I didn't expect to be hovering over his sickbed when he said it.

"For how long?"

"The war is not just coming anymore. It's here. Whatever

happens will shape the future of Wickery. This position won't be temporary."

Though the weight of his words doesn't crush me, I still consider what my response will mean. I will be taking Naupure to war. I'll be their leader. I will make decisions that affect how my people will fight—how some will die. Yet at some point, when I was facing Moolek, I made my decision. No more evading. No more living on the defensive. And to blood with another voice inside my head besides my own.

This is my destiny. My father needs me. My country needs me.

"I'd be honored."

◈ ◈ ◈

I'm surveying my father's torn-apart office when a knock echoes through it.

"May I come in?" a familiar voice asks.

Fiza stands there in loose, dark blue Naupure silks. She looks better than one would expect for someone who was tortured by Maharaja Moolek himself. Yet the bandages on her wrists stand out, the yellow bruises even more so. I gesture to the partially destroyed door and the half-open threshold. "Of course, Fiza. Who's going to stop you?"

She steps over the wooden debris gingerly. "You could. Very easily." She looks me in the eyes. "And with every right to tell me never to come here again."

"My father owes you his life. And I owe you—"

"An apology?" she says without her usual note of one-upmanship. She sounds resigned.

"Yes."

"What if I told you I didn't want it?"

This is a new Fiza. Still complicated and hard to read, but there's something else. A wall has come down. "I'd still want to give it," I respond.

"And what if I wanted to say I'm sorry?"

"Then I would listen." I tilt my head. "I promise."

"The Bloodlurst, that facility." She takes a deep breath. "I was ashamed. My father gave me the substance months ago to toughen up, to get stronger. After graduation, I was falling behind, not progressing quickly enough for my title, my father said, or to even attempt my royal ceremony. Even so, I stopped taking it eventually. Bloodlurst, it . . . I could feel it draining me. I burned what I had." Fiza clenches her fists. "Then the news arrived that a red forte, the witch I envied more than anyone, had failed her own ceremony. I panicked and sought out the source of the Bloodlurst. I didn't care about the effects, and even though I didn't know the full extent of what they did at that facility, I didn't care enough to stop it. I couldn't be like Adraa Belwar. I had to be better."

My sympathy runs dry at that last part. "No, you couldn't be like her."

"I get that now. But at the time, when Mount Gandhak blew, we bought into the lies. I bought into them until that trial. Then I knew something was very wrong. The illusion was the best I'd ever seen, but the voice—the voice was off."

"What does your father know of all this?"

"My father is ignorant of most of what Bloodlurst can do to the body. He only saw the enhancements. He thinks strength and power come only from magic. The Vencrin cut him in on supplies for his people, and he let them have that run-down prison and enough security to produce what I'm sure was triple what they were making before."

Just what I thought. More corruption. Another mess to clean up. "We'll have to destroy it. From the roots up."

"I'll help you."

"You have your alliance, Fiza, but you should know that it'll be Adraa, me, and you working together."

She smirks. "Good. I may like her better than you, anyway."

My eyebrow arches. Well, this is new.

"Okay, that's a lie," she says. "But I can understand the hero worship. I mean, a bloody mind caster? I didn't think it was possible."

"I never thought I'd live to see the day Agsa was willing to go to war."

"Farming is harder than it looks. We'll have a strong army. I simply have to convince my family."

"I believe you can." And I mean it.

Fiza pauses and takes another breath, her humor gone. "I'm sorry you had to put up with me. You've always been kind. Do you know how rare that is?"

"What do you mean?"

"My whole life, my brothers, my father, uncles—they are perfectly calm and sweet to me when I'm obeying them. But

when I stand up for myself? When I speak out and push back?"
She shakes her head. "They don't like that very much." She
bites her lip and goes on. "I wanted to tell you something. For
once, I hope you hear me out without thinking I'm trying to
manipulate or ambush you."

"Okay." I nod. "I'm listening."

"I love you," she says. "I truly do. And it's because of your
kindness."

I school my expression and try to remain calm. She wants
me to listen, and I will.

"I know you strive to be like Adraa. This daunting, confident
force of a wizard who can stand up to any problem and solve
any conflict. But underneath all that power, you are kind. You
treat people like you see them. And I liked being seen by you."
She pauses, fills the space between us with a vulnerable shrug.
"You've asked and I thought you might want to know now that
I can articulate it. You'll make a great maharaja. Don't forget
your kindness when you are ruling over Naupure." She holds
out her forearm. "Political allies?"

I step toward her. "Friends?" I ask, pressing my forearm to
hers.

"Okay. Though I can't promise I'll come to your wedding."
She straightens and heads for the door. For a second, I think
about letting her just leave.

"Hey, Fiza."

She turns back, but I can see it's out of politeness, that she
doesn't expect anything.

"Thank you. There is more to you than anyone will ever know."

"I know." She smiles.

"And I hope you can find someone someday who can see it all a whole lot quicker than I did."

"Ah, but what's the fun of that?" With that, she steps over the broken door and walks away. For the first time, I wouldn't mind if she came back.

◇

CHAPTER FIFTY-FIVE

What It Means to Be a Rani

Adraa

In the end, Raja Dara fundamentally changed the system. There will be a vote to determine who leads Belwar. Though I'd like to think it wasn't him but the people of Belwar who brought about the real change. That in those rallies filled with anger were people with good intentions and a desire to have a say in who governs them.

My family and I throw our voices behind the movement, which sets it in motion quickly. I campaign for my mother, but my name gets brought up again and again, which shows me that Belwar understands the truth and, more importantly, believes it.

If Raja Dara was a less selfish, power-hungry person, I'm sure he'd be pleased with the upcoming election. But it becomes clear as he's led away by trusted guards to a prison cell under Belwar Palace that he didn't want to incite change for the good of the people. He wanted it for himself. Moolek convinced him long ago he could have a title handed to him through murder and deceit.

Hiren proclaims his innocence, that he didn't know what his father had done or what he had planned. The council is wary. But after I explain it was Hiren's spells that saved me, they ease up. Prisha also vouches for him, reiterating how close he was to death by her own hand on that rooftop when she thought he had betrayed her. Even after all that, a truth spell is cast and Hiren is more than cleared. In an embarrassing moment during the proceedings, he admits his feelings for my sister. *Intense* feelings. I've never seen my sister blush so hard or smile so wide. Afterward, Jatin smirks and says, "That could have been me."

◇ ◇ ◇

Riya recovers in the clinic next to her father. A few hours after Maharaja Naupure took the cure and awoke, Mr. Burman opened his eyes after a year in a coma. We're by his bedside when it happens. For once, my eyes are filled with tears of happiness.

After they've had a moment to reunite, he touches Riya's bandaged arm. "She saved my life," I say. "She's a wonderful head guard."

"Trained by the best," Riya whispers.

He smiles as the words sink in. Then Mr. Burman, the wizard who taught me some of my first beginner spells, who protected me for years, notices my father's absence. "What else have I missed?" he asks.

"There's a lot to catch you up on," Riya says sadly.

Harini decides to stay in Belwar. I make a point of giving her one of the large windowed rooms and press the key into her palm.

"We can get you on a ship to Pire Island anytime. You can go home. Be truly and wholly free."

We've fought together through prison and a coup and now you're trying to kick me out?

"You want to stay?" I laugh. It's the most unexpected news I've heard all day. "I thought you would have gotten sick of me."

Oh, I have. My life is constantly in danger being near you. But we need to make sure you got all that Bloodlurst. Can I help?

I hesitate for a second, knowing that an agreement could mean feeding her designs for revenge. But I've grown to care for Harini, and I need all the help I can get. Plus, I would like to get her thoughts on overhauling and reforming the prison system.

I'd like to learn your language, I sign.

She raises her eyebrows. *I'll make a lesson plan.*

"And I'll make a plan for everything else."

Oh, I'm sure you will. You and your plans.

"They weren't all bad."

Not all. She smiles.

✦ ✦ ✦

Large clinics are set up across Belwar, and as soon as I'm able to, Prisha and I visit each and every one to lend our mother's expertise. I'm happy to report that no one spits in my face. I even cast firelight and hand it out. Children squeal in delight and for a few moments the sadness dissipates.

But it doesn't go away entirely. Jatin talks of time and how grief never really disappears, just changes, becomes manageable. Though my family supports me, and I them, I often slink off to be on my own. I only have to give Jatin one look and he'll nod and release my hand. I've made a habit of traveling up to the newest flying station. The one in the west, which crumbled under Mount Gandhak and my father rebuilt only three months ago. It was the last big project he helmed, one of the last great illustrations of his power and his contribution to his people.

I stare down at Belwar. To my left, Mount Gandhak stands tall; to my right, Belwar Palace and the mountains beyond it are outlined by sky. The breeze has been constant all day, yet I still embrace it, let it flutter against my clean sari and ruffle my hair, dry my tears.

It's Mr. Burman who finds me. He always was good at that. For a second I wonder whether I would have gotten away with any of the Red Woman exploits if he had been around.

"You still have Hubris?" he asks.

I pull out my skyglider and place it in his sturdy hand. "It's Hubris the Fifth now."

He gives me a look. "Some things never change."

I turn back to Belwar. "And some things change completely." We stand there for a moment. "You know I started all this, the Red Woman, because I didn't know what to do when you went into that coma. A part of me realizes it wasn't *just* because you told me a real rani helps the people. At the very beginning I wanted to prove, to make sure . . ." I choke. "I wanted to make sure it wasn't my fault."

"It wasn't, Adraa. And your father's death wasn't either. Bad people are always trying to corrupt good things. Your father wasn't just a good thing, he was a great one. I was willing to sacrifice my life for him."

"And he did the same for me."

Mr. Burman's eyes fill, and he slowly nods. "And he did the same."

"He had that same saying, about corruption," I tell him.

"Well, I got most of my sayings from him."

I'm taken aback for a second. "I always thought . . ." Suddenly, with that one piece of information, the tears come again. "There's so much I didn't know. So much I'm not ready for and I need . . ." My voice cracks. "I need him."

"And so does Belwar. Thank the gods they have you."

"Or whoever they elect." People, Touched and Untouched, have been voting all week. Now we wait to see whether my mother or one of the rajas has pulled ahead.

"I think they know you'll always be here for them, though." I look over at him, knowing what he is about to say. I know because I've been waiting for it my whole life.

"You have turned out to be a true rani. But that saying was never a lesson I needed you to learn. I was reminding you of what you already do. I am honored to serve you." He pauses. "Maharani Belwar."

I jolt at my mother's title. "What are you talking about?"

"The vote is in. It has been counted and verified. Belwar wants you."

"What? I can't believe . . ." I look down at my country, waiting for the punch line. There's no answer, just the wind. They . . . they voted for me. In the aftermath of the battle, they had bowed when the truth came out. But to honor me in battle is very different from wanting me to lead them.

"It's everything you wanted, Adraa."

"It's everything I *used* to want," I clarify. Jatin's news of becoming maharaja strikes a different chord inside me now. What does this mean for us? I can't be Maharani Belwar *and* Maharani Naupure. A thousand thoughts tumble through my head. One finally sticks, and I can't help but smile. For once, I can say with complete certainty that this wasn't in Moolek's plans. The South won't be his puppet, that's for sure.

"Riya is my head guard, but there's someone I need your help finding." I pause, considering. "Actually, two someones."

◇ ◇ ◇

There's a lot to do as maharani, especially in a country devastated by a near coup. But before my father's funeral, before all the meetings and the plans, there are a few things I want to get under way.

"Thank you for coming to see me on such short notice," I say, peering down at the judge who sentenced me to the Dome.

His fingers tremble as they press against his pulse point and he bows.

"Maharani." He dips all the way to the floor. He doesn't waste a moment. He thinks he knows why he's here. "Please understand. I thought—"

"I know what you thought. It's a marvelous excuse, how we can all say we were under Moolek's influence. How we can say he made us do what we did."

"Please."

"I'm not punishing you. I need someone to help make sure that no one is using this to get out of other crimes, past or present. You will never judge over prolific cases again—that much power will never rest on one person's shoulders. But I want you to contribute to the judicial system. Are you interested? I was thinking of an elected board of wizards, witches, and Untouched."

His head bobs upward. "So . . . you aren't going to have me killed?"

Where does this perception that I'm evil really come from? Gods. "No, Judge. I hope you realize soon that I am not a murderer nor have I ever been. I hope I will never have to be one."

Fear touches his eyes at that last phrase. It's worth it.

I sit up straighter. "The truth accords, my father's law, was not bad, but it was corrupted. As he liked to say, bad people are always trying to corrupt good things. So we change that. Find a way to employ truth casting and balances of power without those in control trying to overpower the others. Do you think you could do that?"

"Yes, Maharani, I do."

"Good. I want justice, and I want you to help me achieve it."

◇ ◇ ◇

My second act as maharani is calling Basu to the throne room. A team, with Riya and Mr. Burman in charge, hunted him down and he comes in with cuffs glinting on his wrists. The sight should draw pleasure, but I can't muster up any satisfaction.

"You can leave us alone," I tell the two guards. They obey without even a glance at one another.

"There's no warden here to save you this time," I say as Basu's eyes dart around the throne room.

"Lady, please."

"I'm not a lady anymore."

He surges on. "I was under orders."

"That does not justify what you did. I've protected you from death for far too long. And I told you I would come for you."

"I saved you." His hands bob like he's trying to snap his fingers. "From your pierced lung. You couldn't breathe, and I saved you."

"Only so they could drain me of my magic like an animal."

"I'll be better. You've shown me how."

"Oh, so I've redeemed you?"

He nods, the movement more like trembling.

I didn't think I could get any angrier. "That's not my job. That was never my job." My father's voice shoots through me. *I always thought he was a mucky little fellow.* And now my father is gone, partly because of this muck in front of me. This wizard declaring that my trials and hardships made him a better man. Changed his muckiness.

I hadn't planned on killing him. The notion swirls to the surface with an appealing gleam. Basu notices it. Or maybe it's the flames coursing up my arms as I step forward that he notices.

"Yes, that was never your job," he says. "You're right. But . . . but even so, look how strong I've made you."

"You don't get to take credit," I yell. "You did not make me stronger. This trauma didn't make me stronger. I was already strong." I take another step and my magic unfurls in smoking red tendrils. "All you've done is make me angry."

He jolts backward, as any sane wizard would. But he doesn't see the huge window, the broken one that has yet to be repaired. His arms pinwheel as he stumbles. With a kick of legs and a whoosh of a spell that he doesn't quite articulate, Basu falls.

"*Kasharaw,*" I cast, and a red rope leaps from my arm and wraps around his. The sudden extra weight tugs at my arms, and I yearn to drop it. Basu has a second of relief before I lean forward to peer at him. "I could make this look like an accident."

He swallows and the terror returns. "Your people would know. You will rule through fear and everything you fought against."

"But who would tell them?" I let the magic spool from my

hand, dropping him half a meter. "I can assure you, it won't be you."

His eyes widen, and then harden. "I will not beg." His grip slips. Huh, I didn't expect such resilience in the face of death.

"At least I didn't take away that choice."

I let go.

◇
The Weight of the Throne

Jatin

A fine line of morning sunshine has slipped past the mountains. Adraa sits on the throne like a true maharani, staring out the arched windows. For what won't be the last time, I wonder what she's thinking, how I can help her. I've been going back and forth between palaces, cleaning up the courtyard, helping her mother in the clinics. Anything to let her know I'm still here when she's ready. We'll need to talk eventually. About how this will all work. I've been avoiding it until now.

She sees me then and jerks up from the throne.

I lift a hand. "No, don't get up. I was just admiring the view."

"No, I need to—"

Moans emanate from right outside the window. I walk over to it and glance down. A red rope of magic hangs over the broken frame, supporting a cage-casting sphere. It houses one sad, hairy-armed man. Basu.

"What's going on?" I ask, though I can surmise. I already know he deserves worse for what he did.

"I'm interrogating Basu about where all the Bloodlurst is. I'm trying to make sure there's none left, but he's just whining. I think I really terrified him. It's my first time without the mask and I went a little overboard." Adraa smiles. "Though it was quite satisfying when I dropped him."

I measure the height. One story, maybe one and a half. "You *dropped* him?"

"Don't give me that look. Kalyan caught me up on all the interrogating you two did."

I lean forward and kiss her. "You should have pushed him," I whisper in her ear.

She laughs, a wondrous sound. Then her mouth twists into a frown, and suddenly I don't quite have to imagine what she was thinking. Is it weird that the thing I hate most about death is this beginning, when laughter still feels like a betrayal? Like feeling happiness without them, feeling anything but grief, can be misconstrued as a lack of love and caring? I lived within ice walls filled with the absence of laughter for years after my mother passed. Adraa will never encounter that, I vow.

She eases away from the window, stares at the rising sun on the wall. "I never . . ."

"I know." She was supposed to be a rani, always. Even maharani of Naupure when she and I marry. But not of Belwar. And not like this.

Adraa takes a deep breath. "This wasn't the plan."

"I know," I say again.

She rubs the gold bangle I gave her in the mountains. My stomach coils into a knot. I meant to prepare for this better, but my heart is too fragile when it comes to her. I can't act like I don't care. "Please keep it. I don't want it back. I swore to myself I would never marry anyone besides you, and I meant it."

Adraa's hand jerks away from the bangle. She turns to me, stricken. "Wait, no! Jatin, I don't know how this will work. I don't know how we can marry, with each of us leading our countries, but I still want to marry you."

Breath gusts out of me, and I smile. "That's a relief." I step forward, lacing my fingers through hers. "We will. But first you have to do this. We've got countries to run and then . . ." I don't really know about the "and then," to be honest. Wickery is on the brink of all-out war. Naupure needs me, and Adraa isn't just some placeholder. She's been elected, for the first time in history. Belwar did right in my book by choosing her. Yet the future is more uncertain than ever.

"And then we will complete the blood contract when things are settled. After we figure everything out," she finishes.

"That sounds pretty easy," I joke.

She gets the reference immediately, the words she threw back at me the day before the trial, before this whole mess began. "I know. Coming up with solutions like that? I think I just proved that if *I* had gone to the academy you wouldn't have graduated top of class."

"Oof, coming for my honor like that, huh?"

"I'd get used to it. As ruler of Belwar I can't have foreign leaders thinking my country is weak. Naupure won't be getting our support *just* because our maharani loves their maharaja."

"And I was hoping that would be the main perk of my new position."

Adraa wraps her arms around me, pauses to look me in the eye. "It can be—on a personal level." She leans forward, her face very close to my mine. "But I don't think I'll ever go easy on you."

"Think we can leave him for a little bit?" I nod to Basu and his cage. "I brought you something."

"Oh, he can definitely sweat it out a little longer."

We go upstairs to her room. She turns to me after she shuts the door. "This better be good, Naupure. I do have a prisoner to threaten."

I pull a bunch of letters from my pocket and spread them out like a fan. They're pristine, the Belwar seal perfectly sliced in half. "I brought these in case you thought we couldn't be together. But since you caved so easily, I think it's time I showed you the proof." The letter with the silken fish curry stain lies on top and I present it to her, pointing at the evidence.

Adraa barely glances at it. "So easily you say?"

I step closer. "Well, I am quite the catch. A maharaja of a country six times the size of Belwar."

"But who can mind cast? Who's more powerful?" she jests, a flutter of red swirling from her fingertips.

"You are," I say instantly, abandoning humor to deliver the compliment, the truth.

She laughs but can't conceal the surprise in her voice. "Giving in that easily, huh?"

I lean close enough to feel her breath on my lips. "We said no more lies long ago."

I tilt forward a centimeter more and then our lips connect and I'm kissing her.

Adraa pulls away first. "I'll be right back." She rushes to her closet and returns with a box. Out come piles of my letters to her. I close in, smiling. Wordlessly, I take them from her, noting the hole in the middle of each one. "You really did nail them to a post," I say, laughing.

"I wouldn't lie about something like that."

I arch an eyebrow. "But none of them are burned."

"Yeah, well . . ."

For the next hour we sit and pore over our letters, reliving moments, going into detail about how they may or may not have been exaggerated for the sake of the other. "I still think the curry-stained one is the most embarrassing by far," I argue.

"Oh, that's a lie if I ever heard one." She smirks like she's been waiting for this opportunity, and I notice she has one of my letters tucked under her knee.

"'Dear Adraa, I believe you should know something,'" she begins. I recognize the words immediately and jerk forward, reaching for the parchment. My first love letter, the one admitting . . . everything.

"We don't need to relive that," I say.

She holds the letter above my head, out of reach, and con-

424

tinues. "'I didn't want to tell you before, but I've never been upset about our arrangement. In fact, I—'"

I tackle her to the floor. My body presses against hers. The words are forgotten. All I can think about is our closeness, the warmth of her underneath me. The letter flutters to the ground. "Did you ever think it was real?" I ask, a question I've spent half a lifetime being too scared to say aloud.

She stares. "Was it?"

"Yes." A flutter races through me at my admission.

It seems to affect her too because she blushes as she searches my face. "It took me a week to discover the message beneath," she whispers. "But for a week I was bewildered and surprised. And most of all . . . happy."

The world evaporates as I smile down at her. "Wow, I could tease you about that for probably . . ." I tilt my head like I'm making calculations. "Probably the rest of my life."

She rolls her eyes. "Good Gods. What have I done?"

I lean forward. "I'm happy I didn't screw it all up," I say as I lower my head to kiss her.

"I'll be sure to let you know if you do."

"Oh, well, then. Wonderful." I laugh, but not long enough to stop Adraa from lifting her head and finding my lips again. And once that happens, we don't break away for a long time.

◇

CHAPTER FIFTY-SEVEN

Dawn to Dusk

Adraa

The funerals are at dawn because my father wouldn't want it any other way. We stand on the cliffs of the South Village. The sea crashes against the shore below, a familiar tune no rougher or calmer than on any other day. It's a long service, stretching into morning. Through it all, I turn to the sun, letting it coat me in heat and remind me. The tears were already doing the job. But for the first time since getting out of prison, I can hear my sniffles and I refuse to hide the sound of them, of my grief. I lived too long in silence to dwell in it now. Not today, when most if not all of Belwar hold candles up to the dozens of pyres on the cliffs.

One by one, Belwarians of the same forte cast their colors. I step forward with the red fortes to honor and bless the dead in a red glow. It's a tradition, one to help each soul find their way to their god or goddess. For the first time in my life I understand where my ancestors were coming from.

Then we get to my father. My mother speaks, casting her voice aloud with orange magic like my dad used to do. "My husband was my sun. He knew how to live, to cherish those he cared deeply for. And he cared for Belwar. He understood its flaws, its brilliance, and its possibilities. His light in this world will never set, and I know this because you have chosen the best of us to lead you into a new era. The path will be hard, as all paths through life are, but I implore you to live, to love, to help those in need."

My father's influence touched many. They knew him as a ruler. I knew the crinkles around his green eyes. Now his face is the calmest I've ever seen it. It's the first time I realize that his face was never still. It was always contemplating, always laughing, always living.

What's more, he let me live.

"Just think of this as meeting a new friend, Adraa."

"But, but he's—a boy."

"Yes." Father chuckled, the warmth of his breath marking the frigid air. "Yes, he is a boy. And so am I, and you like me well enough, right?

"Yeah."

"Yes," I whisper now as I touch his hand. "I like you well enough. Always. Thank you for liking all of me." Every part. Every version. Every facet of myself that got me here, that he helped shape. "I love you."

◈ ◈ ◈

I find my mother and Prisha when it's time to throw his ashes. Or maybe we just naturally gravitate to each other. The city and its people have left to mourn in their own way, the fire has died down, and there's only one part left for us to do. We fly back to our home and land on the roof.

I've shown them the ball of magic, the message surely inside. I'm too scared to let it go, let his magic fade, let the one last piece of him go out like a light. I hand it to my mother. It's only fair. I was the one with him. She and Prisha didn't get their final goodbyes.

Slowly, my mother breathes a pink mist over the surface, and it glows awake.

My father's voice fills the air, even though it's a whisper. But it's him. I'd know his voice anywhere. "I hope this finds you, my family, because it's time. I have to leave you. I'm sorry I have to go. I'm sorry for how much I know I will miss. The world keeps changing, new dawns every day, and I wish I could be there for each and every one. But before the end, I wanted to tell you all one last time how much I love you." He stops, and I think that's the end of the message, when suddenly he continues. "Ira, I'm looking at Adraa right now and I know she will save us. We've done two things very right in our daughters. They are powerful and brave, just like you. Thank you for choosing me, for loving me." And that's where it ends—with love and total confidence in us. In me.

"See, I was right," Mother says through her tears. "And he was always right."

We hug each other, a heap of limbs and comfort and

tears. "I'm glad it's you. The new maharani of Belwar," Prisha whispers.

"I still don't completely understand it. I don't know what to say or what to do."

"I'll be here," my mother says. "Everyone will be here for you. Your dad is here for you too."

We collapse on the roof and watch the sunset deepen to the brightest orange I've ever seen. And as night falls, wave after wave of orange fortes shoot streams of magic into the air. For hours, the darkness is staved off by the color of my father, in tribute to him.

❖

CHAPTER FIFTY-EIGHT

My Beginning

Adraa

"They're ready for you," Riya says. "Maharani."

I nod, take a breath.

"I've been waiting for this moment," Riya whispers. "And I'll be by your side. Now and forever." I reach out and squeeze her hand. Her reassurance works.

"I'm ready."

Riya opens the double doors for me, and I step through. Long strides forward into the meeting room I've been in hundreds of times as I listened to my father preside over his council. This time I wear my own colors, bloodred with orange suns embroidered into the pallu and the falls of my sari. And for the first time, I wear a sleeveless blouse with the emblem of Belwar, golden and blazing, stitched on the front. Everyone watches as I take my father's chair at the head of the table.

Riya sits to my right; my mother is already seated to my left. Four rajas, Prisha, and the Burmans take up the remaining seats. I look each one of them in the eye before I get to Jatin, sitting directly across from me and wearing a fine white jacket fit for a maharaja.

He bows his head, giving his respects. You'd figure one of the rajas would do that, but it's Jatin supporting me and setting me up to be the leader I've always dreamt of being.

I sacrificed myself for my country. I sacrificed myself for Jatin and Maharaja Naupure. And maybe I shouldn't have. Maybe I should have stayed and fought my way out of that courtroom. But I can't change the past. All I know now is I'm too valuable. Even as an eight. Even if I fail sometimes. In this world, I don't need to throw myself away or hide behind a mask. I need to live and change the course of this war, maybe destiny itself. And that is what I intend to do.

The next words I speak will not be as Lady Adraa Belwar, the role I was born into. Or as Jaya Smoke or the Red Woman, whom I created. No, now I step into a title not taken but given.

I am the maharani of Belwar. And today is a new dawn.

"Let's begin."

Acknowledgments

I wrote most of this book during the pandemic, at a time when I, like much of the world, felt very alone. But in truth, I was never alone. I've had the support of friends and family, and I now get the chance to thank them. So please bear with me as I get sentimental, because these people deserve to know just how much I care.

To my agent, Amy Brewer, and the entire Metamorphosis Literary Agency team, thank you for being there for me and supporting this book as much as the last. Also, thank you for inventing the title like it was the easiest thing in the world. I love it so much and am so lucky to have you.

My editor, Hannah Hill, has illustrated what it means to be supportive and talented and to deliver the fastest edits I've ever seen. Thank you for helping me dive deeper into the story. To my first editor, Monica Jean, who acquired this series—I will always be grateful to you for starting me off on this journey.

I also want to give a huge shout-out to everyone at Penguin Random House who helped this story become a physical book: Cathy Bobak, Lili Feinberg, Sarah Lawrenson, Drew Fulton, Erica Henegen, Jenn Innzeta, Nathan Kinney, Kelly McGauley, Carol Monteiro, Dani Perez, and Tamar Schwartz. Thank you always to my copyeditors, Heather Lockwood Hughes and Colleen Fellingham, who are magical beings for catching all my mistakes. And my proofreader, Janet Rosenberg, for catching everything.

Special thanks to Casey Moses, who again designed the cover and has shown that her talent knows no bounds. Thank you for always making me feel listened to and coming up with the best ideas ever. Thank you to Virgina Norey again for the wonderful map. To the brilliant illustrator Charlie Bowater, you have now gifted me *two* dream covers. Having absorbed them, I've found I will forever be in a state of shock and happiness you brought these characters and magic to life. Thank you!

The DFW Writers' Workshop has always felt like an extended family, and I'm so happy I was able to attend Wednesday nights when we went virtual. To every member who has been part of DFW Writers' community, listened to my words, and helped me edit this book: thank you! Rosemary Moore, Leslie Lutz, A. Lee Martinez, Sally Hamilton, Sarah Terentiev, and Brooke Fossey, thank you for always keeping in contact and being the best long-distance friends. Special thanks to Katie Bernet, who read through my bad first draft and gave me the encouragement that this story was worth it. I'm forever lucky to call you my friend.

Thank you to all the writer friends I made in California, with a special thanks to Priya Kavina, Persephone Jayne, and Sage Magee. Priya, thank you for always being there for me and again helping me rework the spells. Persephone, thank you for one day posing a question and thus creating the biggest and best plot twist a girl can hope for. This book might have been easier to write without your inspiration, but not half as fun.

Thank you to Kathryn Purdie and my fellow Delacorte Press authors KayLynn Flanders, Kelly Coon, and Amélie Wen Zhao for blurbing *Cast in Firelight* and always being there when I had a question. Thank you as well to my debut groups #theRoaring20s and #the21ders for their advice and support through both books.

To all my family—thank you! Dad, Rae, Austin, Katy, your support has meant so much to me. Mom, thank you for believing in me and this dream and for giving me the chance to live it. You are truly the brightest person I know, and I'm so privileged to be your daughter. To Steve, thank you for being there for me, always.

To all my in-laws—Gokul and Nanda Bysani, as well as all the Bysanis and Janardans—thank you for your continued support and excitement. Kaethan, my husband and my best friend, thank you for always loving me and for being my absolute favorite beta reader. I wouldn't have wanted to be quarantined with anyone else. I'm especially grateful that you let me spoil key events so I could talk through plot points. I love you so much.

And finally, to my readers! I still can't believe I have readers now. Even a year later it boggles me that my words and story have meant something to you. Thank you for reading this book and continuing Adraa and Jatin's story. Please know how much you matter. It is a privilege unlike any other to provide you this book.

About the Author

DANA SWIFT has been making up fantasy worlds since she was eleven years old. She graduated from the University of Texas at Austin and lives in Miami, Florida, with her husband and their golden doodle, Kala. She is the author of *Cast in Firelight* and its sequel, *Bound by Firelight*.

@swift_dana
@danaswiftbooks